A

JASON ELAM
AND STEVE YOHN

NOVEL

PRESENTED BY

TYNDALE HOUSE
PUBLISHERS, INC.
CAROL STREAM, ILLINOIS

A

RILEY COVINGTON

THRILLER

Visit Tyndale's exciting Web site at www.tyndale.com.

TYNDALE and Tyndale's quill logo are registered trademarks of Tyndale House Publishers, Inc.

Blackout

Designed by Dean H. Renninger

Published in association with the literary agency of Yates & Yates, LLP, Attorneys and Counselors, Orange, California.

Library of Congress Cataloging-in-Publication Data to come

Elam, Jason.
Blackout : a Riley Covington thriller / a Jason Elam and Steve Yohn novel.
p. cm.
ISBN 978-1-4143-3172-0 (sc)
1. Football players—Fiction. 2. Terrorism—United States—Fiction. 3. Football stories. I. Yohn, Steve. II. Title.
PS3605.L26B57 2010
813'.6—dc22 2009040053

Printed in the United States of America

16 15 14 13 12 11 10
7 6 5 4 3 2 1

DEDICATION

JASON ELAM

It is to the real Jesus that I dedicate this book.

STEVE YOHN

To Madeline, my girl.

ACKNOWLEDGMENTS

THANK YOU, GOD, for love, patience, and creativity. Use this for Your glory.

When we're writing, we're thinking of our families; when we're with our families, we're thinking about writing. Thanks to Tamy and Nancy and all the kids for putting up with us.

We are deeply indebted to the whole Tyndale family—Karen Watson for making this all happen, Todd Starowitz for getting the word out, Dean Renninger and the design team for producing consistently amazing artwork, and Jeremy Taylor for putting the dress on the pig.

A huge thanks to Matt Yates for your guidance and friendship. Finally, we owe a debt of gratitude to LTC Mark Elam, Joel C. Rosenberg, Amir Tsarfati, and Phil Irwin for your wisdom and depth of knowledge.

CHAPTER ONE

TUESDAY, JUNE 30

The impact was swift and sudden. Muhammed Zerin Khan cursed himself; he should have seen it coming. He had always prided himself on having a sixth sense—a special awareness of his surroundings. But this time, his gift had failed him, and now he would pay for it.

The initial concussion knocked the air from his lungs and left him stunned. A dizzying pain forced him to squeeze his eyes shut until the wave passed.

As he sucked for air, he spun and scrambled to all fours. He knew he had to get into fighting position or it was all over. But as he looked around, he knew he was done for. *Where did they all come from?*

Hands were all over him. Something sharp pressed into his lower back. He tried to squirm away, but the grips on his arms and legs were like iron manacles.

Less than a week ago, Zerin had walked into the Georgia State Prison and sat down in the tight cubicle. His father was waiting for him on the other side of the Plexiglas with the phone already in his hand. Zerin pressed his knuckles to the cool glass as he picked up the phone. His father leaned forward and completed the fist tap. "It's been a while, Son. You good?"

"I'm living. You?"

His father slowly leaned back in his chair, stretching the phone's cord taut. Zerin noticed how the man's age had begun to reveal itself. The wrinkles around his eyes and the gray streaked through his beard made him look much older than Zerin remembered. The look was a little surreal, a little discordant with what he knew of his father's past, because with the white *kufi* and the white prison-issue garb, his father actually looked like one of the wise imams Zerin had seen online.

"Me? I'm doing well. Allah has blessed me. Besides, it does my heart good to know what's on the horizon," his father stated with a definitive smirk.

"'What's on the horizon'? What do you mean?" Zerin asked him, puzzled.

The older man slowly shook his head. "I'd love to tell you, Son. I want you to know—to be ready for—what's coming down the pike. But I can only say so much. Let's just say it's gonna happen. It *is* gonna happen. And you'll know it when it does. And you'll also know that your old man knew about it before it did, because they came to *me* for help. They asked *me* to organize this. *I* am the only one in this whole facility to whom they have entrusted their plan.

"So when it all goes down, you'll know that your broken-down old pops was responsible for everything that takes place in this here facility. You'll know that I was involved in the biggest thing that's happened since . . . well, just trust me, boy, you'll know. Meantime, we just have to be patient, and *insha'Allah*, we will make it count when the time is right."

Zerin said nothing. His father had taken these cryptic turns occasionally during recent visits. The first few rebuffs had taught Zerin not to try to dig for anything deeper than what his dad was ready to willingly offer up.

After a short pause, his father sat upright in his chair, releasing the tension from the phone cord. "Enough of that for now. I want to know how my son is. How's your training going? Tell me everything."

It was now less than one week later, and Zerin was glad he hadn't had *this* story to tell his father. The weight on his back was pressing the air out of his lungs. He fought and squirmed with every fiber of his existence, but there were simply too many of them. There was laughter all around, mocking and cruel, as those in the room started a mini celebration.

Zerin's rage boiled over, and he made a sudden effort to free himself. One arm got loose but was quickly clamped back down. Someone had his head pressed firmly into the short carpet and was rubbing it roughly back and forth, taking the skin off his right cheek directly under his eye.

Suddenly he was flipped onto his side, and he heard the unmistakable sound of someone ripping off pieces of duct tape. Through the bodies, Zerin could see the one with the tape moving toward him. He tried to tuck his legs a bit in order to drive his heels into this man. Maybe he could break his assailant's nose and in the frenzy free himself. It was a long shot, but at the very least Zerin could make them realize he wasn't simply going to let them have their way.

As the others made room for the taper, Zerin saw his chance. He lunged with all his might, kicking straight into what he hoped was the man's face. At the last second, the attacker saw it coming and dropped his head just enough to take the full force on his forehead. While the man stumbled backward, dazed, the pile on top of Zerin grew even larger. Fists were driven into his side, and threats were made against any further resistance.

Zerin had no hope now. His opponents held him firmly, and the tape began wrapping his legs. Once his ankles were secured, his wrists and arms were next. As his arms were pulled tighter behind his back, Zerin felt a piercing pain in his shoulder. He refused to cry out.

Duct tape went around and around his head and eyes, and then a strip went over his mouth, causing his first moment of real panic. He had been breathing deeply through his mouth, but now he had to draw rapidly through his nose.

Now he saw nothing but felt clothes being ripped off him. A chill told him when there was nothing left on his body.

Then he was on the move. The complete darkness was disorienting. He tried to picture in his mind the direction he was being taken but soon got lost. The carpet he was being dragged across was creating more rug burns on his already-reddened body. Zerin was trapped between rage and terror.

After a few more yards, he felt himself lifted off the ground and passed from hand to hand. There was laughing and shouting coming from all around him.

Then, as quickly as he was picked up, he fell back down. His body slammed headfirst into the floor—only now the abrasive carpet had been replaced by hard tile. A searing pain shot through Zerin's brain, and he immediately felt blood rolling across what little skin on his face wasn't covered with tape.

As he tried to collect his wits, hot breath made its way into his ear. "Khan, did you really think you could hide from us? Did you really think we wouldn't get you? We get everybody!"

The duct tape was ripped from his mouth. "You have any last words, Khan?"

Zerin spit, not knowing if he hit anybody. Another big cheer went through the crowd, as well as one loud curse.

Again he felt himself being lifted, and then there came another free fall. Zerin cringed and tried to brace himself. However, the impact was not what he expected. It felt like he had been dropped into liquid fire. The shock sucked all the air from his already-burning lungs.

Then he realized that it wasn't heat but cold—ice cold. He instinctively took a breath, and freezing water rushed through his sinuses. He began to choke. As quickly as he was in the water he was plucked out.

Amid the laughter and cheers, he was flopped on the cold tile, gagging and trying to rid the water from his lungs.

Suddenly the unmistakable voice of Roy Burton, head coach of the Colorado Mustangs, pierced the air. "What do you idiots think you're doing? Get away from him, now! Somebody get some scissors and cut this boy loose."

Zerin heard the mass exodus of people, and by the time the tape was removed from his eyes, the crowd had grown very small.

It was then that Coach Burton noticed the blood. "Get the trainers in here too. Quick!"

Burton leaned down. "Son, you okay? I'm sorry about this."

But Zerin said nothing. What was there to say? He had been hurt and humiliated. They had attacked his body and his dignity. Those were not things he could just brush off and forget. Zerin had heard about rookie hazing in the Professional Football League, but this incident had gone way too far.

Now the seeds of revenge had been sown. On that cold floor, he made a vow—a promise to himself that he would be patient. He would find his time. He would strike! Just as his father had said.

"It is gonna happen. . . . We just have to be patient, and insha'Allah, *we will make it count when the time is right."*

CHAPTER TWO

WEDNESDAY, JULY 1, 5:45 P.M. KST
PYONGYANG, NORTH KOREA

The strip of paper was just durable enough to hold ink without falling apart. Any more thickness and it would lose its most important quality—the ability to dissolve if soaked in water . . . or saliva.

The characters being etched upon this paper with a fine-tip pen were miniscule and seemingly gibberish. The hand writing them was calm and steady.

The same could not be said of the rest of the author.

Kuk Ho mopped his forehead with a handkerchief. One drop of sweat could easily ruin an hour's worth of painstaking work. He stole another quick glance at the small window set in the door of his office. If he were spotted doing what he was doing, it would mean a tortured confession and death—not just for him but for the whole extended Kuk family. *I can't think about that. Just keep writing,* he told himself.

Kuk Ho had been thirty years old when the "Eternal President" died. He had taken to the streets of Pyongyang and cried his crocodile tears along with the hundreds of thousands of others. Later, he cheered and rubbed more hot pepper paste in his eyes in order to show the proper emotion at the accession of the new Dear Leader, son of the old Great Leader. He did it because that was what was expected, and in North Korea, if you didn't do what was expected, then you had better plan on an unscheduled trip to police headquarters to be asked why.

The day that Kim Jong Il had taken over, Kuk Ho's heart had broken. All hope for a new Korea had died. The failing national policy of *Juche*, or self-reliance, would continue with the new Little Dictator. Hundreds of thousands of Koreans had died of famine and disease in the past decade. The economy was failing. Public executions and prison camps were needed just to keep the ruling party in power. And the nation's foreign policy was almost begging for a United States–backed South Korean invasion. *If that's self-reliance, then give me imperialism any day of the week.*

And yet, in spite of this history of failure, many of Kuk Ho's fellow countrymen worshiped the Dear Leader and his father before him as gods. *No more,* Kuk Ho had decided that fateful day that saw the ascent of a leader and the continued descent of a country. *No more will I contribute to the destruction of my homeland. No more will I turn a blind eye to the holocaust directed toward my fellow citizens*. That was the day that in his heart Kuk Ho had become a traitor.

A note slipped into the palm of an assistant to a visiting Western dignitary had sealed the deal. Six weeks later, he received his first contact.

At that time Kuk Ho was just a junior member in the Ministry of People's Armed Forces, but in the intervening fifteen years he had risen in the ranks to his current position of deputy vice minister.

There was a period when Kuk Ho had hoped his treason would be temporary—that eventually, after Kim Jong Il died, there would be hope for a new Korea. But once the Dear Leader had named his youngest son, Kim Jong Un—"Our Commander Kim," as he was already being hailed—his successor, all hope had died. The future ruler was truly his father's son and his grandfather's grandson.

So Kuk Ho continued to use his position to get more and more important information—information that he passed on only when he was sure that the payoff would be worth the risk.

There's no doubting the worthiness of this intelligence, Kuk Ho thought as he penned the last few characters. *How the Dear Leader let himself get talked into this scheme, I'll never know. Although, if this plan of theirs does succeed, it could mean a crippled America. And if America is crippled, there's no one to stand in the way of the Little Dictator as he mows through our southern brothers and sisters and makes them pay for what he perceives as a half century of disrespect and abuse.*

Finished, Kuk Ho gently rolled up the paper and slipped it into a pliable, waterproof sheath barely larger than a wooden matchstick. The sheath was slightly perforated in three places in case it was necessary to quickly dispose of the message. Three seconds of grinding with his molars and the note would be history.

Slipping the note into his mouth, Kuk Ho used his tongue to tuck it up between his gums and right cheek. A mirror from his top desk drawer confirmed that there was no noticeable bulge, and some spoken words assured him that his diction had not been altered.

Kuk Ho reached back into his desk and retrieved his keys, then headed to the parking lot. Although his position afforded him the luxury of a vehicle, it did not provide him a driver. Today, this arrangement suited him fine.

Walking out was always the worst part. It felt as if he had *traitor* written all over his face. With every good-bye he said, he was sure the incriminating evidence would come flying out of his mouth. With every turned corner, he was certain he would face an armed guard ready to escort him back upstairs to the minister's office. Sweat rolled down his cheeks, and the moist heat from his body fogged his glasses. Pulling his handkerchief out, he toweled off his face and cleared his glasses.

Finally he reached his car—a black Pyeonghwa Hwiparam, quite a different vehicle from the vice minister's Mercedes-Benz. His glove box provided him with a fresh handkerchief, which he quickly soaked. Starting the engine, he saw that the gas gauge settled just under half full. *Good enough reason to stop for a fill-up,* he thought with a relieved smile.

CHAPTER

THREE

WEDNESDAY, JULY 1, 6:30 P.M. KST
PYONGYANG, NORTH KOREA

Pak Bae's adrenaline started rushing as soon as he saw the car in line. It wasn't the vehicle itself—Pyeonghwa Motors was the only manufacturer licensed to sell cars in North Korea. *I still don't know how the Reverend Moon was able to pull off a deal that allowed the Unification Church–owned company to be the sole carmaker in officially atheistic North Korea,* he thought. *Money and influence allow for strange bedfellows.* No, what drew Pak Bae's notice were the driver's frightened but hopeful eyes, partially hidden behind thick black glasses and set deep in the jowly face. Frightened eyes were not unusual in North Korea. Nor were angry, sad, resigned, or empty eyes. Hope, however, was not an expression one saw every day.

Pak Bae knew that much of this man's hope was resting on him, and he was determined not to let him down. Trying to keep his focus for the next two customers would not be easy, but he knew he couldn't show a thing. *Steady face, no emotion, business as usual.*

Finally, the nameless man in the black Fiat knockoff pulled up to Pak Bae's pump. Pak Bae waited patiently as the man reached into his glove box to retrieve the key for the gas door. As the window began descending, the man in the car sneezed into his hand.

"Wihayeo," Pak Bae said.

The man acknowledged the blessing with a curt nod of his head as he passed the key out. Transferring the key to his left hand, Pak Bae moved toward the rear of the car. Suddenly, he coughed, covering his mouth with his right hand. As he did, he slid a moist, waterproof sheath into his mouth, tucking it between his gums and his right cheek.

After keying open the gas door, Pak Bae pretended to have difficulty removing the gas cap. This allowed him to pull off the five 1,000-wŏn notes that had been taped to the inside of the small door. Finally, with the nozzle inserted, the gas flowing, and the money safely tucked in the pocket of his coveralls, Pak Bae was able to start planning ahead.

Although taking the money always made him uneasy, he knew it was necessary for him to carry out his link in the chain. But never let it be said that he was doing this for his own financial gain. No, every wŏn, every last chŏn, would be put toward accomplishing his mission.

Pak Bae prided himself in being a patriot, but his loyalty was to the old Korea—the Korea his parents and his mother's parents had told him about when he was a child and the family sat around the huge stew pot in their little corner of the village. That was a Korea of culture, of hope, of faith. When he called himself a Korean, that was the nation to which his loyalties belonged.

Not this new country—this plaything for the powerful. When Kim Il Sung had inexplicably allowed Korea to become a pawn in the chess game between America and the Soviet Union, Korea had been shattered, Pak Bae's family along with it. On the day the border was permanently sealed, Pak Bae's grandfather on his father's side was in Seoul, along with two of Pak Bae's great-uncles. The family had never seen nor heard from them again. *These Kims do not serve Korea; Korea serves the Kims. Well, this is one Korean who will not bow down in his heart to these criminals. If I and my whole family must be sacrificed in the name of a restored homeland—a Korea we can once again be proud of—then so be it!*

After work, Pak Bae would stop at the market and use the 5,000 wŏn to buy some medicinal herbs, a new pair of glasses for his uncle, Sam-chon, and a new stew pot for his mother. Then, when Sunday came, he would stuff the pot with the herbs, glasses, and some other items that were hard to get in the rural areas, go to the train depot, and begin the hot, muggy journey north to the border county of Chosan. By the time he arrived in his hometown, he would have only an hour before he had to begin his trip back to the big city. That would give him just enough time to pay his respects to his family, deliver the supplies to his mother, and slip a certain waterproof sheath to his cousin.

Pak Bae knew why he risked what he did, but as he watched the black car drive off, he couldn't help wondering why that man would jeopardize so much. *Most men in such a high position follow the party line. Why does he chance losing his job, his comfortable living, his family, and even his life?*

A horn pulled Pak Bae out of his reverie. He gave an apologetic wave to the driver of the next car in line and hurried to the descending window.

CHAPTER FOUR

TUESDAY, JULY 7, 10:00 A.M. MDT
PARKER, COLORADO

Riley Covington's body was burning, but it was a good burn. With his toes balanced on a large blue physio ball, he was seeing how many push-ups he could do in sixty seconds.

"Look at the boy go," said Keith Simmons, his fellow Colorado Mustangs linebacker, kneeling about fifteen feet from Riley. Keith had just finished a second set of eight reps on the cable row and was drying his face with a towel.

Riley turned and gave him a wink, then began adding claps to his push-ups. *Let's see the old guy do this,* he thought with a smile. He knew that Keith, who had played in the Professional Football League four years longer, was really starting to feel these off-season workouts.

Suddenly, in the middle of a clap, his body crashed to the ground.

"In the old country, we call that the Persian Flop," said a laughing voice behind Riley. "But you do it pretty well for a Wyoming farm boy."

Riley rolled over and spotted Afshin Ziafat just in time to see the younger linebacker rifling the exercise ball back his way.

Afshin was a rookie—twentieth player taken in the draft—and Keith had taken the younger man under his wing.

Initially, Riley had struggled with having Afshin on the team. But soon he came to realize that his hard feelings toward the kid were based solely on his name and Iranian heritage. After Riley had done some serious repenting to God and apologizing to Afshin, the two had become fast friends. Now these three linebackers, who shared a mutual faith in addition to a love of the game, had bonded to form a team within the team.

"Now, Z, that's what I'm talking about when I say you've got to think ahead in the game," Riley said, using the ball to lift himself up. "You're two exercises behind me doing what?"

"Physio ball push-ups."

"Which is done with . . ."

"Uh . . . a physio ball?" Afshin responded with a barely suppressed grin, knowing where this conversation was going.

"Exactly," Riley said, bouncing the large ball next to him. "Two exercises from now you will be doing . . ."

"Okay, Pach, I get the point," Afshin said as he watched the ball bounce up and down. *Pach* was Riley's nickname from his time playing with the Air Force Academy Falcons and came from a comparison to the fast, hard-hitting Apache attack helicopter.

"You will be doing . . . ," Riley repeated, forcing an answer from Afshin.

"What you were just doing—physio ball bridge push-ups," Afshin quietly answered, still grinning.

"Which means that I have two opportunities to get you back in painful and borderline evil ways, and which makes you . . ."

"El Stupido?"

"Si," Riley said, drilling the ball back at his friend, then moving to his next exercise.

"Come on, amigos, this is America. Speak American!" Keith complained as he grabbed the v-bar for another set of kneeling rows.

"Lo siento," Riley called back as he placed his face between the split pads for the first of four directions on his neck machine. The conversation ended as each man worked through his set.

While the workout room at the Mustangs training center in Dove

Valley was bigger and better equipped, it also tended to be loud and crowded. So two years ago Riley had converted his basement guest suite into a weight room. It wasn't huge, but it was big enough, and it had all the equipment Riley needed for his off-season workouts. Along with the weights and workout machines, he had installed a booming sound system and a large-screen television that he usually kept muted and tuned to ESPN or FoxNews so that he could watch the crawl.

Off-season workouts were required four days a week by the Mustangs organization, but they didn't necessarily have to take place at Dove Valley. So Mondays and Wednesdays, Riley, Keith, and Afshin worked out down at the training center. Although the training center wasn't as convenient as Riley's basement, they wanted to keep their connection with the team. Tuesdays and Thursdays, however, they met at Riley's.

Since they all played the same position, the workouts, while varying from day to day, were identical for each man. They started with movement exercises—deep squats, diagonal arm lifts, rotational stretches—then moved on to strength training: weights, kettlebell exercises, and ab work, as well as presses, pull-ups, and push-ups. Finally, they'd end with a restoration period that included a hurdle series, Gatorade recovery shake, stick and soft tissue work, and then a 3x cold tub–hot tub contrast, which could best be described as misery to ecstasy to misery to ecstasy to misery to ecstasy in one-minute intervals.

Now, as he rested between sets on the neck machine, Riley bobbed his head to TobyMac and Kirk Franklin singing about not wanting to gain the whole world while losing their souls. From the first time Riley had heard the song, it had resonated with him. As a professional football player, it would be easy to get caught up in himself—to believe his own press. *It takes a lot of prayer and perspective to keep your head small enough to fit through a doorway when everyone's calling you a hero and telling you how wonderful you are,* Riley thought. *And it takes good friends like Keith and Afshin, who are more than happy to make sure I stay humble.*

After finishing his last neck set, Riley sat down on the padded floor to do the exercise he hated most—Russian twists. *No wonder they call these Russian twists; they're worse than being sent to the gulag!* Picking up a medium-size weight ball, Riley lifted his legs and his upper body, balancing himself on his rear. Then he held the ball out at arm's length and began twisting his torso side to side. He counted to himself as he touched the ball to the ground on either side, *one, one, two, two, three, three,* all the way up to fifteen. When he was done, he collapsed to the floor.

"I hate them; I hate them; I HATE THEM!" Riley yelled, while his abs and obliques screamed.

"Oh, come on! Man up, pansy-boy," Keith taunted from the neck machine.

Riley shot him a dirty look and saw Afshin watching him from the corner of the room while quickly finishing the last of his physio ball sets. "Don't worry, Rook," he called out, "I won't mess with your ball. I'm much too creative to do something that obvious."

Afshin slid off the ball and stretched out on the floor. "Oh, great—now I'm going to have to be Mr. Paranoid, watching your every move. Can't you just get it over with? Here," he said, putting his feet back on the ball, "come and get me."

"Sorry, son; don't play the game if you can't pay the price," Riley said as he picked up the ball for his second and final set of twists.

CHAPTER FIVE

TUESDAY, JULY 7, 10:35 A.M. MDT
PARKER, COLORADO

Later, when Riley, Keith, and Afshin were relaxing in the backyard hot tub, letting the jets work through their sore muscles, Keith asked Riley, "So how're you doing, man?"

"I'm doing good," Riley answered quickly. "A little sore, but good."

Keith rolled his eyes. "Okay, now that you got the pat answer out of your system, let me ask you again: how're you doing, Riley?"

Riley put his head back and sighed. Just over a month had passed since his father had been murdered—blown up—by a terrorist group trying to flush Riley out of hiding. *Collateral damage,* he had thought at the time. *That's all my dad was to them—collateral damage.*

Then, less than a week ago, Riley's best friend, Scott Ross, and Riley's . . . *What? Girlfriend? No . . . Girl friend? Maybe . . . Who knows?* Khadi Faroughi had been suddenly transferred out of Denver, along with the whole counterterrorism division they were part of.

Khadi and Riley had hit it off last January and had only been growing closer since. The only thing that kept them from establishing a true romantic relationship was the huge chasm between their two faiths—Khadi was a Muslim. Her move to Washington, D.C., with the rest of the CTD team had already been misery for Riley, as it added physical distance to the existing emotional and spiritual canyon.

The only team member left was Riley's bodyguard and good friend, Skeeter Dawkins. Tilting his head, Riley looked over at the big man, who was sitting in an Adirondack chair, scanning the trees at the back of the property. *If you ever want a picture of loyalty and trustworthiness, there's your man.*

"I don't know," he finally answered Keith. "Don't take this the wrong way, but I guess I'm a little bit lonely. And while I'm so thankful that all the killing is over with, I also get the feeling that it's not really over with. Does that make any sense?"

"Yeah, I suppose," Keith said. "I'm not sure that I'll ever get past what's happened in the last year. I have no idea how I'm going to feel the first time I walk back into Platte River." Last December, Keith had taken some shrapnel to his thigh during an attack at Platte River Stadium during a Colorado Mustangs *Monday Night Football* game. The physical damage had healed completely, but the emotional wounds were still open and raw.

Afshin, who was the only one of the three who had not been in the stadium that night, said, "I can't imagine, guys. I mean, I don't even know what to say when you start talking about it. But you know I'll be there for you both, praying you through and encouraging you however I can."

Keith and Riley nodded their appreciation. Silence surrounded the men for a time.

Riley took a sip from his protein smoothie, then asked, "So what do you guys think of Zerin?"

"Man, if I could take back any moment . . . I can't believe how I let that taping get out of hand," Keith said. "One minute I'm laughing, holding on to one of his legs. The next minute I'm wondering what just happened."

"We were just as bad," Afshin said. "We just sat back and watched. We should have stepped in and stopped it."

"I tried apologizing," Keith continued, "but he'd have no part of it. He just turned and walked away."

"Yeah, me too," Riley said. "I even invited him to come to our workouts, but I got the same response."

Afshin shook his head. "Don't expect much else from him. It's an honor thing now. That's one thing about us Persians and the Arabs. If you insult our honor, then it's game on."

"So what do we do?" Riley asked.

"Yeah, is there any way to repair the damage done?" Keith added.

"Time and prayer. That's how I got over your warm little welcome, Riley," Afshin kidded.

Shame circled through Riley's stomach, even as he laughed with the others. *Forgive yourself and let it go. Z's forgiven you and moved past it; you've got to move past it too.* But even as Riley thought those words, he knew it would still be a while before he would get over the guilt of his prejudice.

"Speaking of repairing the damage," Riley said, turning to Keith and changing the subject, "how's the work coming on your cabin? I still feel bad over that." During the events of a month ago, Riley had holed up in Keith's mountain cabin/mini mansion, trying to draw out the terrorists who had killed his father. Unfortunately, Riley's plan had worked a little too well, and Keith's home had burned to the ground.

"Well, don't," Keith said. "I told you, it's just stuff. Besides, I had some sweet insurance on the thing. They're just finishing clearing the rubble from the old place, and we've already got the plans for the rebuild. Puts the old one to shame. Seriously, it's almost embarrassing. Hey, why don't you cook me and Z some barbecue this weekend, and I'll bring over the blueprints?"

"Sounds like a date," Riley said.

As he slid a little deeper into the hot water, Riley said a quick prayer of thanks for good friends. *Maybe things really can get back to normal for me,* he thought with a smile.

CHAPTER

SIX

TUESDAY, JULY 7, 7:15 P.M. EDT
WASHINGTON, D.C.

The brilliance of the halogen lamp shining on the kitchen table banished any sign that outside the windows the sun was setting. Not that Hassan al-Aini could have seen the oncoming darkness anyway with the window shades drawn and fastened down with duct tape. On the side of the brown brick building ran a fire escape, and the very thought of a fleeing drug dealer clomping down the metal stairs or a love-struck girl cautiously sneaking her way past the window on her way to a secret rendezvous was enough to cause Hassan's brother, Ghalib, to take the extra precaution.

Hassan secured the soldering iron in its metal stand. Just below the tip were two brown-edged scars that had been burned into the table earlier in the day when the tool had slipped from its makeshift holder. Two teaspoons and more tape were all Ghalib had needed to reinforce the stand and make it stable. Hassan flexed his hand, trying to release the tension of the last five minutes' white-knuckle session.

Ghalib crossed the room to admire his older brother's work. "Is it done?"

"It is done," Hassan said with a sigh.

Ghalib placed his hand on Hassan's damp shoulder. "Then we are ready to go?"

"Tomorrow, Ghalib. We will do it tomorrow." Hassan patted his brother's hand, then stood and took Ghalib by both shoulders. Although only six years separated the two siblings, the premature gray around Hassan's temples and the extra three inches of height seemed to triple that spread. "Father would have been proud of you, little brother."

"And of you," Ghalib replied with a heavyhearted smile.

With one final shoulder clap, Hassan walked to the kitchenette and put a pot of water onto a hot plate. As he stood leaning on the narrow counter, he noticed that his right leg was bouncing up and down. He forced himself to stop. Ghalib needed to see strength and confidence, not this nervousness.

Tomorrow didn't scare him—death held no fear anymore. Hassan just wanted to make sure that they would die in such a way as to further Allah's cause. If only he could be certain that they were doing the right thing. Just a quick phone call, a brief *"Is this okay?" "Yes, it's okay"* would set his mind and heart at ease. But that was impossible now.

Two months ago, all communication had halted from the leadership of the Cause to Sheikh Hamza Yusuf, the leader of the madrassa where Hassan and Ghalib had been taught the truth about Islam and what Allah expected from his followers. Then, two weeks ago, the madrassa and its accompanying mosque had been raided. Sheikh Yusuf had disappeared during the raid—whether into the hands of the American government or through one of the escape routes, Hassan did not know.

For days afterward, Hassan and Ghalib had remained paralyzed in their apartment, waiting for the inevitable knock. Hassan knew that the amount of explosives and accompanying electronics squirreled away in their small living space was enough to send them both to prison for many years. The television said that the raid on their madrassa had been just one of a massive series of raids across the country that had effectively put an end to the Cause in America.

Confused and frightened, the brothers had prayed for direction for their next steps. It had all seemed so right and so clear as they'd listened and studied and grown through the wisdom of Sheikh Yusuf. Step one, step two, step three—it was a formula that would lead them directly to paradise. But now they were on their own. Allah knew their hearts, and he knew the paths they should take. He must speak to them now.

The beginnings of their answer came one night as they were watching the television. A special report broke into the investigative crime show, telling of a suicide attack on a bus in Portland, Oregon. Two days later, word came that another bomb had gone off at a religious music festival in Illinois. A day after that, two more explosions took place in Dallas, Texas, and Charlotte, North Carolina.

That was when Hassan realized that Allah *was* speaking to him. Leaderless cells like his were no longer looking to men for guidance. They were looking directly to God. And what would God have Hassan and Ghalib do? Finish what they had started!

That "aha" moment had taken place three nights ago. Now Hassan and Ghalib were ready to make their own mark in the cause of Islam. Tomorrow the brothers would each don a vest containing twenty-five pounds of explosives and several thousand flathead screws, travel to the National Zoo, and then continue their journey to paradise. On a crowded Saturday, the death and mayhem left behind would be considerable. And if a few wild cats happened to escape in the aftermath, well, the terror would just be prolonged.

Hassan reached into a doorless cabinet to get a tin of tea and two cups. As the kettle began to whistle, another sound struck Hassan's ear—a slight scraping sound on the wooden floor. He turned in time to see a thick, black wire sliding back underneath the front door.

"What . . . ? Ghalib!" he yelled as the door burst open.

Three masked figures dressed all in black and carrying automatic weapons rushed into the room. A confusing cacophony of orders filled the apartment: "Drop!" "Don't move!" "Get on the floor now!" Hassan froze in place as one of the barrels trained itself on his chest.

Then he saw something that caused his heart to sink at the same time that it swelled with pride and envy. Ghalib was diving for the vest nearest himself. The tall man in the middle of the group fired two quick shots, striking the young man in the head and chest. Hassan closed his eyes, and when he opened them again, he saw Ghalib on the ground—blood rapidly pooling around him. Thankfully, the shots had spun him the other direction, so Hassan didn't have to see what the bullets had done to his brother's face.

"I said get on your knees now!" The rifle stock of the man nearest Hassan drove into his thigh, dropping him to the ground and bringing his attention away from Ghalib's body. Two more dark figures had entered the room, and he could see more movement outside in the hall.

"Clear," one of the men said as he came out of the apartment's bathroom.

"Clear," another echoed as he exited the bedroom.

"Cuff him, Tommy," the tall man said as he made his way toward Hassan. Hard plastic encircled Hassan's wrists and pinched his flesh as it was pulled tight. "Let him stand."

Hassan felt a hand slip under his armpit and easily lift him to his feet. The man giving the orders reached up and pulled his mask off, revealing a face highlighted by distant, melancholy eyes; a slight, wry smile; and a goatee that hung four inches below his chin.

"Why'd your brother have to go and make me shoot him, Hassan? If only he'd stayed nice and calm like you." The man accentuated the last words by patting Hassan lightly on the face. Then he grabbed Hassan's face tightly and turned it toward Ghalib. Together they stared at the body.

Finally, he spoke. "*Tsk, tsk, tsk.* What a waste." Then, with a quick sigh, he released his grip. "Tell you what, Hassan: Mr. Li here is going to take you on a little drive to a place where we can talk more privately—you know, sort of like a get-acquainted session. You might not be surprised to find out that I have a few questions I'd like to ask you."

With that, the man turned and walked out the door, leaving Hassan dizzy, scared, and more than a little sick to his stomach.

CHAPTER SEVEN

TUESDAY, JULY 7, 7:25 P.M. EDT
WASHINGTON, D.C.

Scott Ross cursed under his breath as he left the room. For all his bravado, the truth was he hated taking a life. It didn't matter what the person had done or was planning to do; every time he pulled that trigger, it put a little more darkness into his soul.

Realizing that his exit from the room had been a little premature, Scott said into his comm system, "Gilly, secure the apartment, then wait for the tech geeks to get there."

"You got it, boss," came Gilly Posada's voice through Scott's earpiece.

A lot of changes had taken place in Scott's life recently. After Jim Hicks, the former head of the counterterrorism division's experimental Front Range Response Team, had ignored established jurisdictions and broken every interagency rule by hacking other intelligence agencies' information—and then had the audacity to get himself killed in an unauthorized covert operation on foreign soil—the upper mucketymucks of Homeland Security had decided that enough was enough. Maybe their CTD response teams were a little too Wild West. Eventually, the whole concept was scrapped, the people reassigned.

Although Scott had been able to keep his analyst and ops teams together, they had been transferred en masse to Washington, D.C., where eyes and ears could keep tabs on them. Those eyes and ears were stifling. Political correctness ruled the capital. Public opinion seemed to be determined more by George Soros and the *Huffington Post* than by the public itself. As a result, Scott found himself having to analyze his every move before he made it just to decide whether the political fallout was worth the end result.

The big move had occurred just under a week ago, and Scott's team had hit the ground running. This was the second terrorist cell they had broken up in as many days. And as long as they were out hunting bad guys, the new situation was tenable. But back at the office, things were very different.

After the absolute freedom of the brief Jim Hicks era, Scott was finding his new situation extremely confining. He could already imagine the reports he was going to have to write and the hearings he would have to endure for shooting this kid. At least he still had some autonomy as a special operations group leader. Stanley Porter, the head of the counterterrorism division, gave Scott's SOG team more leniency than most. But Porter could only allow the lines to be stretched so far before he felt the wrath of his own superiors at Homeland Security.

This kid . . . that's what ticked Scott off so much. Ghalib al-Aini had been only nineteen years old. *And you killed him . . . put a gun against his head, pulled my trigger; now he's dead.* Since coming to CTD, Scott had killed more people than he had in all his years with the Air Force Special Operations Command—not necessarily a statistic he had anticipated when he had e-mailed his résumé for the analyst desk jockey job.

And it wasn't just the killing that got him down. It was seeing the wasted lives. *Hassan al-Aini is going to disappear into some prison, never to be heard from again. His whole life is done—he's never going to have a wife, never going to have kids, never going to contribute to society. That's it,* no más, *exit stage left and Heavens to Murgatroyd!*

As he stepped from the building into the warm night air, Scott thought, *You're going to have to decide how long you're gonna keep at this. Is this really the life you want? All this killing's making you into someone you don't want to be. All these wasted lives are turning you into a cynic. Now you know why Jim drank so much.*

Until last week, Scott could relieve some of this pressure by hopping into his '73 Chevy panel van and driving over to Riley Covington's house. Scott would stretch out on the leather couch in Riley's great room, feet kicked up on the coffee table, and settle in for an evening of chatting. Eventually perspective would begin to take hold. By the time Riley dead-bolted the door behind him, Scott would be in a much better frame of mind.

But now fifteen hundred miles separated Scott from that sofa. He leaned against the building and tried to shut out the flash of police lights and the bustle of activity all around him. *Well, if you don't have the hand you want, you just gotta work with the hand you're dealt.*

Reaching into his pocket, he pulled out a cell phone. He pressed speed dial three, and after two rings a voice answered, "Yo, Homeslice, what up?"

Scott breathed a sigh of relief when he heard his friend's voice. "Pach, dude, you gonna be home later tonight? I think I need a little couch time, even if it's only by phone."

A minute later Scott slid the phone back into his pocket. The wry smile gently began tugging again at the corners of his mouth. Riley Covington's last words to him—*Anything, anytime, anywhere*—echoed in his mind, and the elusive peace that Scott so desperately needed slowly began to make its migration back home.

CHAPTER

EIGHT

SUNDAY, JULY 12, 11:30 P.M. KST
NORTH KOREA–CHINA BORDER

The sounds of dice and laughter announced the patrol boat minutes before it slowly drifted into view on the Amnok River. There was just enough light on the deck for Pak Kun to make out two men on watch—one manning the spotlight and one the mounted gun.

Pak Kun huddled down in the fetid mud on the North Korean side of the river. His makeshift raft had been almost completely uncovered when he first heard the sounds of the approaching boat. Panicking, he had hastily thrown the branches back on. Now he prayed that the covering would be enough.

It was one week ago that Pak Kun's cousin, Pak Bae, had come to Chosan bearing gifts for the extended family. Nearly twenty family members had shown up at the railroad station to celebrate this rare visit. Even the cousins' great-grandfather, Pak Bae's namesake, had shuffled his way to the reunion.

Pak Bae was led to an old tree where a picnic had been set up. For the next hour, while everyone feasted on *cheonggukjang, kimchi,* and the wonderfully sweet *tteok,* laughter and the occasional gasp filled the air as stories were told of city life. Pak

Kun laughed until his sides hurt as Pak Bae, who from childhood had always had a gift for impersonations, imitated some of the important men who came to get gas at his station.

As always, the time had passed much too quickly, and soon it was time for Pak Bae to catch the train for his return trip to Pyongyang. Hugs, kisses, and blessings were given all around. After Pak Kun received his hug, he separated from his cousin but still held on to his hands as they spoke their words of farewell. When he finally let go, Pak Kun stepped away, turned to cough, and slipped a small, waterproof sheath into his mouth. As the family waved at the departing train, Pak Kun was already planning the journey he would take one week later.

Now, as the river mud oozed up between his toes, Pak Kun's tongue slowly ran along that sheath. He wondered what secrets were held in that soft little container—diagrams for a weapons system, plans for an attack, petitions for helping a people's insurrection? *Sure, an insurrection—that will be the day,* he thought, shaking his head. *Our army is too strong, our leaders too corrupt, and our people too used to being beaten down. Any change for our country is going to have to come from the outside, not the inside.*

Pak Kun's body tensed as the sweep of the spotlight got closer. He tried to sink deeper into the mud and rotting vegetation. He knew what would happen if he was caught. In his mind he replayed the vision from two years earlier of four badly beaten bodies hanging by their necks from a tree in the town square for three weeks before the police finally cut them down.

Something brushed against Pak Kun's ankles, causing him to gasp. He looked down to see a water snake slowly gliding between his legs. He dared not move. He prayed the noise he'd made hadn't been enough to attract the attention of the boat. But a moment later, everything around him lit up like the middle of the day.

It took all his self-control to hold still the last few seconds until the snake glided into the water. Then Pak Kun eased down to his stomach. While he inched his way deeper into the brush, he heard soldiers' voices. Then a large-caliber gun began firing.

All around him bushes and trees shredded. Branches, leaves, and bugs fell over him. *Be invisible,* he thought. *Please let me be invisible.*

Then, as abruptly as the firing began, it ended. Pak Kun could hear an angry voice coming from the boat.

"What are you shooting at, you toad?"

"I heard a noise, then saw that raft, sir," a second voice said.

"Where? What raft? That little thing? That's it? That's probably just some peasant's fishing boat."

"But I heard a rustling, sir!"

"A rustling? You heard a rustling? Imagine that. There are bats and weasels all around this river, and you heard a rustling! Did you see anything?"

"No . . . no, sir."

"Then why did you scare us all half to death by firing at an empty riverbank, you ignorant fool? Idiot! Double shift for you tonight! Who knows, maybe you'll discover a rebel band of river otters preparing for a sneak attack!"

Laughter sounded from the boat as the engines started up. From his hiding place, Pak Kun watched the spotlight continue its sweeping of the shore as the patrol slowly floated downriver. He waited a few extra minutes, and then carefully slid back down to the raft.

While there were definitely some chunks taken out of it, it still looked seaworthy enough. Even if it did sink, the place where Pak Kun made his crossings was only a third of a kilometer across. He had just finished hiking through seven kilometers of forest. Surely he could swim that short distance if need be.

After pulling the brush off the raft, he eased it from the mud and into the water. Using a small, homemade paddle, he pushed himself away from shore and into the lazy current.

As he paddled, Pak Kun thought of the day his cousin, Pak Bae, had first asked him to become part of this treason. Although they had been like brothers ever since they were babies, Pak Bae's voice was noticeably shaking as he explained what he had recently become involved in. It was obvious he knew that with one word from Pak Kun to the authorities, he would be a dead man.

Pak Kun was stunned as he silently listened to his cousin. Sure, everyone broke little laws here and there. You did what you had to do to survive. But treason? Espionage? That was dangerous.

Pak Kun had not given his cousin an answer immediately.

Instead, he had wrestled with the decision for a night. *Do I really have the right to put my whole family at risk? Can an insignificant peasant like me really stand up against the Kim regime?*

By the time the first rooster crowed, Pak Kun had made up his mind. There were millions of his fellow Koreans standing by and not doing anything—many because they were afraid, but many others because there was nothing they could do. If he had a chance to make any sort of difference, he owed it to those helpless millions, he owed it to his ancestors who had built this country, and he owed it to the future generations of Koreans.

But if he was caught, he would be just another nameless sacrifice to the Great Leader.

Today was his fourth trip across the North Korean–Chinese border since that day eighteen months ago. Although each trip left him with physical and emotional scars, he still hoped there would be many more.

Finally Pak Kun's raft slid onto the muck of the opposite shore. He hopped out and pulled it into the bushes. After climbing up the steep banks, he made his way to a barbed wire fence. *It's interesting,* he thought as he snipped away with his cutters. *Our troops patrol the rivers to keep our people in, and the Chinese build fences to keep our people out.*

After widening the hole he had just created, Pak Kun crept through the fence. A moment later, trusting in the darkness of the night, he left the security of the brush. In his hand he carried eight small river stones.

About five hundred meters from the small delta on which he had made his landing was a dirt road. The road was narrow and consisted of two ruts dug into the soil from centuries of cart wheels. Pak Kun found a place on the side of the road that was clear of decomposing ox dung, then laid out the stones, forming a small *T*.

Pak Kun quickly made his way back to the riverbank and found a particular tree. He walked around to the river-facing side, removed the sheath from his mouth, and tucked it into the crook of a branch.

Silently asking his ancestors to protect the message, he slipped back through the fence and onto his raft. Pak Kun still had a dangerous and exhausting journey ahead of him before the new sunrise came, and with it another long day at the textile factory in Chosan.

CHAPTER NINE

MONDAY, JULY 13, 10:45 A.M. MDT
INVERNESS TRAINING CENTER,
CENTENNIAL, COLORADO

Riley's eyes opened, and the first thing he heard was shouting off to his left. He shook his head and tried to clear the cobwebs. Then the pain hit. It started like a small seed just under his right ear and soon grew to encompass everything from the neck up. His jaw felt like it had been nailed with a Kathy Bates sledgehammer swing, and he could taste blood in his mouth. There was a tickle under his nose, and when he went to wipe it, his hand came away red.

What is all that shouting? he wondered. A hand slid under him, helping him to sit up on the grass.

"Pach. Pach, you okay?" Afshin was asking him.

"Yeah, I'm fine. Help me up, would you?"

"Don't you think you should—"

"Just help me up!"

Another arm slipped under his opposite shoulder. "You heard the man, Rook. Up we go," safety Danie Colson said.

Riley's world spun, and he felt for a moment like he was surfing the earth's rotation. He was finally able to steady himself by picking a point on the north goalpost and fixing on it until his brain caught up with his body.

Turning around, he immediately saw the source of the racket. A scuffle was being broken up as one group of large bodies tried to pull apart and hold back a second group of large bodies. When things sorted themselves out, Riley could see linebackers coach Rex Texeira and several defensive players holding Keith Simmons and center Chris Gorkowski. Facing off with them and being restrained by two other players was one man—tight end Muhammed Zerin Khan.

Like a light being switched on in a dark room, the last several seconds came back to Riley with sudden clarity. It was minicamp, and the Mustangs were running a touch drill—no pads, no hard hits. Riley had spotted Zerin cutting across the middle. But the ball was thrown downfield to Jamal White, so Riley had let up.

Zerin hadn't.

The last thing Riley remembered was Zerin's head hitting his cheek. Then came the waking and the spinning.

Ted Bonham, the head of the medical team, came running up and set his bag on the grass. "Riley, you all right?"

"I'm fine," Riley replied, unsure whether his answer was true or not.

"I want you to look at my finger and—"

"Hold on, Bones," Riley said, pushing past the trainer and moving toward the crowd of players. "I'll be right back."

Bonham's protests were quickly drowned out by the curses of various players as Riley approached the group. Standing just outside of the melee was Coach Roy Burton. He raised his eyebrows to Riley, and Riley nodded that he was okay. *He must be waiting for everything to calm down and disperse before he gets his pound of Zerin's flesh.*

Riley put his hand on Keith's chest and then reached over to Gorkowski's. "I'm fine, guys. Really, it's all right. Back off."

Both reluctantly stood down.

Riley spotted Texeira, who had found the receivers coach. Riley let them keep on arguing—that was none of his concern.

Turning to Zerin, who had quit yelling but was still pressed up against the hands of two other players, Riley said, "That was quite a hit."

Zerin just stared at him silently.

The look in his eyes—angry, yet somewhat amused—unnerved Riley a bit. "Don't worry, man; accidents happen," Riley said, walking up to Zerin with his hand held out.

Zerin's eyes never left Riley's. "Wasn't no accident."

"I should have held you under the water while I had the chance!" came Gorkowski's voice.

Riley turned to see the center straining again against the hands that were holding back his attack.

"Snap! Leave it alone!"

But even as he said it, he could hear Zerin saying, "I'd like to see you try! How many steps have you lost now?"

Riley whirled around and walked directly up to Zerin until they were almost nose to nose. The crowd suddenly fell silent. Riley spoke quietly so that only Zerin and those holding him could hear. "Zerin, I forgive you."

Zerin continued to fix Riley with his hard stare. "I didn't ask for no forgiveness," he said with venom in his voice.

"That may be, but I'm forgiving you anyway, so you better get used to the idea. And if you cheap-shot me again, you know what? I'm going to forgive you again." Then Riley broke into a grin that killed his jaw and cracked the drying blood on his mouth. "Sorry, man, but I'm not going to let you get in my head. You're just plumb out of luck."

Riley turned and started walking to Ted Bonham. "Okay, Bones, now you can check me. Let's see just how badly Mr. Universe scrambled my already-mixed-up brains."

As Bonham ran him through a series of tests, Riley could see the crowd breaking up. But one thing never changed—Zerin never took his eyes off Riley. At least until Coach Burton walked up to him, and then the volume increased all over again. This time, however, the conversation was completely one-sided.

CHAPTER TEN

MONDAY, JULY 13, 11:30 A.M. MDT
INVERNESS TRAINING CENTER,
CENTENNIAL, COLORADO

After the drills, Riley wanted to get home as quickly as possible. But when he saw defensive lineman Tony Hawker, the team's only Muslim other than Zerin, getting a rubdown, he decided that his muscles felt pretty sore too. He stepped in front of a rookie tailback who was about to hop up on the adjoining table and took it for himself.

"Sorry, Rook," Riley said, not really feeling sorry at all. *What can I say? Tenure has its privileges. Besides, the chances of this kid still being here in September are slim to none.*

"Give me the works, Fletch," he said to trainer Russell Fletcher, who was standing by ready to work on whoever took his table.

"You got it, Pach."

As Riley stretched out, Hawker was already waiting for him. "I don't understand him either, man."

"What?" Riley asked. "Who?"

Hawker chuckled. "Come on, Pach, I can read you like a book. You want to ask me about Zerin, and I'm telling you I don't understand him either."

Riley laughed. "I'm that obvious?"

"You're so transparent, you're see-through."

"Well, I guess that's not altogether a bad thing. I think the main thing I'm wondering is whether this is a—*uhhhh!*" Fletcher had just hit a spot on Riley's calf that made it feel like he had plunged his thumb through the skin, under the muscle, and onto the bone. That was the thing with these trainers. It felt great when you reached your destination, but sometimes the journey itself could be murder.

Hawker, white-knuckling the sides of his own training table, waited Riley out.

"What I'm wondering is whether this is a Muslim thing or just a Zerin thing?"

Hawker quickly sucked in air as his trainer began working on his quads. "I don't know," he said through gritted teeth. "Both, I guess."

"Go on," Riley encouraged, his eyes just beginning to water—"involuntary eye sweat," they liked to call it.

"I mean, he and I follow a different kind of Islam from each other. And while it's true that you've got to look a little harder for the 'turn the other cheek' kind of forgiveness you guys have, it's there. I know you're kinda familiar with the Koran. Surah 42:40 says, 'And the recompense of evil is punishment like it, but whoever forgives and amends, he shall have his reward from Allah.'

"But mostly, though, I just see my faith as trying to emulate the character and qualities of Allah. God is forgiving, so I too should be forgiving. God is merciful, so I too should be merciful. God is generous, so I too should be generous."

"But Zerin doesn't see it that way. . . ."

Hawker gave an involuntary twitch as hands began probing his ribs. "No, he doesn't. I talked to him after the taping incident. I could see his heart was going the wrong way. He didn't say much, even to me. But what he did say got me a little scared for him. He's big into the whole honor thing, which I know is important among Middle Eastern Muslims. But the kid's from Atlanta!

"Still, he feels like his honor has been wounded and he needs to avenge his name. So you got that, and you combine it with his focus on the more controversial parts of the Koran, and you got trouble."

"Controversial how?"

"Well, you got passages like Surah 22:60—'He who retaliates with the like of that with which he has been afflicted and he has been oppressed, Allah will surely aid him.' And 5:45—'Life is for life, and eye for eye, and nose for nose, and ear for ear, and tooth for tooth.' But you guys got that one, too, don't you?" Hawker said with a grin.

"Yeah, that's Old Covenant. Hey, Fletch, any farther center and you'll have to buy me dinner," Riley called back to Fletcher, who was working his fist into Riley's glutes.

"Old Covenant, New Covenant. You Christians make things so complicated. We've got one God, one book, and one truth—there is no God but Allah, and Muhammad is his messenger. Plain and simple."

Riley chuckled. "Yeah, one God, one book, one truth—and five pillars and five prayers and six articles of belief and two descending lines from Muhammad and twelve imams . . ."

"Okay, okay," Hawker laughed, "I guess we both have our little complications."

"But that's just the thing, Hawk. Christianity isn't complicated. It's the simplest belief system in the world. It's all about a free gift of salvation you don't have to work for."

"Yeah, I know. Believe me, I've heard it all before. But, Riley, man, if it's all the same to you, I'm not in the mood to get all theological right now. You wanted to know about Zerin, and I told you what I know. Let's leave it at that. Cool?"

"Cool with me," Riley said just as Fletcher reached his fingers into Riley's armpit. "Ow! Come on, Fletch, do you love me or do you hate me? You gotta decide, because I can't take this split personality thing you're giving me much more."

A sharp dig into his serratus anterior gave Riley his answer, although it wasn't the answer he was hoping for.

CHAPTER ELEVEN

MONDAY, JULY 13, 12:10 P.M. MDT
INVERNESS TRAINING CENTER,
CENTENNIAL, COLORADO

As Riley toweled off from his shower, he thought about what Hawker had said. *How do two followers of one religion have such different opinions on how it should be lived?*

He tossed his towel into the hamper in the center of the room, then began pulling his clothes out of his locker. As he did, he saw his ever-present Bible sitting on the top shelf. He picked it up and held it in his hand. *But I guess that's not too different from how people have used this over the centuries. In these pages, people have found excuses to go to war and slaughter innocents. Yet others have found reasons to go and tend to the wounded and dying that were left behind by the first group.*

Putting the book back on the shelf, he thought, *I guess while there are huge theological differences between Islam and Christianity, there isn't necessarily that much difference in the people.*

I mean, look at Khadi. She is one of the best people I know, and she is a good Muslim. At that thought, sadness came over Riley. *Unfortunately, being good is not enough. And believing in something false is also not enough, no matter how passionate your faith.*

As he finished getting dressed, Riley prayed for Khadi as he often did throughout the day. He also prayed for Tony Hawker, and he even forced himself to pray for Zerin.

Just before reaching *amen*, Riley's prayer was interrupted by a voice. "Covington!"

Turning, he saw Zerin walking by on the other side of the locker room. Suddenly, he underhanded something at Riley. Instinctively, Riley reached out his hand and caught the item—a mini bottle of Gatorade. He was so stunned that he didn't look back up to say thanks until Zerin had already walked out the door.

Dropping to the bench in front of his locker, Riley began laughing. He twisted the cap off the bottle and chugged the drink in one pass. *Wow, maybe things are starting to look up.* He put the cap back on and launched the bottle with an NBA-quality flip of his wrist. The empty sailed across the room, hit the rim of a trash barrel, and bounced to the ground.

"Missed it by that much," Riley said, getting up to retrieve the bottle. But before he had a chance to collect it, defensive coordinator T. J. Ceravolo walked up and lifted it off the ground.

"Thanks, Coach. I think we need to put a backboard on that barrel," Riley said, laughing. However, his mood quickly changed when he saw the look on Ceravolo's normally friendly face.

"Coach Burton needs to talk to you, Riley—ASAP."

"Of course. What's up?"

"Just get up there," Ceravolo said, not looking Riley in the eyes.

"Sure, Coach," Riley answered, his anxiety level starting to rise.

As he traveled down the halls of the training center, his mind raced. A player never got called to the coach's office for good news. Typically, it meant you were leaving the team for one reason or another—suspension, cut, or trade. But none of those options made sense to Riley.

He hadn't done anything suspension-worthy—although his brain rapidly processed through every supplement and pain remedy he'd ingested over the past six months. He couldn't imagine getting cut, unless it was because he was becoming too dangerous to have around. And the thought of trading him, when the off-season talk had all been about designating him the franchise player, made absolutely no sense.

Franchise player—that's it! The July 15 deadline is only days away. These bums are going to go through with franchising me!

Up until recently, the Mustangs had been telling Riley that he was their franchise player. But for some reason, they had been holding off on making the final decision. The coaches had told him it was a done deal, his agent had told him it was a done deal, but Riley kept on holding out hope that it would fall through. It's not that he wanted to leave the team. Far from it—he couldn't imagine playing anywhere else. But while being franchised offered a player job security, it stunk in the financial department. Between salary and signing bonus, a "franchise player" designation could cost him upwards of seven million dollars this year.

"But now they're going to do it," Riley grumbled under his breath as he opened the door to the coach's reception area. *I guess I should have expected it.*

Karen Watkins, the same secretary Coach had had since coming to the team years ago, said, "Go on in, Riley. He's waiting for you."

"Thanks," Riley said as he knocked, then opened the next door.

Coach Burton was sitting behind his desk. Behind him was a bank of video screens that received feeds from each of the position meeting rooms. The desk itself was piled with large stacks of paper, and the bookshelves surrounding him held playbook binders and DVDs.

"Sit down, Riley," Burton said.

As Riley moved to a chair, he decided to take the upper hand in the conversation. He was an elite veteran player, after all. Shouldn't he have some say in his contract designation? "Listen, Coach, I think I know what this is about, and you need to know that I'm not happy about this whole franchising thing. First of all, I think the whole rule is—"

"You're being traded," Burton said.

Riley stopped cold. He wanted to ask the coach if he was joking, but Burton's face made it clear he wasn't. "I'm being . . ."

Burton leaned back in his chair. "I'm sorry, son. This is not my decision. You are a great player and a good person. You're also an American hero, and it's been an honor to have you playing on my team."

"I'm being . . ." Riley's body had taken on a lightness that made it feel as if he were dreaming. *Wake up! Come on—wake up!*

"I don't even know the terms of the deal—it's something Mr. Salley and the Washington Warriors' owner, Rick Bellefeuille, have worked out."

"Washington?" *Wake up; wake up; wake up!*

"And I know this is a lot to ask, but Mr. Salley is insistent. Because of the fallout that's going to result from this, Mr. Salley has asked that you don't mention the trade to anybody—particularly not to your teammates or the media. You're obviously excused from any more practices or workouts, and you don't have to report to the Warriors until training camp starts. Take the time to get away. To process. To get used to the idea."

"I still don't understand. Why?"

Burton, who was obviously disgusted by the whole thing and just wanted it over with, finally lost his patience. "I don't know why, Riley! It's the nature of the game! Players come and players go, and it's your time to go, okay? I'm not happy about this; you're not happy about this. But what am I going to do?"

Riley sat glaring at the man. He wanted to throw something, maybe sweep the stacks of papers and binders off the desk, break a monitor or two. But he just sat. *The man's right. What's he going to do? What am* I *going to do?*

"When you leave today, just make it seem like any other day. Don't clear out your locker. We'll do it later and send everything to you. Mr. Salley wanted me to threaten you with all sorts of financial things if you say anything, but I know you better than that. You're a man of integrity. I know you'll do the right thing."

Yeah, you know where you can stick that "man of integrity" thing! I'll say what I think I need to say to anyone who I think needs to hear it, Riley thought, knowing deep down that he was going to end up doing exactly what was asked of him. This was the nature of the game, after all.

Coach Burton stood up and extended his hand across his desk.

"It's been a pleasure coaching you, son. I hope someday to get a chance to do it again."

Riley stood also and shook Burton's hand, all the while mumbling something about it "being an honor" and "let's hope so."

As he walked out of the office, he was in a daze. He heard Karen Watkins say something to him, but he didn't acknowledge her.

For the past few months, he had been wrestling with whether football was still for him. Many times he had considered leaving the Mustangs and moving into counterintelligence or even high-tech private security. But now that the Mustangs were being taken from him rather than him leaving the Mustangs, he was devastated.

The Mustangs had been his team from the time he was a small child in Wyoming. He'd grown up wearing orange and blue pj's and T-shirts and undies and jerseys and ball caps. He'd drunk his hot chocolate from a Mustangs mug and celebrated his birthdays with Mustangs cakes. He'd painted his body, colored his hair, and even considered getting a homemade tattoo with a few of his high school buddies until a friend's dad had told them a tattoo horror story that had scared some sense into them.

Now he was going to play for the Washington Warriors. *The Warriors? Really? They're not a rival. They're not a contender. The Warriors just kind of fall into that "who-gives-a-rip" category of PFL franchises. They're paragons of mediocrity.*

Riley struggled with feelings of loss and betrayal as he packed his day bag and left the locker room for his car. *They may think they hold all the cards and can play them however they want. However, I still hold one big ace in the hole. There's nothing that says I have to be anywhere but in my living room when the next season starts.* And the farther Riley walked away from that locker room, the farther it felt like he was walking away from his football career.

CHAPTER TWELVE

TUESDAY, JULY 21, 5:45 P.M. AKDT
KIIRAURAQ BAY, ALASKA

"Look out for the rope, Pach!" Skeeter yelled. "You got that one there? There's another one. What about the boulder at twelve o'clock? You see that?"

"Why, Mr. Dawkins, I've never heard you talk so much," Riley laughed as he watched Skeeter clutching the v-bar with a death grip. Riley sat directly behind Skeeter in the tandem aircraft, manipulating the controls.

This was something Riley had looked forward to for a long time. That last day of minicamp had been tough—physically and emotionally. And the emotional struggles went far beyond just the final meeting with Coach Burton.

Every time he stepped onto that practice field he had been reminded of his former best friend, Sal Ricci, who had turned out to be his worst enemy. He was reminded of Khadi's bloody body and Sal's blown-out skull. He was reminded of Jim Hicks and Billy Murphy and Chris Johnson and Jay Kruse—all members of his band of brothers, all dead in this past year.

But mostly he remembered his dad. All the afternoons playing catch, all the hours spent coaching his teams, all the love and support and encouragement—all now gone.

And now my team has been taken away from me too. I still . . . I just don't understand! Burton said he had nothing to do with it, and that might be true. But Salley? What was he thinking? More than once, Riley had mollified himself with the thought that this could very well be the stupidest move since the Twin Cities Norsemen had notoriously bankrupted their future by sending three number-one draft picks, three number-two draft picks, a couple of lower picks, and five players to the Texas Outlaws for Henry Walters and a smattering of lower-round picks. Sure, Walters was a great player, but come on!

Stop thinking about football, you idiot! Take a look at the beauty around you! Live in the here and now!

Alaska was an outlet for him—a way to relax, unwind, and at least for a time, forget. When he was flying this little plane, his mind cleared, and he felt truly peaceful.

Skeeter, on the other hand, looked like he was feeling an emotion as close to terror as Riley had ever seen him express. Riley couldn't help laughing. That this very large, very dangerous man who had been involved in countless military special operations was acting so much like a scared little girl was something Riley would not soon let him forget.

Over the past months, Skeeter Dawkins had become more than just Riley's faithful bodyguard. He was his most trusted confidant. Time and time again Skeeter had put himself in harm's way to protect his captain. The deep scar on Skeet's left arm gave testimony to the big man's devotion.

The two men had served together in Afghanistan and had seen things, experienced things, and done things that bonded soldiers in a unique way. Riley had been his lieutenant, but the bond now was much deeper than simply soldier and officer. Skeeter had once expressed an insight about Riley Covington that Riley didn't even see himself. He'd said that one of the greatest attributes any real leader could have was a heart of servanthood. When you find someone who passionately serves and truly cares for those around him, then you have found a leader worth following.

Right now, I have a feeling Skeeter's questioning his commitment, Riley thought with a smile.

Riley knew the compassionate thing would be to lighten up on the aerial cowboy act and just put the plane down.

"But what fun would that be? Right, Skeet?" Riley said out loud as he dropped the aircraft down so that the wheels were just above the water.

"Pach!" Skeeter yelled from the front.

The PA-18 Super Cub seemed to be an extension of Riley. He flew with no fear and felt he could do almost anything with it. The little plane, known for its short takeoff and landing capability, was perfectly maneuverable. And its massive tundra tires allowed it to put down almost anywhere, including the small beach just to their left.

The Super Cub had dual controls, and Riley was sitting in back because he thought Skeeter might enjoy flying the plane. Unfortunately, it became very clear very quickly that Skeeter wanted nothing to do with that special little opportunity. So instead, Riley had given his friend the task of watching for any boulders or set nets that he might not be able to see from behind Skeeter's hulking frame.

This small Alaskan beach was littered with ropes that began close to the adjacent bluffs onshore and led out into the ocean to a net system used to harvest the massive salmon run that traveled through the area each summer. The nets were operated and maintained by various native people groups and could be extremely dangerous to unsuspecting pilots.

Alaska was a truly unique place. It was not unusual to see small aircraft landing on beaches or pulling out onto state highways for takeoff. It was a mecca for general aviation pilots and outdoorsmen, and Riley had made this pilgrimage annually since he mustered out of the Air Force Special Ops.

This particular beach was one Riley knew well, and he wasn't as concerned about the obstacles as Skeeter apparently thought he should be.

Riley slowed the plane to 40 knots and picked a spot directly in front of one of the set-net ropes. He had done this so many times he could tell by the coloration of sand and gravel that it was a firm touchdown point. For added safety he would keep an appropriate flying speed so he could be airborne again in an instant with a quick jolt of the throttle if necessary. If everything seemed fine once they touched down, he'd simply close the throttle and steer the tail-wheel Cub to a stop with the rudder pedals.

"Okay, Skeet, we've got a slight crosswind from the left, so we'll use a bit of right rudder. A little less power—looks good."

"I don't need a play-by-play! Just get us down!"

As the giant tires began to roll across the beach, Riley backed off the throttle, eased the stick into his lap, and applied the heel brakes. A moment later, the plane was still as the propeller came to an abrupt stop.

Silence. Only Skeeter's heavy breathing interfered with the sound of waves lapping the shoreline.

Skeeter struggled to turn around in the small cockpit. "Now what?" he asked, trying to seem tough once again.

"You okay, Skeet?" Riley asked with a grin.

Skeeter glared at Riley.

"'Cause you almost sounded a little scared," Riley continued.

"You gave me a job, and I did it. Now are we getting out of this thing?"

Riley scanned the beach. "You sure you want to get out? There could be scary birds out there or maybe even a ferocious baby seal."

The two men stared at each other, albeit with very different expressions on their faces.

Riley broke the standoff, saying, "Okay, my friend, if you think you can handle it, let's get out. I want to show you something."

Riley swung open the door next to Skeeter, and the big man lumbered out of the tiny airplane. Riley followed with much greater ease. At the tail of the Cub, Riley grabbed a handle, lifting the plane's rear section off the ground and pulling it further from the surf.

"That should be good," Riley said admiring his work. He looked at the sun and at the water. "We only have about forty minutes before we'll get run off by the incoming tide."

He went back to the plane's cabin and reached behind the backseat to pull out a bucket and two small shovels.

"Let's go," Riley said with a smirk.

As the two men walked toward the water, Riley explained what came next. "This area is known for very large razor clams. As you can see, right now it's low tide. As the tide begins to come back in, the water pressure will force the clams to the surface. You'll know you've got one near you when you see small air bubbles in the sand.

"When you see one, take your shovel and dig very quickly just to the side of the bubble. When you've got a small hole, drop the shovel and begin digging with your hands. Once you feel the hard outer shell, grab what feels like the clam's tongue and pull. The clam will be digging too, so you need to be quick."

"Grab the tongue of a digging clam? Be honest—this is kind of like snipe hunting, isn't it?" Skeeter said suspiciously.

"No, I'm serious. We can get close to seventy, but we have to be fast. Then when we're done, we'll clean them up, and I'll make a seriously rocking clam dip," Riley bragged.

Skeeter didn't move.

"Still don't believe me? Here, watch."

Riley, hitching up his chest waders, dropped to his knees next to a dime-sized hole. After two quick shovel motions, Riley thrust his hand down into the sand. Moments later, he pulled his hand back proudly and revealed a nine-inch oval creature.

"Your turn," Riley said as he tossed the clam up to a surprised Skeeter. "Once you get one, throw it in the bucket, and move to the next set of bubbles."

Skeeter reluctantly dropped to his knees and began the muddy process. At first he was clumsy with the shovel, flinging sand on himself and Riley.

"Lighten up, Francis!" Riley laughed. "That's the only shovel I have for you. You break it, you're digging with just your hands."

Tossing the shovel aside, Skeeter plunged his hand into the wet sand, mumbling incoherent curses all the while. Finally, his hand came out, and he stretched it over his head. In it was an enormous clam. "Woo-hoo!" Skeeter uncharacteristically called out.

"Shhh! You'll scare away the rest of the clams!" Riley chastised him.

"Oh, sorry," Skeeter whispered.

Riley started laughing as he rifled a handful of wet sand

against Skeeter's waders. "Come on, Skeet! You see any ears on that thing?"

Skeeter looked at the clam, then threw it at Riley—pegging him in the chest.

"Ow," Riley yelled, still laughing. "What kind of bodyguarding is that?"

Without answering, Skeeter began scouring the sand for more air bubbles. Quickly, he got the hang of the process and began tossing clams into the bucket at rapid intervals. By the time the tide returned, the two of them had filled the big metal container to the brim.

Riley got to his feet and saw Skeeter in a tug-of-war with one last clam. The water was up to Skeeter's armpits, but he would not let go.

"Hey, Skeet, it's just a clam. We've already got plenty. We need to get airborne before the tide gets too high."

"I've almost got it," Skeeter said with determination. But he spoke too soon. In the epic battle between man and clam, it was the clam that lived to see another tide.

Skeeter wasn't happy about his loss, but he couldn't help but smile at the full bucket.

Riley laughed at the muddy blob standing before him. "Welcome to clamming, my friend," he exclaimed, clapping his friend on the back.

The two men walked back toward the Cub, loaded up, climbed in, and were airborne in a matter of seconds for their twenty-five-minute flight back to Kenai Airport.

CHAPTER THIRTEEN

TUESDAY, JULY 21, 7:00 P.M. AKDT
KENAI, ALASKA

"Kenai Tower, Cub November One Romeo Charlie, five miles south low level inbound with information Alpha, full stop," Riley announced over the radio.

"November One Romeo Charlie, Kenai Tower, roger. Enter straight in final for runway One. Clear to land. Be advised once on the ground proceed to ramp and park next to the Air Force Learjet."

Air Force Learjet? Riley wondered. *What's that all about?* Nevertheless, he acknowledged the instructions. "Clear to land on One and park next to Learjet. One Romeo Charlie out."

Moments later, Riley greased the plane onto the asphalt. As he taxied toward the Air Force plane, he saw four men waiting, two dressed in flight suits and the other two in business suits. Each of the business suit guys had a bulge from a vest holster, sunglasses, and—*Are you serious?*—an earpiece.

"What, did the president come all the way up here to go clamming with us?" Riley asked Skeeter in an attempt to be funny. Skeeter, on full alert, didn't acknowledge Riley's little quip.

Riley shut down the engine, and both men

began the process of extracting themselves from the small cabin. As they emerged, sand and mud dropped off their chest waders onto the ground below.

One of the suits stepped forward, ignoring the filthiness of the men, and asked, "Riley Covington?"

"That's me. What's this all about?"

"I'm Agent Devoe of the FBI. This is Agent Benson." Without saying anything else, Devoe handed Riley a sealed envelope.

Riley took the packet and opened it, stealing a quick glance at the four men's serious demeanor. He read the enclosed paper and then looked up at Agent Devoe. "I don't quite understand. Do you have anything else for me?"

"Yes, sir, but I've been given instructions to not give you the orders until airborne. This mission is strictly classified."

Skeeter became noticeably fidgety.

"Do I at least have time to run home and change?" Riley asked.

"I'm afraid not, sir," Devoe said. "As you can see by the orders, we need to depart immediately."

Skeeter couldn't help himself any longer. "Sir, my name is Sergeant Skeeter Dawkins. Mr. Covington's safety is my direct responsibility—"

"My apologies, Sergeant, but we are taking over the security of Mr. Covington. Rest assured, he will be safe."

"But, sir," Skeeter protested, putting a hand on Devoe's arm.

"Sergeant, I must respectfully ask you to stand down," Agent Benson ordered, speaking for the first time.

Skeeter was quickly becoming extremely agitated. All four of the visitors tensed up at this large man, who was visibly upset and was, for some reason unknown to them, holding a very short, muddy shovel.

Seeing the potential escalation, Riley quickly took control of the situation. He grabbed Skeeter by the shoulder and said, "Hey, Skeet, it's okay. I have to follow through on the orders. You know that. We both do. I'll let you know something ASAP. Take the truck, head back to the house, and I'll call you when I know what's going on."

"But—"

"Skeet, an order's an order. I'm sure everything is fine."

Skeeter said nothing.

The two pilots turned and quickly ran up the steps of the Learjet as the other two men escorted Riley onto the plane while keeping an eye on Skeeter. Once on board, Riley unhooked his chest waders and folded them down to his waist. Clumps of mud fell on the jet's plush carpet.

"Oops," Riley said with an apologetic grin. "So have you guys been to Alaska before?"

The two FBI agents said nothing.

"Great. I move from one great conversationalist to two more," Riley said grumpily as he turned toward the window.

Within seconds, the engines were roaring as the plane taxied out to the runway. Riley saw Skeeter still standing by the Super Cub in his waders with his clamming shovel in one hand and his bucket beside him on the ground. He knew Skeeter was weighing all his available options. *Poor guy,* Riley thought. *And all those clams gone to waste.*

The Learjet powered up, and soon it was screaming down the runway and into the air. As they climbed out of the Kenai area, Riley noticed they turned southeast. He'd initially thought they may be headed to Elmendorf Air Force Base near Anchorage, but that was north.

Agent Devoe leaned forward and handed him another sealed envelope. Riley opened it and slid a paper out. He read it, then read it again. He looked up at the man, who offered him nothing in return.

Riley's mind spun as he slowly turned to the window. "What the—" He stopped in midsentence, then leaned back into his seat as he pondered the implications of having an F-16 escort.

WEDNESDAY, JULY 22, 5:30 A.M. EDT

Riley was incredibly uncomfortable when he woke up the next morning. He had shimmied out of his waders before falling asleep but was still muddy from his and Skeeter's clamming escapade, and his shirt smelled like two-day-old sweat.

The flight had been long—very long—and he still didn't

understand what this was all about. His orders were vague and incomplete. They simply said he would be transported to Andrews Air Force Base in Maryland, where he would receive further information.

Riley was stumped. He realized there had to be some type of terror threat. But why him? He glanced out the window and again saw the escort off the left wing. New fighter, same mission. *But what in the world could that mission be?*

It was early morning when the plane touched down. The Learjet turned off the runway and taxied directly to a pristine hangar. When it came to a stop, the agents motioned for Riley to exit.

Riley stepped to the top of the stairs and looked down at a man who had just gotten out of a black Suburban. He was wearing a familiar Blue Öyster Cult T-shirt and flip-flops.

"Welcome to Washington, D.C., Lieutenant Covington," Scott Ross offered with his familiar sarcastic grin.

"Scott, you've got some 'splaining to do," Riley said, confused and exhausted but happy to finally see a friendly face.

CHAPTER

FOURTEEN

WEDNESDAY, JULY 22, 6:15 A.M. EDT
ANDREWS AIR FORCE BASE, MARYLAND

The two men grabbed each other's shoulders at the foot of the Learjet's steps. Riley was excited to see his friend again, but he also felt he was waiting for the other shoe to fall.

After they separated, Scott looked around Riley at the plane. Agent Devoe had already deplaned after Riley had stepped off, and through the windows Agent Benson could be seen talking to the two pilots.

"Where's Skeeter?" Scott asked.

"That's 'splaining number one. Skeeter's in Alaska, where these two little chatterboxes left him," Riley answered, motioning to the FBI agents. "And I'm thinking he's probably going to want to take his abandonment issues out on you because of it."

Scott's face reddened, but Riley wasn't sure whether it was from anger or from fear of what Skeeter was going to do to him the next time they were together. "Devoe, didn't I tell you to bring the big dude that was going to be with Riley?"

Devoe walked toward Scott and held out some papers. "Sir, our written orders were for

Riley Covington to be transported to Andrews Air Force Base. Riley Covington is now at Andrews Air Force Base."

Scott brushed the papers away. "But I specifically told you that Riley doesn't go anywhere without Skeeter!"

With a quick nod to Riley, Devoe said, "I think I'd have to challenge you on that point, sir. Now, if you'll excuse me . . ." And the FBI agent turned to walk away.

"Sure, whatever," Scott said, dismissing the agent with a wave of his hand. Riley could hear him mumbling, "Skeeter is going to freaking kill me" as he stared at the ground. Suddenly Scott's head popped up. "Devoe, where are Riley's bags?"

As Devoe turned around, Riley said to Scott, "That's 'splaining number two."

"What? You don't have a bag?" Scott asked as the color drained from his face.

"He does have these," Agent Benson said as he exited the plane. He tossed Riley's waders to the hangar floor, sending chunks of dried mud skittering across the clean surface.

Devoe held out the papers a second time. "Sir, our orders were to expedite Riley Covington. Taking time to go to his house so that he could pick through his wardrobe would not have been expeditious."

"Oh, brilliant! Way to think out of the box, Devoe," Scott complained, rolling his eyes. "I guess if my orders had been to pick up Riley and run him back here, you guys would be on foot about seventy-five miles down the Alaskan Highway."

Devoe clearly wanted to extricate himself from the situation and move on to bigger and better things than chauffeuring a football star from one end of the country to the other. "Sir, if you're through, we've got—"

"Yeah, I know, places to go and wires to tap," Scott interrupted. "Thanks, Devoe and Benson, you've been real gems. It's good to know the domestic safety of our nation rests in creative minds like yours."

Benson seemed about to say something, but Devoe stopped him. They walked to a waiting black sedan and drove away.

Scott turned to Riley. "I'm so sorry, Pach. If I had known . . ."

Scott's voice trailed off as he stepped back to take a good look at his friend's apparel—a dirt-stained T-shirt, clean khaki shorts, and mud-caked rubber galoshes. Suddenly Scott began chuckling.

"What?" Riley asked self-consciously.

As his laughing grew, Scott tried to speak but couldn't. Soon he was doubled over with his hands on his knees. Tears poured down his face.

"Come on, man, it's not the best look, but it's not that funny," Riley protested.

Scott tried to speak. "If . . . if only . . . if you only knew where . . ." He couldn't continue. Taking Riley by the arm, he stumbled over to the Suburban.

CHAPTER FIFTEEN

WEDNESDAY, JULY 22, 6:30 A.M. EDT
WASHINGTON, D.C.

"I'm going to see *who*?" Riley asked, panic quickly setting in.

Riley's reaction to the information Scott had just given him sent his friend into another fit of hysterics.

"Scott, it's not funny! There's no way I can go there looking like this!" Riley's voice was pleading now. He currently had a galosh on each hand and was slamming them together, futilely trying to knock the caked-on mud from the boots.

In the last row of the Suburban, Scott half stood from his seat so that he could tuck his dress shirt into his suit pants. Riley watched him in a mix of anger, horror, and envy.

"Couldn't we just pull into a Target? I'd be in and out in like five minutes max!"

Stealing a quick glance at his watch, Scott answered, "Pach, dude, you know I'd love to, but we can't. We're already running late. If we miss our time, there's no telling when we'll get on the schedule again. Besides, I doubt anything's open yet."

Scott's grin made Riley question the veracity of his friend's claim. *But he's not really that cruel,* Riley thought; *is he?* He turned in his seat and dropped the galoshes to the floor. He looked out the window; off in the distance he could see the Washington Monument standing strong against the July sunrise. *It doesn't matter how many times I see this city, it never gets old—the monuments, the Capitol, the White House . . .* A sudden wave of dread washed over Riley. *Ugh, the White House.*

"Scott, there's absolutely no way I can meet with the president looking like I just got out of—well, like I just came off of a muddy beach after a day of clamming," Riley continued his protest.

"Sorry, buddy, but we don't really have a choice. Besides, he'll probably just think you're an eccentric sports star. Don't worry about it."

"That's easy for you to say! You're wearing the suit," Riley argued, watching Scott clip on his tie.

"Quit acting like such a diva. You look fine."

Or at least Riley thought he said "fine." Scott's laughter made it difficult to fully decipher his final words.

With a sigh, Riley resigned himself to his fate. "Okay, can you at least tell me why I'm meeting with President Lloyd, or is that beyond my security clearance?"

Scott sobered up quickly. "Believe it or not, this all has to do with your senior thesis at the Air Force Academy."

A fist clenched Riley's stomach. What in the world could his thesis have to do with anything? Did they think that he stole someone else's ideas or plagiarized someone's quotes? *Yeah, brilliant deduction. The president of the United States is now doubling as the academic dean for the Air Force Academy. Besides, you know you never did anything like that.* "Go on," he prodded Scott.

"You remember you wrote about strategic defense against EMP bombs?"

The fist that had clenched Riley's stomach now gave it a twist. "Please tell me they're just taking some of my advice and shoring up our infrastructure against potential electromagnetic pulse strikes?"

"Unfortunately, it may be a little too late for that," Scott said as he finished wrestling his right foot into a dress shoe and sat up in the seat.

Riley's heart sank. "What do you mean? Are we in danger of an EMP hit?"

Scott shrugged. "Unfortunately, we just don't know for sure. MI6 got some information from . . . You know what? We really shouldn't be having this conversation here. The White House has an SCIF where I could fill you in on the whole backstory."

An SCIF, Riley knew, was a sensitive compartmented information facility. These rooms were built for privacy and secrecy. The walls were made of reinforced concrete at least eight inches thick, and it was regularly swept for bugs. If Scott or someone else at CTD had received intelligence from MI6, the British secret intelligence service, it would be highly classified and then some. Proper procedure would have any conversation of this clearance level taking place in one of these specialized rooms.

But Riley knew that time was short, and the last thing he wanted to do was go into a meeting with the president of the United States not only looking like a fool but sounding like one too.

"Scott, I need to know what's going on. Do you really think we need to worry about a security breach in this Suburban?"

Scott looked around and dropped his voice to a low whisper. "Okay. So MI6 got some info from a North Korean mole via a Chinese pipeline. Apparently, Pyongyang saw fit to sell two EMP devices to a terrorist group that is intent on bringing them here to the U.S."

Fear stole into Riley's heart. Depending on the type of device, this could mean the end of the United States as it currently existed. Even a small EMP weapon could knock a major city back to the Stone Age for months or years to come. "What's the size of the device? What sort of delivery system was sold with it? How high in the atmosphere could it get?"

"Like I said, we just don't know for sure. We don't even know if it's nuclear or nonnuclear. All we think we know is—" Scott held up a finger for each point—"two EMPs, headed for the U.S., North Korea to terrorists."

"What kind of pressure are we putting on North Korea?"

"Come on, you know North Korea. It's already the most sanctioned country on the face of the earth. Besides, right now this is still an intelligence rumor. It's completely uncorroborated. Without more evidence, if we acted against the DPRK it would cause a firestorm of international protest."

"But—"

"I know this MI6 analyst. I trust her. Her name's Anna Zeller, and she and I have traded information for years. She's not one to fly off the handle or run after cheap leads. Pach, she's scared. Scared for us."

Riley paused to let the information sink in. Writing that thesis had been one of the first eye-openers he'd had as a young cadet as to how dangerous a place the world was. EMPs could mean millions dead, America gone, the world changed. The scenario was so extreme that he had never been able to shake it from his mind. Back home in Parker, he had a shelf on his bookcase devoted completely to books, reports, and videos discussing the EMP threat.

He stretched his arm across the back of the seat, but the smell from his armpit caused him to drop it again. Then a thought struck him. "But what am *I* doing here in D.C., going to see the president?"

Scott's crafty smile spread across his face as he reached into his shaving kit and tossed Riley a stick of Right Guard Xtreme Power Gel. "I need someone to fill President Lloyd in on worst-case EMP scenarios."

With a nod of thanks, Riley popped the cap, twisted up the gel, and glided it under his arms. Then, taking one more whiff of himself, he rubbed it over his chest and stomach and put a little on the outside of the shirt, too. As he rubbed, he said, "But, Scott, I wrote that thesis years ago, and since then I could hardly be described as an EMP expert. Shouldn't you find some egghead PhD who's made the study of electromagnetic pulse weapons his life's work?"

"No, I need *you* in there. First of all, EMPs are still an understudied and underappreciated technology. So, sure, there are a handful of eggheads out there who are experts in this. However, between your thesis and your continued research, you're probably barely behind the curve. But, more importantly, an egghead is not going to help me with what I have planned," Scott said firmly. Then his resolve faltered a bit, and he added, "And this is where things could get a little bit dicey between us."

"Dicey how?" Riley asked suspiciously. He recognized the tone in Scott's voice. It often accompanied major changes that Scott had planned for Riley's life.

"Oh, Pach," Scott began with a little chuckle, "you are seriously gonna laugh. At least I hope you're going to laugh." Scott looked at Riley with a big grin, apparently hoping that his humorous demeanor would at least get a smile out of his friend. Riley tossed the deodorant stick back to Scott and continued to stare.

"Okay, man, it's like this. I need you in there because I need to establish you as an expert on EMP weapons. So while you're in with the president, if you don't know something, fake it."

Riley was about to protest, but Scott pushed on. "The reason I need to establish you as an expert is because I need *you*. You're the only one I trust to lead the operations side of the team. I can't put some dude with a pocket protector in with the guys. If the terrorists didn't rip him to shreds, the ops team would. You, however, have proven your leadership, and the guys on the team already practically worship you. So you've got the ops cred. However, I also need someone leading my team who understands EMP weapons inside and out and can recognize one when he sees one. I know enough about EMPs to be dangerous to our team; you know enough to be dangerous to the terrorists."

"Scott, you forget one thing," Riley said. "I'm a football player with the Colorado Mustangs. You've been to the games. You've seen me out on the field, remember? I was the guy with the number *50* on his back and a big *Covington* written across his shoulders. I am not, nor do I have any current desire to be, a member of the counterterrorism division. I play football, Scott. That's what I do!" But even as Riley was saying the words, he knew they were going nowhere.

"Yeah, right . . . well, you see . . . ," Scott hemmed and hawed.

Exasperated, Riley ordered, "Just say it!"

"Okay, Pach, don't hate me for this. I kind of asked Stanley Porter to pull a few strings. And he kind of got Homeland Security involved. And they kind of got the FBI involved."

"Scott! Just tell me what you've done to screw up my life!"

"Okay, so it's like this. You know you don't still play for the Colorado Mustangs—and I'll be more than happy to forgive you that little lie. And in return, I hope you'll be willing to extend me some forgiveness when I tell you that . . . well . . . you know the little football trade that you haven't mentioned to me because I'm not supposed to know about it?"

Riley didn't answer.

"Well, believe it or not, that was sort of my idea."

"What?" Riley was in shock. Scott had done things in the past to mess with Riley's life, but this far surpassed them all—this was beyond the pale. This was just plain wrong!

"I'm sorry, Pach, but I had to do it!"

Riley leaned way over the back of his seat, and Scott sank back into his. "You had to do it? Okay, you tell me why you had to do it! You tell me why you had to uproot my life and pull me away from the team I love and the teammates I love! Go ahead, *friend*, tell me!"

Scott was angry now too. He sat up right in Riley's face. "Because your country needs you! Because I need you! And even if you aren't feeling it right now, I know you well enough to believe that you would much rather be here saving lives than in Denver playing games!"

Riley leaned back into his own space. "Well, I sure appreciate having someone in my life who can force the big decisions on me, because heaven knows I couldn't handle them myself! I mean, don't you think you could have at least asked me? Couldn't you have given me at least that much respect?"

Scott's anger deflated. "You're right, Riley; you're right. I'm sorry about that. Things just got going so quickly that I've just been in action mode. I should have asked."

Riley looked into Scott's eyes and could see the sincerity of his apology. But he also got the sense that there was more that Scott was hiding from him.

But before he had a chance to pry deeper, Scott said, "If all goes well with the meeting with the president, he's prepared to give you full security clearance. You'll be living a very busy life. In the hours you're not with the Warriors, you'll be working with us preparing the ops boys."

Riley sat there letting the information sink in. At least he had an answer to why such an illogical trade had happened. And, he had to admit, spending time with his buddies on the CTD ops team again did hold a definite appeal. Then a thought struck him.

"And Khadi? Is she on board with this?"

Scott gave a soft laugh. "You know, it was all I could do to keep her from telling you. I finally had to threaten her security clearance. But, yeah, Khadi's on board.

"Like I said earlier, you're the only one we—that's both Khadi and me—can fully trust with the special ops. You have our respect and the respect of the men. If this EMP thing is for real, I want somebody leading the team who fully understands what's happening and knows the full ramifications if it actually goes down. Nobody else I know has that knowledge base. Remember your words to me: 'Anything, anytime, anywhere'? Well, this is the thing, now is the time, and here is the where."

Riley shook his head, angry at the way Scott had thrown his words back at him. *How? How in the world did this happen again? Lord, this is getting too much for me. For once, can't my life follow my plan?*

Riley sighed, resigned. It was a fait accompli. Fighting it was going to get him nowhere. Quietly, he said, "But I'm just a football player. I'm just a dumb football player."

"First of all, Pach, you're not dumb," Scott said, giving Riley's shoulder a shake, then leaning back in his seat. "You know that already. And second, if these two bombs are big enough and have a high enough atmospheric detonation, not just professional football but American civilization as we know it will, in the blink of an eye, totally cease to exist. Doesn't really matter who you're playing for then."

CHAPTER SIXTEEN

WEDNESDAY, JULY 22, 7:20 A.M. EDT
WASHINGTON, D.C.

Any self-consciousness Riley had felt in the Suburban was multiplied exponentially as he and Scott walked through the White House. He could hear people all around him whispering and snickering. One staffer made a crack about Riley being a "Gitmo reject" a little too loudly, drawing an admonishing look from their escort, a woman in her midfifties who walked with the authority of someone who had been ushering people through these sacred halls for years.

It was becoming more and more obvious that Riley's deodorant bath was only partially working, and his right galosh had developed a bit of a sucking, popping sound as he walked, which only added to the nightmare.

As he passed the portraits on the walls and the curios set on small tables, he could feel the history of the place. It was like walking into the past—all the events that he had read about for years in dry textbooks were coming alive all around him. A visit into the inner sanctums of this building was a dream come true for Riley. And here he was experiencing it while looking way too much like Tom Hanks's castaway, albeit only four days into the bushy beard.

Riley tried to put the situation out of his mind by concentrating on what Scott had told him about the people they were about to meet. President Lloyd was a liberal, antimilitary Democrat elected based on his promise to bring peace to the country and harmony with the world. However, Riley had heard that Lloyd's "Give Peace a Chance" bubble had burst during his first presidential intelligence briefing, during which he learned what was really happening throughout the world.

Then the attack on Platte River Stadium took place. Several thousand people were killed. Not many months following came terrorist attacks on the subways in Philadelphia and Washington, D.C., and at a movie premiere in Hollywood. And now, recently, were the multiple small-scale attacks taking place throughout the country that had many Americans feeling as though they were living in Jerusalem during the intifada. All these things had combined to change President Lloyd's view on the military and Homeland Security, and while he certainly couldn't be described as a hawk, he now wasn't afraid to do what needed to be done to keep the country safe.

According to Scott, Gordon Carroll, the secretary of defense, was a great ally in the fight against terrorism. A civilian, he had started his career as a K-9 cop in Des Moines, Iowa. Eventually he entered politics, and his reputation for fearlessness and straight shooting led him into Congress, the Senate, and now into the president's cabinet. Rumor was he didn't speak much in meetings, but when he did, the commander in chief listened.

In contrast, Secretary of Homeland Security Dwayne Moss was a weasel. In Scott's words, he was an "obnoxious, narcissistic stuffed shirt whose main concern is climbing over the people above him while protecting his backside against anyone or anything that might drag him down." Scott had said Moss would be their biggest opponent in the meeting today.

Finally, Stanley Porter would be there. He was the director of the counterterrorism division. While Secretary Moss was Porter's direct superior, there was probably no one on earth who had a greater disdain for the secretary of Homeland Security than Porter himself. In what now seemed like a previous lifetime, Scott had worked directly under Porter in the CTD Midwest Division Headquarters in St. Louis,

Missouri. There, the two of them had clashed repeatedly. But over the last few months, the two men had developed a mutual respect for each other's commitments and styles. Porter would be the CTD pit bull in the meeting if some biting was needed.

As their escort led them to a door, Scott whispered, "You know you ought to get that boot fixed. You sound like a walking suction cup."

"Shut up, Raggedy-Man," Riley answered, taking a quick glance at Scott's grinning profile. This was only the second time Riley had seen Scott in a suit, and while it was better than his typical rock-and-roll T-shirt and torn jeans combo, he still had the discordant look of a high school burnout wearing a graduation gown.

"Gentlemen, this is the Roosevelt Room," their escort said as she opened the door for them. "Please make yourselves comfortable until the president is ready for you. You'll find water and coffee in the carafes on the conference table."

They thanked her and entered. Riley was immediately taken by the large portrait of Teddy Roosevelt in his Rough Rider garb hanging over the fireplace. Riley had always admired the country's twenty-sixth president. His independent spirit, fearlessness in battle, and amazing sense of adventure were all qualities that Riley strove to emulate in his own character.

Movement caught his eye, and in a moment all focus on the historicity of the room flew out the window. Standing up from a couch on the far side of the long conference table was Khadi Faroughi. Her eyes were wide and bright, and a smile filled her face. The look of excited expectation, however, quickly evaporated when she saw Riley.

"Scott, what did you do to him?" she asked in disbelief as she made her way around the table.

"Uh, just a little mix-up with our friends in the Federal Bureau of Literal Interpretation."

"Riley, you're a mess," she said as she reached out to him. It had been nearly a month since they had seen each other, but as soon as he touched her, it felt like they had never been apart.

When they separated, Riley said, "Oh, I don't know. It's not so bad. I like to think of it as clamming chic. Like the boots?" he asked, lifting one up. But as he did, he accidentally kicked one of the conference chairs, leaving a dirt scuff and dropping bits of dried mud onto the immaculate carpet. Immediately he dropped down to wipe the scuff and pick up the mud, saying, "Great, we'll never get invited back here."

Scott laughed. "Riley, they've got people with vacuums who can do that."

Khadi bent down to help Riley. "Where's Skeeter? Did they make him wait in the lobby?"

"Ask Mr. Detail there about Skeeter," Riley said, nodding toward Scott.

"Skeeter? You want to know about Skeeter?" Scott paused for a moment. "Well, he sort of got left behind."

Khadi let out a sigh of exasperation. "And Porter chose you as team leader of our special operations group? Unbelievable!" Khadi still bristled a bit at her title of assistant team leader, considering her more extensive experience, more extensive education, and more extensive knowledge of counterintelligence.

"Hey, it's not what you know; it's who you know," Scott jabbed back, affirming what they both already knew to be true. Scott was team leader because he had more history with Stanley Porter—pure and simple.

"Yeah, well, soon enough it won't matter, because when Skeeter gets here, he's going to kill you, and I'll inherit your position," Khadi muttered. Then she looked up at Scott and they both started laughing. True, it was unfair, but they both genuinely respected each other, and their growing friendship went a long way toward helping them work effectively with each other despite the circumstances.

Turning serious, Khadi asked Riley, "So has Scott filled you in on the situation?"

"With the EMP threat? Yeah. We have to find a way to make that a nonstarter. If it goes off, it could potentially knock us back to the nineteenth century," Riley answered as they both stood up with little handfuls of dirt. They looked for a place to put it and finally settled on giving it to Scott, who proceeded to drop it into his pants pocket.

"Scott also told me about his wonderful plan for my life," Riley continued, letting a little of his anger slip out. He had determined in the truck that he was going to put aside any of his feelings about what Scott had done until the meeting was over. There would be time enough to deal with his friend then.

Khadi reached out and took hold of Riley's arm, "I'm so sorry about that. I wanted to tell you, at least to warn you. Scott just thought it was better to wait until you were here, and he pulled rank."

"Honestly, he was probably right. But he and I are still going to have a bit of a chat when all this is done." He turned to Scott, who pretended to admire a large grandfather clock.

The door opened, and the woman who had brought them to the room stepped in. "The president is ready to see you now," she said.

CHAPTER

SEVENTEEN

WEDNESDAY, JULY 22, 7:30 A.M. EDT
WASHINGTON, D.C.

Scott straightened his tie, Khadi pulled down on the bottom of her dress suit's jacket, and Riley took one more quick sniff of his armpits, rolling his eyes and resigning himself to his impending embarrassment.

"Just follow my lead," Scott whispered to Riley as they crossed the hallway to the open doors of the Oval Office. "And try not to say anything stupid."

"Thanks for the confidence," Riley whispered back.

As Riley stepped across the threshold into the Oval Office, his breath caught. *What is a small-town Wyoming boy like me doing in a place like this?* He was overwhelmed by a sense of the importance, the history, the absolute power of the decisions that were made in this room. *Wars were declared and peace was won all from the desk in this office. And now they want to talk to me!* Riley felt himself getting swept up in the moment, until he took his next step and heard the *mmmup!* of his heel pulling up in his galosh. *So much for history-making moments,* he thought as his face reddened.

"Ross, what is wrong with you, bringing someone looking like that into the office of the president of the United States? Have you no respect?" To Riley's right, a thin, immaculately dressed man had jumped up from his place on a couch and was rushing toward Scott. *That must be the weasel.*

"Sorry, Secretary Moss," Scott answered, "but I thought Khadi looked pretty good."

"That's enough," said both President Lloyd and Stanley Porter, although they each said it to a different man.

Moss glared at Scott another second before returning to the group of men who were now all standing. Scott, Khadi, and Riley walked around a second couch, and introductions were made.

Speaking to the president, Scott said, "I am truly sorry, sir, for Riley's attire. There was a mix-up in the rush to get him here. It's my fault."

"Don't worry about it, Agent Ross," the president said with a smile. "You should see what I sometimes wear in here—or don't wear," he whispered with a conspiratorial wink toward Riley, "when I'm up late working."

Riley wasn't sure if he should laugh or be creeped out by the president's remarks, but before he had time to decide, the president had taken his hand. "And it's a pleasure to meet you, Riley. I've always enjoyed your football play, but in this last year I've gained a whole new kind of respect for you. On behalf of the American people, I'd like to thank you for what you've done in saving so many lives."

"Thank you, sir," Riley managed to stammer.

Then, turning to Scott and Khadi, the president said, "The same goes for the two of you. I've read about your actions. We owe you a debt of gratitude as well."

Scott and Khadi shook the president's hand and acknowledged his words.

"I've been very proud of them too," Secretary Moss interjected. "They were a key part in *my* plan to stop the attacks on our soil and to bring down the Cause."

Riley saw Scott give a quick, angry glance to Stanley Porter, who returned a barely perceptible eye roll and shake of the head. *Smart move,* Riley thought. *Let the boss take the credit, which keeps you in good with him.* Those in the know—and the president definitely seemed like a man in the know—would be able to discern who was really doing the work and who was just blowing smoke.

The president sat down in his chair under the famous Rembrandt Peale portrait of George Washington. On the chair next to him sat Secretary of Defense Carroll. Moss and Porter took seats on one of the couches, leaving the other for Scott, Khadi, and Riley, who couldn't help wondering what his grimy T-shirt was doing to the cream-colored fabric.

Once everyone was settled, President Lloyd said to Scott, "Well, Agent Ross, I read your briefing, yet through Mr. Porter here I got word that you still insisted on a meeting. While it's possible that this is all part of an elaborate plan to give Riley here one of his most embarrassing moments, I have to assume that this is something more than that. So, with the most detail in the least amount of time, why don't you tell me why you're here?"

[illegible]. Then, at the window and the president [illegible] in the [illegible] would be able to [illegible] around where he was last Friday night.

The president sat down in his chair and [illegible] Upon Washington's [illegible] Secretary of Defense [illegible] of the [illegible] leaving the other for Scott [illegible] wondering what his mind [illegible] white.

One [illegible] everyone was seated, President [illegible] said to [illegible] I read your briefing [illegible] word that you all agreed on a decision. While it's possible that this is all part of a democratic plan to give [illegible] embarrassing moments, I have the feeling that [illegible] more than that. So I'd like most of all [illegible] you tell me why you're here.

CHAPTER EIGHTEEN

WEDNESDAY, JULY 22, 7:35 A.M. EDT
WASHINGTON, D.C.

Riley heard Scott take a deep breath and exhale his nerves, but before Scott could say a word, Secretary Moss jumped in. "Agent Ross has received information that—"

President Lloyd held up his hand and interrupted Moss. "Dwayne, I've heard enough from you for right now. Let's hear what Agent Ross has to say."

Riley saw the icy glare Moss directed at Scott. *The guy seems like an impossible friend to make and a dangerous enemy to keep. Gotta keep an eye on him for Scott's sake.*

"Thank you, sir," Scott said. "We have received very strong intel that an attack with electromagnetic pulse weapons is imminent. We believe that the devices originated in North Korea but are now in the hands of a terrorist group."

"So said your report. And where do you believe these weapons are now?" President Lloyd asked.

"Sir, we don't know. Our information is just that they left North Korea and are bound for the United States. We don't even know what terrorist group has them. It could be al-Qaeda, Hezbollah, Hamas, or even some new Mexican terrorist drug cartel. All we know about is the departure. We're in a fog after that."

The president picked a piece of lint off his pant leg and flicked it to the ground. "And you're sure that the DPRK is behind this? That's a pretty serious accusation—one that could get a lot of people killed. There's no telling what that crackpot Kim might do with his recently honed nuclear capabilities."

"All I can tell you is that's where the intel originated, Mr. President. Apparently MI6 has a mole fairly high up in North Korea's government. He used a pipeline to get the information to a runner in China, who got it to the Brits. An analyst friend of mine called and gave me the heads-up. Technically, we're not even supposed to know about this."

Moss, who had been fidgeting in his seat, spoke up again. "You see, sir, that's why I hesitated to hold this meeting. I hate taking up your time on supposed 'North Korean moles' and information from 'analyst friends,'" he said, air-quoting the appropriate phrases.

"In the past, the information from *this* source has been nothing but credible," Scott countered.

"But credibility has been an issue with *you*, hasn't it, Agent Ross?" Moss sneered. "I seem to remember hundreds of thousands of dollars of taxpayer money wasted at the Rose Bowl stadium based on supposedly credible information from another of your buddies, a certain Riley Covington."

Riley's eyes jerked toward Moss, but before he said anything to defend himself, he spotted Porter, who was fixing Riley with a hard stare and giving him a furtive shake of the head. Riley swallowed his anger and let Scott answer Moss.

"Did we or did we not stop the attack by Hakeem Qasim?"

"But it wasn't at the Rose Bowl!"

"Did we or did we not stop it?"

"Enough!" The president stood from his seat and had a finger pointing at each of the two men. "Now you're both wasting my time. Agent Ross, you *will* remember that Secretary Moss is your superior. And, Dwayne, *you* will do me the courtesy of letting my questions get answered uninterrupted. Do you understand?"

Although both men were still seething, they each managed a "Yes, sir."

The president sat down, crossed his legs, and straightened the crease in his pants. "Good. Now, Agent Ross, there are threats against our country every day. If you saw even half of the reports that came across my desk, you'd be wondering how it's possible that our nation is still in one piece. What makes you feel that this threat is worthy of extra attention?"

"First of all, let me apologize both to you and to Secretary Moss." The president nodded his pardon, but Moss's head remained still.

Good move, Riley thought. *Maybe the boy's growing up after all.*

Scott continued, "But it's because of the nature of the weapon that my emotions are so high. The results of an EMP attack on our nation would be nothing short of catastrophic. However, I'm not the best person to tell you about that. Riley?"

Riley spun his head to look at Scott. Scott gave him a wink and a nod. Riley turned back toward the president, but before he could say anything, President Lloyd said, "Listen, Riley, there's no offense meant, and I've already told you I'm a big fan, but I've got four members of Homeland Security in here, two of whom I understand are a couple of the best analytical minds in the whole country. Why in heaven's name are you the one briefing me on EMPs?"

Exactly, Riley thought and was about to say so. Instead, the words that came out of his mouth were, "Because I'm the only person in this room who has the depth of knowledge to help you understand the gravity of our situation."

A smile spread across the president's face, and he nodded for Riley to continue.

CHAPTER

NINETEEN

WEDNESDAY, JULY 22, 7:45 A.M. EDT
WASHINGTON, D.C.

Sweat and heat slowly began spreading over Riley's body, causing the thinly masked stink of his T-shirt to break free from its bonds. Riley futilely tried to ignore it. "As you know, Mr. President, prior to joining the PFL, I was in Air Force Special Ops. Much of what AFSOC does is weather-related—high-altitude drops into hostile territory in order to gather necessary meteorologic information and the like for aerial and ground attacks.

"During my senior year at the Academy, missile defense was a major topic, so I decided to write my thesis on the atmospheric ramifications of the destruction of ballistic missiles while in a sub-orbital flight path. However, as I gathered information, I became aware of a phenomenon known as electromagnetic pulse. As I read more about it, I ended up changing my thesis to a study on EMP devices and their potential impact on American culture."

"Riley, you may want to move it along just a bit," Stanley Porter said.

"Of course, sir. Sorry. So the electromagnetic pulse was first discovered by accident in 1962 during a high-altitude nuclear detonation, code-named Starfish Prime, off Johnston Atoll in the Pacific Ocean. The blast could be seen clearly eight hundred miles away in Hawaii—that part was expected. What wasn't expected was the damage to electronic equipment on the islands. More than three hundred streetlights no longer worked, many televisions and radios fried, and power lines fused together.

"What was ultimately determined was that the detonation's rapid acceleration of charged particles caused a burst of electromagnetic energy that shot out across the visual horizon line. This energy has the potential to fry any and all electronics and crash electrical grids."

President Lloyd shot a quick glance to his watch. "Interesting stuff, Riley, but let's get down to the nitty-gritty. What could an EMP do to us?"

Riley took a deep breath. "First of all, it would depend on the type of weapon—nuclear or nonnuclear—the size of the bomb, and the height of the blast. A small nuclear device with a low-altitude detonation—say thirty kilometers—could affect an area 250 miles in diameter. However, a large nuke detonated four hundred kilometers over America's heartland could potentially take out the whole continental United States."

"What do you mean by 'take out'?" the president asked, looking sharply at Riley.

"Imagine every piece of electronic equipment suddenly stopping. The initial impact will be devastating enough—you'll see everything from people with pacemakers falling over dead to planes falling from the sky. Roads will be filled with cars that just stopped, stranding people miles from their homes. Panic will set in quickly as parents aren't able to get to their children at school or day care. They won't even be able to call to make sure they're all right because phones—cell and landline—will no longer function. Many people undergoing even the most routine of surgeries will die on the operating table because the hospital's lights and equipment will fail, and even the required backup generators will be toast too. Fires from the airplane crashes will consume city blocks because the fire trucks won't be able to start. It won't be long before rioting and looting will fill the streets. But that's just the beginning.

"Realize, sir, that it will be months, if not years, before we can recover from this kind of destruction. When electronics are hit with an EMP, they never function again. We'd be thrown back into the nineteenth century with a society that is not used to providing for itself. Because there's no refrigeration, food will run short. Clean drinking water will be hard to come by.

"As far as long-term health care, dialysis patients will be the first to go, and soon after, death will spread to diabetics and cancer patients. Disease will run rampant, and simple ailments that were once cured with antibiotics will cause tens of thousands of deaths. Anarchy and mob rule will become the law of the land, because without communication or transportation, Washington, D.C., becomes just another starving, backwater town."

Riley paused to collect his thoughts. "I know I'm painting a doomsday scenario, but, sir, that's because that's exactly what it is. Hundreds of thousands, if not millions, will die, and American civilization as we know it will come to an end."

"And these weapons exist," the president said quietly.

"Anyone who has nukes and the capability to send them to altitude can create one of these high-altitude, doomsday-type EMPs—us, Russia, China, Israel, North Korea, the U.K., France, and possibly India and Pakistan. And that's just the nuclear EMPs. For little more than four or five hundred dollars for explosives and copper tubing, any person with the know-how and even minimal intelligence can build what's known as a flux compression generator, or FCG. One of these homemade mini EMPs has the power of up to a thousand lightning strikes and can wipe out the electronics of city blocks.

"Add to that the new nonnuclear EMP technology. North Korea, Russia, and the United States have been working hard on NNEMPs that can be detonated at fairly low altitude—say thirty kilometers—and still have a hundred-mile-plus footprint—sort of like an FCG on steroids. These—in a sense—'surgical' EMPs can be used to impact major population hotbeds, political centers, and key military bases. Imagine what would happen to our efforts in Iraq if Camp Liberty were suddenly and permanently off-line. And rather than needing an ICBM delivery device, a smaller missile or even a Scud could loft an NNEMP to where it needs to be."

"And do we know that North Korea has this EMP-junior capability?" Lloyd asked.

"Sir, as of now, I'm not cleared to know if even we have this type of capability," Riley answered, watching as Defense Secretary Carroll gave a slight nod to the president. "But every indication I've read recently is that if the DPRK doesn't have the technology yet, they will soon. It's amazing how starving your people can up your research-and-development budget."

Silence hung in the air as Riley's information sank in. Finally, President Lloyd turned to Defense Secretary Carroll. "Gordy, what are our defenses against this?"

"Honestly, I'm not up on the countermeasures against the small FCGs. As far as high-altitude EMPs, if it's just one missile, the chances are fairly decent that we could take it out—given enough warning. But with every additional warhead, our odds decrease. And, unfortunately, it only takes one. If it's a smaller, low-altitude attack, the chances of our catching it in time are slim to none.

"And, if I may, there's one more thing you need to think about. If we have the doomsday scenario that Riley spoke about, that would open the door for other nations to roll in and take over parts of our country. We could easily see Russia in Alaska and the Pacific Northwest, Mexico up into the Southwest, and even Canada into New England, assuming our border allies weren't taken off-line by the same weapon that was directed at us. We couldn't even defend ourselves if Cuba decided to annex Florida.

"The only defenses we would have are those that were overseas during the time of attack. But realize, even if we brought them all home, how would we provide upkeep? How would we get them fuel? How would we feed the troops? Riley is exactly right, sir. A large-scale EMP attack could mean the end of America."

The president abruptly got to his feet. "One bomb? Seriously, with all our weapons, with all our defenses, you're saying one bomb could spell the end of the strongest, most technologically advanced nation this world has ever seen?"

"If I may, Mr. President, that's the problem," Khadi spoke up. "Our whole society is based on technology. Take away the technology, and what are we left with? If you detonated one of these devices in the heart of the Amazon or in the African bush, things would pretty much go on as they have for centuries. But for most of us? We wouldn't know how to find a single meal without a nearby Chili's or a Super Walmart."

"Well, I'll tell you this, the end of the world will not come on my watch," President Lloyd said, as much to himself as to everyone else. "And it very well might be the end of the world, because there's not a chance with all of our Ohio-class subs out there carrying their Tridents that I'm going to let any nation come rolling across our borders without giving them something to think about back home!"

Secretary Carroll paled at the president's words. "Sir, I don't think—"

"Oh, come on, Gordy! I'm just venting!" President Lloyd stood quietly for a moment. Nobody dared say a word. Finally, the president turned to Scott. "And how sure are you of this information?"

From behind the president came Secretary Moss's voice, "See, that's what I'm saying, Mr. President. Agent Ross is giving you this doomsday scenario, trying to incite panic, based on one person's word. It's ludicrous to be getting all worked up over—"

The president held up his hand, silencing Moss. He continued to stare at Scott.

Slowly moving his head side to side, Scott said, "Basically, he's right, sir. It is just one person's word, based on information MI6 has received from a North Korean mole. The whole thing could be a setup by the DPRK to embarrass us somehow . . . but I don't think it is."

It was obvious Scott had more to say, so the president waited him out.

"Because it's coming from North Korea, I'm guessing the devices are small. They keep trying to show their power with their tests, but I have serious doubts as to whether they have anything that is both big *and* portable. Their Taepodong-2 ICBMs are well over a hundred feet long—not something easily hidden away. But their Scuds—the Rodongs and Hwasongs—are only about a third that size. Any of them would be capable of setting up an NNEMP blast. And even a small detonation over a major city like New York or L.A. could cause tens of thousands of deaths and could put our already-damaged economy into a death spiral.

"I also think it is probably an NNEMP because if a terrorist group launched a North Korean nuke on our soil, we'd know it by the weapon's inherent identifiers. That's the whole reason we haven't seen a Russian-made nuke fall into some *hajji*'s hands. The world would know it was Russian, and the political fallout for them would be enormous."

The president sat back down, again taking time to fix his crease. "Stanley, you've been pretty silent. What's your opinion?"

"Sir, I know Scott and Khadi well enough to realize that if they are scared, then we should be too."

"Fair enough. Dwayne, how are you addressing this?"

With barely concealed contempt, Moss answered, "I can assure you that we are dedicating the resources appropriate to pursuing an unconfirmed rumor."

"Which is about a quarter of what is needed for this kind of threat," Stanley Porter added.

Before Moss could respond, President Lloyd said, "Fine. Dwayne, do what you have to do. Quadruple the resources if you need them. Stanley, I want you heading this up. If you find any roadblocks to getting what you need, I want you to contact me directly."

Riley could see Porter suppressing a smile while Moss fumed next to him. *The conversation between those two is far from over.*

Turning back to Scott, the president said, "Agent Ross, you and Agent Faroughi still could have briefed me on this through Stanley, or even come in by yourselves. You brought Riley here for a reason."

After clearing his throat, Scott said, "Well, sir, I brought Riley here so that you could witness his expertise. Otherwise, you would have thought it ridiculous when I told you that I need your permission to form a carte blanche black ops team and that I need Riley to be part of it."

"Wouldn't having one of the most recognizable faces in professional football as part of your secret team be sort of defeating the purpose?" Secretary Moss asked.

Ignoring his superior, Scott continued, "Please trust me when I say that Riley is necessary to the success of the team. Not only do the members of my team trust him with their lives, but he will be the one with the greatest knowledge of just what it is we're looking for. You've heard today his expertise on the subject. You've already mentioned your awareness of his courage and leadership skills. Sir, I don't exaggerate when I say that Riley is an essential element in our plan to thwart this attack."

The president nodded, then stopped suddenly. "Just how do you plan on getting him out of football without . . . never mind. I don't want to know," he said as he stood, indicating that the meeting was over. Everyone else stood with him. "You just do what you need to do to stop those weapons from reaching our soil. I'm counting on all three of you." President Lloyd shook each of their hands, looking directly into their eyes as he did so.

As he shook Riley's hand, he said, "Riley, have Agent Ross take you to get some clothes. It's the least the taxpayers of our great land can do for you."

Great, Riley thought as he stammered out an embarrassed thank-you. Then President Lloyd turned to hold a private discussion with Secretary Carroll.

When they were in the hallway with the Oval Office's door closed behind them, Moss put his finger in Scott's face. "You may have won this battle, but believe you me, you're going to lose the war!"

Scott took a step forward so that Moss's finger was just inches away from his nose. "That's funny. I wasn't aware we were in a war except with the people who are trying to destroy this country! But if you really do want a war, *Mr. Secretary*, then I'm more than happy to oblige!"

"You best watch the way you talk to me, Ross! I'm not your boss—I'm two levels above your boss! That means that if I decide it's time for you to go, I only need to say the word and you're gone!"

"Then say the word! Go ahead—open my weekend schedule a bit; say the word!"

"Back off, Ross," Porter said, stepping between the two.

"And you," Moss continued, now directing his finger at Porter's nose. "Let me assure you that your career is over! I will not have insubordination in my department, particularly in front of the president! You think I can't find anyone who can replace you? someone who knows how to follow orders? someone who . . ."

As Moss continued his rant, Porter put a hand up behind his back and motioned for the rest of them to make their way out. Riley, Scott, and Khadi didn't have to be told twice. They slowly backed themselves down the hall, turned a corner, then got out while the getting was good.

CHAPTER TWENTY

WEDNESDAY, JULY 22, 10:30 A.M. EDT
WASHINGTON, D.C.

Riley gave the bellman a generous tip, even though all the kid had done was open the door to his room. *Best to make friends of the staff now, since you'll probably be staying here awhile.*

Riley's suite was 1002, but he also held the key to the adjoining top-floor room. Even though he had been unable to get Skeeter on the phone—which meant that Skeet was either on a plane or dead—he had no doubt that sometime in the next few hours his friend and bodyguard would be showing up at the Quincy looking for him. *Better to risk paying for an unused room than to have Skeeter show up with no place to put him other than the other half of the suite's king-size bed.*

Scott and Khadi had wanted Riley to come with them, stick his head in, and say hey to the rest of the analysts, but hard as it was to separate from Khadi after so short a time, he had declined the invitation. Too much had happened in the past day, and he desperately needed time to process.

After a stop for some clothes and food and other necessities, Scott and Khadi had dropped him off at the downtown hotel. Earlier, Scott had tried to talk Riley into staying with him, but Riley had visited Scott's place back in Denver and knew that their two differing definitions of "living conditions" would only cause them to clash. Better to keep some space.

After cranking up the air-conditioning against the humidity, Riley put his new clothes in the closet and the food in the refrigerator. Then, following a thorough search through the kitchenette for the necessary equipment, he opened a can of SpaghettiOs, dumped the contents into a pan, and slid the pan across the stove's cooktop. It had been years since he had had this childhood favorite. He knew its nutritional value was just above eating paste, but for some reason it sounded good to him tonight. As he stirred, he smiled, thinking about Khadi's grimace when he had reached for the can. He had been tempted to grab a can of the SpaghettiOs with sliced franks to mess with her even more, but in the end he was simply too tired to play around.

While his dinner cooked, he explored the rest of the suite. Trendy but comfortable. Huge television that he didn't feel like turning on. Nice bathroom with a thick robe and slippers. All in all, not a bad place to hole up for a few weeks.

He lay back on the bed and immediately missed home. This was one of the worst things about road trips—the mattresses. The expensive hotels made them too soft, and the cheaper ones made them too hard. This one wasn't bad as hotel beds went, but still, it was different from home.

The smell of tomato sauce cooking forced him to get up. After pouring the pasta into a bowl and pulling a Diet Coke out of the fridge, he sat at a table by the window and looked out at the monuments only minutes from his hotel.

Now that all the activity of settling in had ceased, it was only him, his SpaghettiOs, and his thoughts. He had to admit, he was still angry with Scott. But it wasn't so much at what Scott had done. Every step his friend had taken had been well planned out, which told him it wasn't just Scott's brainchild. Khadi, too, had probably been involved from square one but was afraid to admit it.

His anger came more from the fact that his brief moment of serenity had been taken from him. For a short time it had felt to him like everything was going to be okay. He was starting to heal from his father's murder. He was beginning to get excited about football again. He had been entertaining the hope that maybe—just maybe—everything could possibly return to a seminormal state.

Then came Scott.

Suddenly, civilization is about to end, America is about to be EMPed back into the Stone Age, and millions of people are about to meet grisly deaths. Of course, technically, none of those things were directly Scott's fault. But still, being close to Scott was like having Jessica Fletcher from *Murder, She Wrote* as your best friend. Every place Jessica showed up, you knew that someone was going to die. Riley just hoped that he, or more so Khadi, would not be the one to get hit with the rock or stabbed with the letter opener or poisoned with the merlot or driven off the cliff in the convertible with the cut brake lines.

Without Scott, Riley would have remained blissfully ignorant of the threat, like all the other 300 million Americans. *But is that really what I would want? Would I rather be clueless, caught unawares, or be one of those in the know that is given an opportunity to do something about it? When it's put that way, I guess I should be thanking Scott instead of cursing him.*

Riley got up and put his bowl and spoon in the sink next to his dirty pan—one of the benefits of living in a place with maid service. His body was telling him that it needed activity, and the hotel offered free guest passes to the Bally's two blocks down. But for once he ignored what he needed and instead chose what he wanted. And what he wanted was sleep—blissful, quiet, escapist sleep.

He stripped out of his filthy clothes and dropped them in the trash can. *Actually, I probably should burn those!* He showered, then slipped under the covers in his now-arctic-chilled room. A thought crossed his mind: *I'm no longer a Colorado Mustang. I'm a Washington Warrior!* A knot set in his stomach, and he felt his throat begin to constrict. The Mustangs had been Riley's team from the time he was old enough to know what a football was. He had followed the team religiously, and the day he was drafted by his favorite team was one of the best of his life.

And now that was gone. *Pfft,* just like that.

Again the emotions against Scott began to rise. But this time they were combined with something else. Sorrow mixed with fear. Well, maybe not fear, but definitely nervousness. *What will it be like when I walk into that new locker room? Will I get along with my teammates, with my coach? How quickly will I be able to pick up the new defensive scheme?*

Fat chance going to sleep now, he thought with a sigh. Getting out of bed, he dressed, grabbed some of his new workout clothes, and walked out the door to do what his body had been telling him he should have done in the first place.

CHAPTER TWENTY-ONE

WEDNESDAY, JULY 22, 11:00 A.M. EDT
WASHINGTON, D.C.

When Scott and Khadi opened the door to the Room of Understanding (a term coined by analyst Evie Cline because *War Room* had sounded too violent), the five people inside quickly turned their heads. Then, seeing that Riley wasn't with the two, they just as quickly let out a collective groan.

"Oh, it's only you," Joey Williamson complained.

"What, no hugs? No kisses? Not even a 'Welcome home, Daddy'?" Scott said sarcastically. For once in his life, he wasn't in the mood for the banter that usually took place around the office. And seeing the "office" he was in just soured his mood more.

Back in Denver, they'd had a roomy, state-of-the-art facility. Now the team was crammed into an undersize workspace, the analysts working in back-to-back cubicles and Scott and Khadi each stuffed into a separate closet-size office with walls so thin they constantly got distracted by each other's phone conversations. What little extra room there had once been was now occupied by a laminate-topped conference table. *And they expect us to save the world from this little space? Unbelievable!*

"Meeting in five minutes," Scott said as he walked through to his office to change out of his suit. Slamming the door behind him, he yanked off his clip-on tie and threw it across the office—which wasn't a great feat, since if he stretched both arms out to the side at once, he could almost touch both walls.

Soon his suit pants were replaced with ratty-bottom jeans and his dress shoes with Birkenstocks. He flipped through the assortment of black T-shirts hanging from a pole he had strung from the ceiling and pulled one out. *Nice! Uriah Heep—Heep '74. My favorite Dickens character turned progressive rock band.* After slipping it over his head, he walked back into the main room.

"Drop what you're doing, and gather round, kids!"

"That was only three minutes," Evie Cline whined. "You said we'd have five."

"I lied. Let's go!"

"Apparently Pa had a bad meeting today at work," Virgil Hernandez said.

"Can it, Virgil." Senior analyst Tara Walsh was the one who cracked the whip around the RoU. Her stunning looks reminded Scott of Jaclyn Smith in her *Charlie's Angels* days, but her personality was at times closer to the Wicked Witch of the West. Still, if he was forced to admit it, Tara's face was the one that most often visited him as he drifted off to sleep at night.

"Yeah, what she said," Scott commanded. "Besides, it was an excellent meeting. Couldn't have gone better."

"Then what's got you down, Scottybear?" asked Evie, who hated to see anyone feeling low.

"'Scottybear'?" Khadi said, giving Scott a curious look. Scott just shrugged in response.

"I know what it is," Hernandez answered. "He's got the Riley Covington blues!"

"Hernandez, just leave it alone," Scott said angrily.

Gooey, the fifth and most recent addition to the analyst crew, cleared his throat and began playing a blues riff on an air guitar.

Dom dom dare dare, doe doe doe doe doe dom dom dare dare

Wellll, I kidnapped my best friend while-a he was a-clamming.

Dom dom dare dare, doe doe doe doe doe dom dom dare dare
Yeeaah, said I kidnapped my best friend while-a he was
a-clamming.
Dom dom dare dare, doe doe doe doe doe dom dom dare daarre
Dom—Thought he'd be glad,
Doe doe doe dom—Turned out he was mad.
I guess I just gots me them, uh, Ri-ley Co-ving-ton blues.

Evie, Hernandez, and Williamson all put down the cell phones they had been waving and burst into applause. Soon Khadi joined in. Scott, who desperately wanted to unleash a biting comeback to Gooey, instead found himself laughing. Tara, who was giving him an exasperated, can't-you-control-your-children look, only made him laugh harder.

"Okay," Scott said when he finally caught his breath, "so today what I learned is that I have the absolute power to totally destroy my best friend's life, but for some reason I can't seem to find a way to make him like it."

"Have you tried drugging him or possibly beating him into submission?" Gooey suggested.

Scott looked thoughtful. "Props on the ideas, Goo, but unfortunately Khadi keeps the key to the pharmaceutical cabinet and Riley could probably kick my butt from here to next week. But way to think out of the box." The rest of the team congratulated their fellow analyst.

Once they were all seated around the table, Scott began his debrief of the meeting with the president. Other than the team's occasional comparison of Secretary Moss with various bodily parts, Scott was able to get through it without interruption—a sign that this group of social misfits fully understood the gravity of the threat facing the nation.

"So your job is to find those weapons," Scott concluded.

A rare silence surrounded the table, until Williamson spoke up. "Bypassing any tired needle-in-haystack clichés, do you have any suggestions as to how we might accomplish said task?"

"Well, gee, Joey, for some reason I thought that was your job."

"I know, boss," Williamson said, sounding unusually flustered.

"But where in the world do we begin? I mean, this is like a global *Where's Waldo?*"

Scott sat back for a moment to think, then said, "First off, I think your *Where's Waldo?* simile comes dangerously close to qualifying as a needle-in-haystack cliché. Second, I would start by checking shipping manifests. The weapons could have been taken out of the DPRK by boat, but with the way the world is watching that country, I'm guessing they were trucked to another port. Khadi, who else could have a vested interest in this little scheme working?"

"Well, it could have shipped from China or continued south to Southeast Asia. Or maybe northwest to Russia—no doubt they'd like a shot at finally being the number one dog on the block. Possibly it could have gone west to the Indian subcontinent, Pakistan, maybe even to Iran and the Middle East. I don't think there's any need to go into their feelings toward us. From there you've got Egypt and North Africa—all of whom would probably be dancing in the streets if America crashed."

"So, Khadi, let me get this right. Basically you've narrowed our search to the Eastern Hemisphere," an exasperated Hernandez said.

"Look at it this way: I just ruled out half the world in one fell swoop. Not bad for a day's work," Khadi answered with a smile.

Despite the daunting task that had just been laid out for them, the analysts had to nod their heads in appreciation of Khadi's mighty display of analytical prowess.

"Listen, gang, I realize what I'm asking you to do is a near-impossible task," Scott said. "But you guys understand what's at stake. I've got every confidence in you. Tara, you divvy up continents and then keep the kids on task. If you reach a roadblock, come talk to Khadi or me."

Everyone stood with Scott as he rose to go, but then dropped into their chairs when he sat down again. "You know, in this past year, the intel you guys have come up with has saved thousands of lives. Now I'm asking you to save millions."

"No pressure," Evie said with a grin.

Scott smiled grimly. "Actually, I hope you feel more pressure than you've ever felt in your life, because finding these EMPs is probably the most important thing you'll ever do. It's even more important than breaking into the top five of the *WarCraft III* global ladder."

"Seriously? Wow," Gooey answered.

"Wow is right." Again Scott stood. "Now get out there and find me two EMPs. And if your computer screen should happen to go blank, you'll know you were just a little too late."

CHAPTER TWENTY-TWO

THURSDAY, JULY 23, 9:30 A.M. MDT
INVERNESS TRAINING CENTER,
CENTENNIAL, COLORADO

Keith Simmons's face contorted as he squatted, then pushed himself back up. Sweat had completely darkened his clothing, and his right leg had just the slightest tremor. On the bar across his shoulders hung 625 pounds of black metal weight. Normally he could get eight to ten reps without too much trouble, but today he was straining just to get to number five. Letting out a yell from the depths of his being, he pushed his body to standing position and stepped back, indicating for Afshin Ziafat to guide the bar down onto its pegs.

Keith tried to hide a limp as he slid out from the apparatus, but obviously he didn't do a good enough job because Afshin asked him, "Are you sure you don't want to have a trainer look at that ankle?"

Last Saturday, Keith had gone to his sister's house to hang out for the evening. After dinner, he and his two teenage nephews and young niece had walked up to the neighborhood school to play some soccer. As usual, Keith had begun messing around and showing off, and at one point he broke away and ran down the field, dribbling the ball all the way.

Just before he shot into the open goal, his right foot hit a dip in the grass. Even as his ankle was turning, Keith knew it wasn't good. He fell, shouting out a few words for which he'd later had to ask forgiveness from God and the kids.

As he lay in the grass, he kept praying, *Please let it be nothing; please let it be nothing.* But when he stood up, his fears were confirmed. He hobbled back to his sister's house and began a regimen that he had been following during all of his off-hours since then—ten minutes ice, ten minutes heat, ten minutes ice, ten minutes heat—over and over, trying to get the joint back into shape before training camp started in another week and a half.

Grabbing Afshin by his damp shoulder, Keith said, "Rookie, you've got to learn now. Never—I mean *never*—let a trainer know you are injured if you can help it. Letting a trainer know means letting the coaches know, and letting the coaches know means letting the owner know.

"Soon you'll lose all your free time. Unless it's surgery-worthy, you'll end up having to come in at least an hour early every day for rehab. Then it's practice with everyone else. Then afterward, it's another hour or two of getting rubbed, twisted, and yanked. Trust me, kid; it's not worth it. Besides, I'll be past this in no time." Keith laughed. "Come on, it's your set."

But underneath Keith's surface of confidence was a sea of doubts. As he helped Afshin pull fifty pounds off the bar for his own set of squats, he pondered the future of his career. Five years ago, he would have bounced back from something like this in no time. Now it seemed every little injury turned into a rehabilitation. *What is it Riley's grandpa always says? "Why does everything have to be a project?" No doubt! Especially in football. Nothing's easy anymore.*

So why keep doing it? he wondered, even as his mouth was automatically encouraging Afshin. "Push it! Push it! C'mon, Rook!" *It's certainly not the money—I've got plenty of that. And while I enjoy the fame, I'm getting to the point that a little anonymity might be nice for a change. So what is it?*

Suddenly the answer came to him, and with it came a feeling of sadness and frustration. *It's because I have nothing else! Look at Riley; he's got meaning to his life—real meaning beyond just hitting people for the sole reason that they're carrying an oblong ball. He's shown that he can take or leave football. But me? This is all I have. If I weren't playing football, what would I be doing other than sitting around playing* Guitar Hero *and hoping my phone would ring?*

The thought so depressed him that he missed Afshin's step back.

"Keith!"

Keith quickly took hold of the bar and set it in place.

"Come on, man, you can't leave me hanging like that," Afshin said angrily.

"Sorry, Z, my mind drifted off."

"Well, let it drift off when the bar's on your shoulders," Afshin replied, walking off to find an open stationary bike.

Not good, Keith thought. He had broken one of the cardinal rules of the weight room. If you're spotting someone, you have to keep your head in the game, because you might be the only one keeping a friend from an injury, possibly even a career-ending one.

Frustrated, Keith leaned against the cold metal squat rack, rehearsing in his mind his nonlimping walk across to the bikes. As he did, he absentmindedly watched one of the weight room's six flat screens. All were tuned to ESPN and were muted with the closed-captioning on. Suddenly, a uniformed Riley appeared in a box next to the SportsCenter anchor.

Keith chuckled to himself. *As much as Riley tries to stay out of the spotlight, his face probably shows up on this channel more than anyone else's.* But then he saw something that made his heart sink. Through the magic of Photoshop, Riley's Colorado Mustangs uniform transformed into a Washington Warriors uniform. Keith's eyes dropped to the captioning in time to read, *"We'll let you know as soon as we hear if the trade rumors are confirmed."*

A string of profanities came from across the room where Chris Gorkowski had thrown down a set of dumbbells. All around, guys began talking, but Keith was too stunned to move. Afshin came running over, but by the time he arrived, Keith's shock had transformed into anger. Pushing past the rookie, Keith strode toward the door of the workout facility—all pain in his ankle forgotten.

CHAPTER TWENTY-THREE

THURSDAY, JULY 23, 11:40 A.M. EDT
WASHINGTON, D.C.

Riley leaned back on the leather couch, savoring the combination of flavors in his corned beef Reuben. The meat was lean and perfectly seasoned, the sauerkraut still had the slightest of crunches, and the dark rye bread was toasted to perfection. *Just think, I could be sweating with Keith and Afshin back in Denver!*

He lifted the sandwich from the table he had pulled over by the couch and took another bite, dropping a big glob of Thousand-Island-dressing-infused pickled cabbage on his plush white robe. *Bummer,* he thought with a smile, picking up the blob with two fingers and popping it into his mouth. *Gonna have to make sure the laundry service knows to soak that.*

Riley knew he should probably be up and doing something, but he so rarely had any time off. Besides, Scott had interrupted his vacation. He deserved a little bit of R & R.

He also knew that a lot of what he was feeling was just plain tiredness. Between his whirlwind two days and Skeeter's knocking on his door at 2:15 that morning to let him know he had made it, Riley was simply exhausted.

That late-night meeting with Skeeter had been interesting. It had been obvious that Skeet was still angry. He had wanted to go immediately to Scott's house. When Riley told him that there was no way he was getting dressed so that Skeeter could go give Scott a pounding—as deserved as it may be—Skeeter had demanded a first-thing-in-the-morning smackdown.

Riley knew that the best thing he could do would be to keep the two men apart as long as possible. The fireworks resulting from that initial meeting could leave a bad taste for months to come. So while Riley made the excuse that he was extremely worn-out and needed to sleep late, the real reason he was still lounging in his room was to let Skeeter calm down before meeting with Scott.

However, Riley would have a hard time convincing anyone that he was making any sort of sacrifice by keeping the peace. He had told Skeeter that he didn't want to be disturbed until 1:00 p.m. That had given him time to sleep in, brew up some coffee and have some cereal, get some reading in, then order up this incredible sandwich from Mackey's Pub downstairs.

As he ate, he casually watched SportsCenter. Scott had asked him to wait until the trade was announced before he called anyone back home in Denver. He felt bad knowing that his teammates and friends would be caught totally off guard, but he understood Scott's reasoning. This was a very delicate negotiation that Scott, Khadi, and Stanley Porter were involved in. If word got out and then the deal fell apart, it would be embarrassing for all parties, particularly if there was any hint of governmental involvement.

But Riley had a feeling that everything would work out just how Scott wanted it—it always did, didn't it? *After all, I'm a Warrior and not a Mustang. I'm here in muggy Washington instead of beautiful Colorado. And they call* me *a golden boy!*

But here he was, and here he would stay, because he had every confidence that Scott, Khadi, and the gang would work the negotiations. And also because he had a feeling that if need be, the talks would broaden to include one owner's tax problems and the other owner's son, who had just been convicted of an intent-to-distribute-cocaine charge.

Yep, I'm a Washington Warrior. No two ways about it. The same feeling of nervousness that he had felt the previous night came back. *Thankfully, I don't have to report until Monday. But still . . . isn't that just putting off the inevitable?*

Something on the television pulled Riley out of his musings. On the screen he saw a picture of himself dressed out as a Mustang. Then, as the anchor spoke, his uniform slowly morphed him into a Washington Warrior.

". . . unconfirmed report that Riley Covington has been traded to the Washington Warriors. If this is true, it would cause a general outcry of 'What are you thinking?' among the Mustang faithful and would probably lead to a marked increase in lottery sales among the Warrior fans who have just hit their lucky day. The terms of the alleged trade have not been announced, but word is that Washington is considering sending Denver four senators, two congressmen, and the Lincoln Memorial. We'll let you know as soon as we hear if the trade rumors are confirmed."

Guess that means I can call Keith now, he thought, reaching for the phone. But before he had a chance to dial a number, the phone rang. *Whitney Walker,* the caller ID said.

Riley debated whether or not to answer it. Whitney was a sports reporter from the local Fox News station in Denver. She was a class act and had helped Riley out of a major jam just a couple months ago.

Riley's hesitancy came not from the fact that she was media. She had already proven to him that she could be trusted to quote him accurately and in context—something that was a little too much of a rarity among many in the journalistic field. His concern was that since meeting Khadi seven months ago, Whitney was the only female who had piqued his interest. In fact, it was piqued enough that even though he and Khadi were only in the loosest of relationships, he had felt a lot of guilt over his two or three coffees with Whitney—*all of which were media-related,* he reminded himself, *purely professional. Still, there's something about those green eyes of hers and the way she laughs that just brightens up a whole room—and she knows football!*

"Aw, heck," he said, punching the Send button. "Hey, Whitney! Long time no talk!"

"Riley Covington," Whitney answered with a bit of playfulness in her voice, "do you mean to tell me that you've been traded to Washington and you didn't give me a heads-up? That's not very nice, you know."

Riley smiled in spite of himself. He had been determined to keep things purely professional and to end the call as soon as possible. But Whitney had a way of flirting with him that got through whatever defenses he could put up. *Come on, Covington, don't be a sap. You're not that easy of a mark, are you?*

Actually . . . you probably are. "What makes you think that I've been traded? Have you been listening to the Denver rumor mill?"

"I think you've been traded because I have ears, and what makes you think I'm still in Denver? Don't you pay any attention to the media news?"

"You're not in Denver? I had no idea. Media comings and goings are right below British royalty on my list of things I feel I need to keep up with. So where are you?"

"I'm going to try not to be offended by your comments, Mr. Covington," Whitney said with a little pout evident in her voice. "And, just so you know, I arrived last week in Bristol to work at ESPN."

"Seriously? The big time? Congratulations," Riley said, half of him thrilled that she was again so close and half of him terrified that she was again so close.

"Thanks. But remember, this call isn't about me. So what is it? Are you a Warrior or not?"

Riley thought. He didn't want to cross any lines he wasn't supposed to. But he knew how an exclusive like this could help Whitney in her new job.

"Tell you what," he said, "this has got to be off the record—"

"Come on, Riles. Then what good is it?" Whitney interrupted.

Riles? "Let me finish, missy. Off the record, I'm 90 percent sure that I'm a Warrior. However, there are extenuating circumstances that make it impossible for me to say any more. But . . ."

"But . . . ?" Whitney repeated hopefully.

"When everything is announced—which will probably be later today—I'll give you the exclusive interview on how I'm feeling about the trade, about leaving Denver, etc. Also, from here on out you can be my primary pipeline into the network. Fair enough?"

Whitney was ecstatic. "Thank you, thank you, thank you! Honestly, part of the reason they hired me was because of my promise of access to you; did you know that? Oh, I hope that wasn't too presumptuous of me. But you'll forgive me, won't you? Oh, Riley, this will be huge for me."

Riley couldn't help but smile. He could picture her face all lit up, her green eyes beaming. "This is the least I could do. You helped me when I really needed your help."

"I've told you not to mention that again," Whitney lightly scolded him. "I was just doing what any friend would do. Now, how about we meet for coffee tomorrow? I'd be happy to drive down your way."

Too dangerous! Say no; say no; say no! "Sure, that'd be great," Riley answered, grimacing even as he did so.

"Fabulous! I can't wait to see you again!"

"Yeah, me too." As soon as he hung up the phone, Khadi's face popped into his mind. *Come on, it's only a cup of coffee. Purely professional.*

Maybe, but are you planning on telling Khadi about it?

Riley picked up his sandwich to take another bite but found he wasn't hungry anymore. He pushed the plate to the other side of the table so he wouldn't have to smell the food.

You're a football player, and she's a reporter. It's as simple as that. This is just a part of my job. And if Khadi can't understand that, then she needs to reevaluate our relationship!

What relationship? Do we even have a relationship?

And whom exactly are you trying to convince—Khadi or yourself? Especially since you are the only person involved in this internal monologue.

"Whatever," Riley said out loud as he picked up the phone to call Keith Simmons. "Everything will work out."

But even as he dialed the numbers, the half-finished Reuben began turning somersaults in his stomach.

CHAPTER TWENTY-FOUR

THURSDAY, JULY 23, 9:45 A.M. MDT
INVERNESS TRAINING CENTER,
CENTENNIAL, COLORADO

As Keith burst through the weight room door, the summer heat hit his face. Typically he took great pleasure in that feeling, especially when it combined, as it did today, with the smell of freshly cut grass from the manicured practice fields. Right now, though, all of those sensory pleasures were lost on him. He wove his way through the German luxury cars, the Italian sports cars, and the Japanese and American SUVs parked in the players' lot. As he passed Coach Burton's Capri Blue Mercedes S600, he was glad he wasn't carrying anything sharp and metallic.

There is no way it can be true! Burton wouldn't let it happen; Mr. Salley wouldn't let it happen. Keith knew A. J. Salley was an unbelievably shrewd businessman, and the presence of American hero Riley Covington on the Mustangs meant millions to the franchise through ticket sales and merchandising. But deep down, Keith also knew it was a very rare occasion when ESPN had to go back on one of its rumors.

Cutting through some picnic tables, he approached the facility's main building. He pushed through the doors and into the cafeteria. The large room was nearly empty; only a few players sat with reporters or with their agents. To his right, second-year offensive tackle Travis Marshall was talking with his agent.

"Hey, Simms, did you hear—yeah, I guess you did," Travis said as Keith brushed past his table without a second look.

Keith punched the crash bar to the inside doors, sending them slamming against the hallway wall. After rounding a corner, he flew up a flight of stairs and marched his way down a long hallway filled with offices and decorated with jerseys of eras past. At the end of the hallway was Coach Burton's office—a place Keith usually tried to stay as far away from as possible. Most often, if you were summoned to the coach's office, the news was not good.

Without thinking of the consequences, Keith opened the door into a wide reception area. Karen Watkins, the coach's secretary, was stunned; no one ever burst into the coach's office. Finally, she called out, "Wait, you can't go in there!" just as Keith threw open the door to the forbidden sanctuary.

Coach Burton was sitting on his desk. Seated around him were Rex Texeira, defensive coordinator T. J. Ceravolo, and team general manager Anthony Lawrence.

All eyes were on Keith, but now that he was in the office, he realized he had no idea what he was going to say. Texeira, Ceravolo, and Lawrence were obviously shocked, but Burton looked just plain angry.

"What?" Burton growled.

Keith opened his mouth, and words came falling out. "Coach, is it true? Did you just trade Riley? I mean, I can't believe that it would be true, but they're saying it on ESPN, so I'm not sure what to believe. A bunch of the guys and me were wondering whether the rumor is actually true . . . sir."

"It's true," Burton said matter-of-factly.

"It's true?"

"That's what I said," Coach answered, his face starting to color a deep red. "Now get out of my office. And if you ever barge in here again uninvited, I'll see to it that you spend the last few years of your career playing in Detroit!"

To his left, Coach Texeira was nodding and motioning with his hand for Keith to leave, but Keith stood there not moving. He knew he should defend his friend. He should tell Burton what a mistake he was making and that he needed to rescind whatever deal he had made. He should threaten the coach and tell him that if Riley went, so would he! He should . . . he really should . . .

But in the end, he simply turned and walked out of the office, closing the door behind him. Karen Watkins looked like she was going to let Keith have it, but after seeing his face, she sat behind her desk and let him pass.

In the hallway, waiting for him, were Afshin, Danie Colson, Travis Marshall (who must have left his agent sitting all alone in the cafeteria), and Chris Gorkowski. At the end of the hallway, right at the top of the stairs, stood Zerin, but as soon as Keith's eyes met his, he retreated back down the steps.

"What'd Burton say?" Afshin asked for all of them.

"Get out of his office," Keith said quietly. "And the rumors are true."

"What?" Gorkowski yelled. Turning, he punched a hole through the drywall, causing a 1974 team picture to fall to the ground and shatter its glass. As soon as he did, his face fell. "Oh, crap; I'm going to pay for that!"

Sure enough, offensive coordinator Brandon Murray stormed out of his office, which just happened to be on the other side of the offended wall. "Snap, was that you?"

"Uh, yeah, Coach," Gorkowski answered sheepishly.

"Get into my office! And the rest of you, get out of my hallway!"

As Gorkowski followed Murray through the door, the rest of the guys made their departure. When they reached the stairs, Keith was peppered with questions from the other guys.

"I don't know!" he snapped. "I've told you all he said! Riley's gone! That's all there is to it, so you might as well start getting used to the idea!"

Keith pushed past them and made his way to the locker room. All the pain in his ankle that had been hidden by the adrenaline was now back in spades, and there was no masking the limp anymore.

Quit your bellyaching! Players come and players go. It's happened before, and it will happen again.

But this time was different. For once in his life, Keith had felt that he had a friend who was going to help him be a better man, someone who would lift him up rather than drag him down. Now that friend was gone, and Keith was faced with trying to live a right life without his external conscience near him.

God, I gotta tell You, this really sucks! I mean, how could You take Riley away just when I was starting to really learn how to live the way You want me to? Now how am I going to figure out all that Bible stuff?

Suddenly he stopped in front of the team equipment room. *Oh, man! All I've been thinking about is myself! This has got to be horrible for Riley! God, forgive me for my selfish attitude. Riley needs You more than I do right now, and I know he's struggling to get adjusted to life without his friends and teammates. Go get him, God; he really needs You!*

CHAPTER

TWENTY-FIVE

MONDAY, JULY 27, 7:45 A.M. EDT
WARRIORS PARK, ASHBURN, VIRGINIA

Riley sat in a rented Chevy Trailblazer, staring at the front of the building. The entrance had a large, caricatured Indian face on both sides of the doors, and a giant spear was cocked at a twenty-degree angle over the entrance. The words *Warrior Pride* were printed on a vinyl banner that hung from the spear.

Classy, Riley thought, shaking his head. People buzzed all around the front of the building on this unofficial first day of training camp—unofficial because training camp didn't technically start until 5:00 tonight. However, the players were still expected to be here for today's practice.

Mapquest had told Riley to plan for forty-five minutes to make the drive from Washington, D.C., out to the Washington Warriors training facility in Ashburn, Virginia. However, having heard about the notorious D.C. traffic, he'd decided to leave at 6:15, and he was glad he did. His SUV had rolled up only about ten minutes ago.

He had not moved since.

All sorts of emotions shot through him—sadness, frustration, nervousness. Getting to know the players wasn't a big deal. He already knew four or five guys who were former Mustangs and another couple whom he had gotten to know a bit during his college days. Besides, the turnover in the PFL was so great, a player had to get used to seeing new faces.

No, it wasn't the players who were causing the anxiety. Riley was much more concerned about getting to know the owners and the coaching staff. During training camp, a player's every move—on and off the field—was already scrutinized, but a new guy was truly under the microscope. And even though Riley had a strong record of achievement behind him, that could be a double-edged sword. Playing professional football was very much a "What have you done for me lately?" proposition. He was going to have to prove himself to the coaches just like everyone else on the team—maybe even more so.

A call yesterday to tight end Don Bernier, a former Mustang who now played with the Warriors, let Riley know that both the coaching staff and the players expected him to be a bit of a prima donna. A little self-righteous anger crept up in Riley as he worked that through his brain. *I may be a lot of things, but I'm no prima donna! In fact, I try to be the farthest thing from it.*

Idiot Scott! Him and his stupid ideas! I shouldn't even have to be dealing with this! I should be back in Denver, laughing with Keith and Afshin as we watch the rookies scramble to make it out onto the field on time. Instead, I'm stuck here with a bunch of teammates I don't know, playing for coaches I don't know, in a city with enough water in the air to turn the whole Sahara Desert into an oasis.

But those thoughts were quickly followed by a wave of conviction. *Yeah, I know, Lord. You've got me here for a reason. Forgive my lousy attitude. Help me to take hold of the plan You have for me. Make me open to Your will!*

With a deep breath, he turned to Skeeter, who had been patiently waiting in the passenger seat, and said, "What do you think? You ready to do this thing?"

"Warrior pride," Skeeter answered without looking at Riley.

"So according to Bernier, these guys already think I'm some sort of a diva."

"And they're wrong how?" Skeeter asked, the slightest of smirks showing in the corners of his mouth.

"That's cold, Skeet," Riley said, feigning a hurt look. "All I got to say, though, is that my private locker area better be ready for me, and if I find any red M&Ms in my candy dish, heads are gonna roll."

"Rightfully so." Skeeter nodded.

Riley sat for another minute trying to will himself out of the SUV. *I hope I don't have to deal with the media today. That's going to be the worst part. If they'd just ask about football, that'd be fine. But they're going to ask about my dad and about Sal Ricci and about the bombings and about the torture.* Riley fought the urge to hit the ignition, throw the truck in reverse, and take a road trip back to Denver.

Finally, looking at his watch and seeing that he had five minutes to get in, he said, "So what I was going to say earlier is that since they're already thinking I'm a prima donna, walking in with a bodyguard is not going to help that perception. Would you mind giving me an hour or two? Then you could go in and get to know the security folk at the facility. From what Scott said, they should be expecting you."

"Sure," Skeeter replied, but Riley could see that he wasn't really happy with the plan.

Sorry, buddy, but that's the way it's got to be.

Riley appreciated Skeeter's protectiveness—it had saved his life more than once in the last year. But sometimes having a six-foot-seven-inch walking shadow could feel just a wee bit confining. Although where he was going, a six-foot-seven-inch giant would actually fit right in.

Somewhere along the line, though, Riley was going to have to start separating himself from Skeeter—if not for his own sake, then for Skeeter's sake as well.

Riley smiled as he pictured himself, old and wrinkly, in a bed in a nursing home, and Skeeter, just as old and just as wrinkly, lying in the next bed over with his feet hanging off the end of the bed and an M4 strapped across his sunken chest. The smile left him quickly. *Yeah, but with the way things are going, the chances of either of us living to be old enough for a nursing home are pretty slim.*

"Pach," Skeeter said, nodding toward the dash clock, which now read 7:58.

"Yeah, yeah, yeah. You're right. Can't be late for my first day."

But still he sat there.

Finally Skeeter said, "Go!"

"I'm going! I'm going!"

Thankfully, it looked like the media must be setting up around the practice fields, because the entrance seemed to be fairly free of big-haired gals and jock-wannabe guys. So if he was quick, he might be able to make it in without having to deal with any obnoxious questions. Riley opened the door and quickly retrieved his bag from the backseat. With a sigh, he jogged to the entrance, under the mighty spear, and in to meet his new team.

"Good morning, Mr. Covington! Welcome to the Washington Warriors," said a perky receptionist from the middle of a long half-moon desk set in the middle of the spacious lobby. "Coach Medley and Mr. Bellefeuille are waiting for you in Mr. Bellefeuille's office. Let me show you the way."

"Thank you." *Oh man, right into the fire!*

Coming around her desk, she held out a dainty hand. "My name is Madeline. May I take your bag and leave it up front for you to pick up after your meeting?"

"No thank you. I'll keep it with me," Riley said, not wanting to leave his gym bag and the concealed Smith & Wesson .357 Sig around for potential prying eyes.

As Madeline began narrating the club's history while they crossed the tiled logo on the floor and ascended a flight of dark wood-paneled steps, all the nervousness Riley had felt outside in the truck multiplied tenfold. Scott Medley had the reputation of being a "players' coach," which Riley thought was kind of a misnomer. A players' coach would fire your butt just as quickly as any other coach. But at least Coach Medley seemed like a fair man and would hopefully be a little easier to get along with than Coach Burton had been.

Rick Bellefeuille was another story. He had made his hundreds of millions in the sign business—*which makes the cheesy Warrior Pride banner out front that much more out of place.* Bellefeuille had bought the team twelve years ago and was very involved in the day-to-day operations. He could be seen on the sidelines at some point every game yelling at the players or laying into the coaches—sort of like the NBA's Mark Cuban, but with more self-control and less legal trouble. He was the guy that Riley was the most worried about.

". . . and this is the owner's suite," Riley's cheerful little escort announced as they walked into a room decorated in faux rustic and animal-head chic. *I wonder if he shot all these himself,* Riley thought, admiring the mounted head of a large sable. The way the ticks had chewed away at the antelope's ears answered his question. *This was not a farm-raised animal. Maybe I'll get along with Mr. Bellefeuille after all.*

"Let's see if they're ready for you," Madeline said as she turned toward a frosted-glass door.

"Yes, let's," Riley said with a smile, causing her to quickly glance back to see if he was mocking her. Riley just winked and nodded toward the door.

Just as quickly, Madeline's smile returned, and she knocked, then opened the door when a voice from inside called out, "Come in."

CHAPTER TWENTY-SIX

MONDAY, JULY 27, 8:05 A.M. EDT
WARRIORS PARK, ASHBURN, VIRGINIA

All Riley's hopes for getting along with Rick Bellefeuille flew out the window as soon as he saw the man's face. In that moment Riley remembered that this trade was not the idea of either PFL organization but was the brainchild of a goateed analyst in the counterterrorism division of the Department of Homeland Security.

"Mr. Bellefeuille, this is—"

"I know who he is," Bellefeuille interrupted Madeline. "Close the door behind you."

"Yes, sir," she replied as she quickly retreated out the door.

"Welcome, Riley," Coach Medley said, walking over to him, shaking his hand, and leading him to a dark leather chair in front of the large desk. "It's good to have you as part of the organization."

"Thanks, Coach, it's good to be here."

"Okay, let's cut the bull," Bellefeuille interjected. "We all know the score here. You didn't want to come here. And, while I'm happy for what you could be adding to our defense, I don't like being told what to do with my organization. If it wasn't for some legal issues my family is facing—which, by the way, makes this whole thing feel like it's just a step above common blackmail—without those issues, there's no way I would have let you on my team."

"Fair enough," Riley said. It was all he would allow himself to say. The fact that this guy was treating him like he was doing Riley some huge favor by letting him be part of his team rubbed Riley the wrong way.

"And I also don't like being kept in the dark about things that affect the Warriors organization. So before I let you into my locker room, I'd like for you to tell me what's really going on here," Bellefeuille demanded, leaning back in his deep mahogany chair.

Riley took a deep breath to steady himself. "I'm sorry, sir. I'm sorry you've been put in this position. I'm even more sorry that I've been put in this position, because believe me, this would not have been my choice.

"Now, I'm not sure what you know, but whatever it is, it's what Homeland Security has determined you need to know. You can keep me out of your locker room if you like, but the fact is, I'm not at liberty to say anything beyond what you've already been told."

Bellefeuille's hand slammed the top of his desk. "Don't you talk to me about what you are and what you're not at liberty to say! This is *my* team! This is *my* facility! I know enough about your history to know that the Mustangs kept you out of minicamp earlier this year because of concerns for the safety of the club and their training center! I will not have you risking the lives of my people just so that you can keep playing Captain America!"

Captain America again, he thought. *Enough with the Captain America already.* Ever since *USA Today* had run a front-page picture of him wearing a computer-generated cape and bearing that caption, the moniker had stuck. And it drove him crazy.

As much as Riley wanted to lose his cool with Bellefeuille, he couldn't. Rick Bellefeuille's concerns were well-founded. While the target on Riley's back was smaller than it had been a couple of months ago, it was still there. The *fatwa* that had been declared against him in May had not, as far as he had heard, been called off. The very fact that Skeeter was sitting out in Riley's rented SUV attested to his still-precarious situation.

"Mr. Bellefeuille, I'm truly sorry for the situation that you're—that we're—in. Truth be known, you're right—I'd rather not be here. While I have respect for you and your organization, I would much prefer to be sitting in Denver right now.

"But because of circumstances beyond either of our control, I'm stuck here now, and you're stuck with me. However, I can promise you one thing. I will give you 100 percent every day. I will work like a dog to learn Coach's system. As far as I'm concerned, I am a Warrior now, and I will do everything I can to make your team—our team—better."

"Yeah, rah, rah. Go team." Bellefeuille sat for what seemed like an eternity before continuing. "I've been in business long enough to know that when life hands you crap, you make crap sandwiches and sell them for three-fifty a pop."

"Okay," Riley said tentatively, not sure where the owner was going with this.

"As I've said, I don't want you here, but since you are here, I'm going to make the best of it. So expect to fulfill every media requirement in your contract, plus some more that I will ask you to do as a personal favor to me. Captain America comes to the nation's capital," Bellefeuille said as he ran his hand through the air like he was reading another of his cheap vinyl banners. "Got any problems with that?"

Riley's heart sank. *Nothing like feeling like a piece of meat in a butcher shop. But that's the nature of the biz.* "No, sir."

"Good. Medley, you got anything you need to go over with Riley before he leaves us?"

Coach Medley, who obviously had learned to wait his turn with Bellefeuille, answered, "Not really. We'll talk later, Riley. Head downstairs and find your locker. Then go to the equipment room and get what you need. Someone will come for you for a uniformed photo shoot at 11:45. No pads, but with your helmet. You can join up with the team after lunch."

"Yes, sir."

Medley stood. "Good to have you on board, Riley."

Riley stood too and shook Medley's hand. "Thanks, Coach."

When he turned to say something to Bellefeuille, the owner just nodded toward the door. Riley picked up his bag and walked out of the office.

Well, that couldn't have gone much worse. As he walked past the mounted animals in the outer room, Riley couldn't help feeling that his head was about to join the others on the Warriors owner's wall—a new trophy for all the world to see.

CHAPTER TWENTY-SEVEN

MONDAY, JULY 27, 6:20 A.M. MDT
CENTENNIAL, COLORADO

Muhammed Zerin Khan listened to the automated voice, then agreed to accept the charges for a long-distance collect call.

"Hello, Zerin," Hamza Yusuf Khan's low, scratchy voice said over the line a moment later.

"Dad," Zerin responded tentatively.

Zerin still struggled with what his relationship with his father should be. Zerin had grown up in Atlanta, Georgia, living with his mother. She was still there in the same small, dingy apartment complex.

Mom had lived a tough life after Dad had been imprisoned for drug trafficking in the late eighties. For as long as Zerin could remember, his mother had worked two and three jobs at a time just trying to keep things together—waiting tables at the local diner, selling cigarettes and candy as a cashier at the corner gas station, cleaning trains for the Metro Atlanta Rapid Transit Authority. As he had watched his mom struggle, the resentment he held for his dad had grown. Because of his dad's stupid choices, Zerin was watching her work herself to an early grave.

Whenever Zerin visited Atlanta, his mom still encouraged—pressured—him to visit his father in the Georgia State Prison. Somehow, in spite of her hard life, she continued to love the man who was the cause of it all. So Zerin made the drive from time to time mostly for her sake, although if forced to admit it, part of him still felt an obligation to honor his dad simply because he was his father—a lesson his mother had taken great pains to instill in him.

Lately, though, if Zerin was completely honest, the visits to his dad had begun to hold a little more interest. In the last few years he had begun to notice a difference in his father. The way his mom told it, before going to prison, his dad had never been a very religious person. There was a brief stint with the Nation of Islam back in Chicago in the 1970s. But he had become disillusioned with the NOI after learning of what he felt was their heretical belief that Allah had become incarnate in Wallace Fard Muhammad. Ultimately he left the organization, though he kept the name change. Since that time he had loosely kept ties with his Muslim beliefs, sort of like someone who moves to another town but still follows the football team of the city he left.

Now it seemed like every time Zerin visited his dad, he saw bigger and bigger changes—changes in how his father dressed, changes in how his father talked. This man who previously had kept himself meticulously shaven had grown his beard out and always seemed to have his head covered.

After one visit, Zerin went online to do some detective work to try to uncover what was going on with his dad. What he learned surprised him. He discovered that in prison, political correctness was out the window. Instead segregation was the norm—whites stayed with whites, blacks with blacks, browns with browns. Among the prisoners, the color code was strictly enforced.

In the power struggle within the prison walls, each group fought to create their own distinctives, whether it was in the way they wore their clothes, the ink they embedded into their bodies, or the belief systems they held to. Recently, among many of the African-American prisoners, a harsh form of Islam had taken root.

This radical Saudi doctrine of Islam was known as Wahhabism and had been made infamous by Osama bin Laden. The followers of this sect never masked their desire to put America under Islamic control by the year 2025, saying things like, "Muslims must raise the banner of jihad until America falls under the one-world Islamic caliphate," and "Islam is the answer, and jihad is the way."

Zerin's father was fully immersed. In fact, to hear his dad tell it, he was the Wahhabi imam for all the Muslim prisoners at Georgia State Prison. He was a big man—a man who knew things, a man who controlled things, a man who made things happen. People listened to him, and nobody crossed him.

Now Zerin's dad was in the midst of something huge, and Zerin was dying to know what it was. *Could I possibly even be part of it?* Maybe this big thing, whatever it was, could help restore a relationship that never really was and give him a father he'd never really had.

Just gotta control the temper. Don't let him get under your skin. Try to draw him out.

"How goes football?" Hamza asked his son.

"It's fine," Zerin answered as he slipped out from under his comforter and made his way to the kitchen of his two-bedroom apartment, where his timered coffeemaker had a fresh pot waiting for him. "Big news around the locker room is Riley Covington getting sent to the Warriors."

"Good! That man is pure evil! A tool in Satan's hand!" Hamza responded with venom in his voice.

"Actually, he's really not that bad when you get to know him. Of all the guys—"

"Shut up, boy! You don't know what you're talking about. Do you know how many of our brothers he has killed?"

"Our brothers? He hasn't killed any of my brothers! In fact, I don't have any brothers, because my father decided to get himself locked up before he could give me any," Zerin said, angry not just at his father but also at himself for feeling the need to defend Riley Covington.

"You know exactly what I'm talking about! You keep away from him!"

Zerin slammed a mug down on the kitchen counter. "Or what? Since when have you been able to tell me who I can associate with? Listen, this conversation is going nowhere, and it's way too early to stand here and argue with you. Let's just call it a—"

"No, wait . . . wait," Hamza said quickly. "My bad, Son. I let my emotions overtake my head. Let's start this conversation again, all right?"

After a moment, Zerin answered, "Sure. So what's new there?"

"What do you mean?" his father asked with a playful lilt to his voice. "I'm locked away in the same place I've been for the past twenty years. What could be new?"

"You know what I mean," Zerin said, frustrated that his dad was making him pump him for information. "With the project. What's new with the project?"

"Well, since the 'man' is listening in—right, Mr. Man?" Hamza said to whoever's job it was to monitor inmate calls that day, "you know I can't say much. But just know that things are continuing to move. When the time comes, I'm going to want you to come down here to me. I don't care if it's in the middle of the season and you have a game the next day. You drop everything and get yourself down here. Am I clear?"

Obviously he has no clue about the PFL rules. I can't just up and skip a game to visit my inmate father. Zerin shook his head, imagining how that conversation would go with Coach Burton. "Sure, Dad, I'll see what I can do."

"Stop! I won't have you patronizing me. This is not something you can just laugh off, Zerin. You *must* come when I tell you to come. Please!"

Zerin was taken aback. This was the first time he had ever heard that word come out of his father's mouth. "Sure. Like I said, I'll find a way to get there."

"Good, good. Listen, there are others waiting to use the phone, so I must go. You take care of yourself, Son. Follow the pillars, pray the *salat*, and *insha'Allah*, we may be together soon."

"Sure thing, Dad. You take care too." It wasn't until he had hung up the phone that his father's last words hit him. *"We may be together soon"? What's that all about?* He poured himself a cup of coffee and sat down at the table in the kitchen nook. *I'll never understand that old man, so it's no use trying to figure him out. I'll learn everything in its time.*

As he sipped his coffee, his mind shifted to trying to figure out if there really was a way to disappear from the team when his dad called without totally destroying any chance he had at a future PFL career.

CHAPTER TWENTY-EIGHT

MONDAY, JULY 27, 8:25 A.M. EDT
WARRIORS PARK, ASHBURN, VA

Riley was running about 70-30 on his warm reception–cold shoulder ratio as he walked through the Warriors locker room for the first time. However, even the warm receptions consisted of little more than a handshake or a fist tap or a "Hey, Riley." But since it was the first day of training camp and everyone had to be out on the field in five minutes, Riley knew he couldn't have expected much more. He just thought back to how he had acted whenever a new face showed up in the Mustangs locker room. If he wasn't in a rush, they got a "Welcome to the Mustangs." If he was, then they got nothing. Add to that the nerves of training camp—a place where everyone had to be ready to prove himself at all times. *Not the most social of situations,* Riley thought.

"Pach," a friendly voice called from behind him. Riley turned and saw his old teammate, Don Bernier, coming his way.

"Nails," Riley responded, giving his friend a handshake and a one-arm hug. "Still got the garage?"

Most people thought Bernier's nickname derived from him being "tough as. . . ." But its origin was actually found in his hobby of building huge pieces of woodwork in his garage, then placing them around his property—or giving them to friends, whether they wanted them or not. Riley still had an eighteen-foot Celtic cross tucked among the rows of ponderosa pines on his property back in Parker. When Riley had shown him where he wanted it, Bernier had protested at its hidden location until Riley convinced him that he wanted it there as a place where he could go for private prayer retreats. That seemed to satisfy his friend, and Riley had been sure to go out there once to pray just so that he wasn't technically lying.

"Oh, the garage is alive and kicking! Got a guy on the team who's a big Monty Python fan, so I'm building him a giant Trojan rabbit for his backyard," Bernier said proudly.

"Wow, he'll be thrilled," Riley said, thinking that he might want to live without a backyard for quite a while longer.

"No, he won't," Bernier said with a smile. "He'll hate it, just like you hated that big cross I gave to you."

Riley tried to come up with words he could say that would convince Bernier otherwise, but since it was so completely true, he just started laughing. "You know, I'm not even going to try to deny it. So if you know your buddy hates it, why are you doing it?"

"Two reasons. First, I've only got so much room at my own place, so after I build these things, I have to put them somewhere. Second, the looks on the faces of you guys when I pull up in your driveways with my trailer behind me is absolutely priceless. And you were one of the worst! 'Uh . . . I'm putting it back here . . . uh . . . for a . . . a . . . a private prayer retreat! Yeah, that's it!' Heather and I laughed at that one for days!"

By this time they were laughing so hard that other players who were on their way out to the practice field started looking at them. Typically there wasn't too much laughter on the first day of camp.

When Riley finally could speak, he asked, "So how are Heather and the kids?"

"Great! Hey, listen, I want to catch up and all, but I got about two minutes to beat the buzzer. You cool? You need any directions or anything?"

"Just looking for my locker; then I got to get to the equipment room."

After glancing up at the clock on the wall, Bernier started backing toward the door. "Linebackers are on the other side of the locker room, toward the back corner. Then, if you go out the door right by your locker and head left down the hall, you'll find the equipment room. The equipment manager is named Stump—he's a good guy. Gotta go!"

"Thanks," Riley called as Bernier slipped out the door.

Riley walked through the now-empty locker room. Thirty seconds later a horn blew, indicating the beginning of practice. Anyone not out there was one step closer to the end of his football dreams and could also expect his wallet to be $1,500 lighter come tomorrow. Although training camp didn't officially start until tonight, the pressure and the fines started this morning.

It didn't take long for Riley to find his locker. At the top was a piece of athletic tape with *Covington* written across it. It had been a number of years since he had seen his name on anything other than a laminated plaque. A weird feeling of déjà vu caused him to pause for a second and reorient himself.

Placing his bag on the ground, he lifted the bench seat at the front part of his locker. After looking around, he reached into the bag and pulled out the .357 Sig. He quickly pulled the paper coating off the Velcro strips that were attached to the holster and secured the weapon on the underside of the top of the storage area. Mr. Bellefeuille and Coach Medley knew about the gun, but no one else—and Riley really wanted to keep it that way.

After a few minutes of emptying out clothes, deodorants, and lotions from his bag, he found the door Bernier had told him about and went to find out why they called the equipment manager "Stump."

CHAPTER TWENTY-NINE

MONDAY, JULY 27, 11:41 A.M. EDT
WARRIORS PARK, ASHBURN, VA

Riley found it bizarre being in the red and yellow of the Washington Warriors instead of a blue and orange Mustangs uniform. In fact, as soon as Riley had gotten back from seeing Stump—*I'm still not sure why they call him that, and I probably don't want to know*—he had quickly dressed out, taken a picture of himself with his cell phone, and texted it to his family and friends.

Then, after the initial excitement of the new uniform wore off, he had spent the next couple hours studying the playbook that had been left at his locker. Many of the plays looked familiar because both clubs ran the same type of defense. And even though the codes were different, Riley was used to that. The Mustangs had gone through two defensive coordinators while he had been there, and with each new administration came a new playbook.

There had been a brief flurry of excitement in the locker room when the players had come back from the field at 10:30 and moved into position meetings. But other than that and the occasional trainer or equipment person coming up for a quick introduction, Riley had had the place to himself.

When the third staff member introduced

himself, it really hit Riley that he was a stranger in a strange land. Back in Denver, he had known all the trainers, equipment managers, field personnel, and media people—everyone from the front office to the janitorial staff. Trying to get to know all the members of the new organization seemed a near-impossible task.

Glancing up at the wall clock, he saw that it was 11:43 a.m. Time for the photo shoot.

Sure enough, a kid in his early teens came walking toward him. "Mr. Covington? My name is Brad Wiens. I'm supposed to take you to your photo shoot," the boy said in a nervous voice.

"Good to meet you, Brad," Riley said, shaking his hand. He reached back and grabbed his helmet out of the locker. "Let's go."

As they walked, Brad said, "It's just so awesome to have you here. I've got so much respect for you—like, not only as a player, but as a person, too."

"Thanks, Brad. That's nice of you to say."

"No, seriously. All my friends couldn't believe it when I told them I was going to meet you today. . . ."

Brad's voice faded into the background as soon as he turned Riley toward the practice field. Riley had thought the shoot would be indoors, but it looked like they were heading right out to the media. *Here we go,* he thought as Brad opened the door for him, saying, ". . . autographs for all my friends, but my dad said that wouldn't be cool to do."

Immediately, camera flashes started going off all around Riley. His name was called out by hundreds of different voices. He smiled, keeping his head down, and gave a quick wave.

In the midst of the crowd, a hand grasped his, and a man said, "Riley, I'm Jonny Wiens. I'm the head of PR here. I hope you don't mind me sending my son to get you. He couldn't give a flying flip for any of the Warriors players, but as soon as I told him you were going to be here today, he was practically on his knees begging me to let him meet you."

"Dad!" Brad protested through the noise.

"Don't worry, Brad," Riley said. "It was a pleasure to meet you, too. And you tell your dad how many autographs you need for your friends, and I'll be sure to get them to you."

Brad's face lit up but fell again when his dad said, "I'll take him from here. Thanks, buddy."

Brad nodded, then faded into the crowd.

Wiens put his arm around Riley's shoulders and led him toward the practice field. Walking through the media reminded Riley of being at a movie premiere—all the shouts, the flashes, the microphones, everything except the tuxedos and the red carpet.

Once they cleared the press gauntlet, Wiens turned and put his arms up, quieting the mass of people. "If you'll check your schedules, you'll see that Riley will have a press Q&A tonight at six. Until then, I've asked him not to answer any questions. However, you're welcome to take all the pictures you want."

Leaning into Wiens, Riley asked, "Any chance I can get one of those little schedules, Jonny, so I don't miss any of the wonderful things you've already got planned for my life?"

Flustered, Wiens said, "Oh, sure, sorry. I'll get one to you as soon as we finish here." As he answered Riley, another man with a camera came out to them. Wiens introduced him. "Riley, this is Mack Kinsey. He's the team photographer. I'm going to leave you in his hands. After you're through, you can grab some lunch with the rest of the team."

Riley and Kinsey shook hands. "Good to meet you, Riley. Let's get you in the center of the field here, and I'll snap a few pics and get you on your way."

"No problem."

Except there was a bit of a problem. Now that he was away from the roar of the press contingent, other voices began calling out to him. It was only then he noticed a bunch of the players eating lunch at some tables set out on a long, second-level balcony.

"Strike a pose, superstar!"

"It's a bird; it's a plane; it's Captain America!"

"Come on, Covington, smile! No, bigger! No, bigger!"

"Look at them pearly whites!"

"Oh, be still, my heart! He's beautiful!"

And right in the middle of them was Don Bernier, who seemed to be the most vocal out of all of them. Riley couldn't help but laugh. How many times had he done the same thing to his buddies on the team? He probably couldn't count that high.

Riley pointed to Don and gave him a threatening scowl. That set off a whole new round of taunts.

"Better watch it, Nails; Covington's probably packing heat!"

"He's coming to get you, Nails."

"Best be careful; I heard Captain America can shoot lasers out of his eyes!"

As embarrassing as it was to be standing in the middle of the field posing for pictures and looking like a doofus, it was also good to hear the taunts. That meant that at least the ice was broken. After a couple more days, the novelty of having Captain America in the locker room would fade, and the players' attention would go back to where it belonged—torturing the rookies.

CHAPTER THIRTY

SATURDAY, AUGUST 22, 6:45 P.M. MDT
PLATTE RIVER STADIUM, DENVER, COLORADO

Riley shook his head to clear the cobwebs. Something about his situation seemed extremely familiar, but his brain felt too fuzzy to put the pieces together. The rich smell of the bluegrass blend that was separated from his face only by the side of his helmet's cage told him that he was home. *But home isn't really home anymore, is it?*

An arm reached down and hit him on the chest, then stayed low to help him up. As Riley's eyes followed the arm up to its owner, everything fell into place. He laughed to himself as he let the hand pull him up.

When he was back on his feet, he reached over and slapped the opposing player on the helmet. "Ain't gonna be no third time, Zerin."

"We'll see about that, old man," Muhammed Zerin Khan answered, then turned to go back to his huddle. However, he stopped and faced Riley. "You sure you're okay?"

Riley laughed. "It'll take more than you to put me out, Rookie."

"I may not have put you out, but all it took was this rookie to put you down . . . twice," Zerin answered with a wink and a turn.

Although it was all in good fun, Riley could feel the teasing starting to get to him. Sure, this was only the second preseason game, but Riley still felt like he had something to prove coming back home. After all, in many ways this game really was all about him.

Tonight was the first game in Platte River Stadium since the terrorist attack last December that had killed more than two thousand people. There had been talk about closing down the stadium, but the public outcry against letting the terrorists win had finally convinced the city and the Mustangs organization to repair and reopen the stadium.

Originally some genius at PFL headquarters had thought it would be a splendid idea if the Baltimore Predators—the Mustangs' opponents on the fateful Monday night when the bombs started going off—returned to Denver to play the first game back in the venue. But player complaints had begun as soon as the schedule was released. The situation came to a head when the Predators organization flat out refused to return to Platte River Stadium.

This put the PFL into quite a quandary until Rick Bellefeuille jumped in to save the day. True to his word to exploit Riley as much as he possibly could, Bellefeuille offered to let the Predators play the Warriors' scheduled opponent down in Dallas, while the Warriors would take the game in Denver. The PFL jumped at this solution, and the public ate it up. It was estimated that this would be the most-viewed preseason game in professional football history.

In order to remember those who had been killed that horrible night, a ceremony had been held prior to the game. It began with a police honor guard marching out to bagpipes. This was followed by a reading of the names of the deceased by some of the wounded who had survived. The first name was read by a ten-year-old girl in a wheelchair who no longer had legs below midthigh. Next, five more victims joined her, reading off more names. With each new set of names, five more survivors joined in until the stadium rang out with 150 voices simultaneously reading out names of those fallen. This was immediately followed by the release of 2,223 white balloons. All the while Riley, along with most of the players on the opposing sideline, wept openly.

When the ceremony was over, Riley had asked, and been granted, permission to cross the field and join his former team for a pregame prayer. The crowd had erupted in cheers when he had run across the field and again when he came back—facts that both embarrassed him and gave him an even deeper love for the people of his former hometown. By the time he reached his new teammates, he was wondering how he could possibly be able to control his emotions enough to play the game.

Riley's emotional struggles had started the moment the buses had first pulled up to the stadium. As the doors *shooshed* open, part of him wanted to just stay on the bus. He could feel himself sweating, and his right leg was bouncing up and down like he had springs on his shoe. When he finally stepped off the bus, he found himself anxiously scanning the underground corridor for anything that might seem suspicious or out of place. *Got a little post-traumatic stress going on here? Lord, give me peace in my heart, and please protect us all.*

Riley began to calm a little bit when he saw how much tighter security was now than it had been last season. Police were everywhere. Every bag was checked, and every player was wanded. The team was then escorted en masse from the buses to the visitors' locker room.

At one point before the game, Riley had tried to go stick his head into the Mustangs' locker room. It had been a month since he had seen Keith Simmons, Afshin Ziafat, and the rest of the team, and he knew they would be having just as difficult a time as he. But when he stepped through the door into the corridor that ran under the seats, he was met by the head of security, who approached from one of two lines of police that formed a pathway from the locker room to the field.

"Sorry, Riley, but the visiting team doesn't have access beyond the locker room and the playing field," his old friend said apologetically.

"No need to apologize, Pat. Believe me, I understand," Riley said as he clapped him on the back and turned around. And that was at least partly true. Mentally, he was very thankful that the PFL had taken the events of last season so seriously. But truthfully, he hated being confined to the visitors' locker room in what he still considered his stadium.

Yeah, but that was two hours and twenty-one points ago, Riley thought as he leaned into the huddle. *Cry your tears later, boy. Now it's time to get into the game.* Although he could see the irony of getting clocked by Zerin again, he was angry at himself for letting it happen—same play, same pass to Jamal White, same letting up by Riley, and same hit by the rookie. *Stupid. Fool me once, shame on you. Fool me twice, you deserve to clobber me.*

But Riley couldn't really blame himself, just like he couldn't blame the rest of his former teammates for the current rout being inflicted upon them by a far inferior team. This was anything but a normal preseason game.

"You all right, superhero?" asked Dave Edwards, the guy who played Riley's old position. Since the Warriors already had a Pro Bowl–quality inside linebacker, Coach Medley had moved Riley to the strong side, a position that he was still getting used to.

"Yeah, just getting acquainted with old friends," Riley answered.

Edwards nodded, then gave the call for the next play. "Okay, Tite Mocka Blitz, Tite Mocka Blitz! Break!"

On two of the three previous first downs, the Mustangs had come out with short screens that had netted them eight and six yards respectively. Apparently Coach Medley was banking on Coach Burton trying to capitalize on his success with another screen.

Knowing what he did about Burton, Riley highly doubted that the Mustangs coach would go for it again. But a play call was a play call. So he readied himself as the Mustangs came to the line. Zerin moved to the right side of the line, and Riley heard Edwards call out, "Rudy! Rudy!"

At the start of quarterback Randy Meyer's call, Riley and the two other linebackers rushed the line, timing their arrival just right with the snap of the ball. Immediately Riley knew that it wasn't going to be a screen. He tried to adjust as he watched Meyer hand the ball to running back Bob Rhine, but before he could shift his body, Travis Marshall wrapped his beefy arms around him, taking him out of the play.

"What? You losing a step, Pach?" Marshall asked after Rhine had gained seven yards and the play was blown dead.

"Just be careful, Marsh. Sometime this half, I'm going to embarrass you," Riley said as he turned to trot back to his huddle.

"You better hurry," Marshall called after him. "You've only got six minutes left."

Yeah, the whole country is tuning in to watch you, Riley thought, *and so far you've pretty much done squat!*

"Rip Tomahawk Double Quad Set! Rip Tomahawk Double Quad Set! Break!" Edwards called out. The team clapped once and moved to their positions.

This play called for a strong-side blitz, which would give Riley a chance to take his revenge against Travis Marshall. *Kinda feel sorry for the boy—but only kinda.*

"Lenny Tiger! Lenny Tiger!" Edwards called out.

Sure enough, it was a two-tight-end package, and Riley could see Zerin lining up on the left side next to a second rookie tight end whose name Riley couldn't remember.

As soon as Meyer began his call, Riley began easing toward the line.

"Green 23! Green 23! Go! Go! Go!"

Riley had heard Meyer use that cadence many times before, so he bolted on the first *Go* and reached the line of scrimmage just as the ball was snapped.

Travis Marshall barely had time to come out of his crouch before Riley's hands reached his shoulders and pushed him back down to the grass. Riley was past him in a flash and saw that there was now nobody between himself and Randy Meyer. He saw Meyer spot him, but the quarterback didn't seem concerned about him. Suddenly Riley understood why. A huge body moved into Riley's path.

Great, Gorkowski. Riley ran into the oversize center's chest at an angle, rolled off the man's left side, and wrapped his arms around a surprised Meyer, pulling him to the ground.

A cheer echoed through the stadium, then died quickly as the crowd remembered that Riley had just sacked *their* quarterback. But as Riley stood up and pulled Meyer back to his feet, a chant began to build until it thundered through the venue. "Riley! Riley! Riley! Riley!"

Riley stood in the middle of the field with tears again forming in his eyes. *These are my people. What am I doing in Washington when my people are here?* Slowly he turned and took it all in.

"Wave to them, you idiot," Chris Gorkowski yelled into the ear hole of Riley's helmet so he could be heard over the cheer.

Feeling like a fool, Riley half raised his hand and gave a little wave. The crowd exploded. People were going crazy cheering in the stands. The tears were flowing down Riley's cheeks now.

Finally a ref came over, took Riley by the arm, and guided him over the line of scrimmage and to the Warrior huddle.

Dave Edwards put his hand on Riley's face mask and pulled him down into the huddle. "Hey, Captain America, it's great they love you and all, but it's still only third down. Forty-four Reader Long Cover One! Forty-four Reader Long Cover One! Break!"

The rest of the game was a blur for Riley. He got two more sacks and four tackles in the three quarters he played of the Warriors' 44–17 victory.

Immediately after the game ended, Riley met up with his former teammates and a number of his new ones for a prayer of thanksgiving in the middle of the field.

When the prayer broke up, Riley visited with Keith Simmons, Afshin Ziafat, Travis Marshall, and others for about ten minutes before he was ushered off the field by Jonny Wiens. Apparently Mr. Bellefeuille had let it be known through Wiens that Riley would be available for any and all large-market media opportunities following the game. This included eleven television interviews while still in the locker room, a postgame press conference, and a multitude of print interviews on the flight home.

When Skeeter finally pulled into the Quincy's parking garage, it was 7:15 a.m., and Riley was dozing in and out in the passenger seat. Skeeter roused him enough to get him to his room. Since the team had the day off, Riley didn't bother setting the alarm and slept until 2:30 p.m., at which time he got up, scarfed down a peanut-butter-and-jelly sandwich, climbed back into bed, and slept until his alarm woke him again early Monday morning.

CHAPTER THIRTY-ONE

SUNDAY, AUGUST 23, 10:15 A.M. EDT
WASHINGTON, D.C.

On the computer screen a headline announced "Riley Covington's Homecoming." What followed in the ESPN.com story was a very detailed, very personal look into what superstar and American hero Riley Covington was feeling as he entered Platte River Stadium for the first time since the attack. It told of his joy at seeing his old teammates, his tears during the reading of the victims' names, and just how much fun he'd had embarrassing his former nemesis, Chris Gorkowski, and sacking Randy Meyer. All in all, it was a very well-written article that provided interesting insights into the mind and heart of Washington Warrior Riley Covington.

However, as Scott Ross watched Khadi Faroughi staring at the monitor, he somehow knew that her eyes were not on the text. Instead, they were fixed on the picture by Whitney Walker's byline—a picture that showed Whitney with a microphone in one hand and Riley's arm in the other.

Scott, too, had stared at the picture for a long time while in his office. There was something more there than just the hand on the arm. Maybe it was the way Whitney was looking up at him—such a deep admiration in her bright green eyes. Maybe it was the laughter on Riley's face—easy, comfortable.

Or, maybe . . .

Scott couldn't help thinking of a scene in the movie *While You Were Sleeping*—a movie Scott never missed when it was on late-night television, although he would never admit it to any male friend—where Sandra Bullock's character was accused of "leaning." She was told by the character who was in love with her that "leaning" involved more than just hugging; "Leaning is whole bodies moving in. . . . Leaning involves wanting . . . and accepting. *Leaning.*"

Maybe I'm overanalyzing—although I guess that's what analysts are supposed to do—but I could swear that both Whitney and Riley are leaning *in that picture,* he had thought.

Scott cleared his throat.

"I know you're back there, Scott. You're about as stealthy as a water buffalo," Khadi said, keeping her eyes on the screen.

"Sorry. Asian bovine characteristics tend to run in my family."

Khadi chuckled softly. "You know, I was just looking at this picture of Riley and Whitney. Is it just me, or do they look like they're *leaning*?"

"*Leaning*? What do you mean by leaning?" Scott asked, feigning ignorance.

Khadi finally turned around and said, "Oh, come on, Scott. Don't try to pretend you don't watch *While You Were Sleeping* every time it's on TV. It's the one chick movie every guy likes but is afraid to admit it. It's been scientifically proven or something." She turned back toward the monitor. "So are they leaning or not?"

"Yeah, they're leaning," Scott admitted.

Khadi sighed. "I guess they are."

She reached across her keyboard and turned the monitor off before turning back to Scott. "You know, I really like Whitney. After everything calmed down back in June, she and I even went out to lunch together. She is a smart, beautiful, funny woman."

"But not at all Riley's type," Scott said, hoping to lift Khadi's spirits.

"Oh, really? And just what is his type?" Khadi responded.

Scott remembered reading a study that had recently been

completed that found that two to three times each year every male on the planet finds himself in a conversation with a female during which he would willingly commit Japanese ritual *seppuku* if it meant extracting himself from the situation. *Or maybe I didn't read about it; maybe I just thought the study should be done. Either way, it doesn't matter; the truth still stands. I guess it's a good thing that I'm not wearing a sword today, although she does have a pretty mean-looking letter opener on her desk. . . .*

"Scott, come back from your own little world—you're not getting off that easy. I asked you just what is Riley's type."

Khadi's question pulled Scott back from his struggle to remember if the ritual went "plunge, then left, then right" or "plunge, then right, then left." *Doesn't matter! Right now I'd just settle for the plunge!*

"Uh, what is Riley's type? Well, it's like this: in *our* conversations, he's told me . . . he's said that . . . the . . . the girls he likes . . . are . . . are . . . smart, beautiful, funny . . . and Persian! Yep, he always added Persian. Don't know why. I don't know any Persians. Do you know any Persians?"

Khadi couldn't help but laugh. Scott relaxed when he saw her softening up. *Might it actually be possible to survive this?*

"Khadi, I don't know what's going on with Riley right now," Scott said, leaning against the doorframe. "I doubt Riley knows what's going on with Riley. We've—I've taken his life and turned it upside down. Then, no sooner does he get here than he's thrown into training camp with a new team, then preseason. Plus he's got all the memories of his dad and of what he personally has gone through this last year. I think Riley's a struggling boy right now."

"I know," Khadi said sympathetically, "and I want to be there to help him through it. But between his schedule and my schedule here, we've only seen each other three or four times since he's arrived in Washington." Then, motioning back to the computer screen, she added, "But he does seem to find time for Whitney."

Khadi fell back into her chair and started laughing. "Listen to me. I sound like a teenager with a schoolgirl crush. Riley and I don't even have an actual relationship going, and here I am acting like a jealous little girl."

"Listen, Khadi," Scott said, taking a step into her office and lowering his voice, "I don't know what's going on with Whitney, but I'll tell you what I do know. I know how Riley's face lights up when you show up. I know how he watches you when you're across the room."

"Like you do with Tara."

"Right, like I do with—wait a minute, I do not watch Tara from across the room," Scott defended himself.

"Oh please, Scott. Everyone sees it except Tara."

"Listen, if I'm watching Tara Walsh, it's because she is an exceptional analyst and I am admiring her skill and womanly fortitude."

Khadi just smiled at Scott.

"You really don't think she knows?"

"She's clueless."

Scott gave a sigh of relief, then said, "Good. Now where was I?"

"You were telling me how much Riley digs me."

"Exactly. Listen, if you two kids didn't have this whole religious rigmarole between you, Riley would have been down on one knee with you months ago."

"You really think so?" Khadi asked with her eyes wide.

"I really think so."

A genuine smile filled Khadi's face. "Thanks, Scott; I guess I needed to hear that."

"Anytime," Scott answered, amazed at how quickly he could move from the brink of ritual suicide to chick-hero.

"And by the way, nice use of the word *rigmarole*," Khadi complimented him.

"Thanks," Scott said proudly, "I've been wanting to use it in a sentence for a while."

"Hey, you two, am I interrupting anything?" Tara Walsh asked from behind Scott. This was the first he had seen her today, and she was more beautiful than ever. The August humidity had caused her to temporarily give up her usual pantsuits in favor of cooler fare. Today she was wearing a sleeveless black and cream empire jersey dress and had her hair pulled back in a loose ponytail. The whole package together caused Scott's tongue to temporarily stick to the roof of his mouth.

"No, we're just chatting," Khadi answered, saving Scott.

"Good, because it looks like Evie may have found something."

"Seriously? We'll be right there," Scott said, having managed to pry his tongue loose.

"Okay, I'll let everybody know," Tara said, turning to go.

Scott watched as she walked away. When she finally rounded the corner, he looked back at Khadi, who gave him a wink.

"Doesn't Tara look nice today in that summer dress?" Khadi asked innocently.

"I hadn't noticed."

"Obviously."

"I have to run to my office," Scott said as he started out the door. "I'll see you in there."

"Scott," Khadi called out, causing Scott to stop midstride and peek his head around the doorway. "Thanks again. I needed that."

"Anytime. You know where I'm at," Scott answered, then was out the door and back to business.

CHAPTER

THIRTY-TWO

SUNDAY, AUGUST 23, 1:45 P.M. IRDT
TEHRAN, IRAN

Looking out the window, Ayatollah Allameh Beheshti could see the embassies of the Vatican, Italy, and France. Just beyond his sight line, he knew, were the delegations of the Russian Federation, the United Kingdom, Armenia, Germany, and—way off in the distance—the United States of America.

So much of the world, so close! What will be happening in those buildings in the days to come? What panic will take place? What threats will be made? Will those complexes even be standing at the end of the year?

Who will be ruling Iran . . . Islam . . . the world? Which reminds me . . .

"Close your books," Beheshti said to the teens sitting at two long tables. Immediately, all thirty-two books snapped shut. He examined his students—all male, all aged thirteen to eighteen, and all wearing long white kurta shirts with white kufis on their heads.

These young men represented some of the cream of Iran's future. They all came from extremely wealthy and influential families; while there was a lot of oil money represented, there were also two brothers whose father owned a chain of electronics stores throughout Tehran and the surrounding provinces, four students whose fathers were either governmental ministers or deputy ministers, and one boy, the youngest of the class, whose father was the owner of the third-largest television network in Iran.

That was why the textbooks were new, the madrassa was clean, and all five of the Islamic school's classrooms were protected from the oppressive August heat by air-conditioning.

Ayatollah Beheshti had set no standard tuition rate, but the student selection process was very strict, and the families were expected to donate generously to the upkeep of Jomhouri mosque and madrassa. This expectation allowed Beheshti to live a very comfortable life. It also helped to fund his personal projects—the most important of which was currently aboard four separate freighters, each of which was on a long ocean journey to America.

"Farid," Beheshti called out to one student whose upper lip was covered with a dark, soft down, "how many imams have ruled Islam from the time of Muhammad, peace be upon him, until now?"

Farid stood and answered confidently, "There have been twelve, *sayyid*."

Some of the students giggled at his response, and Farid whipped his head around to find the offenders.

Beheshti singled one out. "Namvar, since you find Farid's answer so humorous, please do him the favor of telling him why he is incorrect."

Namvar stood and turned to his classmate with a smug look on his face. "There have been only eleven imams who have ruled Islam, starting with the Prophet's cousin and son-in-law Ali ibn Abu Talib al-Murtadha, peace be upon him, and continuing until Hasan ibn Ali al-'Askari, peace be upon him. The final imam, Muhammad ibn Hasan al-Mahdi, never had a chance to lead Islam."

"And why is that?" Beheshti asked, scanning the room, bypassing the anxious eyes that were trained on him and searching for those that were averted. "Pasha?"

The boy stood up timidly. "Because he was killed?"

More laughter told him he was wrong, and he sat down.

Beheshti fixed him with an angry glare. "Could you please tell me what you were doing for the last half hour while everyone else was reading about this subject?"

"Daydreaming about Danush's mother," a voice called out from the back of the class.

While the class erupted in laughter, Pasha and Danush both pushed their chairs across the tile floor and leaped up, ready to pounce on the one who had said such a vile thing.

"Stop it." Beheshti's voice echoed through the room. "You young men forget where you are and who I am!" Calm was instantly restored to the class. "Now, Yahya, perhaps you can tell me what happened to the young imam."

Yahya stood and cleared his throat. "When the Mahdi was seven, Caliph al-Mu'tamid tried to kill him. His mother tried to hide him, but the caliph would not rest until he was dead. So Allah in his great mercy granted him invisibility, and the Twelfth Imam disappeared from humanity until such a time as Allah sees fit to restore him to his rightful place as ruler of all Islam."

"Very good, very good. You have studied well." *Maybe there is hope for this next generation after all,* Beheshti thought with no small amount of self-satisfaction. "The Mahdi has been hidden away by the hand of Allah for more than a millennium. But the time for his re-emergence during the End of Days is near—very near. Quick, what are the signs we are to look for?"

"The hero Yamani will fight the enemies of Islam," one boy called out.

"Sofiani will fight against Islam," another said.

"Jibril will call out from heaven!"

"Sofiani will be destroyed!"

"The Pure Soul will be killed!"

"Iran will win the World Cup!"

Again, laughter filled the room.

"Excellent, excellent," a smiling Beheshti said. "Except for you, Namvar; I'm afraid when it comes to football, you have put patriotism ahead of common sense."

While he much preferred teaching adults, guiding the children of the wealthy into the truth was what drew the fathers—and their money—into the mosque. So this was an obligation that Beheshti accepted only reluctantly. But there were times, like now, when watching a class full of youths really grasping his lessons gave him a joy that surpassed anything he felt when he led in the mosque.

The ayatollah stood at the head of the two tables and tried to let his pleasure show on his face. All eyes were on him as the students waited to see what he would do next. He slowly smoothed his long beard, grabbing a handful and gently pulling it down, as he prepared his final flurry of questions. The teens, who were used to these rapid-fire sessions, waited on the edges of their seats, each ready to jump up if his name was called.

"Anoush, where will the Mahdi appear?"

"Mecca!"

"Rahim, will he remain in Mecca?"

"No, he will conquer the enemies of Islam and finally rule from Samarra in Iraq!"

"Youness, will he come alone?"

"No, *sayyid*, the prophet Jesus, peace be upon him, will appear with him!"

"Jamshid, will Jesus fight against the Mahdi as the Christians believe?"

"On the contrary, Jesus will lead the final jihad, destroying all those who do not accept the truth of Islam!"

"Mansoor, what time is it?"

The boy leaped up before realizing the question had nothing to do with the lesson and hesitated just long enough for the classroom to break into laughter. Looking at the wall clock, Mansoor answered sheepishly, "Two o'clock, *sayyid*."

Beheshti smiled. "It's good to know you can handle even the most difficult of questions, young man."

Again the students laughed as an embarrassed Mansoor slowly sat back down.

"For tomorrow," Beheshti said, pausing long enough for everyone to reach for pen and paper, "make sure you have Surah As-Saff and Surah Al-Fath memorized, and write down passages from each which you think might refer to the Mahdi. Good work today for most of you. You are dismissed."

The students filed past him with a respectful bow. Farid and

Pasha each received a light slap on the back of the head and a stern look from the ayatollah.

When they were all gone, Beheshti made his way down the corridor toward his office. This was the time of day that he cherished most. The meetings were finished, the classes were taught, and there were still three hours or so until the *'Asr* prayer time. Now was when he could think, pray, and plan for the future.

CHAPTER

THIRTY-THREE

SUNDAY, AUGUST 23, 10:30 A.M. EDT
WASHINGTON, D.C.

Scott wedged himself into the tiny corner of Evie Cline's cubicle that had been reserved for him. Khadi was pushed up against him, and Tara Walsh was on the other side of her. Virgil Hernandez and Joey Williamson stood on chairs, looking over the back and side walls respectively. Gooey, however, sat at his workstation tucked into a far corner of the room. Apparently he had found a way to monitor Evie's screen on his own computer and was listening to the conversation on the in-house communications.

This office is ridiculous, Scott thought. *Jim would have never stood for this.* Jim Hicks, Scott's late boss and friend, had been as tough and hard-nosed as they came. He would fight for, and usually get, what he wanted and whatever he thought his team needed. His death three months ago during an operation in Turkey had been a huge blow to Scott and had thrown him into an identity crisis. When Scott inherited leadership of the team, he initially tried to emulate Jim's leadership style. But soon he found that rather than being a new hard-nosed Jim, he was just being a jerk. *Some people naturally have the hard-nosed gene; some people don't. Maybe if I just had a little more of it in me, we wouldn't all be crammed into this glorified closet!*

"You know, Scott," Hernandez said from over Scott's right shoulder, "if you'd be a little more hard-nosed with the higher-ups, maybe we wouldn't all be crammed into this—"

"Shut up! I know," Scott replied angrily.

"You almost got it just then, although that made you sound a little more like a jerk," Hernandez said.

Scott turned and glared at him. Then he said to Evie, "Okay, let's see—"

"Tara, are you able to see from there?" Khadi asked from right next to Scott. "Why don't we change places? I'm used to eyeballing the side of a monitor."

"Really? Thanks," Tara said as she and Khadi wedged past each other. Now that Tara was pressed up against Scott in the tiny space, Khadi turned to him and gave him a little grin.

Oh, great! Me and my big mouth! Now I'm going to have to deal with Khadi trying to put Tara and . . . What's that . . . ? Tara's hair smells incredible, Scott thought as he leaned in closer for a deeper whiff.

"Should we get this—," Tara said as she turned around to Scott, her face now inches away from his. "What are you doing?"

"Uh . . . I was thinking. . . . You know, processing through about how . . . about how we might be able to better utilize our office space," Scott said, feeling the color rush to his face. "What do you think?"

"Oh, well, actually I do have a few thoughts on the subject," Tara answered, leaning away just a touch. "But don't you think since everyone's here, we should see what Evie's found? Maybe we could meet up later and talk through the office layout."

"Sure, you're exactly right. Evie, show us what you got."

As Tara turned around, Khadi gave Scott a subtle thumbs-up. Quickly, her thumb was joined by thumbs belonging to Hernandez and Williamson. Even Evie's thumb showed her approval below Tara's sight line, and back at his station Gooey gave a barely audible "Woop, woop!"

Lovely, just lovely, a thoroughly embarrassed Scott thought as Evie began her presentation.

"Okay, so a while back we decided that the weapons probably didn't go by plane, ship, or train out of the DPRK. The international community has the North Koreans so tightly monitored that it would be too big of a risk. So the only other option is truck."

"Right, I remember that," Scott encouraged.

"East is the ocean, and south is South Korea. So the only options are northeast into Russia and north or west into China. Russia didn't seem plausible because of the difficult terrain going up through the north part of the DPRK and into Primorsky and Khabarovsk. But Joey's still been following up that route, and he's come up empty. Am I right?"

"Empty as Stalin's cold heart," Williamson confirmed.

"Interestingly antiquated metaphor, Joseph. Minor props," Evie said appreciatively. "So the rest of us have followed the China route. Our hypothesis has been that China would probably have to know about what was being shipped through their country—there are too many checkpoints along the way, not including the two borders, to think otherwise. However, they would also want plausible deniability. So we figured there would be no rigging of the shipping manifests or load documents."

Tara, her head filling Scott's senses with a coconutty piña colada scent, said, "Right. This way they could apologize, say that there were mistakes made—maybe execute a border guard or two—and they'd be golden."

"Exactly. Now, comparing manifests from the North Korean border crossings with all of China's other border crossings was crazy hard, but Gooey created a filtering program that really sped up the process. Right, Goo?"

A click was heard on Evie's speakerphone as Gooey took his phone off mute. "Yep," he said, then clicked back off.

However, Scott thought there was something in the background during that short moment. . . . "Gooey," he called out, "are you playing Halo over there while we're meeting?"

"Uh, no, sir," Gooey replied, clicking on and off.

"Let me rephrase. Gooey, are you playing any computer game while we are holding this all-important strategic meeting during which we might just come up with a plan that could save our entire nation?"

Click. "Uh, maybe, sir." *Click*.

"Well, stop!"

Click. "Uh, yes, sir." *Click*.

Crazy multitasking freak, Scott thought, secretly wishing he too could divide his mind so effectively. "Go on, please, Evie."

"Right," Evie said, obviously enjoying every minute of this. "Gooey's filter left us with just over six hundred manifests for the last three months."

"Why so few?" Khadi asked.

"First of all, North Korea is much more an importer than an exporter, both because of economy and because of the global political climate against them. Second, what they do send out primarily goes out by water or rail. And third, most of what they send into China by truck stays in China. The country is too big and too inhospitable to traverse by road unless you really had a fear of railroads or—"

Click. "Siderodromophobia." *Click*.

"What?" Scott asked.

Click. "Fear of railroads." *Click*.

"Don't be too impressed," Virgil Hernandez said. "He just sits there with Google open waiting to look something up so that he can sound really smart."

Click. ". . ." *Click*.

"Or . . . ," Khadi said, prompting Evie to continue.

"Or really had something to hide," she said with an appreciative nod toward Khadi. "We were able to rule out all but twenty-two of the manifests by following them to their destinations—mostly all down into Southeast Asia. The twenty-two open manifests were primarily from the western border of China. We set aside the six going into India and Kashmir because of our good relations with them. Then also set aside the five countries that only had one truck going in on the premise that whoever is masterminding this wants to deal with as few governments as possible."

"Aren't you making a lot of assumptions in this?" Khadi asked.

"Definitely," Evie answered. "We haven't ruled out those others, just set them aside while we follow one strain of hypotheses."

"Fair enough," Khadi said.

"So cutting to the chase, there were four trucks that have stood out from the rest," Evie said, bringing a map of Asia up on her computer screen. "They all crossed out of China and into Tajikistan, then into Afghanistan, where they've now disappeared."

"Are you sure about Tajikistan?" Tara asked. "Our relationship with them has been pretty solid lately. We've even got troops stationed there."

"Honestly, that's the only big question—why Tajikistan? Then we got thinking about their history. Who are the Tajiks most closely related to?"

Click. "Iran." *Click.*

"That's no fair, Gooey," Evie complained. "You were in on that discussion. Quit stealing my thunder."

Click. "Sorry." *Click.*

Evie continued. "And what country is on the other side of Afghanistan from Tajikistan? Iran. You see, the Tajiks are Persian. They even speak Persian, although they call it Tajiki. The roots between the two countries are very strong, and they seem to be strengthening. Just a couple years ago, Tajikistan threw its support behind Iran's bid for membership into the Shanghai Cooperation Organization."

"And remind me what the Shanghai Cooperative thingy is?" Scott said.

"The SCO is made up of China, Russia, Kazakhstan, Kyrgyzstan, Tajikistan, and Uzbekistan. And their whole reason for forming was to oppose American interference in Central Asia. So, as you can see, the Tajiks are certainly not our best friends."

"So bring me up-to-date. What's the status of your search now?" Scott asked.

"Well, like I said, we'd lost the four trucks . . . until now," Evie said.

Her words were followed by a clatter from across the room, followed by some rapid, heavy footsteps. Suddenly Gooey's oversize head popped up next to Williamson's.

"Say what?" he said, slightly out of breath.

Evie smiled. "I thought that might get you moving. I think that I just now might have found one of the trucks. And if I'm right, it shipped out from Bushehr, Iran, just six days ago."

Scott was elated. *This gang is unbelievable! I've got to get word up the chain as soon as possible. If we're going to do anything to stop these shipments, it's going to take some serious international relations!*

"How sure are you of this?" Scott demanded.

"Probably about 25 percent right now."

That deflated Scott just a bit. But he knew that analyzing intelligence was a volatile business; one new piece of information could bump a percentage up to 100 or drop it to 0.

"Do everything you can to increase that. There's no way I can ask for a raid in international waters on a ship flying a different country's flag based on 25 percent," Scott said as he started to squeeze himself out of the cubicle. "Joey, you keep the sweep going for other options. The rest of you join up with Evie."

"Wait," Evie called out to a rapidly departing Scott. "Don't you even want to know how I found it?"

"Write it in a memo," Scott called back as he entered his office. He reached for the phone to call Stanley Porter, but it rang just before he picked it up.

"Ross," he answered.

On the other end of the line he heard a sigh, then an angry voice. "Did you not get the telephone etiquette memo that was sent around?" Scott immediately recognized Secretary Dwayne Moss's voice.

"I believe I did get it and placed it in my very important—"

Ignoring Scott's words, Moss continued, "You answer the phone by department, division, title, and name. So your greeting should be what?"

"I'm sorry, sir. I will read the memo."

"Your greeting should be . . . ," Moss prompted him again.

"Department of Homeland Security, Special Operations Group Bravo, Director Scott Ross," he answered, thinking that by the time he got that out, whatever threat they were being called to stop would have already occurred and now be in the cleanup stages.

"How . . . ," Moss continued to push.

". . . de-do?"

". . . may I help you! How may I help you? Is that really too difficult for you, Ross?"

"It is a little long, sir, but maybe if I write myself a cheat sheet and keep it by the phone, I'll be okay," Scott suggested, knowing that the next phone call he received would be answered with the same one-word greeting he'd always used.

"Listen, Ross, I don't need your sarcasm or your back talk! So knock it off!"

Scott kept silent.

"The reason I'm calling is that I've decided I want daily updates of all your work on this whole EMP thing. Each of your analysts will write up a detailed update of their day's activities, time allocation, and findings. Then you will collect them, summarize them, and have them in my in-box by 8:00 the next morning. Do you understand?"

Scott couldn't believe his ears. "But, sir, do you know how much of my evening that will suck up, let alone the time that will be taken away from the analysts doing what they're supposed to be doing?"

Moss's voice went shrill. "I am the United States secretary of Homeland Security! What the analysts are supposed to be doing is what I say they're supposed to be doing! This is not up for debate! I expect the first set of reports to be in my in-box tomorrow morning! Do I make myself clear?"

"Couldn't I just give you a daily status—"

"Do I make myself clear?"

Scott paused to control his emotions. "Crystal."

"And I know you, Ross. You best not be thinking that this is something that you can just blow off. Don't mess with the bull, young man, or you'll get the horns."

"Yes, sir," Scott said, his demeanor suddenly changing from outrage to barely controlled laughter. *How bizarre, yet how appropriate, that Moss should be quoting threats from Mr. Vernon of* The Breakfast Club. *I should ask him if Barry Manilow knows that he raids his wardrobe.* But instead of digging his hole deeper, Scott asked, "Is that all, sir?"

"That'll be all."

"Okay. Department of Homeland Security, Special Operations Group Bravo, Director Scott Ross . . . out!"

Scott quickly hung up the phone before Moss had a chance to

respond. He jotted himself a note to call Stanley Porter later in the afternoon to prepare him for Moss's inevitable tirade when he discovered that there was no report in his in-box in the morning.

What an idjit! What a maroon, Scott heard Bugs Bunny saying in the back of his mind. Scott knew he was playing with fire when it came to Moss, but he just couldn't help himself. *Stupidity breeds contempt. And this man is most contemptible. I may get bit on this one, but so be it. There's no way that I'm going to pull my gang away from their work just so this buffoon can get a report each morning that he probably won't even read.*

Resolved in his course of action, Scott leaned back in his chair, kicked his sandaled feet up on the desk, and began tossing a pen in the air. *Now for more important things. It looks like it just might be time to consider unleashing "The Acquisition of Riley," phase two.*

CHAPTER THIRTY-FOUR

SUNDAY, AUGUST 23, 2:05 P.M. IRDT
TEHRAN, IRAN

Ayatollah Allameh Beheshti's heels clicked down the hallway until he turned into his carpeted office. His secretary, Bahman Milani, a young man who had been a student of his less than ten years ago, left his own workspace directly across the hall and followed Beheshti. In his hands, he held a silver and glass tea set with the pot freshly filled from a small, antique brass samovar that Beheshti kept in his own office. The samovar used to belong to Beheshti's grandfather, himself a well-known cleric in his hometown of Esfahān. The tea set was a priceless gift from the Grand Ayatollah Ruhollah Khomeini.

When Beheshti was a student at Faziye Seminary in Qom, he had studied Islamic law and philosophy under Khomeini, who seemed to take a special interest in his brilliant young student. Then the shah had banished the spiritual leader from the country.

The day Khomeini left Iran was one of the worst Beheshti could remember. Suddenly he was on his own, his leader, guide, and protector gone. Ultimately, though, his mentor's exile had been one of the best things for young Beheshti.

He was suddenly forced to stand for himself and make his own way in the world rather than just riding the train of Khomeini's robe. Twelve years later, when Beheshti's own political activity got him into trouble with the government, he was able to join the ayatollah in his exile in Najaf, Iraq, as a true, mature man of God.

Those three years in Iraq teaching alongside Khomeini were the best of his life. He was amazed at the great leader's wisdom and awed by his presence. When the shah fled Iran in 1979, Beheshti was on the plane that returned the Grand Ayatollah to his home. He could still close his eyes and visualize watching through his window on the Air France jet as the seventy-seven-year-old leader was aided down the stairs to the ramp. That was the beginning of a new dawn for Iran.

The days of Grand Ayatollah Khomeini as Supreme Leader were a blessing for the country. Radical reforms were made. All the Western-influenced moral pollution was rooted out of society. Once again, the Koran became the basis of the legal and political system. There was little doubt that Allah was smiling upon the great nation and upon its glorious leader.

But now, things had changed. Grand Ayatollah Khomeini was gone and a new Supreme Leader sat in his place. Beheshti held nothing against the new leadership. The very fact that the current Grand Ayatollah had been in power more than twenty years was a testimony to his skills and wisdom. There was no doubt that he had been a strong, competent leader. It was just that anyone short of one of the great prophets would have paled in comparison to Khomeini. And lately it seemed the Grand Ayatollah was making some very wrong decisions, particularly when it came to his choice of president.

The president had been hand-picked by the Supreme Leader, but he was not the man to take the country to the next level of power and influence. He was an obnoxious little man who had let power go to his head—an unthinking zealot with a one-track mind. And when the Supreme Leader had a chance to get rid of him in favor of a man who could bring respect to the leadership of the country, he instead chose to keep the status quo—even being forced to rig the elections to keep the clown in place.

The Supreme Leader lost big in that election. Even though he kept his man in office, he lost some influence among his people, who took to the streets for months afterward to protest his manipulations.

It was almost as if the Grand Ayatollah had known right away that he had made a mistake—the way he didn't allow the president to kiss his hand after the election but only his shoulder. *I think the protests surprised him and shook the usual confidence he had in his decisions. But that is water under the bridge now. What's done is done, and what's rigged is rigged. The election was rigged; the protesters were beaten and shot; the world's outrage was ignored.* And in Beheshti's mind, the Supreme Leader had done that all so that this wonderful country with millennia of history and glory, this bastion of Islamic strength and piety, could be led by a man of half-truths and gimmicks.

This country needs more than gimmicks, Mr. President, Beheshti thought as with a nod he took a freshly filled teacup from Milani, who then left the room. *And it needs more than just a single-issue national policy.*

He sipped the scalding red liquid, feeling the burn wash down his tongue and against his throat, and placed the silver-rimmed glass cup on his desk. He took a handful of *ajeel*—a mixture of dried fruit and nuts—from a dish that Milani somehow always seemed to keep full and began popping it in his mouth as he continued thinking.

The failure by comparison of this Supreme Leader to the first—that was the reason, despite his status as an ayatollah, Beheshti shunned politics and kept off the Islamic courts.

It certainly wasn't theological differences that caused Beheshti to separate from Iran's leadership. Like the president and the Supreme Leader and 90 percent of the population of Iran, he was a Shi'ite Twelver—a follower of Shi'a and a believer in the imminent return of the Twelfth Imam, the Mahdi. Also, like the country's leaders, he believed that it was possible to hasten the Mahdi's return by bringing about worldwide turmoil and mass destruction. Where he parted with them was simply in methodology.

Beheshti looked at his watch and sipped his tea.

It was quite obvious that the president's sole focus was on developing nuclear weapons. And he was willing to risk everything to get them—the stability of his government, Iran's world reputation, the lives of hundreds of thousands, if not millions, of his fellow Persians.

The problem was that his motivations for going nuclear were so obvious. Everyone in the world knew that the first thing he would do with his newly acquired weapons would be to drop one right on Tel Aviv.

If that happened, the mass destruction the president hoped for would certainly take place. Israel, and possibly the United States, would respond with their own nukes, and most of Iran would be laid waste. Was that an acceptable cost in light of the greater goal of the Mahdi's return?

Even if the president somehow managed a nuclear strike on America, the Great Satan would survive, while Iran would be wiped off the map.

This direction was so shortsighted! It would never succeed! There was no way the United States and all its toadies would allow Iran to go nuclear. Either they would strike, or more likely, they would use their angry little dog Israel to do their bidding.

But . . . what if there was a way to take the American military out of the picture, at least for a time? What could be accomplished then?

If that happened, Iran would be able to solicit the help of other Islamic countries who were currently too afraid of the Sleeping Giant to assist them in taking out Israel. Nuclear deals could be made with Russia, who would jump at the chance to retake all their former breakaway republics while maybe even expanding into Poland and farther west.

China, too, would most likely be willing to assist with developing a nuclear arsenal. Without the American deterrent, Taiwan could quickly be reabsorbed back into the mainland as just the first step in Chinese expansion into Southeast Asia.

And even if Russia and China weren't willing to part with their nuclear weapons or secrets, they most certainly could be persuaded to turn a blind eye to Iran's continuing scientific progress.

If America was laid low, by the time she was able to act, Iran would be nuclear, Israel wouldn't exist, and the European and Asian maps would look very different. Then, if the little president or the Supreme Leader wanted to launch their great nuclear holocaust to usher in the new golden age of Islam, they would at least have the weapons to do so. If they continued to pursue their present course, they would end up with no weapons and no End of Days.

But how to accomplish these goals? How could one country bring America to her knees? The answer to those questions was one of Allah's great miracles!

Three years ago, Beheshti had attended a symposium in New York City entitled "The Future of Global Terrorism." He had come, ironically, with the reputation of a voice of Iranian moderation. During one of the sessions, a general from the United States Air Force spoke about electromagnetic pulse bombs and how one large high-altitude nuclear blast could wipe out the nation. American culture was so technologically dependent, it would collapse without power. Even smaller bombs could shut down large metropolitan areas and electrical grids, wreaking havoc on the country financially, industrially, and militarily.

The EMP—this was the answer to Beheshti's prayers, and in the ultimate example of America's stupidity, it came from the mouth of one of their own military men.

A year ago, Beheshti had presented his plan to the Grand Ayatollah, who, because of Beheshti's former association with Khomeini, had granted him an audience. The Supreme Leader had made no comment at that time but said only that he would have a reply to him in a matter of days.

Beheshti was sure it wasn't until after a conference with the president that the Grand Ayatollah issued his reply a few days later. "We have chosen not to sanction or participate in your plan. However, if you decide to proceed on your own, neither will we block your efforts."

Blessings upon you for your help, O Great Leader! It's up to me to raise all the funds myself, make all the arrangements, take all the risks, suffer all the consequences, and let you reap the rewards! Bless you for your cowardice, because now I need not answer to anyone except my God!

That very day Beheshti had started making contacts and raising funds. Someone from Hezbollah, an organization that had taken on the role of terrorist matchmaker for the past few years, got him in contact with North Korea.

Dealing with the DPRK's weak-minded dictator had been a piece of cake. All the Dear Leader could think of was revenge against the United States, never realizing that in the aftermath of the attack North Korea would probably become no more than a Chinese colony. But because of that passion for vengeance, Beheshti was able to negotiate the acquisition of two EMP weapons and the accompanying launching devices for a much better price than he could ever have imagined.

The operational team Beheshti had put together—all brilliant former students of his—took the logistics from there. They monitored the progress and gave him daily updates. And, praise be to Allah, according to the piece of paper that Milani had delivered with the tea, America had not much time left of their fat, comfortable existence before all hell was going to break loose and their lives would be changed forever.

CHAPTER

THIRTY-FIVE

TUESDAY, SEPTEMBER 1, 12:45 P.M. EDT
WASHINGTON, D.C.

Riley tried not to flinch when a hand slipped into the back pocket of his jeans and gave him a little squeeze. He just kept smiling and stepped away as soon as he heard the sound effect of the camera clicking.

"Thanks, Riley," the too-old-to-be-wearing-what-she-was-wearing woman said with a wink, approaching him for one final hug.

"Anytime, and thanks for your support," Riley replied, quickly blocking her way by holding out a signed picture. The photo was of Riley in his Warriors uniform. At the top were the words *Warrior Pride*, and at the bottom was printed, "Thanks for supporting YOUR team!"

Disappointed, the woman took the picture but then began giggling like a little schoolgirl as she retrieved her bebe and Restoration Hardware bags from her friends and walked down the street in the middle of the Georgetown shopping district.

Riley looked over at Skeeter, standing guard a few paces away, and shook his head with a wry smile. He barely had time to be thankful for her departure before a man and his two young boys stepped up. Riley glanced at Christel Barber; the

Warriors' young PR intern was clearly out of her depth with the size of the crowd. He gave her a light shake of his head, reminding her not to send anyone forward until he was ready.

Christel waved apologetically, and Riley smiled back his forgiveness. *Poor girl.*

"Say hi to Riley, guys," the dad said.

"Hi," the boys said shyly. Riley guessed their ages at about four and six.

He squatted to eye level. "How you gentlemen doing?"

"Fine," they both said.

"Those are really nice Warrior jerseys you're wearing. But who's number 50?"

"Wiley Covington," the younger one said as he spun around a couple of times trying to point to the *Covington* on his back.

"Riley Covington? Who's he?"

"He's you! Look," the six-year-old said as he pointed to Riley's jersey.

Riley looked shocked as he spotted the number on his chest. "Well, blow me down! It *is* me!"

The boys giggled. Their dad said, "We couldn't believe it when you were traded to Washington!"

"Yeah, you and me both," Riley said.

"I can imagine. As soon as we heard, we ran out and got the shirts right when they came out. My little one here hasn't taken his off for what seems like weeks."

Looking at the various shades of stain on the yellow and red jersey, Riley had no trouble believing it.

"Well, I sure appreciate having two true-blue fans like you guys," Riley said, putting one hand on each boy's shoulder.

"What's 'too blue'?" the four-year-old asked, looking at his arms.

"I'll tell you later, Joshy," the dad answered. "Mind if we get a picture?"

"Of course," Riley said, turning the two boys toward their dad. "Okay, on three say, 'Go, Warriors!' One, two, three . . ."

The three of them said, "Go, Warriors!" as the dad took the picture.

"Thanks, Riley," the dad said. "Say thanks to Riley, guys."

"Thanks, Riley."

"Keep up the Warrior pride," Riley said as he handed each boy a picture.

Sweat poured down his back as he stood up. *Of all places for Bellefeuille to put me, it has to be outdoors right on the congested Georgetown corner of Wisconsin Avenue and M Street on what feels like the hottest, muggiest day of the year! Well, he said he was going to get his pound of flesh out of me—this pound is coming out in liquid form.*

Each player had a minimum number of public relations events that he had to do each year. Most were obligated for six to ten. Riley's new contract, however, had fifteen mandatory free ones, plus an option for five more paid appearances. A player usually didn't get to choose his events, and today was one of the worst Riley had ever been part of.

Typically, an event might be an appearance at a local school or autographing pictures at a sporting goods store or swinging a hammer at a community revitalization project. Riley was more than happy to do those kinds of appearances.

But today the geniuses at the Warriors' PR mind trust had unleashed something totally new. Each player had been assigned a street corner where he had to stand with his jersey on and hand out autographed pictures to passersby. They were even coached in what they were supposed to say.

"Warrior pride! Thanks for supporting *your* team!" The PR geeks had made it very clear that the word *your* had to be emphasized. This stressed possessive adjective was specially chosen as a means of reminding the fans that the Warriors really were the people's team. *Yeah, if that's true, why do the people have to pay an average of $80 a shot just to see* their *team play?*

All the guys had laughed as they exited the PR meeting. Riley would have been surprised if today the words *your team* had crossed the lips of any player other than the most desperate of rookies.

Looking at the crowd around him, Riley knew it was going to be a long afternoon. He groaned inwardly. The schedule of football player by day and CTD ops training guy by night was catching up to him. He didn't feel that he was doing either job as well as he could. Stupid things like this afternoon only added to his exhaustion.

Somehow, even as he watched, the crowd seemed to multiply. Skeeter had protested at the outdoor setting. "Too uncontrollable," he had said. "Too many X factors." Now, as Riley watched him scanning the surroundings, he could tell that his friend was extremely agitated.

Riley nodded to Christel. She, in turn, nodded to a teenage boy and his girlfriend, who both seemed very excited to meet the team's newest superstar. *All in all, other than botoxed shopaholics with wandering hands, I guess things could be worse. Just grin and bear it—it'll be over soon enough.*

"What's up," he said to the young couple.

Suddenly a man wearing a black fabric mask burst through the crowd just to Riley's left. He rushed Riley, carrying something shiny in his right hand.

"Allahu alayla!" he cried out, then punched Riley hard two times in the side. The blows knocked the breath out of Riley, and he dropped to his knees. In his peripheral vision, he watched as his attacker ran down Wisconsin Avenue and disappeared behind the bank Riley had been standing in front of.

What just happened? Riley thought as he gasped for breath. He grabbed his side where the man had hit him, felt a strange sensation, and pulled his hand back. It was completely red. Screams erupted around him as the shock began wearing off the crowd.

Skeeter arrived just as people started rushing to Riley's aid. He pushed Riley all the way to the ground and stood over of him. With his HK45 out, he looked like he was just dying to shoot somebody.

"Everybody back! Now!"

Two burly men stood their ground.

"Who are you?" one of them demanded.

"None of your business! Just back off!"

"We're not moving until you show us some ID!"

"All the ID you need is sitting in my hand," Skeeter said, waving his .45. "Now back off and do something useful like calling 911!"

The two men finally backed up a couple of steps; one took his cell phone out.

All the while, Riley watched, unable to say anything. Finally, he started getting his breath back.

"Pach, you hurt?" Skeet asked, not looking at him.

"I must be, man. I'm bleeding like a dog!" Riley said through gasps. Pain shot through his ribs.

"Hang in, buddy!"

All around, people were slowly pushing forward, and Skeeter had to keep threatening with his gun.

A security guard came running out of the bank with his gun drawn and trained on Skeeter. "Drop the weapon," he yelled.

"Yeah, drop it, or I swear I'll put a hole smack-dab in the middle of your head," another gun-wielding man said as he stepped out from the crowd.

"Lower *your* weapons," Skeeter yelled back. "I'm a federal agent assigned to protect this man!"

"Show me your ID," the security guard commanded.

"I've already been through this! I ain't showing you jack until the cops come! Now lower your weapons and call 911!"

"He's with me," Riley managed to croak out, his mind running through what had just happened. Hearing his words, the two men reluctantly holstered their guns and moved toward Riley.

"Stay back," Skeeter, who had not holstered his gun, demanded. The men stopped in their tracks. "Go back and control the crowd before they start pressing in!"

The two men complied and started pushing the mass of people back. Riley heard concerned fans calling out his name as well as more than a few hysterical screams.

So this is what it feels like to be stabbed, Riley thought. *I've been shot, blown up, beaten, and cut but never stabbed. All in all, I've felt worse. . . . Either that, or what I'm feeling is just shock setting in. Wow, I never noticed the beautiful golden cupola on top of the bank building. Here I was standing right next to it, and I never even saw it.*

"Excuse me! Move aside; I'm a doctor!"

Riley turned to see a woman push her way through the crowd and approach him.

"Stay where you are," Skeeter yelled, aiming the gun right between the lady's eyes.

"I'm a doctor, and this man's hurt! Now either shoot me or move out of the way, because I'm not stopping!"

Skeeter hesitated, then stepped aside.

"Got a knife?" the doc asked.

"Yeah," Skeeter replied.

"Well, since you probably won't hand it to me, I want you to cut his shirt top to bottom. And be careful; he doesn't need you slicing him up too."

Riley couldn't take his eyes off the doctor. She met his eyes for a moment, then turned back to watch Skeeter.

When Skeeter was done, the woman carefully lifted the left side of Riley's shirt and examined the damaged area.

"How are you feeling, Mr. Covington?" she asked.

"Been better."

"Well, you've been better because right now you have two deep puncture wounds. You know, from what I read, you seem to have a hard time making friends wherever you go." Then, turning to Skeeter, she said, "Hey, Andre the Giant, give me your shirt!"

Skeeter whipped off his shirt, revealing a very well-sculpted, thoroughly scarred torso.

"Wow," the doctor said as Skeeter handed her his shirt. "It's guys like you who keep docs like me in business." She folded up Skeeter's shirt and pressed it against Riley's side. Riley winced in pain. "Easy, tough guy, help should be here any moment."

Even as she said that, the sound of sirens cut through the air. While the security guard and the other guy formed a path in the crowd, three sets of tires could be heard screeching to a stop. A moment later, the cops ran through the gap. The security guard met them and explained the situation and who Skeeter was. Two of the cops ran off in a vain pursuit of the perpetrator, and the other two helped with the ever-increasing mass of people.

Fifteen seconds later, two white-shirted paramedics ran in, wheeling a gurney between them.

"What's up?" asked one of them with tattoos covering his arms and creeping up his neck.

"Two stab wounds, unknown depth of penetration or organ damage," the doctor answered. "He's also bleeding like a sieve. We've got to transport him fast."

"We drive to keep them alive," tattoo guy said as he hit the one-hand release, dropping the gurney to ground level.

As Riley was lifted on, he looked at the people who were watching the action. Some looked genuinely concerned; a few were even crying. But a vast majority were on their cell phones narrating the events to their spouse or buddy or kid.

Why do people like to see trouble? Is it the blood? Is it the gore?

Well, whatever it is, consider this just another part of the big freak show, folks. You all were the lucky ones; you'll have a story to tell your kids and grandkids. "I was there when Riley Covington got stabbed right on the street corner by some lunatic." Glad I could make your day like this.

Now, do I give them the coup de grâce? the icing on the cake? Sure, why not?

The onlookers, who had begun applauding as he was wheeled away, erupted into frenzied cheers as Riley's thumb slowly rose up from his fist.

CHAPTER THIRTY-SIX

TUESDAY, SEPTEMBER 1, 1:10 P.M. EDT
WASHINGTON, D.C.

Skeeter and the doctor followed the gurney into the ambulance. The rear doors slammed, the siren began crying out, and the ambulance began its journey.

As soon as they rounded the first corner, Riley looked up at the woman who had been trying so hard to stem the flow of his blood and said, "Dr. Faroughi, I presume?"

Immediately, everyone in the ambulance burst out laughing.

"Oh, Riley, you should have seen your face when I came walking out of the crowd," Khadi finally managed to say.

"My face? What about Skeeter's?" Riley said. "I honestly thought he was going to shoot you."

"Nah, I knew she was there the whole time," Skeeter said.

Riley whipped his head around to face his most loyal and trusted friend. "What? You knew about this? Why didn't you tell me?"

Skeeter just smiled his answer.

"Come on, Pach. You're the worst actor in the world. If we had told you ahead of time, you would have been all tense, looking around, waiting for it to happen," paramedic Scott Ross said, mimicking Riley with jerky movements reminiscent of a squirrel surrounded by a pack of angry schnauzers.

"No, I . . . well, actually yeah, I probably would have," Riley laughed. "So who clobbered me?"

"That was Ted Hummel. He hit you with one of those retractable-blade stunt knives that you can load up with fake blood," answered Kim Li, the tattooed driver of the ambulance. Li and Hummel were both part of Scott's ops team, along with Gilly Posada, Matt Logan, Carlos Guitiérrez, and Steve Kasay. "Gilly picked him up a couple of blocks down. I got him on the line right now, and he says to tell you he's sorry, but he had to make sure you were stunned enough to not mess things up until you could figure out what was really going on."

"Yeah, well tell him I owe him one—actually, two. Oh, and ask him what 'Allahu alayla' means."

"He says he was so nervous he was going to screw things up that he forgot what he was supposed to say, so he just winged it."

Scott, ever the linguist, said, "Tell him that he attacked Riley with a blended Arabic/Turkish battle cry of 'God is sardonic!' Words sure to strike fear in the hearts of all who hear."

As Riley laughed, he looked down to where Khadi's hands were still pressing against his side. Watching his eyes, Khadi's face colored, and she pulled her hands away, disappointing Riley immensely.

"I'm assuming this is your way of taking me out of football," he said to Scott.

"Yeppers. A wound this severe will put you out for weeks, if not months."

Scott's words were bittersweet to Riley. As much as he loved the idea of not playing for the Warriors anymore, he was still going to miss the game itself. But before he dealt with those emotions, there was something else he had to clear up.

"I knew you weren't telling me everything, Scott," Riley said, his attitude suddenly serious. "We've always been honest in our friendship, even going back to Afghanistan. If you want me to work with you, I need to know I can completely trust everything you're telling me. I don't want to be wondering whether or not you're keeping something back from me. So, is this all, or are you still holding out on me?"

"This is it. I swear it. I'm sorry for the deception. There's no more."

Riley nodded his belief in Scott's words, then asked, "Can I ask you something, O great puppetmaster? Why'd you have to make it so dramatic? Why not just let me slip in my shower?"

Scott smiled a smug little smile—the one he used when he felt he had all the answers figured out, the one that drove Riley absolutely crazy. "It's simple. If you had just slipped in the shower, the team would have wanted you to be checked by their doctors and in for physical therapy practically 24-7. We would have had you less than we have you now.

"Something this major, though, you'd not only be in the hospital while recovering but also under double-secret government protective custody. 'Where'd Riley go?' 'Don't know; he's in double-secret government protective custody.'"

Even Riley had to admit that was pretty good thinking. Although there was one wild card that Scott hadn't factored in—Rick Bellefeuille. *We'll just see how this plays itself out.*

"So what now?" Riley asked Mr. Smug.

"First, we get Atlas there a shirt," Scott answered, nodding toward Skeeter. "Next we get you down to the RoU to get caught up on what's going on. Then we get you rested and healed from Ted's little love tap. Finally, at 0600 Thursday—and I hope you brought your swim trunks along for this part of our vacation itinerary—we hop a ship and head out to sea."

Sea? Why? For what? Riley was about to barrage Scott with a bunch of questions when he suddenly realized that the gurney he was on was really quite comfortable, the ambulance was well air-conditioned, and Khadi's hand had managed to find its way back onto his arm. *The time for getting answers to your questions comes later. Now's the time to just kick back, close your eyes, and enjoy the ride.*

CHAPTER THIRTY-SEVEN

TUESDAY, SEPTEMBER 1, 12:15 P.M. MDT
INVERNESS TRAINING CENTER, CENTENNIAL, COLORADO

"Listen, Ziafat, I've had just about enough of you missing this coverage! How many times has it been now—ten, fifteen, twenty? This organization isn't dishing out two and a half mil a year for some rookie who can't figure out how to adjust to a freakin' Tre package!"

The three-tight-end offensive setup that the Mustangs were running had given Afshin fits for the last two weeks, and right now, linebackers coach Rex Texeira was letting him know that it had been noticed.

"This is PFL football 101—no, I take that back; this is *high school* football 101! What's Coach supposed to do? Every time he sees the other team lining up in a Tre, should he quickly call a time-out so he can put in someone who knows how to cover what to you obviously must seem to be the brilliant grand-master wizard formation of all time?"

Keith Simmons looked at Afshin and could see the kid was struggling to keep his composure. Every player had received reamings like this before, and it was always telling to see how guys would react. Some would just take it, some would yell back, and Keith had even seen some break down in tears of frustration. Right now, it looked like Afshin was teetering between options two and three.

This verbal assault was taking place in the linebackers' meeting room. The entire linebacker corps had been watching film of the morning's practice. However, for the last five minutes, the screen had been filled with the Afshin Ziafat Tre package blooper reel—all Afshin, all the time. The first time through the video loop, Coach Texeira had simply narrated the plays and the ensuing mistakes. However, for the last two loops it had been "tear Afshin to shreds" time in the old meeting room.

"You know every game's the real thing here in the PFL! There ain't no minor leagues! We can't send you down to some double-A Pueblo Ponies until you can figure out how to play this sport! Every mistake you make can cost us points! Every time you choke, it can cost us games!"

"Hey, Tex-Rex, you've made your point," Keith finally said. Texeira whirled on Keith, but before he could blast him, Keith continued, "I'll work with the kid. Don't worry, Coach; I'll get him ready."

Texeira glared at Keith, apparently weighing whether backing down was worth Keith's offer to be a scapegoat. "Okay, the kid's yours. But if he blows it this Saturday, both of you are going to answer to Burton."

As Texeira moved on to Garrett Widnall, a second-year man who was barely hanging on with the team, Afshin leaned over to Keith. "Thanks, man."

"He made his point five minutes ago. After that he was just being an idiot," Keith whispered back.

The two half listened to the coach for another minute until Afshin again leaned toward Keith. "Listen, I know I blew it sometimes on the Tre, but was I really that bad?"

"The eye in the sky don't lie," Keith answered, nodding toward the screen. The "eye in the sky" was what the players called the video camera mounted high on a portable lift over the practice field. The eye caught every move—and every mistake—of every practice.

Afshin straightened, obviously not having heard the response he was hoping for.

Better toughen up, kid. The PFL is the real thing. This is The Show. It ain't your backyard, it ain't high school, and it ain't college ball. "What have you done for me lately?" applies even to rookie first-round draft picks with multimillion-dollar contracts. You better fix what's broke, or you're going to discover just what that nonguaranteed contract'll get you out in the real world, where people don't care how much you press or how fast you run the 40.

Almost as if he heard Keith's thoughts, Afshin leaned over one more time. "Keith, thanks for working with me. I know if anyone can drill that coverage into my thick skull, it's you."

"Don't sweat it, Z. It's my pleasure."

"Hey, if you girls are through having your little tea party, maybe you can join the rest of us," Texeira called to the two.

Before Keith answered, he took a glance at the fines list that was written on one of the whiteboards—more precisely, at the Banned Words & Phrases section that had been created to "promote civility between players and between players and coaches." *Yeah, there's a good one, and it'll only cost me two bills.*

But just as Keith started to spend his money, one of the assistant trainers opened the door and said, "Sorry to interrupt, but Coach wants everyone in the main room immediately."

In all Keith's years playing football for the Mustangs, never had Coach Burton called a team meeting in the middle of position time. Surprised and confused, the linebackers all got up and filed down the hall to the team meeting room. The offensive players were already sitting in the front four rows. The rest of the defense followed Keith's squad in.

Coach Burton was waiting up front, and as soon as the last guy sat down, he said, "You guys need to know that Riley Covington was attacked today on a street corner in Washington. He was stabbed twice in the side. They don't know who did it."

A surprised and angry murmur rose from the players. Keith spotted Chris Gorkowski looking back at him. He nodded to him, and Chris turned around.

"As of right now, we don't know his condition because apparently he's under protective custody, and nobody seems to know where. We've been promised word of his condition within the hour, and I'll be sure to let you all know as soon as I hear anything."

Burton paused and took a deep breath. Keith was surprised to see that Coach actually seemed to be getting emotional as he spoke. "You guys know how we all feel about Riley. Even though he's with another team right now, he will always be part of our family. Now, I've asked Walter to say a prayer for Riley. Walt?"

Walter Washburne, the team's chaplain, stepped forward. "Thanks, Coach. Let's pray.

"Lord, we pray for Riley right now. We ask for Your hand of healing upon his body. We pray for wisdom for the doctors who are working on him; guide their hands. We pray for diligence for those who are protecting him; sharpen their sight. We pray for those who are caring for him; fill their hearts. We also pray for Riley's mom. She's been through so much this year with the loss of her husband. Give her peace as she trusts You with her son.

"Lord, You have promised us in Your Word that in all things You'll work for the good of those who love You. None of us in this room have any doubt of Riley's love for You, so we trust that You will keep Your promise and make something good come out of this. Thank You for what You're going to do. Amen."

Muted amens could be heard throughout the room. Quite a number of the players were clearing their throats and wiping their eyes.

"Thanks, Walt," Coach Burton said. "That was nice. Listen, gang, I'm giving you all the rest of the day off. I've asked Walter to stick around if any of you want to talk. You're dismissed."

Keith and Afshin sat stunned. Soon they heard cursing and jostling and saw Gorkowski come bounding through the lines of guys filing down the rows. Right behind him was Travis Marshall, traveling in his wake.

"Keith, what do we do?" Gorkowski asked in a near panic.

"Dude, there's nothing we can do except pray," Keith answered.

"Come on, man, you know that's not what I'm about! We gotta do something—help Riley out somehow!"

"Believe it or not, Snap," Keith said, "there's nothing better we can do for him right now."

Frustrated, Gorkowski started making his way through the door. "Well, I'll leave you guys to your little prayer meeting while I figure out something that'll really help!"

"If you think of anything, let me know," Keith said, too softly for Gorkowski to hear. *Man, it's tough being your friend, Pach. If you ain't off getting shot, you're getting kidnapped by terrorists. If you're not getting kidnapped by terrorists, you're getting stabbed by unknown assailants. I remember when my friends in the PFL got injuries like pulled muscles and torn ligaments.*

"Hey, Simms," Marshall said, "I was thinking we should get together tonight and spend some time praying for Pach."

"Good call," Keith agreed. "I'll snag us some Chili's To Go, and we can meet at my place around seven. Sound good, Z?"

Afshin was picking absently at his armrest and didn't respond.

"Hey, Z, did you hear me? Dinner and prayer at seven?"

"What? Yeah. That'd be great. Mind if I ask Garrett to come along?"

"Definitely; the more the merrier," Keith answered, thinking just how inappropriate that phrase was for the circumstances.

The three men filed out of the meeting room, giving a final wave to Chaplain Washburne, who was standing up front by himself. After walking down the hall, they passed through a pair of frosted-glass doors displaying the Mustangs logo and into the locker room.

Inside, the typically raucous room was silent. Some guys were stripping out of their practice clothes and heading into the showers. Others were quietly going to the training tables to get worked on.

Keith and Afshin went to their lockers, and Keith, out of habit, grabbed his phone to check for messages. *One text message,* it read. Pressing the envelope icon, Keith immediately saw the name of the sender—Riley Covington. Keith's heart began to beat faster, then increased even more when he saw the time it was sent—thirty minutes ago.

Taking a deep breath, Keith finally allowed his eyes to move down to the body of the message. He read: *4 u 2 only. Im fine. Cant say more.*

No way! I mean, thank You, Lord, and all, but no stinkin' way! Keith didn't know what to do. He was elated yet furious. He wished Riley were here so that he could give him a huge hug, then pummel him into the ground.

Wait . . . "4 u 2 only"?

Doing everything he could to keep a somber face, he glanced two lockers down. Afshin was looking at him with the same expression, but there was a sparkle in his eye that made it perfectly clear to Keith that he had found the other member of the *2*.

CHAPTER THIRTY-EIGHT

TUESDAY, SEPTEMBER 1, 4:15 P.M. EDT
WASHINGTON, D.C.

Scott picked up the phone, then put it back down. *Come on, don't be a wuss! What would Jim Hicks do?* He picked up the phone . . . then put it back down.

Scott had received an urgent message from Rick Bellefeuille. *Of all people to deal with today, why him?* Back when Jim Hicks was in charge, Scott would have handed the message off to him, and Jim would have been glad to have a little confab with the Warriors owner. But now Scott was the big kahuna, and there was no one else he could drop it on.

What would Ozzy have done? he thought as his fingers scratched at the rectangular artwork on the front of the Black Sabbath 1978 World Tour T-shirt he was wearing. *I mean the old Ozzy, not the embarrassingly burned-out, caricature-of-himself TV Ozzy. Actually, come to think of it, the old Ozzy would probably have dropped another tab of acid, then called his manager to take care of the problem.*

Oh, just make the call! How bad could it be? Resolved, Scott picked up the phone and dialed. He had a brief moment of regret after touching the last number, but the first ring sealed the deal—he was in the whole way.

A pleasant-voiced woman named Madeline told him that Mr. Bellefeuille was expecting his call and asked him very kindly if he would please hold. *See, it's already better than—*

"Ross, you overinflated rent-a-cop, what have you done with my player?"

"Uh . . . good afternoon, Mr.—"

"You can stuff your good-afternoon! What have you done with Riley Covington, you second-rate G-man wannabe?"

"What do you mean? Haven't you listened to the news?"

"What do you mean, what do I mean? You and I both know that the news stories are a load of crap! You know, I'd been wondering what your endgame was in this whole trade thing you forced on me. Now I know! Well, let me inform you of something, Mr. Ross: I'm not playing your game! You can take your little agenda, roll it up, and sit and spin, because I've got an agenda of my own!"

Scott could feel his face starting to burn, and sweat had begun trickling down his neck. "Mr. Bellefeuille, I don't think you understand—"

"Oh, believe me, I understand! I understand more than you think! So here's how it's going to be. You can have Riley during the week to do whatever it is you want to do with him. But starting the first regular season game, I better see Covington on the Warriors' sideline—and the more bandages and casts on him the better! And after the game, he's going to give the interviews that I choose for him to give. You following me?"

"But, sir, that's just not possible!"

"Oh, it's possible, all right! In fact, it's going to happen. And you know why? Because if he's not on that sideline, I'm blowing the lid off this whole thing. How do you think that'll play? The government's already taking over health insurance and the banks and the carmakers—now they're stepping into the business of professional sports. How do you think that'll help the president's reelection bid?"

"But, Mr. Bellefeuille, you forget about—"

"I forget about what—my son? To tell you the truth, some time in the slammer'd probably be the best thing for the kid. He could use a wake-up call to the real world with the way his mother spoiled him."

"But, sir, if it wasn't for your son, why—"

"Why'd I do it? Are you really that stupid? Riley Covington is the biggest PR commodity this country has seen since space flight. He's going to make this team millions—tens of millions. So what's it going to be, Ross? Yes or no? Am I going to see Covington at the season opener?"

"But, Mr. Bellefeuille, it's not that easy—"

"Sure it's that easy. You either say yes, and you can carry on your little shoot-'em-up games Monday through Saturday, or you say no, and I make a call to my buddy at the *New York Times*. So which is it? Yes or no?"

Trapped, Scott had no choice but to quietly say, "Yes."

"Good," Bellefeuille said, then hung up.

Scott sat there in a daze, clenching the phone. *What just happened? Did I really just agree to have Riley attend all the Warriors' games? Am I really that much of a—*

Stop! Whatever you were going to say, the answer is yes. In fact, whatever it was, you're probably the telethon poster boy for said quality, you idiot!

As he slowly returned the phone to his desk, a worse thought came to him. *Who's going to tell Riley? Aw, man, where is Jim when you need him?*

After taking a deep breath, Scott willed himself to stand. With one more curse at Jim Hicks for dying on him, he headed out to find Riley, fully prepared for an already-terrible day to get a whole lot worse.

CHAPTER THIRTY-NINE

TUESDAY, SEPTEMBER 8, 2:15 A.M. GMT-1
EASTERN ATLANTIC OCEAN

The SH-60 Seahawk cruised low over the choppy seas. Forty minutes ago it had begun its hundred-mile journey from the deck of the Oliver Hazard Perry–class frigate *Kauffman*. Now, five miles ahead, the lights of a freighter grew bigger and brighter in the moonless night.

"Three minutes," Riley heard in his headphones. He reached to his left, slapped Skeeter in the chest, and held up three fingers. Because there were more passengers than headphones, hand signals were the order of the day. Skeeter passed the message to the next person, and the message sped through the helicopter's crowded cargo hold.

Along with Riley's ten-person team, the Navy had insisted on sending two of their SEALs on the mission. The CTD team could hardly say no, since they were making use of a Navy ship and a Navy helicopter. Besides, the addition of two highly trained, highly lethal SEALs could only help the mission. Still, in order to fit twelve troops into a space designed to only hold eleven, the crew had been forced to leave their sonar operator behind so that one of the SEALs could take his seat.

Riley watched as the three-minute message circled around to Khadi, who was sitting across from him. A black fabric mask covered all but her eyes, but those eyes looked hardened and ready to go.

He had wrestled with having her along. She had an extremely strong ops history and was the best sniper on the team. But despite that solid résumé, Riley was hesitant to allow her to come. It wasn't until Scott and Skeeter had both teamed up on him and told him he was letting his heart get in the way of his head that he had given in.

Khadi looked up and saw him staring at her. She met his eyes for a moment and then looked down. Riley knew she was still a little angry with him. *She'll get over it. Her hurt feelings are the last thing I need to worry about right now.*

"One minute! Harness up," came the voice of the tactical operator, a young Navy man named Frank Wilson.

Riley, Khadi, Skeeter, and Scott all latched themselves to zip lines. Riley and Skeeter were designated Botox 1, while Scott and Khadi were Botox 2. The Botox moniker had been suggested by Scott after Riley had told them the story of the lady with the wandering hands.

The plan called for Botox 1 and 2 to drop to a wing that jutted out from the starboard side of the freighter's bridge. The rest of the teams would then be lowered down to the deck, taking care to avoid the ship's two massive cranes.

Tonight's operation was the culmination of a difficult and at times exhausting process. Once Evie had confirmed that the container from North Korea was aboard the MSC *Shirley*, a Panamanian-registered cargo ship, the next ten days had been a pure logistical nightmare. Scott had asked CTD head Stanley Porter to push everything through with the Navy and Secretary Weasel of Homeland Security. Meanwhile, Riley and the rest of the ops team had developed a mission plan, then drilled and redrilled.

The reason for the sneak attack had nothing to do with any fear of the captain or crew, although one could never fully anticipate the reaction of a seaman when his ship is being taken over. International law allowed weapons on container ships, but when these boats pulled into port, they had to follow the laws of that particular country—many of which didn't allow weapons of any kind. So even if the captain tonight was thoroughly hacked off, there probably wasn't much he could do about it.

Instead, the justification for stealth was the real possibility that the container in question could be rigged to blow if anyone got too close. The doors could be wired, or someone on board could have a detonation device. If it did blow, the worst-case scenario was that everyone could be killed immediately or end up receiving a fatal dose of radiation. Best case, they would lose evidence critical to tracking down the other containers.

That was why the frigate kept its distance, and that was why the chopper was flying low and dropping in hot.

"Thirty seconds," Wilson said.

Riley put his fist up, and the four stood by the doors. Adrenaline surged through his body as he prayed silently for the safety of his team. He gave one last nod to Khadi on his right, then Skeeter on his left, and looked around to Scott, who gave a thumbs-up.

Nothing like jumping out of a perfectly good helicopter! I hope they remember to keep us clear of the communications equipment on the roof of the bridge! . . . Come on, this is the longest thirty seconds—

Behind him, Wilson threw the door open. Gilly Posada whirled his hand above his head, signaling them to jump. Without thinking, Riley launched himself away from the helicopter and immediately started falling. No matter how many times he'd done this, he always found his stomach in his throat.

He looked down to see the rapidly approaching bridge. *Looks like the pilot's got us right on target!* He landed hard at the end of his zip line and dropped to a squat, letting his knees absorb most of the jolt. He'd learned that lesson the hard way on a painful landing back at the Air Force Academy. Quickly he unlatched himself and saw that the others had done the same. He circled his hand toward Wilson, and the lines began the rapid ascent back into the helicopter.

A door to the left opened, and a surprised face stared out. Riley let his Magpul Masada assault rifle drop against his chest and lunged toward the door, arriving just as it was closing. He grabbed the wet metal handle and slowed the door just enough for Scott to get his boot into the opening.

"Auugghh!" Scott cried out as the heavy metal door slammed against his foot.

Skeeter got his fingers into the opening and pulled, and both the door and Riley flew backward. When Riley caught his step, he saw Scott and Khadi going through the opening with Skeeter following behind. By the time he got himself inside, four crewmen were standing with their hands up. One man was down on his knees, holding his hands over his bloody face.

Scott remained by the door they had just entered, while Skeeter headed to the opposite side of the bridge to cover that entrance. Khadi stood ten feet inside the doorway with her weapon pointed at the crew.

"Who's in charge here?" Riley yelled.

"I am First Officer Marvin Jiménez," one man said, stepping forward, "second-in-command of the MSC *Shirley*, a lawfully registered container vessel flying the Panamanian flag! What is the meaning of this invasion of my ship and assault upon my crew?"

"Where's your captain?" Riley demanded. Out of his peripheral vision, he could see through the windows of the bridge eight black shapes gliding through the air to the deck below.

"I refuse to answer any of your questions until you tell me—"

Immediately Riley was on the man. He took hold of him by the front of the shirt, causing the stench of the man's sweat-stained uniform to launch into the air.

Leaning forward until they were almost nose to nose, Riley again demanded, "Your captain—where is he?"

Suddenly the door nearest Skeeter flew open, and a man wearing shorts and a T-shirt came running in. Skeeter's hand flew out and caught the man by the neck, stopping him in his tracks.

"Captain," Jiménez called out, trying to break free of Riley's grasp.

Riley recognized Captain Tony Blanco from his mission file. He pushed the ship's second-in-command backward so that he fell in a chair in front of the control board.

Walking across the rough metal floor, Riley said, "Skeeter, let him go!"

Skeeter removed his hand, and the captain doubled over, coughing.

Riley took Blanco by his thick salt-and-pepper hair and lifted him straight. Pushing the barrel of his rifle against the underside of the captain's chin, he commanded, "Tell me where the container is!"

"What container? This ship is full of containers," the captain pleaded.

"Don't feed me that! You know what I'm talking about! Where is the container you picked up in Bushehr with the special instructions?"

"Please, sir! I don't know what you're talking about! We picked up many containers! There was nothing out of the ordinary! Please!"

Riley saw the terror in the man's eyes and knew he was telling the truth. *This just made our mission way harder! Don't let up on the pressure, though. Right now, he's ready to do whatever he can to keep himself alive.*

"Did you pick up any new crew in Bushehr?"

"Three . . . no, four," Captain Blanco said. Looking down at Riley's assault rifle, he pleaded, "Please, put the gun down so that we can talk like civilized men."

"Trust me, you haven't seen uncivilized yet," Riley said, pushing the barrel harder into the man's flesh. "Give me their names."

"Omidi, Zamaani . . . Marvin, help me!"

"Hemmati and Seddigh," the second-in-command called out angrily.

Riley toggled his comm. "Botox team, look for crewmen Omidi, Zamaani, Hemmati, and . . ."

"Seddigh," Blanco said.

"And Seddigh. When you find them, cuff them immediately and isolate them."

Riley pulled a piece of paper out of a pocket in his vest and held it in front of Blanco's face. "I need to know where this container is! You do this, and no one will get hurt! Do you understand?"

Each container had a number, and Riley knew that somewhere

on the bridge was a manifest that would tell them exactly where their prize sat.

"Yes, sir," the frightened man said, rapidly shaking his head as he examined the number on the paper.

"Good. Now I'm going to let you go, Tony," Riley said, purposely not using the man's title. "If you give me any trouble, I will kill you and your whole crew. Do you understand?"

"Yes, sir," Blanco replied. Then, turning to one of his men, who had stood immobile under Khadi's watch through the whole exchange, he held out the piece of paper. "Agüero, find this."

Agüero looked at Khadi, who motioned with her gun for him to take the piece of paper. He hurried over, retrieved the number, and slipped behind a computer.

Now that the situation on the bridge was under control, Riley turned to look out the bay of windows. Down below he could see two shadows moving toward the front of the ship. That would be the SEALs. *Hopefully the rest of the guys have the engine room and the remainder of the tower under control.*

Although there were only twenty crewmen on board, it was difficult to know exactly where everyone was on the massive ship. At this hour, the majority of the men should be in the sleeping quarters, but there still would be a skeleton detail spread throughout the freighter. The job of the rest of Botox team was to round up all twenty as quickly as possible.

The sound of automatic weapons fire echoed from below. Riley looked down, trying to see through the darkness.

"This is Botox 1; what's happening?"

"We got a runner!" Riley recognized Hummel's voice.

Turning around, he said, "Captain Blanco, hurry your man up, and get me that information!"

"Yes, sir. Agüero, what is taking you so long?" the captain said as he leaned over his crewman's shoulder.

Riley looked back outside in time to see a man running toward the side of the ship. He had a thick black brick up to the side of his head. *A satellite phone!*

"Botox 4, there's a guy on deck with a sat phone," Riley called into his comm system.

"We're on him," Hummel and Logan replied in unison.

Sure enough, two men came sprinting out onto the deck but were immediately spotted by the runner.

"No," Riley yelled as the man threw the phone overboard.

The bad guy dropped to the ground just as Logan and Hummel began firing. Riley watched as he scrambled between the forty-foot containers just below the bridge.

"He's heading toward port, down the first row of containers," Riley said into his comm. "Now he's turned forward!"

Riley watched helplessly as his team members gained on the runner, only to see the man pull a small box out of his pocket, turn a key, and rising up to his full height with his arms outstretched, push a button.

CHAPTER FORTY

TUESDAY, SEPTEMBER 8, 2:23 A.M. GMT-1
EASTERN ATLANTIC OCEAN

"Drop!" Riley yelled just as the windows blew in. Glass showered down, and Riley heard one of the crewmen cry out in pain. A fraction of a second later, a deafening sound blasted through the room.

"Khadi," Riley called out.

Frantically, his eyes searched the room until he saw her getting to her knees. Riley was about to run over to her when a weight flattened him back down to the floor. Hands reached around him, grasping for his Magpul.

I don't have time for this!

Riley managed to push himself to his knees. A fist rained down punches on the side of his head. With one hand Riley was holding his weapon, and with the other he reached around toward his assailant's head. He twisted his head to protect it from another blow and saw a crewman on his knees in front of Khadi, holding his midsection. Two others stood a few feet back from Skeeter, and one of them held a knife. Scott had the last crewman's head under his arm and was landing blow after blow on his face. The one person he didn't see was the captain, so he figured that's who was riding his back.

Riley finally managed to wrap his fingers around the captain's neck. He clamped down, then pulled as hard as he could, all the while rolling his body forward. The captain flipped over Riley's right shoulder, and Riley let the man's weight flip him over also. He landed hard with his shoulders on the captain's head. After a quick roll, Riley pressed his forearm onto the captain's throat. The man grasped at Riley's arm, desperately trying to get air into his windpipe. Within seconds, the captain's movements began to slow until he passed out.

Riley leaped up to run to Khadi's aid but instead saw her already standing, a motionless crew member at her feet with blood on his face. As Riley looked around, he saw Scott driving his gun butt into his adversary's stomach. Skeeter was already moving out the door he had been guarding, leaving two more unconscious men in his wake, the knife kicked to the side.

Turning around, Riley looked out the now-glassless windows. Fire raged at the front of the boat. A huge chunk of the starboard bow of the ship had been ripped out, and the hole extended below the waterline. Riley didn't know a lot about ships, particularly cargo vessels, but he knew that didn't look good.

"Report in," Riley said to his team.

"Botox 3, clear."

"Botox 4, down but clear."

"Botox 5, clear."

They all waited for the sixth team—the SEAL team—to respond.

"Botox 6, report in," Riley said. "Botox 6!"

Finally, a weak voice said, "Six down. Can't . . ."

Riley grimaced; Botox 6 had been assigned to lock up the front of the vessel, right where the blast went off. "Five, get up there and find those guys."

"Roger," Kasay said.

"Three, get as close to the fire as you can and check levels," Riley commanded Li and Posada, who were carrying one of the team's two Geiger counters.

"On it," Li said.

"The rest of you, get the crew moving! We're going to have to abandon this ship, and I don't want us anywhere near it when it goes under. Send some of them up here, enough to get the captain and four others. Then follow their lead. They'll know how to get us off this thing better than we do."

Then, remembering Logan's report, he asked, "Four, what's your status? How bad are you hit?"

Riley was relieved to hear Logan say, "Hummel's taken a good wallop, but he'll be fine. What doesn't kill him only makes him more obnoxious."

"Get him back to the aft lifeboats; then see what you can do to keep the herd moving."

"You got it!"

Riley turned around to see only Scott standing behind him.

"Where's Khadi?"

"She followed Skeet down to see if she could help any of the wounded."

What's that crazy woman trying to prove? I knew I shouldn't have brought her along!

Then he mentally slapped himself upside the head. *She's only doing what she's supposed to be doing. You didn't mind Skeeter running off, did you? Get with the program!*

"Scott, get the *Kauffman* on the horn and let them know our situation."

"Already done. They're steaming our way; ETA is about two and a half hours. In the meantime, they're turning the Seahawk around to pick up any wounded."

"Good work, Scott," Riley said. "Let's get ourselves downstairs and see what we can do."

As Riley took the last of the five flights of steps, he found himself off-balance and fell hard against the side of the tower. After steadying himself against the railing, he looked out toward the black water and could see that the boat had already begun listing heavily starboard.

The deck was a flurry of activity as several crewmen hustled to make sure everyone was accounted for, while others readied the lifeboats. Riley was pleased to see a number of his men taking orders from the ship's personnel.

Excellent! This is definitely not a time for pride or attitude.

"Botox 1, I found the SEALs," Kasay's voice said in Riley's ear. "Schab's bad, but he'll live. Rasenjunge's dead."

"Get them both to the aft boats as quick as you can!"

"Roger."

Another man gone under my command. You're like a walking death sentence!

"I know what you're thinking," Scott said from next to him. "It's not—"

"If you tell me that it's not my fault, Scott, I swear I'll deck you right here."

The two men stared at each other as men ran all around them.

Finally Scott said, "Let it go, man. Let it go and lead." Then he turned and walked away.

Scott's right. You've got a whole team here that you need to watch out for. Beat yourself up later.

Li's voice broke into Riley's thoughts. "Radiation levels are negative, One. Repeat, levels are negative."

"Got it," Riley answered. "Get yourselves back to the boats."

Smoke was billowing from the forward hold, and Riley heard an ominous creaking from the bowels of the ship. The listing was getting more and more pronounced, and Riley felt the uphill angle in his calves when he walked toward port.

"Come on! Move it; move it," he yelled to anyone he passed.

The insanity on board continued until the last person was safely on the boats. Everyone accounted for, Riley finally stepped into a lifeboat and closed its door behind him.

He quickly secured himself and gave a nod to a member of the crew. The crewman released a lever, and the freefall lifeboat plunged down to the water. The impact jarred them all, except the experienced crewmen, one of whom proceeded to start up the diesel engine and race the lifeboat away from the sinking ship.

Out his window, Riley was gratified to see two other boats bouncing across the waves. Turning around, he looked at the faces of those inside his own craft. There were two members of the ship's crew, plus Captain Blanco, who was only now regaining his wits. Scott and Khadi flanked Riley, while Skeeter sat next to the captain. Toward the front of the boat were the wounded SEAL and Carlos Guitiérrez, who was busy working on him.

Beyond them, in the absolute fore of the boat, lay the lifeless body of the other SEAL. Skeeter had covered the man with a Mylar rescue blanket, but Riley could still see his outline very clearly. Riley closed his eyes. Rasenjunge's face floated behind his eyelids. Quickly he opened them and locked them on the dead man.

I didn't even know him. Did he have a wife? Does he have any kids? Where's he from? I know nothing about him, except that he was just a piece in my plan—a pawn for me to move around.

"I didn't even know Rasenjunge's first name," Riley said aloud.

"Wes," Khadi said softly. "His name was Wes."

Riley turned to Khadi, who had a soft, sympathetic smile on her face. He nodded, then lowered his head in his hands.

The mission had been a qualified success. On the positive side, they had destroyed one of the containers.

The negative list was much longer. First, they had strong suspicions that there were still three more containers out there somewhere, but they had gained absolutely no information about where they might be.

Second, the lack of any radiation told them that whatever had been blown back there, it was probably not one of the two primary targets.

Third, the loss of the satellite phone and the container itself meant they had come away with scant evidence of the overall plot.

And finally, he had lost a member of his team. *Another death to add to your tally. Another one to put on your shoulders. How many more can you handle before you break under the weight?*

As he sat there hunched over, Riley felt Khadi's hand on his back. He appreciated her sympathy, but her touch only made him think about what Wes Rasenjunge's wife or mom or kids would be feeling tonight. It also made him wonder just how long it would be until it was Khadi's lifeless body he was looking down on.

CHAPTER FORTY-ONE

TUESDAY, SEPTEMBER 8, 9:15 A.M. IRDT
TEHRAN, IRAN

"So, we see that there are two jihads spoken of in the Koran," Ayatollah Beheshti told his students. "There is the Greater Jihad and the Lesser Jihad. Rahim, tell me the difference between the two."

Rahim stood next to his chair. "The Greater Jihad is the struggle of the believers against the wrong beliefs, evil, and desires that fill their hearts. The Lesser Jihad is the struggle of Islam against the infidel."

"Very good," Beheshti said as Rahim returned to his seat. "Another way to say it is that the Greater Jihad is internal, while the Lesser Jihad is external. The question I have for you is whether, in a sense, these names are reversed. In other words, should the internal jihad be lesser, and the external be greater? Namvar, give us your thoughts."

Namvar looked down as he pushed his chair back, but Beheshti could see the smirk on his face. "*Sayyid*, I think they should stay the same. These are the names given to the two struggles for centuries. It would be arrogant and presumptuous for *anyone* to put himself above our forefathers."

Beheshti threw the erasable marker that he had been holding, hitting Namvar just above the eye. "Impudent child! Go sit in the hall until I call for you! This is an academic exercise, and I will not have you challenging my integrity in such a way!"

For good measure, he threw an eraser at the boy as he was hustling out the door, missing to the right and leaving it lying on the floor. All the other students looked stunned. The ayatollah was well-known for his verbal outbursts, but very rarely did they turn physical in any way.

Beheshti scanned his students as he sought to regain his composure. He could tell they were all praying he would not choose them.

"Now, Yahya, please try to give an intelligent answer to my question."

Hesitantly, the young man answered, "The Greater Jihad is well named because it is an epic battle in the heart of all men. It is the lifelong struggle to draw closer to Allah."

Beheshti stroked his beard. "Very true. There is an internal battle within every soul. And it is very important. But is it the most important? Youness, tell us what Surah 4:95 says."

Youness slowly rose to his feet. Beheshti could practically see the wheels turning in his student's brain. Then a smile appeared on the boy's face, and he said, "'Not equal are those who sit at home and receive no hurt, and those who strive and fight in the name of Allah with their wealth and their selves. Allah has favored those who strive and fight with their wealth and their selves above those who sit at home . . . um . . . To both hath Allah promised good; but to those who strive and fight hath he favored with a great reward above those who sit at home.'"

Proudly, Youness started to return to his seat, but Beheshti stopped him. "So, my young student, according to our present definitions, which group is fighting the Lesser Jihad?"

"The ones who are striving and fighting?"

"Very good; and which ones are fighting the Greater Jihad?"

"The ones who are sitting at home."

Beheshti nodded as he walked to the whiteboard and picked up another marker. Everyone in the room tensed. "You may sit down, Youness. Now, Yahya, would you please stand again? Which group does the Prophet, peace be upon him, say that Allah favors with special reward?"

"Those fighting the Lesser Jihad."

"So I ask you again, are the names reversed? But don't answer me now." Turning to write an assignment on the whiteboard, he said, "I want all of you to spend the next hour writing your thoughts on the subject. I expect your answers to be well thought out and to have scriptural backing."

Normally there would have been a collective groan at this type of written assignment. However, the memory of Namvar's recent departure kept the room silent except for the rustling of notebooks and the clicking of pens.

The ayatollah rounded his desk and was about to sit when his assistant, Bahman Milani, entered the room. Hustling to where Beheshti stood, he leaned in and whispered, "Saberi is in your office."

"In my office? Now?" Nouri Saberi was the leader of the team Beheshti had put together for the project. For him to show up in the middle of the morning could mean only one thing—trouble.

"Class, I must leave you for a moment. I expect you to continue quietly with your assignment until I return." Then, turning to Milani, he said softly, "Call Namvar's parents and tell them that I am fed up with his attitude, and unless they can come up with a *sizable* reason why I should keep him at the madrassa, he is finished at my school."

"Yes, *sayyid,*" Milani said, following Beheshti out the door but halting to confront the humbled young man.

All sorts of scenarios ran through the ayatollah's mind as he hurried down the halls. *Did the shipments not make it? Have the packages been compromised? Please, don't let it be serious! We don't have the resources to start over!*

His heart sank when he entered his office and saw the man waiting for him. Saberi looked pale and very nervous. As soon as he saw Beheshti, he leaped to his feet.

"*Sayyid,* I don't—"

Beheshti silenced him with a wave of his hand. He closed the door, then sat behind his desk.

"Get control of yourself, Nouri; then tell me what has happened," Beheshti said in the calmest voice he could muster.

"Yes, *sayyid*; I'm sorry. As you know, we have four containers on four ships, all currently nearing the American coastline. We have placed a man among the crew on each vessel. A little over an hour ago, I received a satellite call from one of our men. His ship had been boarded by what he believed to be American forces. I instructed him to destroy the container. Then I heard gunfire, and the line went dead."

The ayatollah slammed his hand on his desk. He took a deep breath to calm himself, then asked, "Was the container destroyed?"

"I don't know for sure, *sayyid,* but we did receive a report that distress signals were being sent out from a cargo ship that was sinking in the eastern Atlantic."

"Which container was it?" Beheshti asked, afraid to hear the answer.

"It was one of the delivery systems. It was not one of the warheads."

Beheshti exhaled a huge sigh of relief. Then another frightening question struck him. "How did they know, Saberi? If it was the Americans, how could they possibly have known? This was no routine search and seizure, particularly if the ship was in international waters!"

Saberi, whose face had started to return to normal color when he saw Beheshti's relief, immediately went white again. "*Sayyid*, I . . . I have no idea. I'm certain it didn't come from us . . . or as certain as I can be."

The ayatollah knew Saberi's team. All good men. All true believers. But the leak had to come from somewhere. *If we don't find it and plug it, all our future efforts could be in vain.*

In the meantime, though, keep moving forward. If you stop the momentum, you may never gain it again. And if you give your team too much time to think, fear will creep in.

"Get word to your men on the ships. Tell them to increase their vigilance. They must be ready at a moment's notice to destroy any evidence of our plans.

"Then get back to our connections at Hezbollah. Tell them to contact North Korea immediately. I want them to know I hold them personally responsible for what has happened. Order another rocket. Make sure they know we want it expedited so that it will meet the other shipments. You figure out the logistics of getting it to its destination; then have Hezbollah dictate them to the Koreans. Tell them that if they receive any pressure from the DPRK, they should threaten to go public with their selling of weapons specifically designed to harm America. If they still refuse, we can use our contacts to acquire a Shahab-2 missile from our own military. These are the same as the Hwasong Scuds—we just renamed them after North Korea sold them to us. So the warhead will be transferable. But that is only a last resort!

"Also, I want the Koreans to know they have a leak. They must be reminded that if word gets out and our effort fails, they will be rebuked by the world and quite possibly destroyed by America. However, if this plan succeeds and America is taken down, they will be hailed by all nations as true and courageous heroes."

CHAPTER FORTY-TWO

WEDNESDAY, SEPTEMBER 9, 3:30 P.M. EDT
WASHINGTON, D.C.

Riley sat at a picnic table in the large, square courtyard. Surrounding him on all four sides was the Homeland Security building that contained in one small corner the Room of Understanding and in another the tactical team of Scott's special operations group. Riley's sweaty head was in his hands, and his cell phone lay on the table in front of him.

He took a deep drink from a bottle of Gatorade that sat next to his phone. The humidity of the September day was sucking the fluids out of his body, and Riley needed the electrolytes from the green liquid to keep his mind sharp and his body ready.

That was a rough one, he thought as he took another pull from the plastic bottle. *I can't imagine what she's going through.*

Riley had just got off the phone with Kellee Rasenjunge, the widow of the SEAL who had died under his command yesterday. It had been a frustrating conversation, but not because of Kellee. She had been wonderful—keeping her Southern dignity through the whole conversation, even telling Riley a few stories about Wes from when their little daughter had been born. She seemed genuinely appreciative of the fact that this football player and American hero would call to give his condolences.

But that's what had been so frustrating. Riley could only talk to her as if he were on the outside looking in. He couldn't tell her that he had been there when her husband died. He couldn't explain the man's heroism right up to the time that his life was snatched from him. He couldn't reassure her with the knowledge that he himself had stayed with Wes's body on the USS *Kauffman*, keeping his hand on the man's forehead until the time he had to pull it away so they could finish zipping the bag. He couldn't confess to her that he was the one responsible for his death.

Instead, he could only offer platitudes about her husband's bravery and generalizations about things he had "heard." *Lord, grant peace to that family. Watch over Kellee as she starts a new life as a single mother. Be with those two little kids, who are now facing the future without a father. God, it's such a tragedy; I've got no other words. Just be there.*

Riley looked up and caught the eyes of two young ladies who were watching him from behind some windows that were just beyond a narrow sidewalk. They quickly turned away, but Riley could see them whispering back and forth as they pretended to be doing their work.

He felt a bit like a zoo exhibit. *What am I, a trained monkey, here for your amusement? Want me to juggle some bananas?* He picked up his phone and his bottle and moved to a table on the other side of the courtyard—one that had a beautiful view of a redbrick wall. *Just a little privacy—that's all I'm asking for!*

When he cooled down a bit, he began spinning his phone on the recycled-plastic table as he prepared himself for his next call. Whitney Walker had been leaving him messages since last Tuesday, when he had been attacked on the D.C. street corner. At first the messages had been full of concern. Lately, though, she had begun sounding more annoyed than anything else.

Gotta be careful with what you say. Remember, no matter who she is or what remarkably unique shade of green her eyes are, she's still a reporter. Give her just enough to let her know that you're okay, then plead the Fifth on everything else.

Whitney answered on the first ring. "So you do still have my number."

Something about the way she said it made him want to say, "Yeah, because you've left it on my phone twenty times in the last eight days."

Instead, he said, "Sorry, Whitney. As you can imagine, things are pretty weird around here right now."

"How are you feeling?" she asked, still with the same edge in her voice.

Someone is definitely not herself today, Riley thought as he stood and walked to the path that ran the perimeter of the courtyard. "Doing okay. Getting better. I plan on being at the New York game on Sunday—not playing, obviously."

"Obviously. Listen, Riley, I'm going to get right to the point."

Riley decided to take the let's-get-it-all-out-on-the-table approach. "Please do, because right now, honestly, I'm not getting the best vibe from you."

"You're not getting the best vibe? Really? I wonder why that could be. Can you think of any reason?"

Riley stopped on the path. Having been on the receiving end of female attack mode enough times to gain a touch of practical male wisdom, he kept his mouth shut. He did a couple of deep knee bends to release some of his tension, then continued his slow walk.

After ten seconds of silence, Whitney apparently decided to answer her own question. "I'll tell you the reason! You get attacked, and I have no idea what happened to you! I try to get information, but there is none to be found. You just disappeared! I call the police, I call the FBI, I call Homeland Security; I explain to them that we're . . . close. But nobody knows anything about you.

"So I call the hospitals, and I learn that you were not admitted anywhere within a hundred-mile radius. That's when my reporter 'something-smells-fishy-around-here' sensors started going off."

Riley was still trying to process what she meant by *close*, but when she took a brief pause, he saw his opportunity to jump in. "I appreciate how worried you were, and I'm sorry you couldn't get any information. The folks here decided to clamp down on security until they're sure the threat is neutralized."

"I assume your friends Scott and Khadi just stitched you up good as new? I am correct that they've been transferred there, am I not?"

"There's nothing secret about that," Riley confirmed, his mind sorting out what information was classified and what was public knowledge.

"So you receive two deep, life-threatening wounds to your side, and Scott and Khadi just take you back to the office and fix you right up?"

"It wasn't like that at all—"

"Of course it wasn't like that, because it never happened! Come on, Riley, wasn't that attack a little too convenient? Unknown Muslim wacko stabs football star and vanishes into thin air. Then Riley vanishes too."

"I didn't vanish. I was—"

"But then rumors start popping up," Whitney said. "Rumors about Riley Covington being seen around the Homeland Security building; Riley Covington at the shooting range in the J. Edgar Hoover Building; Riley Covington seen through a crack in the curtains of his room at the Quincy, shirtless and seemingly without any bandages or visible signs of trauma."

"What? People are spying through my curtains?" Riley had stopped again but noticed he was in front of the windows of the voyeur girls and quickly hurried on.

"Oh, grow up, Riley. This is the real world. You are the hottest media thing going right now. If someone were to prove that attack was faked, their career would be made for life."

Why? Are other people's lives so miserable that they've got to ruin mine, too? Will knocking the legs out from under someone they perceive as a hero really make them feel better about themselves?

Whitney's voice interrupted Riley's thoughts. Her tone was softer now, like she was finally getting past the anger and moving toward the hurt.

"Did you hear the latest story, Riley? Don't worry, this is just going around between a few of my press friends. They haven't put two and two together like I have, but I know you a lot better than they do.

"It seems there was a container ship that had a big hole blown in it and ended up going down in the Atlantic. Some people are saying it was the result of a U.S. military special operation. According to their reports there were two strange things about the team. One was that Khadi Faroughi was on it—by the way, you should let her know that with all the news and special-interest stories that have been done about her in the last eight months, her face is becoming almost as recognizable as yours.

"But the second thing—that was the stranger of the two. It had to do with the leader of the team. Apparently he was a big guy, built like a—I don't know—like a linebacker, maybe. Oddly enough, it seems that this big leader guy was the only member of the team who never took his mask off. Don't you find that strange?"

Riley was getting angry now. Whitney was butting into things that were way over her head, and that could cause both of them a lot of problems. "What do you want me to say?"

"I want you to tell me the truth!"

"Come on, Whitney! I told you from the beginning that there are things about my life that I can't and won't ever talk about. It's not like this is a big surprise."

"I know you said that, but that was before . . ."

"Before what?"

"Do I need to spell it out? *Argh,* you're such a guy! Okay, that was before there was something special between us."

Riley was back at his table and stood facing the wall. "Special? Special how? Like you're my main media person?"

"Seriously? Do you really think that's what I'm talking about? Riley, you can be so exasperating! Special as in we love being around each other. I never laugh with anyone like I do with you. I never feel as safe as when we're together. There's a chemistry between us. I feel it, and I know you feel it too. I've seen the way you look at me. It's right there in your eyes. I *know* you feel it. Just try telling me you don't."

"I'm sorry, Whitney, but I don't," Riley said firmly, convincing himself in the same moment that he tried to convince her. Softening his voice, he continued, "You're an incredible friend, and I truly enjoy the times that we spend together talking and drinking coffee.

But that's all it's ever been and all it will ever be. I'm sorry if I ever made you believe we could be more than that."

"It's because of her, isn't it? It's because of Khadi."

Is that really it? Am I really turning away an incredibly bright and attractive woman for a woman I know I can't have? Yeah, I guess I am. "Yes, it's because of her."

They were both silent on the phone for a minute. Riley took the time to sit at the table and take another swallow of the now-lukewarm Gatorade. *There are a lot of things I need in my life right now, but this conversation is not one of them!*

As he was trying to come up with a way to close the phone call, Whitney said, "Guess you think I'm quite the idiot."

"Not at all," Riley responded, forcing himself to sound sympathetic. *Please, just make the phone call end!* "I'm the one who's been the idiot."

"Yeah, I suppose you have," she agreed with a sad chuckle. "Can you at least tell me the truth about what's going on? Totally off the record. I'm just worried about you."

"The truth, *if* it's any different from what you're already hearing, isn't going to come from me. I can only say what I'm allowed to say. I'm sorry, Whitney."

"I know. I understand. Again, Riley, I'm sorry that I . . . I don't know."

Enough already! Take the blame and end the call! "Whitney, you're fine. It's just—things aren't always the way they seem. I should have been more careful."

"Are you still going to let me be your favorite obnoxious, hard-hitting, in-your-face reporter girl?"

"I wouldn't have it any other way," Riley said, feeling right now like he would rather have it *any* other way.

"Good. Well, I guess I'll probably see you in New York."

"Definitely. It's a . . . Let's plan on it."

Riley hung up the phone and put it on the table.

Well, off the top of my head, I can't think of any way that could have gone worse.

He started spinning his phone again.

At least the Whitney issue is finally resolved in my own mind. I was stupid to have ever entertained any thoughts about her. She's press, and that means arm's distance. Besides, she's not the one that's got my full attention anyway, is she?

So if it's over and done with her, why am I so uptight? The spying; that's it. Are people really watching me—like those two earlier in the window? Seriously, can't people mind their own business? Trying to dig up dirt about me and spying through my curtains? I've gotta find a way to put a stop to it, and I mean now!

Riley's frustrated final spin on his phone was a bit too hard, and he watched helplessly as it skittered across the table, flew off the edge, and shattered on the cement below.

CHAPTER FORTY-THREE

WEDNESDAY, SEPTEMBER 9, 3:50 P.M. EDT
WASHINGTON, D.C.

While he was still brooding about the phone call with Whitney, Riley felt a sensation on his neck that made him spin around angrily. Khadi stood behind him with an ice-cold Gatorade bottle in her hand.

"Are we a bit uptight?" she asked with a laugh.

"Sorry; I guess I am," Riley answered, taking the bottle from her hand. "Thanks." He gave her a little toast before he twisted the cap off and drank deeply.

Khadi stooped down and began picking the pieces of the phone off the ground.

"No, wait," Riley said, jumping up and joining her. Together they lifted bits of the shattered phone from the cement and pulled them from the grass and the flower bed.

Khadi handed Riley her pieces, and he felt the brush of her fingertips across his palms. He emptied his hands on the table and then bent back down and snapped two white gardenias from their stalks.

Slightly embarrassed, he silently handed the flowers to Khadi, all the while thinking that this would be an ideal time to say something witty or romantic but coming up with nothing.

With a stern look on her face but a twinkle in her eyes, Khadi said, "Why, Mr. Covington, I do believe these flowers are technically federal government property."

"That's all right. I've got the direct line to the president programmed into my . . ." Riley stopped and looked at the shattered phone. "Oops. I'm busted."

Khadi laughed, then brought the flowers to her face and inhaled deeply. "Gardenias always remind me of home. My mother used to keep fresh gardenias in a small lead crystal dish on our coffee table. The smell would fill the room."

Rounding the table and sitting in his old seat, Riley said, "Sounds nice. My mom was never quite that froofy. Although I do remember having a gardenia-scented Glade PlugIn in our guest bathroom once."

"Oh, please. Your mom is great! I'm sure she had your house looking and smelling wonderful all the time."

"True, but the smells usually emanated from the kitchen."

"I can believe that," Khadi said. She had been the partial beneficiary of numerous care packages that Riley's mom regularly sent to him filled with brownies, cookies, and a chocolate-covered peanut brittle that was downright sinful.

Riley watched Khadi's face light up at the thought of his mom's cooking and again thought, *She truly is the most beautiful woman I've ever met. She's like a great work of art that you never get tired of looking at. She's like a book that you read over and over again, and every time you do you find something new to marvel at. She is more than beautiful; she is spectacular. A visual marvel.*

"What's going through that mind of yours?" Khadi asked with a shy smile, as if she already knew the answer to her question.

"I'm just thinking about books."

"Oh," Khadi said, obviously not hearing the answer she expected or hoped for.

"I mean—really good books. Beautiful books with incredible plots and amazing story lines." Riley's face colored as he heard Scott's voice in his head saying, *"Well played, Casanova!"* Shaking his head, he said, "Wow, I can't tell you how many ways that came out wrong."

Khadi laughed and reached across the table to touch his arm. Riley loved it when she did that. "For a guy who's so strong and confident on the football field and on the field of battle . . ."

Riley joined Khadi's laughter. They'd had this conversation more than once. "What can I say? I've never really been what you might call 'good with the chicks.'"

"Nice. Sounds like something Scott would say."

"As a matter of fact . . ." Riley laughed, thinking back to the conversation when Scott had said those very words. "But no matter how you say it, it's still true. I think the only girl I talked to up until age thirteen was my mom."

"Oh, really. And whom did you meet at age thirteen?" Khadi said, pulling her hand back and pretending to be jealous.

"Mrs. Beasely from next door. I had accidentally thrown a football through her kitchen window."

"Mrs. Beasely, huh? She doesn't sound very exciting."

"*Au contraire!* She was actually quite a looker. And even better than that, she had been divorced for several years, so she was available. From what my friends said, she was hot to trot."

"'Hot to trot'? What does that mean?"

Riley shrugged. "I have no idea. I think my friends picked it up from an episode of *Happy Days*."

"So what happened with Mrs. Beasely?"

"It took me a summer of mowing and an autumn of raking her leaves to pay off the window. At least she made good lemonade. What about you? Who was the first boy you took to?"

Without even pausing to think, Khadi blurted out, "Ronnie Kahiona."

"Kahiona? Doesn't sound very Persian to me." Riley took another drink of his Gatorade. He wanted to suggest they go inside out of the humidity but was afraid one of them would get caught up in something and they would lose this rare alone time.

"Oh no. Ronnie wasn't Persian. He was much more exotic than that. I met Ronnie when we took a family vacation to Hawaii. We were at this traditional luau. I'm busy stuffing my face with huli-huli chicken and char siu when the drums start beating. I turn toward the stage, and out walks this tropical vision. He's wearing a sarong, no shirt, and a kukui nut lei. He's dancing and swinging these poi balls around."

"They always say that poi balls are the quickest way to a woman's heart," Riley said sarcastically, trying to sound like a jealous boyfriend yet feeling like a total idiot for the twinge of real jealousy he was experiencing.

"Well, that certainly was true for this girl," Khadi agreed as she motioned for Riley to pass the Gatorade. When she took a sip, Riley noticed that she didn't bother to wipe the bottle first. *Does that mean something?*

Khadi slid the bottle back to him and continued. "What sealed my undying love for him was his second number, when he asked for a volunteer from the audience. Guess who he picked?"

"Mrs. Beasely?"

Khadi made a buzzer sound. "Wrong! He picked me! So I'm up on stage with him standing behind me. He's got his arms around me, showing me how to spin the poi balls. I'm not hearing a thing he's saying. My whole body must have turned seven shades of red. I just knew that everyone in the whole audience could see that I had this massive crush on Ronnie.

"Finally, I sit back down. My family congratulates me, but I'm mortified. I don't touch another bite of food the rest of the night."

Riley shook his head. "*Tsk-tsk-tsk*. Sounds like an absolute nightmare."

"That's not the worst of it. After the show was over, the performers come out to schmooze the audience. I'm watching Ronnie shaking hands with people—one half of my brain praying that he won't come over and the other half wondering if the name Khadijah Kahiona had a musical ring to it. Sure enough, Ronnie makes his way to the table. Then, in front of my parents and God Himself, he squats down and gives me a hug and tells me what a great job I did."

"So did anything come of you and Ronnie? A little Hawaiian fling, perhaps?"

Khadi looked shocked. "I should think not! Ronnie was probably in his early twenties and I was seven!"

"You were only seven?" Riley said, feeling like the level of his idiocy had just reached epic proportions.

Khadi laughed as her hand went back across the table to find Riley's arm. "Oh, Riley. You weren't really jealous, were you? This was over twenty years ago."

Trying to cover his embarassment with bravado, he answered, "Hey, I don't care how long ago it was. Nobody messes with my girl!"

As soon as he had said the words, he wished he could take them back. The lightheartedness of the moment flitted away. The *my girl* hung in the air, mocking them, touting itself as the only gateway to true love and joy in their lives yet floating just out of their reach.

Riley put his hand over Khadi's. Their eyes met—longing and sorrow in both their stares. Finally, with visible regret, Khadi slipped her hand from his.

"I better get back in," she said. "Are you coming?"

"No. I think I'm going to stay out here and practice spinning my poi balls. Maybe if I get good enough, I can win your heart."

"Don't waste your time. It's already won."

Again their eyes locked until, without saying another word, Khadi walked back across the courtyard and into the building.

With a sad smile on his face, Riley watched her go, all the while wondering what he'd look like in a sarong and what the heck a kuikui nut lei was.

CHAPTER FORTY-FOUR

WEDNESDAY, SEPTEMBER 9, 3:50 P.M. EDT
WASHINGTON, D.C.

Scott leaned over Virgil Hernandez's shoulder while the analyst detailed some recently intercepted communications intelligence. Without warning, the door to the Room of Understanding opened, and a man in an expensively tailored suit walked in flanked by two federal bodyguards.

"Secretary Moss," Scott said, flustered and trying to regain his composure as he crossed the room. "Welcome to the RoU."

"The what?" Moss asked with a scowl.

"The RoU—Room of Understanding," Scott explained, though he could see Moss cared very little about what he was saying. "It's just a nickname that we . . . never mind. So what brings you here?"

Moss pulled on his shirt cuffs until exactly one inch extended from the arms of his suit jacket. "Well, Ross, since I can't seem to get any reports from you, I thought I'd better come and examine your operation for myself." Moss glared at the faces around the room. He ran his finger across a coffee stain on the conference table, then cleaned himself off with a monogrammed handkerchief he pulled from his pants pocket. "I must say that, thus far, I'm unimpressed."

So that's the way it's going to be, huh? Big surprise. "Sorry, sir. We gave the maid service the week off. They're from Mongolia, and apparently it's National Build-a-Yurt week. Who knew?"

Moss wheeled on Scott. "Listen, Ross! I didn't come here to be mocked! I'm here deciding if we have the money to keep this little special operations group experiment funded. And if we do have the money, whether or not you're the one to lead them! So I'd suggest you show me some respect! Understood?"

Scott could feel the eyes of everyone in the room on him. Tara looked ready to jump to his aid, but he waved her off with a quick shake of his head. *Just get through this and get him out the door. Then you can have Stanley Porter work everything out.*

"Yes, sir."

Moss gave a self-satisfied *humph* and said, "Now, who is that?"

Scott followed the direction of Moss's finger. "That's Evie Cline. She is our specialist in electronic surveillance and geospatial reconnaissance. She is also invaluable as a cryptanalyst and regional analyst."

Moss slowly moved Evie's direction, watching her as she worked. Scott knew that the secretary probably understood only one out of every three words he had just used, which was by design. *The guy's one big bluff. Call him on it, and you'll see he's got nothing in his hand.*

When Moss arrived at Evie's workstation, he placed his hand on the back of her chair. Immediately she scooted forward, breaking Moss's contact.

"Good afternoon, Miss Cline," Moss said.

"Good afternoon," Evie answered without turning around.

"May I ask what you're working on?"

"Certainly, sir. I've had some trouble of late linking up with the satellite feeds. So I'm adjusting the hardware using Dr. Emmett Brown's algorithmic hypotheses in hopes of getting the system's flux capacitor up to the ideal 1.21 jigawatts."

Scott heard Joey Williamson stifle a laugh, then cover it with an improvised coughing fit.

"Excuse me, sir," Williamson said to a glaring Moss. "Allergies."

Moss turned back to Evie. "As you may have heard, I am here to evaluate your SOG's operation. What do you think of Mr. Ross's leadership of your team? Is he competent? Is he fair to you both as an employee and as a woman? And please know that I will ensure that you will experience no recriminations for whatever negatives you have to say about him."

Evie finally turned around and said in an icy voice, "Thank you for giving me that peace of mind, sir. But to Mr. Ross's credit, his leadership and integrity make him a joy to work for. And his knowledge of our systems is second to none. In fact, he is so far ahead of the curve that any time we discover some new tool or technology, he's already heard about it and is ready to explain it to us. In a sense, one might say that in order for us to even keep up with him, he's got to step back to our future."

Williamson had another allergy-related coughing fit, and Scott, too, was having a hard time not laughing. *Whatever else these kids are, they are loyal to a fault.*

"I've got problems with Scott," Gooey called from across the room.

Oh no! I don't know what Gooey's up to, but guaranteed, this will not end well.

Immediately Moss left Evie and half walked, half jogged to Gooey's station. Scott watched Moss's face cringe as his nose drew in the funk that permeated the air in that part of the room.

"And what's your name?" Moss asked.

"Name's Gooey. What's yours?"

Moss seemed taken aback, both that someone wouldn't recognize him and that a lowly analyst would address him so casually. "I'm Secretary Dwayne Moss. May I ask your real name—just for the record?"

"Well—just for the record—everyone calls me Gooey, so why don't we go with that? So whose secretary are you, Wayne?"

"It's Dwayne—I mean Secretary Moss. I am the president's cabinet secretary in charge of Homeland Security."

Gooey let out a low whistle. "Pretty impressive. Does that mean you *don't* take shorthand? Nah, I'm just messing with you, Wayne. Now, I heard you asking about Scotty over there, and I've got to tell you, I've got some serious issues with him."

Moss's cheeks tightened and a vein in his forehead began to make itself known. But he kept his anger in check and nodded to one of his bodyguards, who pulled out a small, flip-top notebook and a pen. "Again, it's Secretary Moss. But never mind—please, go ahead."

Scott fought to keep his nervousness in check. Gooey was just so unpredictable. Something was about to go really bad—either for him or for Gooey or both. His teeth clenched and his fists balled up as he watched his analyst begin to speak.

"So a week or so ago, I'm here cruising through craigslist—"

"Wait a minute," Moss interrupted. "Was this on government time?"

Gooey started laughing. "Duh! Of course it was on government time. Why else would I be here? So I'm scanning craigslist and I find this popcorn maker. And it's not like, you know, just this regular old countertop popcorn maker. This thing's like the whole cart—you know, like at the circus or the fair or something. I immediately e-mail the dude; he's still got it, so I bolt out and pick it up."

"Was this on your lunch hour?"

"On my lunch hour? Come on! I eat lunch on my lunch hour."

Moss's face was darkening by the second, turning his artificial tan a deep crimson. "First of all, I don't see what this has to do with the topic at hand. And second of all, I don't know how you can justify using government time to purchase a—a popcorn cart!"

"Hold your water, Wayne. I'm getting to that. So I bring the cart back to the office and put it right over there," Gooey said, pointing to the one corner of the room that didn't have a desk crammed into it. "But no sooner do I get it in there than Scott tells me I have to take it back out. Something about a fire hazard and some muckety-muck's rules. Can you believe that? What kind of idiot makes up a rule against popcorn makers?"

"The rule against appliances of any kind being allowed in Homeland Security offices came from me," Moss seethed.

"Oh . . . well, ask a question, get an answer. So that's pretty much my gripe against Scott. That, and his rule against playing computer games during work hours."

"His rule against . . . Ross!"

Scott hustled over to Moss's side.

"My inspection has confirmed everything that I expected about this operation! It is shoddy and undisciplined from the top down! It is a disgrace both to the president's administration and to my department! I have an afternoon meeting today with President Lloyd during which I am going to report to him all that I have seen here. I would be quite surprised if any of you were still working in this office tomorrow.

"But if for some reason the president decides to keep you open, I expect this chair—" Moss pointed to where Gooey was sitting—"to be empty tomorrow! Do I make myself clear?"

"So you're giving me the day off tomorrow?" Gooey asked.

"I'm giving you your life off, you moron!"

"Score," Gooey said, putting his arms straight up, referee-style.

Moss turned to Scott, gave a disgusted shake of his head, and headed for the door. But before he got there, he turned around and stormed back.

"You know what sickens me most about you people?"

"I can hardly venture a guess," Scott answered drily.

"It's the levity—the joking around. According to your way of thinking, hundreds of thousands of lives could be depending on your work, and all your team seems to do the whole day is sit around and crack your little jokes and play your little tricks. And you," Moss said, popping his finger against Scott's chest, "you are the worst of the bunch. That's why you aren't fit to lead—you don't know when to get serious!"

"Listen, Moss," Scott said, grabbing the secretary's finger but quickly letting go after he saw Moss's bodyguards move toward him. "That just shows how little you understand about what we do. Don't you think we feel the pressure? Don't you think we know what's at stake? Every one of us lives day by day with the knowledge that one wrong decision, one missed piece of information, can result in massive loss of human life.

"So we've got two options. Either we let the pressure crush us and twist our insides until we all have ulcers and high blood pressure, or we laugh. We joke. We release our pressure valves by doing dumb stuff and saying stupid things. We don't do it because we don't care. We do it because we care too much!

"And you very well may be right that I'm not fit to lead. But I can guarantee you that I'm a far sight better than some anal-retentive, ladder-climbing, play-by-the-rules-unless-it-suits-your-own-needs, self-important, self-righteous, bureaucratic stuffed shirt like yourself," Scott finished, immediately wondering if maybe he had gone just a tad too far with that final flourish. *Yeah, maybe. But Jim sure would have been proud!*

Moss didn't move. The vein in his forehead looked like it was in danger of widening to a four-lane highway up and over his scalp. Finally he whispered through gritted teeth, "Start packing your office, Ross. You're done."

With one last look of disdain, he walked out the office door.

"Thanks for popping in, Wayne. Come back anytime," Gooey called after him.

Scott whapped him on the back of the head, then wiped the grease on his pant leg.

As soon as the door closed behind Moss, everyone started laughing. Williamson and Hernandez each did impressions of the great secretary while Evie swooned from awe and fear. Even Tara managed a smile, although Scott knew she understood better than the analysts the trouble they were all in. Especially him.

Eventually Scott calmed them down. "Listen, gang, try to forget this little visit and just get back to work. I'll see what I can do about smoothing this whole thing over."

"Should I get Porter on the line?" Tara asked.

Scott sighed. Sooner or later Porter was going to tire of constantly having to bail him out of trouble.

"Sure," he answered.

As he walked toward his office, he saw Gooey packing up his stuff.

"Where are you going?" he asked.

"You heard the man—I'm getting some time off . . . a lot of time off."

"Put your stuff back. You're not going anywhere."

"Aw, man," Gooey said as he started pulling action figures and bags of Cheetos back out of his plastic grocery bag.

"And, Goo, when you come back tomorrow—because you *are* coming back tomorrow—bring the popcorn cart with you."

CHAPTER FORTY-FIVE

THURSDAY, SEPTEMBER 10, 5:30 A.M. KST
CHOSAN, NORTH KOREA

Pak Kun felt blood on his face and arms, but that was nothing out of the ordinary. The pine trees that forested the region between Chosan and the border could be merciless. And although his salty sweat made the scratches sting, the speed he was traveling at made the pain worth it. There was still nearly an hour until sunrise, and he was only fifteen minutes from home. With any luck, his wife, Son Soo, would already be awake and awaiting his arrival with a warm herbal salve and hot tea.

Tonight was the first time Pak Kun had made the trip across the border during the week, and he had to admit that he was even more nervous than usual. If he were stopped on a Sunday, he could at least try to make the excuse that he had gotten lost hiking in the woods. But there was no good reason for a person to be out in the middle of the forest on a weekday when he had to work first thing in the morning.

Careful; careful; watch your step here, he reminded himself as he leaped over the gnarled roots of an ancient oak tree. Then, cutting fifteen feet to the right, he bounded across a dead tree that stretched over a narrow stream.

The first few times he had made this journey, he had returned bruised and battered from tripping his way to the border and tripping his way back. Now experience and familiarity with the trail meant only two or three headfirst sprawls into the dirt and brush each way.

Why was this message so important that Pak Bae came out in the middle of the week? Pak Kun wondered for the hundredth time. *And why was he so insistent that I take this across the border tonight?*

Pak Bae's sudden arrival less than a day ago had caused a stir throughout the family. North Korea was not a country that lent itself to impulsive, spur-of-the-moment actions. So when Pak Bae arrived unannounced, everyone assumed it was bad news.

But his cousin had seemed his normal, jovial self. He laughed; he gave gifts; he did all his usual things. But after he had left, his mother had worriedly told the family that despite Pak Bae's outward appearance, there was something wrong. She knew as only a mother could.

Well, Pak Kun knew what was wrong. He knew as only a coconspirator in treason could. Breaking all their previous protocol, Pak Kun had walked his cousin around the back of the train station, passed him the message without any attempt to cover it up, and told him that he must get the small packet across the border that very night.

Well, it's there! I have done my part! The rest is up—

A sound in the brush caused Pak Kun to dive up against a large boulder that was embedded into the side of a hill. He flattened himself against the jagged rock and tried to control his breathing. *In, out, in, out . . . in . . . out . . . in . . . out.* Pak Kun held his hand against his chest, willing his respiration to slow down.

Silently he sat, waiting, listening.

A small amount of dirt and grit trickled into his hair, telling him that his efforts at hiding had not succeeded. He closed his eyes and tried not to hyperventilate as he awaited the voice or the blow to the head or the gunshot.

A minute passed, and nothing happened. His legs threatened to cramp from the tension. *Do it! Just do it!*

Finally he could stand it no more. He opened his eyes, leaned away from the rock, and looked up.

Standing above him was a lynx, its yellow eyes reflecting the moonlight. Pak Kun couldn't move, but not from fear. He was transfixed—held by the cat's beauty, by its calm, by the way its eyes seemed to be telling him that there was nothing for him to fear in the woods tonight.

What seemed like hours was only seconds. Its black-tufted ears twitched backward. Its gaze seemed to draw within itself. Then it turned and disappeared into the woods.

Pak Kun wanted to stay right in that spot—playing and replaying in his mind what he had just experienced. *But there's no stopping the sun. I have to get home now if I have any hope of getting to the textile factory in time.* He began to run again, twisting and turning with the well-worn path.

Fifteen minutes later, he came to the base of a low hill. Just on the other side was the village where his family had lived for generations. Excitement filled his heart as he picked up his pace.

But then he stopped. Something wasn't right. In the predawn darkness, a strange orange glow shone from the opposite side of the hill.

Son Soo!

Pak Kun sprinted toward his home. There were no thoughts of what might be waiting for him in the village. There was no fear for himself. All he could think of was his wife, his mother, his family.

As he got closer, the acrid smell of smoke reached his nostrils. It wasn't the smell of the morning wood cooking fires that typically filled the village about this time. It was the smoke that came when they burned trash in the afternoons—wood mixed with plastic mixed with whatever other materials and chemicals made up the contents of the week's garbage.

He rounded the corner of the small Buddhist shrine at the end of his block at a dead run, then stopped in the middle of the dirt street. Movement caught his eye, and he turned in time to see shutters closing on the corner house.

Down the block, he could see his house burning, as well as the houses of his mother and extended family. Bodies lay in front of each doorway. He was still far enough away to not be able to see any faces, but he knew by size and location who each person was.

Pak Kun slowly walked forward. Hanging from a maple tree in front of his aunt's house was a naked man. Although the sun had not come up and the face was twisted and bloody, the light from the fire was enough for Pak Kun to be able to discern the features of his cousin, Pak Bae.

How? How did this happen? How did they find out? Look what they've done to my family! Why did I ever say yes to Pak Bae? Why couldn't I have just gone through life quietly like everyone else in my village? Now look . . .

There was his uncle, Sam-chon. There was old Halmoni, the matriarch of their family. There were his two toddler nephews, Pak Ho and Pak Chul.

He wanted to stop and cover the bodies. He wanted to throw up. He wanted to run. But he just kept moving forward, finally coming to his house.

In front of his door, as he knew she would be, lay Son Soo. Her clothes were scattered around, and her face and body were matted with dirt and blood. The absolute horror of what he was experiencing sucked away any emotion and left him in a daze.

Walking past the little white fence he had built, which now lay trampled in the dirt, Pak Kun knelt beside his wife. He brushed the bangs away from her face, having to tug a little to loosen them from the drying blood. Then, as he gently smoothed her hair back over her head, he reached his other hand down and lightly touched her swollen belly—the belly that up until this morning had been protecting and nurturing their first child.

There was a shuffle to his left, but Pak Kun didn't look up. He had been expecting it and was surprised it had taken this long.

"Get up," a voice demanded.

Pak Kun continued to stroke his wife's hair.

"I said get up!"

With a heavy sigh, Pak Kun touched Son Soo's cheek for the last time. He stood and turned to meet his fate.

There were five brown-uniformed soldiers in front of him. The sound of feet behind Pak Kun told him that they were not alone.

"What is your name?"

"You know who I am," he said wearily.

"Tell me your name," the officer commanded.

"My name is Pak Kun, and my only hope is that you will burn in hell for what you have done and that the Buddha will never allow you reprieve."

The officer nodded to a soldier next to him. Pak Kun prayed for a quick death as the man stepped forward. The soldier raised his rifle, and the last thing Pak Kun saw was the butt of the gun driving toward his face.

CHAPTER FORTY-SIX

THURSDAY, SEPTEMBER 10, 12:10 P.M. EDT
WASHINGTON, D.C.

Riley stood behind Scott Ross and watched the computer monitor on his friend's desk. Next to Riley stood Khadi.

Scott had told Riley about the surprise inspection yesterday and how Porter had saved their backsides again. This time, though, the bailout came with a warning—Porter was running out of chips to play, and next time he might not be able to come through.

But that was yesterday, and today was today. And each day seemed to bring new problems of its own.

"Go ahead and play it," Riley said angrily.

Scott clicked the white triangle that was placed on the middle of Riley's face, and the SportsCenter story began playing.

"Good afternoon, I'm Jackie LeTourneau, and welcome to ESPN's SportsCenter. Leading off today is a troubling story regarding the alleged attack on Washington Warriors linebacker Riley Covington. Here to tell us about it is Whitney Walker."

"Unbelievable," Riley said, as the video switched to a two-shot.

"Whitney, we were all shocked to hear what

happened to Covington last week. But you've uncovered some evidence that might give us a different take. What can you tell us about the alleged assault?"

"Thank you, Jackie. A number of months ago, I met Riley Covington while he was going through a well-publicized, extremely difficult time in his life. Since that time, Riley has confided many things to me about his life. Sometimes he gave me permission to share his stories with the public. Most of the time, though, I simply provided an off-the-record listening ear."

Riley felt Khadi's eyes on him. "Please," he said, disgusted.

"Last May, Riley asked me to do him a special favor—to run a story for him on the local television station where I was employed as a sports reporter. Although I knew certain aspects of the story weren't wholly accurate, I still did it because Riley made it clear that it was a life-and-death situation for him and others. However, at that time I stipulated to him that he must never ask me to be part of something like that again."

Riley was about to defend himself, but Scott said, "Shut up; we know."

"He held to his part of the agreement until yesterday, when I received a call from Riley in which he asked me to participate in the cover-up of the faked attack last Tuesday."

"I'm sorry, did you say 'faked attack'?"

"I'm afraid so, Jackie. I declined to be part of his scheme, reminding him of his promise to me, and he apologized for asking. I began prompting him for information about the Georgetown attack while reaching to activate my phone recorder. By the time it was turned on, Riley was wrapping up the conversation. I believe I captured enough, however, to demonstrate the gist of what took place."

A graphic with a telephone appeared on the screen. Whitney's picture was on the left, and Riley's was on the right. Down below, the conversation was captioned in white letters.

> **Whitney Walker:** *Come on, Riley, wasn't that attack a little too convenient? Unknown Muslim wacko stabs football star and vanishes into thin air. Then Riley vanishes too.*
>
> **Riley Covington:** *I should have been more careful. What do you want me to say?*

Walker: *I want you to tell me the truth!*

Covington: *The truth . . . things aren't always the way they seem. I'm sorry, Whitney; it's not like this is a big surprise.*

Walker: *I'm just worried about you.*

Covington: *I wouldn't have it any other way.*

Walker: *Well, I guess I'll probably see you in New York.*

Covington: *Let's plan on it.*

"I tried reaching the Washington Warriors and the Department of Homeland Security for comment. My calls were not returned. As much as it pains me to report this story, Jackie, particularly as it concerns someone for whom I continue to have the deepest respect, I felt I had to do it. We were all horrified at what we perceived as the events that took place last Tuesday. Now it appears that they were not what they seemed."

"And it seems that maybe Riley Covington is not what he appears to be either. Thank you, Whitney, for reporting what is obviously a very personally painful story."

The picture froze with the anchor's mouth half-open, ready to move on to the next sports event.

Silence filled the small office. Riley held the back of Scott's chair in an iron grip. Khadi's hand reached up and rested on his shoulder, causing Riley's fingers to loosen their grip and his body to lose some of its tension.

"I'm sorry, guys. I let my guard down," Riley said quietly.

"Don't be too hard on yourself," Scott said, turning his chair around. Then, realizing that he was now knee to knee with Riley, he turned it back partway and cocked his head to the right. "Reporters are all sneaky little vermin."

"That's not true," Riley said quickly. "Most of them are honest, hardworking people who can be trusted to keep 'off-the-record' off the record. Of course, there are some that will stab their own mothers in the back to get a juicy story, but this . . . this is beyond anything I've ever experienced before. Actually editing my words—unbelievable."

"Well, she got what she wanted. A news story that should make her a household name, with a dose of revenge on top," Khadi said.

"Revenge? How so?" Riley asked.

"Come on, Riley," Khadi answered, looking at her feet as she spoke, "I know a woman scorned when I see one. She didn't just want the story; she wanted to hurt you in the process."

Riley looked at Khadi, but she would not meet his gaze. He decided not to respond to her comments. *I'm not going to dive into that one right now.*

Instead, turning to Scott, he asked, "What do we do now? Are we toast?"

Scott just smiled and pressed a button on his phone. "Oh, Gooey?"

A click was heard, then the sound of some fumbling around, and finally Gooey's voice saying, "Oh, Scotty."

"I'm assuming you've seen the ESPN story on Riley."

"Man, did he royally screw us up or what?"

"Hi, Goo," Riley said.

". . . No comprende; lo siento," Gooey replied in his best Frito Bandito accent.

Riley had to chuckle. "Don't sweat it. I feel the same way."

"Hey, Gooman," Scott said, "here's the skinny. It seems the fair Miss Walker did a little magic with the editing machine and pieced together the so-called incriminating evidence."

Gooey made his feelings about Whitney known. Then he added, "Uh, excuse my French, please, Khadi. That is, if Khadi's in there, which I just assumed she is since Riley's in there, but I guess that doesn't have to be true because it's not like they're attached at the hip or anything, although I'm still willing to bet dollars to do-rags that I'm probably right."

"It's okay, Gooey," Khadi said. "And I agree with your assessment of her."

"Okay, then. So where was I? Oh yeah—now it makes sense. I thought Riley's inflections sounded off!"

"As only you would know, my friend," Scott said. "Now, obviously this little ruse has put us in a bit of a predicament. So I'm going to put you in charge of a little project that I'm christening Operation Keep the Lie Alive."

"Operation Keep the Lie Alive . . . Gooey likey."

Already Riley felt bad for Whitney. If there was one person he wouldn't want sicced on him, it would be that seemingly harmless blob of KFC grease and Pez that sat in the corner of the RoU.

"Do what you need to do to repair the situation, Gooey, but try not to take Whitney down too hard," Riley said and immediately felt Khadi remove her hand from his shoulder.

"No comprende, amigo. Adios." Gooey clicked off the other line.

Scott's phone rang.

"Excuse me, guys; that's my secure line."

"No prob," Riley said.

"Ross," Scott said after turning fully back to his desk and snatching up the receiver.

Riley and Khadi started to head out the door but were stopped by Scott's snapping fingers.

"Double O, how're things across the pond? Did you get that case of Dr Pepper I sent you? . . . It was no problem. It's like the first time I tried Yoo-hoo—instantly addicted. . . . Definitely, and a lot cheaper, too. Besides, I could never shoot up. I'm terrified of needles." Scott laughed as he wrote, *Anna Zeller, MI6* on a Post-it note and passed it to Riley and Khadi.

"So what's up? You're secure from that end? . . . Yeah, that was us. . . . No, that wasn't part of the plan. They had a guy on board. He confettied the package, along with himself. . . . I knew it! One of our guys said they thought they saw him making a call on a sat. . . . I was afraid of that! And you said they're rushing it out, too?"

Scott passed another paper over. On it he had scrawled what looked like *Sending another lilimrj system*. Riley leaned over his shoulder and pointed at the third word. Scott snatched the note out of Riley's hand, scribbled over *lilimrj*, and wrote *delivery*.

"Ohhh," Riley and Khadi said together.

". . . That's majorly bad news because we're still just sitting ducks. The kids here are hugely frustrated. It was a near miracle finding the one we did find. I hate to ask you this, Anna, but is there any way to get word back to your DPRK muckety-muck guy to see if he can get us any more details about where and when these . . . Seriously?"

Scott quickly scribbled another note and sent it flying over his shoulder. Riley caught it on its way down and held it for Khadi and him to read—*Kor govt mole burned ~ think whole pipeline wiped.*

". . . Oh, man, I'm sorry. That sucks with major suckage. Hey, Double O, I got a couple of folks in here that I need to talk to. Can I give you a call back in about thirty minutes? I'll give you the full scoop on the MSC *Shirley* op then. . . . Yeah, you too. And thanks tons."

Scott hung up the phone, turned around so that he was knee to knee with Riley again, and said, "Just when you didn't think it could get any worse."

CHAPTER FORTY-SEVEN

SUNDAY, SEPTEMBER 13, 9:15 P.M. EDT
NEW YORK, NEW YORK

The football came spiraling right at Riley. The receiver for the PFL Cup champion New York Liberty had let the pass get through his hands, and now there was no one between Riley and the ball. His adrenaline surged, but just before it reached him, he stepped aside and let the pass bounce to the turf.

"Do you know how hard it was to do that?" he asked Skeeter, who was standing next to him on the sidelines.

"Mmm," came the reply.

"Because, you know, I could have had that. Probably would have taken it back for six."

Skeeter didn't bother to respond.

"Nice hands, Covington," called a voice from the stands.

"Shut up! He's a hero," yelled out a defender of his, who then began a chant of "Riley! Riley!"

Riley turned around to give a little wave to the fan, who, it turned out, was holding a large sign that read:

New York
Believes
Covington

The network will love that one, he chuckled to himself, giving the fan a thumbs-up.

This was how most of the game had gone. As Riley and Skeeter wandered the sidelines, people would yell out well-wishes and words of support. But then someone would break through with some negative comment. *(They can't help themselves; this is New York!)* Immediately that person would get verbally jumped on by the people around, and some new chant would break out—"Riley! Riley!" or "Covington! Covington!" or "R . . . I . . . L-E-Y! Riley's New York's kind of guy!"

Every now and then as they slowly wandered back and forth, some fans would start something inappropriate, thinking they were expressing Riley's beliefs—chants like "Islam sucks! Islam sucks!" or "Bomb Iran! Bomb Iran!" When those started, Riley quickly glared up into the crowd and motioned for them to cut it.

I can live with this. At least the believers seem to outnumber the unbelievers. It's too bad they're the ones who are wrong.

Gooey had done a spectacular job with Operation Keep the Lie Alive even after Riley had toned him down a bit. Initially Gooey had done a complete analysis on the sound recording, showing every edit and misplaced word—even using background noise to demonstrate the manufactured chronology of Whitney's tape. He was all prepared to release that to the press when Riley stopped him. He knew if that analysis were released, Whitney's career would be ruined forever. So, although Scott and Khadi both gave it an enthusiastic go-ahead, Riley put on the kibosh.

Grumpily, Gooey had gone back to his corner of the RoU to plot some alternative evil. Six hours later, he emerged with Plan B—a little scheme that involved some fancy computer work and a "leak" to some inquiring minds. Riley was home at the time, but after hearing Khadi's endorsement, he gave it the go-ahead.

Two days later, in supermarkets across the nation, shoppers waiting in line were picking up copies of the *National Enquirer* and reading the headline, "Shocking Riley Covington Photos!" Immediately below, covering most of the page, was a slightly blurry close-up taken in an emergency room. The patient's face, clearly seen under the oxygen mask, was Riley's. Below was written, "Warning, Graphic Photos Inside!"

On page 6 was a series of three more pictures. One was a wide shot showing the medical team frantically working on Riley. The second showed his full left side. His face was visible, as were the stab wounds, and his left hip with a red circle on it. Written next to the circle were the words, "Scar from bullet wound Covington received while serving with the Air Force Special Ops in Afghanistan." The third snapshot was a close-up of the stab wounds—ragged, bruised, and bleeding.

Soon the ER photos were on every newscast in the country—most having the decency to pixilate the wounds. Riley was amazed when he first saw the pictures. If he weren't so sure that he had never actually been stabbed, he would have sworn that was him lying on the operating table.

A firestorm of debate soon arose as to who was telling the truth. The National Rifle Association's press release sided with Riley, while the National Organization for Women's release threw their support behind Whitney. Sean Hannity touted Riley as a Great American. Bill O'Reilly labeled Whitney a Pinhead. The ladies on *The View* proclaimed Whitney Walker Day. Keith Olbermann blamed the whole situation on the Republicans.

Yesterday Riley had received a message on his cell phone. After entering his password, he was surprised to hear Whitney's voice.

"It's me. I . . . I never wanted it to turn out this way. I want you to know that if there was any way to take it all back, I would. I betrayed all my journalistic principles—all my integrity, all the things I swore up and down that I held so dear.

"I don't know what happened. I was just so . . . I still think I'm right, Riley. I really do believe that the whole thing was a setup. But what I did was wrong.

"You may be happy to know that I'm probably going to be let go from ESPN tomorrow—at least that's what the rumors are. . . . This whole thing is just so messed up—so . . . wrong! You really disappointed me, Riley. I thought . . . I don't know what I thought. I don't even know why I called. I guess I just wanted to tell you that I wish I hadn't done it. I know there was a reason why you did what you did, and whatever that reason is, I just hope you come out of it safe.

"Now, I'm going to ask you one more favor—the last one I'll ever ask.

Please don't let anyone else hear this message. I know you could put the final nail in my career's coffin, but . . . but I don't think you will. I really wish things had turned out differently."

When Whitney's voice ended, Riley looked up at the ceiling before pressing 7, deleting the message. *What a shame. One bad play and you blow your career,* he had thought. *Whitney was right; the whole thing is just so messed up.*

Apparently the only ones who were really happy about the attack debate were the owners of the *National Enquirer,* who sold five times their normal circulation run. And Rick Bellefeuille, too, who loved the publicity so much that he even put a link to the photos on the Warriors Web page.

Now here Riley was on the sidelines, watching a team he had never wanted to be part of, not playing because of a faked injury, being cheered on by fans whose very loyalty was based on a deception. *On top of that, this whole double life is going to make me insane! How am I supposed to go from almost getting blown up on a container ship one day to pretending to still be a football player a few days later, then back to shooting up bad guys again when the game is done? It's like stepping from one parallel universe to another and back again.*

Suddenly, a chant started behind him: "Walker was right! Walker was right!" This was countered by a second chant describing Whitney in a far less favorable light. Riley spun in time to see one fan dump his beer on the head of another. The second guy wheeled around and decked the first. Soon an all-out brawl was on, with the spouses and friends jumping in. Eventually security arrived and escorted about ten people out.

Riley turned around and faced the field.

"Unbelievable," he muttered to Skeeter as he scratched at the tape on his left side. Another of Scott's brilliant ideas was to tape a slightly curved metal splint onto Riley, then put his left arm in a sling. That way his slightly bent body would add to the charade of his pain and would keep him from doing anything dumb—like trying to catch an errant pass. This would have been fine with Riley, except his skin was having some sort of allergic reaction to the splint, and the itching was driving him crazy.

How did I end up here? he asked himself again. Part of what made standing on the Warriors' sidelines so difficult tonight of all nights was the fact that somewhere not too far from him, the Colorado Mustangs were on a bus on their way to the airport.

For many years, the New York Liberty and the New York Dragons had shared a stadium. This season, that changed. Earlier this afternoon, the New York Dragons had opened the Dell Dome, located only five miles from their old playing field. NBC had taken the opportunity to celebrate the new state-of-the-art facility by scheduling a New York double-header of Sunday night PFL football: for the first time in history, two professional football games played in two separate New York stadiums all on one big night! Both games were sold out, with fans desperate to show their loyalty to one team or the other. Riley had watched the scoreboard during pregame and was happy to see that the Mustangs had disappointed the Dragon fans by handing the PFL Cup runners-up a 42–17 rout.

So instead of being with the football team I love, or even working with the CTD team doing something meaningful like trying to find the EMPs, I'm here wasting time with a team I don't even like, playing for an owner that I absolutely despise, being heckled by fans who—

Riley's thoughts were interrupted when every light in the stadium went black.

CHAPTER

FORTY-EIGHT

SUNDAY, SEPTEMBER 13, 9:15 P.M. EDT
NEW YORK, NEW YORK

A roar came from the back of the bus, followed by Gorkowski's booming voice, already slipping into a slight slur. "Ten high? How do you take a pot with a ten high?"

"The best way possible," replied defensive end Donovan Williams, the only player on the team with a big enough body and a bad enough attitude to face Gorkowski head-on. "I took it from an idiot who tried to bluff with a nine high!"

The bus roared again, almost drowning out Gorkowski's curses and vows to win his money back.

At the end of last season, the PFL had banned alcohol from all postgame activities and team functions. Too many players were getting picked up driving drunk or crashing their Ferraris into trees. But, not to let something as silly as rules get in the way of their good times, a few players usually smuggled at least four or five flasks onto the bus after each game. Keith Simmons thought Gorkowski sounded like he may have kept a whole one to himself.

Yeah, and who are you to knock them? Last year, you would have been the loudest, drunkest one of the bunch! A lot had changed in Keith since the end of the previous season.

The wound he had received during the attack on Platte River Stadium was the catalyst. His thigh had healed quickly enough, but the injury had left him with a lot of questions. *What if the shrapnel had been a couple feet higher and had hit me in the chest? If I had died that night, would my life have been worthwhile? Have I done anything that makes a difference? Would I have left anything that would last?*

As he analyzed his life, he realized that the answer was no. Sure, his family would miss him, as would some fans. Maybe he'd even make the Ring of Fame, and when some kid asked his dad who that guy was, the dad would have some exciting story to tell. But beyond that, after a somewhat-tearful tribute to him by the Colorado Mustangs, he would soon be forgotten.

Then one night, while venting about the purposelessness of life over at his sister's house, she had suggested that he meet with her pastor, Bishop Ezekiel Jenkins. At first Keith had balked at the idea. He got enough of the religion stuff from Riley Covington, thank you very much! But after an hour of arguing with himself, he had finally agreed.

The next day, he was in Bishop Jenkins's little, old-book-smelling office while the bishop told Keith all about hope and faith and love. Keith suddenly realized that he was putting all his life's eggs into his own basket, accepting all the love he could get but never really knowing how to give love back. The bishop walked him through the example that Jesus gave—total sacrifice, total living for others, total love—then reminded him of the legacy that one man could leave.

In that moment, things became clear to Keith. His life felt purposeless because he was trying to be his own purpose. If he wanted his life to mean anything, it had to become about others, not himself. Never before would a thought like that have held any appeal to him, but that day in that office he knew it was the life he wanted.

Keith shared his epiphany with the bishop, and before he knew it, he was on his knees on the threadbare carpet, giving himself to

Christ. Since that time, his life had seemed to consist of one mistake after another, but in his weekly meetings with the bishop, he was reassured of God's constant love and unending forgiveness.

He also began meeting with Riley, who told him to go easier on himself—God didn't expect perfection, he said; that's why He so readily promised forgiveness. The Christian life was a never-ending process of growing and learning.

Riley helped Keith learn how to be a Christian in an environment like professional football—not always an easy task. There were so many ways to stumble—so many opportunities to do the wrong thing. He struggled with holding on to the guilt when he blew it rather than accepting God's forgiveness and forgiving himself. Ultimately, for him it was much easier to look back and dwell on all his failures, not the least of which was that stupid hazing of Zerin Khan. *Which reminds me . . .*

"Hey, Z," Keith said to Afshin, who was sitting across the aisle from him, "what do you think happened to Zerin? In all my years of playing, I can't remember one time when a guy simply didn't show up for an away game. I've seen guys late who end up having to pay their own way. But just not showing up? Never."

Afshin, who like many others on the bus was checking out the game summary sheet—a paper that was distributed to all the media with each player's stats—put the document down. "I know, and especially with it being his first regular-season game. I mean, this was one of the most amazing experiences of my life! I've always dreamed of playing in the PFL, and here I was tonight actually doing it!"

"Yeah, I remember the feeling," Keith said.

"You can? Really? Because that's a long ways back. Maybe you just remember it because you've seen it in black-and-white highlight reels," Afshin gibed.

"Watch it, Rook."

Afshin shrugged his shoulders. "I can't imagine what happened. Zerin doesn't seem like the kind of guy to get cold feet. Think about it—on top of it being his first game, it was also the first game in the Dell Dome. This was history, man! It's just weird."

Both men leaned back into their seats, each lost in his own thoughts.

Looking out the window, Keith said, "So what do you think about this traffic? It's 9:00 at night, and we're still bumper to bumper."

Afshin took a peek, then immediately returned to the game summary. "That's why I live in Denver."

"No, you live in Denver because the Mustangs had a need at linebacker, and you just happened to still be on the board when their turn came."

Without looking up, Afshin said, "Nah, I think my being in Denver is more than just luck or fate. If you had seen my star chart for that day, you would have recognized that Jupiter had just moved into my seventh house, which, as we all know, is a very auspicious cosmological PFL draft event."

"Yeah, keep talking like that and I'll knock your Jupiter out of that house and into the next galaxy over."

Afshin looked at Keith and grinned.

"Hey, how you guys doing?" asked team doctor Ted Bonham.

"I'm cool," said Afshin, who then turned his gaze on Keith.

"You know, Bones, I'm actually doing all right, too," Keith answered.

Bonham was visibly surprised. On the bus ride to the airport and while on the plane, Bonham made regular rounds passing out Vicodin, Percocet, Valium, and any other legal drug a player might need—or want. The last few seasons, Keith had found himself anxiously anticipating Bones's walking pharmacy rounds and was always ready with real or made-up aches and pains that required an immediate dose of Percocet, plus a few extra doses to last him through the next couple days.

Keith had confessed his growing dependence on the pills to Riley and Afshin, who both had promised to hold him accountable to his commitment to walk away from them. Iron sharpening iron, Riley had called it. *Good phrase! Saying no to Bones is like having Chef Bobby Flay slap me back and forth across the sharpening steel twenty or thirty times.*

"You sure?" Bonham asked.

"Yeah, and beat it before I change my mind," Keith said grumpily.

After he moved to the next row, Afshin said, "Who's better than you?"

"Yeah, that did feel pretty good," Keith said with a smile. "Percocet? We don't need no stinkin' Percocet!"

"Hey, Simms," came Gorkowski's voice. "Get back here! All these guys are cleaning me out, and I need someone I can win some money from quick!"

"Yeah, right! I'll own your truck before we get to the airport," Keith yelled back as he stood up. "Hey, Z, you want to come back?"

"Nah, I think I'll just hang out here and relish my two sacks and six tackles, which—just checking the sheet here—would be about two sacks and one tackle more than—who was that again?—oh yeah, you."

"Yeah, gloat if you want. But if they weren't double-teaming me, you wouldn't have had those clear paths."

"If *ifs* and *buts* were candy and nuts, we'd all have a Merry Christmas, my friend."

Keith laughed, then stopped and said, "You know, I don't even know what that means. But just in case . . ." He flicked Afshin just above his right ear.

"Ow," Afshin said as Keith retreated to the back of the bus. "Yeah, you better run away!"

Keith wedged himself past Bones, who was still making his rounds.

"Here he comes," Gorkowski called out. "Simms, I'm gonna make you my—what's going on?"

The inside of the bus had abruptly gone completely dark—the inside lights extinguished, the brightness of the city gone. The bus itself, which had been traveling no more than ten miles per hour, drifted to the right, then came to a stop against a small pickup truck.

"Hey, bus driver, you have a seizure or something?" Gorkowski called out, causing nervous laughter among some of his more loyal followers.

"Hang on, Snap, the dark isn't just in here! Look outside! Everything is dark. It's a total blackout," Travis Marshall observed.

A thought suddenly occurred to Keith. He fished his BlackBerry out of his pocket and flipped it open. No light. He pressed the power button, but nothing happened.

"This isn't an ordinary blackout," he called back to where he had heard Marshall's voice as he quickly made his way toward the front. "Riley warned me about this!"

He ran into Bonham, knocking him down and then walking over him, all the while yelling, "Everyone, stay in your seats! Stay in your seats!" Although he wasn't sure how that would help anything, he couldn't think of anything else to say.

"Open the door," he commanded the bus driver. "I've got to find Coach—"

"What is that?" Danie Colson yelled out of the black.

A loud *shooshing* noise passed over the bus. Keith looked out the windshield to see a huge shadow, darker than the night, rapidly dropping to earth. Then, no more than three hundred yards away, an enormous fireball erupted. The bus rocked as the wave of heat blasted its side. The sound was deafening.

Once it was safe to look out the windows again, Keith could see three more fireballs rising in the distance with new ones happening in a seemingly never-ending succession.

"We're under attack," Colson called out. "They're bombing us."

"Yeah, we're under attack, all right," Keith loudly answered him, instantly catching everyone else's ear. "But they're not bombing us. It's way worse than that."

CHAPTER FORTY-NINE

SUNDAY, SEPTEMBER 13, 9:15 P.M. EDT
NEW YORK, NEW YORK

Almost home, Jim Babylon thought. *What's that old Jefferson Airplane song? "Give me a ticket for an aeroplane. Da da da da da da fast train. Lonely days are gone; I'm a-going home. my baby just wrote me a letter."*

Well, it all fits, except for the letter, and "my baby just sent me a text message" doesn't quite have the same ring to it.

He checked his watch again. It felt like they had been on approach for hours, even though they had only been in the holding pattern for twenty minutes. *If the gates at Kennedy weren't backed up, I'd be on the ground right now—probably almost at the baggage claim. And maybe . . . just maybe . . .*

Although he had Tamara's address on a slip of paper in his pocket, he still hoped that she would surprise him at the airport. After all, her profile had emphasized the words *spontaneous* and *romantic.*

Jim had met Tamara on eHarmony three months ago. When he first signed up for the service, he had limited his searches to the Kansas City area, but after reading what seemed like hundreds of profiles and even attempting two unsuccessful meetings, he had decided to widen his parameters.

And why not? Owning his own successful business allowed him the freedom and resources to travel wherever he needed to. Besides, how many times had he said he would walk around the world to find that perfect soul mate? *At least flying is better than walking, although being stuck in a coach middle seat is only slightly the better of the two options.*

Matches from all over the country began pouring into his profile page. So many choices; so few possibilities. Just when his frustration level was approaching its highest, Tamara's profile had popped up on his list. Before he was through reading her first-level answers, he knew she was the one. That feeling was confirmed after she gave him permission to read the rest of her information.

"They always said you're just going to know," he had told her during their third multi-hour phone conversation. *"They were right."*

Now, after thirty-eight years of singleness, he was within an hour or two of finally meeting in person the woman he truly felt he was going to spend the rest of his life with. *If they'd only land this plane. "So close, so close, yet so far away,"* Jim sang to himself. *Who was that? Air Supply? No, the singer sounded too much like a man. Oh, I know, it was that duo—one tall, long-haired, blond guy and his short, curly-headed buddy. Hall & Oates! That's it.*

"Are you nervous?"

"What?" Jim responded more abruptly than he meant to.

The old woman next to him nodded toward his bouncing leg.

"Oh, that," Jim laughed, a little embarrassed. "Yeah, I guess I am. But not about the flying."

"Oh?"

"I'm about to meet a woman. I think I'm going to marry her," Jim said, wondering why he was telling this to a complete stranger. Other than a quick greeting when he had sat down next to her and a thank-you when he had moved into the aisle to allow her to get to the restroom, they hadn't said two words to each other.

"Well, it sounds like you've got things in the right order. Meet her before you marry her," the woman said with a little wink. She then turned back to the window to look at the lights of the city below.

Jim smiled. *Yep, meet, and then marry. Probably not all in the same visit, but you never—*

The jet went black. The quietness and the stillness of the air made Jim wonder if he had died. It was like suddenly being buried alive. The only sound was the wind outside.

Then a woman screamed, and several other passengers instantly followed suit. Jim gripped the armrests on either side of him.

What is this? What's happened?

He could feel that the plane was still moving, but he couldn't tell which way—up, down, nose first, tail first. It was like being suspended in a lunar capsule and hurtled through space.

He looked to his left to see if the city lights below could help him get his bearings, but the window was completely black.

When did the old lady pull the shade down? he wondered. He reached over to push it back up but felt only the smooth coolness of the window. *Where're the lights? Where's the city?*

Jim felt his breathing increasing. With the circulation stopped and people screaming all around—loudest of whom seemed to be the businessman next to him—he felt like all the air was being sucked from him.

Suddenly a cold, bony hand laid itself on his, and another placed itself on his neck, tugging him. At first he resisted. Then finally, he let himself be pulled down.

In the midst of the pandemonium, the voice of the old woman, so close he could feel the warmth of her words on his ear and smell the tea on her breath, cut through the noise. "Jesus loves you, child."

The words barely had time to register in Jim's mind, and then nothing else registered at all.

CHAPTER FIFTY

SUNDAY, SEPTEMBER 13, 9:15 P.M. EDT
NEW YORK, NEW YORK

Sarah Gallardo was exhausted. *I don't know how long I can keep this schedule up. Seven days a week—it never ends! Andy's got to get out. I didn't sign on to be a single mom. He needs to be here helping.*

But even as she pressed the elevator's button for the tenth floor, she knew she was being selfish. Her husband, Andy, was currently deployed with the Second Marine Expeditionary Brigade in Afghanistan. He was serving his country, fighting for what he believed in—what they both believed in. *Who am I to complain? I knew I was marrying a Marine. If it was good for me then, it should be good for me now.*

However, while this was true, there was one big difference between the then and the now—a difference she lifted up to her face in a little pink and brown Graco baby carrier.

"Genvieve needs her daddy, doesn't she?" Sarah said, giving her four-month-old a little tickle. Then she sighed and lowered the carrier. "She needs her mommy, too."

Once again Sarah wondered if she should just move back in with her parents. They lived twelve blocks away. Then she could quit one of her two jobs, and that would open up more of her time for her little girl. *Genvieve already spends most of her time there with her grandma anyway.*

Yet as she walked down the hall and unlocked her front door, all the reasons for keeping her own place came back to her—independence, not having to deal with her dad, building toward their future. But the chief motivation for staying away was so that she wouldn't have to hear "I told you so" from her folks.

Her parents had never liked Andy. They wanted her to marry a nice little Jewish boy who worked in a nice little Jewish company, and together they could keep a nice little Jewish home and raise nice little Jewish children. But instead of fulfilling their nice little Jewish plan, she had fallen in love with Andy Gallardo—a nice big Spanish boy who wanted to be a nice big Spanish Marine.

She placed Genvieve's carrier on the kitchen table of the small apartment and pressed the button on her answering machine. *Nada—always a disappointment and a relief.* Walking to the kitchen, she poured herself a glass of apple juice.

"Got to wet my whistle; then I'll let you wet your whistle, baby doll," she called out.

If I moved back home, it would be admitting defeat. And if there's one thing I've learned as a Marine's wife, it's never surrender.

She walked back to the tiny nook and lifted Genvieve out of her carrier. "We're going to make this work, little sweets. Only three more months, and Daddy's back. Then twenty-four months after that, and he'll have done his full four years. You'll only be two and a half then, and you won't even be able to remember life without your daddy around."

After grabbing a small towel from the baby's room, Sarah eased herself down into the glider rocker to feed Genvieve.

Then the lights went out.

Immediately Sarah's mind raced through the checks she had written ten days ago. *Yep, Con Edison was one of them,* she thought, picturing the bill.

"Hold on, sweetie," she said to Genvieve, who was wondering when dinner was going to start. Feeling her way to the window, Sarah pulled back the curtain. Outside was as black as inside.

"Well, at least I know it's not just me. Your mommy pays all her bills on time—well, most of—"

She felt something slam into the building above her. Sarah flew to the ground and felt chunks of the ceiling drop onto her. Something hit her head, and all the noise around her distorted, like somebody was playing a tape at half speed. She pushed a slab of drywall off her and rolled over to her hands and knees.

She reached for Genvieve but couldn't find her.

"Genvieve," she gasped. "Where are you, baby?"

Sarah felt along the floor, cutting her hands on the jagged debris. "Where are you, sweetie? Genvieve?"

Outside the window, something started glowing, giving Sarah just enough orange light to make out shapes around the room. Scrambling on all fours, she raced around the tiny nursery. But it wasn't the light that led her to her daughter. It was the cries.

She had never been so relieved to hear her little girl's screams. Quickly shuffling to the source of the sound, Sarah found her baby tucked neatly under the crib.

It was too dark to check Genvieve for injuries, so Sarah just scooped her into her arms and ran toward the front door. Even though she was moving fast, she still had to pick her steps carefully. Anything that had been on a wall, in a cabinet, or on a shelf was now strewn across the floor.

"It's going to be okay, baby. It's just a place. We'll get another," she said, trying to use her voice to soothe her terrified infant.

When she reached the front door, she saw the same glow that had come through the windows creeping in under the door. Quickly undoing the dead bolts, she flung the door open.

A roll of smoke poured in, and Sarah instinctively dropped to her knees. Under the smoke, she could see flames filling the hallway, which was terrifying enough. But try as she might, her mind just couldn't grasp what else she saw. Across the hall, instead of the apartment of the Kennedys, a sweet older couple who sometimes had Sarah and Genvieve over for Sunday dinner, there was nothing—some fire, some rubble, and nothing else. Sarah could see dark buildings beyond where the wall should have been. *What in the world hit the building?*

As Sarah tried to make sense of what she saw, flames began coming through her door. Sarah ran back into the living room. *What do I do? Where do I go? The fire exits are at the end of the hall, but I can't get out into the hall!*

A crash came from the nursery, and Sarah saw dust, smoke, and flames billow out from the room's doorway.

Genvieve was screaming, and Sarah was trying as hard as she could to keep her voice calm. But even she could hear her rising panic. "Don't worry, baby! Mommy'll get us out of here! I'll . . . I'll . . . Oh please, oh please, oh please!"

The roar of the fire was like a freight train running through the apartment, and the heat was nearly unbearable. Every few breaths she took sent her into coughing fits, and her eyes burned. Balancing Genvieve between one arm and her chin, Sarah snapped her contacts out of her eyes and flicked them to the ground. The world was a little blurrier, but at least her eyes could breathe.

She ran to the bathroom—dead end. She ran back to the front door to see if there was a path through the flames—nothing. She ran to the window to see if there was any help coming; there wasn't.

"Oh, baby! Oh, sweet, sweet baby! I don't know . . . I can't . . . Oh, my sweet, sweet little girl!"

We're trapped! There's no escape! We're going to burn to death in this little apartment! My sweet little baby is going to feel those flames! Please, God, no! Please, no! That's too terrible! Not my daughter! Not her perfect, innocent little face!

Then, with sudden clarity, Sarah realized what she needed to do. She put Genvieve gently down on the sofa and gave her a little tickle under the chin, then walked into the bathroom and swept a candle and a couple of magazines from the top of a tall, marble-topped table.

Despite the deafening roar of the fire, Sarah began singing to her little baby.

"Hush, little Genna, don't say a word, Mama's gonna buy you a mockingbird."

Sarah pulled the curtains back from the window that covered one wall of the living room. That window was what had sold her and Andy on this place. From it you could see for blocks to the left and to the right, and you could also people-watch the crowds ten stories below.

"And if that mockingbird won't sing, Mama's gonna buy you a diamond ring."

Grasping the base of the table, Sarah hefted it up to her shoulder, then swung it with all her might. *Slam!* The protective window glass vibrated under the blow.

"And if that diamond ring turns brass . . ."

Slam!

"Mama's gonna buy you a looking glass."

Slam!

"And if that looking glass gets broke . . ."

Slam!

Finally the window shattered. Using the table, she cleared the rest of the glass from the base of the frame.

"Mama's gonna—" Sarah collapsed to the ground, coughing, gasping for air. Slowly she pulled herself back up.

"Mama's gonna buy you a billy goat."

As Sarah picked Genvieve back up, she said in a hoarse voice, "A billy goat? What's Mama's little girl going to do with a billy goat?"

Genvieve's cries had grown fainter until now they were little more than a whimper. Holding her close with one arm, Sarah began tugging the heavy sleeper-sofa across the carpet and toward the shattered window.

"Unh!

"And if that billy goat won't pull . . .

"Unh!

"Mama's gonna buy you a cart and bull.

"Unh!

"And if that cart and bull turn over . . .

"Unh!

"Mama's gonna buy you a dog named Rover.

"Unh!"

The couch was finally below the window. Sarah looked back to the front of the apartment. Fire had engulfed the kitchen and bathroom and was creeping up the walls from the bedroom hall. On the ceiling above her, flames were spreading, and she could hear groans as the structure struggled to hold together.

"And if that dog named Rover won't bark . . ."

As Sarah stepped up onto the couch, she pressed Genvieve's cheek against her own. It had been a little bit since she had heard anything from her baby, but she still wanted her to know that Mama was there.

Sarah's voice now was so ravaged from the smoke that she could barely get the words out.

"Mama's gonna buy you a horse and cart."

Sarah stepped onto the back of the couch, then onto the windowsill. She looked down at the dark street far below, then looked back at the flames, then back down again.

"And if that horse and cart fall down . . ."

Gently she pressed her lips to Genvieve's lips.

"You'll still be the sweetest little baby in town.

"I love you, my angel baby," Sarah said. Then she stepped out.

CHAPTER FIFTY-ONE

SUNDAY, SEPTEMBER 13, 9:27 P.M. EDT
NEW YORK, NEW YORK

"Skeeter," Riley called out, "check your—"

"Dead," Skeeter interrupted, tossing the worthless iPhone to the ground.

"We're too late! I can't believe we're too late!" *All that work! All those hours! And now the worst has happened!*

The darkness was heavy, as if a wet blanket had been dropped over the stadium. It made the night seem warmer and more humid. Riley felt like the oxygen was slowly being sucked out of the stadium, and he found it difficult to catch his breath.

In the stands, there was a low murmur, with the requisite number of half-drunk fans hooting and hollering. Then a scream cut through the stadium noise: "My husband! Somebody help my husband!"

"It's already started," Riley said, knowing that if the lady's husband had a pacemaker, there was no helping him now.

With that, fear dropped on the stadium like a sudden downpour. Riley felt its chill down to the bone. More screams started as other spouses, parents, and grandparents died in their seats. The tension in the stands started to mount.

"Come on," Riley said to Skeeter, "we better get working. This is going to turn into a full-fledged panic any minute."

Riley blinked and squinted, but to no avail; his eyes wouldn't adjust to the darkness. "Skeet, I'm going to find Coach Medley. Go track down some cops and have them find the head of stadium security and the main PFL security guy. Let them know that all communication systems are dead. Tell them this is a terrorist attack like nothing they've probably planned for, and all protocols are off. Have everyone meet me at center field."

"Done," Skeeter said, disappearing into the black.

Riley reached out, taking hold of the shoulder belonging to the person nearest him, which happened to be that of the Warriors' offensive coordinator. He said, "Go get Coach Kaley and tell him to meet me in the middle of the field!"

He could tell he was about to get a protest, so he shoved the other man in the right direction to let him know that he wasn't fooling around. The coordinator ran off.

Riley knew that if there was to be any chance of things staying under control and the players and fans remaining safe, he had to get both coaches and all the police on the same page at once.

He began feeling his way toward where he knew Coach Medley would be, but before he reached him, a loud explosion boomed through the stadium. *First plane down,* Riley thought angrily. A fireball rose above the walls of the stadium, but it was difficult to estimate how far away it had landed. *If one drops in here . . . I don't even want to think about it.*

The light from the explosion helped Riley see into the stands. It was complete pandemonium. Screams echoed off the cement walls. Half the people were glued to their seats, too scared to move. The other half were crawling over them, trying to get out to their cars, unaware that if they had been manufactured any later than the mid-1980s, they were now just useless hulks of metal, fabric, and plastic.

He spotted the coach. Elbowing his way through the players, he took hold of Coach Medley.

"Riley, what—"

"Coach, I need you to listen to every word I say and do everything that I ask you to do. Do you understand?"

Riley's tone, and the fact that his face was inches away from the coach's, must have let Medley know that he wasn't joking. The coach just nodded his head.

"Good. What's happening here is part of a terrorist attack. It's called an EMP, and it has destroyed everything electronic, from cars to phones to the parts needed to keep those planes in the sky." Another explosion, farther off, drifted across the air as if to emphasize Riley's point. "I'll explain more in a few minutes, but right now I need you to get to midfield and wait for me there. Understood?"

"Understood," Medley responded. Riley released him, and the coach ran off.

As the fireball faded away, darkness returned—heavier now after the temporary brightness. For a moment Riley stood where he was, listening to the screaming and movement surrounding him.

The glow from the distant flames provided just enough light for Riley's eyes to begin to adjust to the darkness. He looked into the stands again and saw his worst fears realized. People were panicking.

Family clusters were scattered throughout the stadium, parents holding on to their kids, reassuring them even though they had no idea what to do next. *They're the lucky ones! What about all the fathers here who won't see their kids for weeks? or the parents who left their kids with babysitters? How long until they can be reassured that their kids are all right?*

An audible snap followed by a scream caught Riley's attention. People were starting to jump down onto the field, and bones were breaking as they landed on the hard track below.

"Where are the security guys?" he said to himself.

Finally, from under the stands, he saw two light beams rapidly making their way toward midfield. *That's right! I forgot about the flashlights working—just batteries and a bulb. That's going to be huge,* he thought, running toward the lights with Skeeter alongside.

"Hey, Glen," he said to Glen Smith, head of PFL security for the game.

"Hey, Riley. What's going on?"

"There's been an EMP threat extant. Looks like they carried it out."

"Riley? I'm Mike Benson, head of stadium security. What's an EMP?"

"Tell you in a minute. Let's meet up with the coaches so that we can all get on the same page."

They fought their way through the growing insanity on the field to where Coach Medley and Coach Kaley were waiting for them. Both were surrounded by assistant coaches, and a number of players were leaning in, ready to hear over the surrounding din. *Not ideal for controlling the flow of information, but it'll have to do.*

"Okay, here's what you need to know about what's happened. We are the victims of a terrorist attack. The weapon they used is called an electromagnetic pulse bomb. Based on what I know of the threat, I'm guessing—hoping—that the effects are localized."

"Define *localized,*" Benson said.

"It will depend—*oof,*" Riley said as a man ran into him. Behind him was a woman who appeared to be his wife. In her arms, she carried a toddler wearing a tiny number 50 Warriors jersey.

"Sorry . . . wait, you're Riley Covington! What's going on? Do you know?"

Skeeter moved to escort the man out of the conclave, but Riley stopped him.

"Listen . . . ," Riley said.

"Gregg. Gregg Daniels."

"Listen, Gregg, what's happened is not good. If you want, you're welcome to stand over there and get the full rundown. But you've got to let me talk to these guys right now. Okay?"

"Sure, Riley," Daniels said, moving to the edge of the group.

"Now, *localized* will depend on the type of weapon, the size of the weapon, and the height of the detonation. If it went off over New York City, then we could be talking New Jersey, eastern Pennsylvania, southeastern New York, Connecticut, Rhode Island, and Massachusetts."

"That's *localized*?" Coach Kaley asked.

"Trust me, if that's all it is, we should feel blessed."

"So how long until we get the lights back on?" Benson asked.

"We won't," Riley answered.

"What?"

"Just give me a chance to explain; then you'll understand what's going on here," Riley said. "Actually, excuse me a moment."

Riley pulled his arm out of the sling and tossed it to the ground. Then he lifted his shirt over his head, dug at the tape attached to his side until he got a corner up, then yanked the whole rigging off his skin. Although the pain felt like he had just gotten a hot wax treatment, it was worth it as he scratched and dug into the rash the metal bar had left him with.

There were a number of gasps from the people surrounding the little enclave, and some of them called out angrily.

"You *were* faking!"

"See, I told you!"

"There's your hero for you!"

"Sorry, Coach," Riley said to Medley, gesturing toward the darkness. "I was trying to stop this from happening."

"Obviously, you failed," Medley replied with a scowl.

"Obviously." *Get over it! I don't have time to deal with anyone's hurt feelings or disappointments.*

"So why should we believe anything you're saying now?" one of the Liberty assistant coaches asked.

Riley wheeled on him. "Because you don't have a choice! Think what you want about me. Right now, I don't give a flying flip! This is real! And you have no idea how bad things are going to get!"

Riley squinted to see the expressions on the faces surrounding him. *These guys are scared and angry and are looking for a scapegoat. Let them hate you, as long as they listen to you and do what you tell them to.*

"Go on, Riley," Glen Smith said.

Riley nodded to him. The noise of panic surrounding him had grown in the past few minutes, and he increased his volume. "Okay, what the EMP does is to basically fry everything electronic. That's why your cell phones don't work. Everything from as small as digital watches to electrical grids are gone." In the dark, Riley could make out a few people checking their wrists, confirming his words. "And these things are not just gone temporarily; they're gone for good."

"What? How?" Kaley asked.

"I don't have time to get into how right now. There will plenty of time for that later. Suffice it to say, that's what's happened."

"If it's just a giant power outage, then what are the bombs going off? It sounds like World War III out there," challenged Liberty running back Matt Tayse.

"They aren't bombs. They're planes," Riley said.

"Planes? You've got to be . . . Those are . . . ?" Even in the darkness, Riley could see the look of horror on Tayse's face. Exclamations of shock and grief from the crowd copied Tayse's expression.

"I told you—*everything* electronic. So you got big buckets of technology like airplanes, and tiny little electrical gadgets that help keep people alive. Already there are probably a few dozen, if not a hundred, dead in the stands whose pacemakers quit on them. And if you think it's bad now, realize that it's going to get worse in the days ahead as food and safe water get scarce. Also, as supplies of medicines like insulin run out."

On hearing those words, a woman turned to her husband and began sobbing. *Lord, help them!* Riley prayed.

"But won't the governor call in the National Guard?" one anonymous listener called out.

"You aren't grasping the scope of this! There are millions of people in the affected area. Everyone is going to need to be evacuated. Think about the logistics of that! New York City is going to be unusable for months, if not years to come. And everyone—*everyone*—is going to need to get out! We are all, in a sense, refugees.

"Those who end up in refugee camps will be the lucky ones, because the death toll for this is going to be big. The dead passengers from the plane crashes and the people they killed on the ground are just the beginning.

"The fires from those crashes are going to sweep through blocks and blocks because the fire department won't be able to get their trucks out to do anything to stop it. The injured will die because the hospitals will have no equipment or power—and their backup generators were taken out by the blast as well.

"Anarchy is going to reign in the streets, and the police will be powerless to stop it with their mobility gone and their communications shot. Looting will be in full force later tonight, and even more so tomorrow. And people you'd never expect will be doing the looting. Once ordinary citizens realize that this is real and long-term, they'll want to stock up on food and water. People will take and hoard what they can. Two days from now, every store in the city will be cleared out."

"Wait, two days from now?" Coach Medley said. "How long—"

"Get it through your heads! This is for the long haul! On the positive side, we're in a fairly good location here. The parking lots will keep us safe from the fires. There is a stock of food and drink that, if rationed, will hopefully last until the government is able to make food drops. And this will be a natural place for a food drop because of the number of people in it.

"The other positive is that this is a natural place to defend."

"Defend? Against who?" Benson asked.

"If this thing is more widespread than I think, we won't be able to expect any government help. Soon people will be demanding to get in because they'll think there's food in here, but we'll have to balance compassion with what few supplies we actually have on hand. If you turn people away, eventually they will organize and come back to take what you aren't willing to give. At that point, you have to be prepared to defend yourself."

"Cut it out, Covington! You're taking this too far! Armed bands raiding stadiums to steal food? This is America," Tayse yelled.

"Tayse, shut up," Coach Kaley said. "Go ahead, Riley."

"You're right on, Matt! This *is* America—the most technologically advanced nation in the world! Which is why this is going to hit us so hard! We don't know how to survive without a McDonald's and our local Walmart.

"But, also because this is America, we will survive this! We will find a way through, because that's what Americans do! Now, I've got no reason to exaggerate this. I'm just trying to prepare you for what's coming. Believe me or don't. I'm going to say my piece, then let you do with it what you will!"

"So what do we do?" Gregg Daniels asked from outside the main circle.

"Okay, here are my suggestions. Benson, first thing is you've got to get runners going to gather up your forces and let them know what the scoop is. Tell them to patrol the underside of the stadium and the bathrooms. As you know, there already is a criminal element here that will try to take advantage of the situation. Have your people use their flashlights sparingly to save batteries, and make sure they always travel in pairs.

"Second, you need to get guards on the food and water. It's going to have to be rationed out. When you do start rationing them, obviously it's perishables first, then the rest. People don't need buns with their hot dogs—those buns could be a separate meal later on. Also, really control the alcohol. You won't want a bunch of drunks running around causing havoc.

"Third, people are leaving the stadium right now. When they learn that their cars won't start, most will be coming back in. Let them for now. In the days ahead, people will get antsy and want to try to get home. Encourage them to stay, but don't stop them from leaving. As a group, you're going to have to decide who you will let in and who you will turn away. Harsh as it is, you have to remember that every person you let through those gates is another mouth to feed.

"I wanted you four here because the coaches are looked to as leaders, and the security chiefs have the best tactical understanding of this stadium and of security protocols in general. You need to establish an ad hoc leadership structure right now and then stick to it. The decisions you make will affect the lives of all these people around you."

Scanning the shadowy faces around him—some set strong to the challenge, others just terrified—Riley said, "Listen, I know you didn't ask for this, but this is your new reality. You're in the jungle now, and it's all about survival."

CHAPTER FIFTY-TWO

SUNDAY, SEPTEMBER 13, 9:27 P.M. EDT
NEW YORK, NEW YORK

"What do you mean, 'it's worse'?" Danie Colson yelled.

"I'll come back later to talk. Afshin, fill them in on what Pach told us about EMPs," Keith Simmons said, finding his friend in the glow of the flames.

"You sure this is an EMP?" Afshin asked.

"Look around, Rook," Keith said. "You tell me!"

Turning to the bus driver, he said, "Open the door!"

"It won't open," the driver replied, pressing the button over and over.

No, of course it wouldn't, Keith thought, driving the door open with his shoulder.

His was the third of a five-bus convoy. As he ran past the second bus, he saw people all around him getting out of their cars and looking toward where the plane had gone down. He glanced over, and what he saw sent chills down his spine. The plane had crashed through two multistory buildings. Flaming debris was strewn down a two-block stretch. The buildings the plane had hit were both on fire, and Keith knew it wouldn't be long before the flames spread to neighboring structures.

He arrived at the first bus just as the door flew open with running back coach Chris Winkler stumbling through it. Keith caught him and stood him up straight.

"You okay, Coach Wink?"

"Yeah, thanks."

Behind Winkler stepped defensive coordinator Jeremiah Weymouth, then Coach Burton. Burton spotted Keith.

"What are you doing up here? Get back on—"

"Coach, let me tell you what's going on," Keith said.

"We're under some sort of attack. I don't need some linebacker telling me that. Now get back—"

"Coach, would you shut up and listen to me?" Keith interrupted, causing both Winkler and Weymouth to turn around. Nobody told Coach Burton to shut up, not even if the world was coming to an end, which, looking around, appeared to be the case.

Keith continued, "Riley Covington warned me about this. He told me what all this is."

At Riley's name, the flush on Burton's face began to fade a bit, and he said, "I'm listening."

Keith proceeded to tell the three coaches all that Riley had shared with him about EMPs—the effects of a localized attack versus a national attack, the immediate issues and the future problems, and the coming dangers and lawlessness. By the time he was done, all the other coaches had stepped off and were crowded around, as were a number of people from the surrounding cars. Burton was leaning up against the bus. His face looked like it had aged fifteen years.

"So what do we do about it?" Burton asked quietly.

"Stay put for now. Tomorrow some of us can go out to try to get some food and water. If it's localized, then eventually some government agency will show up with instructions for us."

"And if it's not?"

"I don't know, Coach," Keith admitted. "I honestly don't know."

"Okay," Burton finally said, "I want every coach to get with his position players. You're their babysitters, and I'm holding you responsible for keeping them from wandering off. Simmons, I want you on each of those buses telling everyone what you've told me. Make sure they all know the dangers of going down into the neighborhoods.

Even if they've grown up in New York, let them know this isn't the same city anymore. I don't want to hear that we've lost anyone due to stupid curiosity, and this isn't a time for heroes. They can get out of the bus to stretch their legs, but no more. Am I understood?"

"Yes, sir," came the group's reply. The men split up, and Keith walked onto the first bus. The low, flickering lighting from the burning buildings reminded him of camping with his uncle and cousins, sitting around a dying fire telling scary stories. The whole effect was utterly surreal.

Keith spent the next hour informing the rest of the team of what had happened. Then he and Afshin held an informal Q&A from the back of a Ford pickup that was parked next to bus two. About half the team listened in—some out of curiosity, some out of fear, and some out of sheer boredom since every last iPod and BlackBerry was dead. A good hundred people from the surrounding cars also crowded around.

Their voices easily carried to the group. The eerie silence was broken only by the distant screams of the injured and the low roar of the burning buildings. The black smoke was thick, and Keith coughed often as he spoke.

Some people wanted to organize parties to go assist those hurt down below until help arrived. Keith had to again explain that help was *not* coming. It had no way to get there, and there would be no functioning lifesaving equipment even if help did arrive. Still, some people left anyway. While Keith respected them for their compassion—deep down, he really wanted to go with them—he knew his place was here. His job was not to help the hopeless but to guide those who could still survive this.

Eventually his audience broke up. Most returned to their buses or cars. A few stayed behind and prayed for a while with Keith and Afshin. Soon even that ended. Once they were the only two left, they too headed back to the bus.

The complete silence inside was a welcome relief from the sounds of despair and agony from the dying and the families of the dead. Most of the guys were sleeping. The ones who were awake gave Keith and Afshin a nod as they passed.

Keith dropped onto his seat, exhausted. A few players who had not bothered to go out to the Q&A had more questions for him, but he waved them off.

"Sorry—you had your chance. Ask me tomorrow," he said, and they wandered away disappointed.

One player, though, stuck around. John Clark, a young defensive back, said, "I've got a family, man. When am I going to see my wife and my kids again?"

"I don't know, John," Keith replied sadly. "I don't know how long we're going to be here or how we're going to get out."

"But my littlest is ready to take her first steps. I can't—I gotta get home, Keith!"

"I hear you. I just don't know what to tell you. I'm sorry, man."

"I gotta get home to my family. . . . I just gotta get home . . . ," Clark muttered as he slowly walked to his seat.

Keith closed his eyes and tried to shut everything out. Part of him knew he should pray, but he just couldn't bring himself to even think about what was going on outside. *What I need now is sleep. Everything will be clearer after some good shut-eye.*

He spent the night drifting in and out of awareness, without ever completely falling asleep. When morning came—and with it the reality of his new world—Keith wanted nothing more than to just keep his eyes shut and never have to open them again.

CHAPTER

FIFTY-THREE

MONDAY, SEPTEMBER 14, 1:45 A.M. EDT
NEW YORK, NEW YORK

The hours flew by as Riley, Coach Medley, Coach Kaley, Glen Smith, and Mike Benson faced one challenge after another. Riley had suggested that one of the first things they needed to do was set up facilities for the dead and injured.

As a result, one corner of the field was cordoned off as an open-air emergency room of sorts. The stadium EMTs, as well as the training staff from both teams, were enlisted to address the many medical needs. They set broken bones from people getting trampled or jumping down to the field. They dispensed Valium and other medications for those having panic attacks. They frantically worked down a seemingly endless line, dealing with any and every injury from cuts and gashes to heart attacks.

When the patient list became too great, some of the players had been sent through the masses of people to draft any doctors or nurses on hand. They struck it rich when they found Dr. Randy Robinson, an internationally known oral and maxillofacial surgeon at NewYork-Presbyterian Hospital. He was asked to oversee the medical efforts and soon had shaped things into a well-staffed and well-organized, if not well-equipped, infirmary.

Sadly, there was only so much the medical

team could do in some cases; a temporary morgue was created in the showers of the visitors' locker room. Initially, Dr. Robinson had wanted to locate the morgue in one of the large refrigerators because of the vacuum seal of the doors, but Riley had lobbied to convince him otherwise. The longer they could keep those big doors closed, the longer the food inside would keep. Soon enough, the refrigerators would start emptying out, and they could be used for other purposes.

Another issue the leadership team faced was security. There had been a number of near disasters as people lit fires in garbage cans for warmth and light. Unfortunately, fire and plastic didn't play well together.

There had also been several attempted assaults on women who had gone into the dark concourses of the stadium to use the restroom. As a result, Mike Benson designated members of his stadium security to act as escorts for those who didn't have anyone to accompany them. Word of these escorts was sent around using the players.

At first Riley had hesitated to enlist the players as "town criers" of sorts, fearful of their safety in the crowds. But Coach Medley, whose idea it had been, won out. And looking back now, Riley was forced to admit that Coach had been spot-on.

The stadium's sections were divided and assigned to different players. The plan was that whenever some new information or rule had to be disseminated, the players would head to their sections to let their people know, then come back to the field to await their next mission. The first time they went out, the players, with their size and well-known faces, immediately drew the attention and respect of those they had to communicate with, and they quickly established a rapport. Soon the players felt a responsibility for *their* people, and the people appreciated the stability and consistency of seeing *their* player.

Brilliant move, Riley thought as the players were sent out to look for volunteers who would help with food preparation the next morning. As he watched them go, he scanned the stands. They were about half-full, with the other half either having left or moved down onto the field. There were surprisingly few loners or small clusters in the stands. Most people had migrated into larger groups with families bonding with other families and opening their arms to those who looked like they were on their own.

That's the American spirit! That's why no matter what they throw at us, they will not beat us!

Riley stopped his perusal of the stands short of the infirmary. The torches that surrounded that part of the stadium were killers to his night vision, so he mostly tried to keep his back to that part of the field.

Yelling on his right caught his attention. As he turned to see what it was, Skeeter appeared next to him. Skeeter had been talking with Glen Smith from PFL security, but anytime something unusual took place—or something more unusual than what was already taking place in this altered universe they were living in—Riley could expect to see him right by his side.

"Hey, Skeet, what do you think it is?" Riley asked, resisting the urge to go over and get involved. He was trying to interject himself in fewer and fewer things, preparing for what he knew was coming soon—an event that he and Skeeter had kept from everyone else in leadership.

"Security doing their jobs," Skeeter answered.

"Yeah, you're probably right."

From one of the tunnels came two NYPD officers, one female and one male, leading a man wearing a torn shirt and handcuffs. His face was bloody, and he was noticeably limping. The way he was cursing made it very clear that he wasn't happy with his present situation. Following behind the threesome was a woman holding a cloth against her hand.

While Riley waited to learn what was going on, something big and white drifted onto his nose. He quickly brushed it away, then looked at his fingers. A grayish-white, powdery smear was left on his hand. *Ash,* he thought, as he saw other flakes begin to drift to the ground like a late-summer snow. The smell of smoke had been strong for a number of hours, but this was the first time that ash had begun to fall.

Glen Smith and Mike Benson walked up next to Riley and Skeeter, brushing the powder from their clothing.

"This should be interesting," Smith said as he watched the group approach.

When they had reached midfield, Benson said to the handcuffed man, "Hey, lower your voice; we got families around here trying to sleep!"

The man spit blood onto the grass. "You think I care about these families? You can take these families and go—"

Riley elbowed Skeeter, who took the man by his hair and then, putting his face inches away, hissed, "The man said to shut up!"

He shut up.

"Thank you, Mr. Dawkins," Benson said. "Now, in a calm, quiet voice, tell me your name and what happened."

"My name is James Crane! And that woman came on to me," the man yelled. "She—"

Skeeter cleared his throat, gesturing for the man to lower his voice.

"She came up to me when I was looking for the bathrooms," the man whispered. "She propositioned me, and when I told her I was a happily married family man, she went all crazy on me. Look at my face!"

"Hmm, I can see why she'd come on to you; you seem quite the catch." Benson motioned for the woman to step forward. "Mr. Crane, I'd like to introduce you to Officer Linette Miller." Crane audibly groaned when he heard her name. Benson continued. "Officer Miller, did you make advances toward this man, then beat him when he turned a blind eye to your amorous intentions?"

"I seem to remember the events differently," Miller replied.

"I thought you might. Take him to the hold, write up a quick incident report, and get back into the concourses. Oh, and get your hand checked out."

Miller smiled. "I'm fine, sir; it's just a little blood. Mr. Crane here has a bony face."

"Well, good work, all three of you."

After they walked away to deliver Crane to the dark cells behind the security office, Smith said, "That's three your bait gals have picked up. With the others we've picked up, we have, what, nineteen, twenty in there?"

"Twenty-two, actually," Benson said.

"You guys are going to have to determine what to do with them. You're going to want to make an example of them," Riley said.

"What are you suggesting? Stocks? Public flogging?" Benson asked sarcastically.

"Stocks actually aren't that bad an idea. Somehow you're going to have to communicate that crime or incivility of any kind will not be tolerated.

"You need to keep reminding yourselves that the old rules don't apply anymore. At some point—the sooner the better—you're going to have to declare martial law in here, because I can guarantee that it's already martial law out there. It's going to be up to you to decide where you draw the line between harshness and civility. You could be here weeks or months, and people need to understand that things from assaults to stealing food will not be tolerated. And if you don't clearly establish those crimes with their resulting punishments early on, then good luck doing it later."

A wail cut through the air from the direction of the infirmary. The four men fell silent, knowing what that meant. That brought the death total up to sixty-seven that Riley knew about.

"I'm going to try to get an hour of shut-eye," Benson said with a deep sigh. "I have a feeling I'm going to need it tomorrow."

"Good call," Smith said, stretching his back, then twisting side to side. "We're gathering at sunrise to formally establish our organizational structure, correct?"

"Yep," Riley confirmed, knowing that the chances of his being at that meeting were slim. "You guys get some sleep."

As they walked away, he couldn't help feeling some guilt. While he tried through the night to guide the team in the right direction, he always deflected their attempts to make him the leader. There was something that he was still holding back from them, a piece of information that had the potential to destroy any chance he had at personally influencing the leadership group.

That mysterious piece of information became a reality about an hour later. Skeeter was the first to hear it. By the time he found Riley, both their eyes were on the sky. Thirty seconds later, lights showed in the distant darkness—muted and shifting because of the smoke. Soon people all around were looking up, trying to find the source of the noise.

The Blackhawk helicopter finally arrived over the stadium three minutes later. By that time, everyone was awake and waving and cheering. As it hovered above, activity could be seen around its payload doors. Then a large pallet slid out and hung just below the helicopter's wheels. Slowly, it began lowering.

A space in the middle of the playing field quickly cleared out. Meanwhile, Riley went looking for Glen Smith.

When he found him, he said, "Glen, I'm taking this chopper out."

"Yeah, I kind of figured you would be," Smith said disappointedly.

"I'm sorry, man, but there were two of those EMPs sent our way. If the other one hasn't gone off yet, I've got to find it."

Smith put his hand on Riley's shoulder. "You don't have to explain anything to me. Just do me a favor."

"What's that?"

Squeezing Riley's shoulder tightly, Smith said, "When you find the person responsible for all this, put a bullet in his head."

Riley nodded. "I'll see what I can do."

A cheer went up from the crowd gathered around where the pallet had just landed; it was filled with bottled water.

Cutting through the mass of people, Riley and Skeeter ran up to the pallet just as Mike Benson was directing his people to unhitch the cables. Strapped to one corner of the flat piece of wood was what they were looking for—two vests.

After slipping the vests on, they took hold of two of the cables and connected them to metal rings mounted on their midsections. Then, giving the thumbs-up to the helicopter, they began their ascent. Riley hoped most people would be too focused on the pallet to notice the two men dangling from the chopper, though he did hear several jeers and catcalls as well as voices pleading to be taken along.

Riley couldn't bring himself to look down at those he was abandoning. He knew this was necessary, but that didn't make it any easier. He looked at Skeeter and was surprised to see tears in the big man's eyes too. Skeeter shook his head and turned back to the helicopter.

Lord, please be with these people. Bring help soon. Protect them. And please, help us to stop this from happening again!

CHAPTER FIFTY-FOUR

MONDAY, SEPTEMBER 14, 3:15 A.M. EDT
NEW YORK, NEW YORK

As Riley winched his way toward the helicopter, he had a chance to see the city for the first time. The view took his breath away. He saw at least forty fires burning across the city. Some looked small and contained; a few looked like they were consuming whole blocks of buildings.

In stark contrast, in the areas where no fires were burning, the city was black. *What must be going on down there? The waiting, the wondering, the fear of the unknown. How many beatings, rapes, and murders are taking place right now? How many parents are holding tightly to their children, afraid of the sounds they hear out in the hallways? How many storeowners are waiting with their shotguns at the ready, determined to protect what they've worked so hard to create? How long will they hold out? When will they finally realize that the power is not returning and help is not on its way?*

A foot tapped lightly on his hip. He looked over to see Skeeter swinging back and pointing over his head. Riley looked up to see the helicopter rapidly approaching.

Soon hands were grabbing his harness, pulling him on board. He was surprised at how good the sharp edge of the helicopter's payload floor felt as it rubbed across his rash. When he finally stood, he saw that the hands that had pulled him up belonged to Scott Ross and Kim Li. Gilly Posada and Carlos Guitiérrez had assisted Skeeter.

"Welcome aboard," Scott said, clapping him on the back.

Riley, overwhelmed at seeing his friends for the first time since the nightmare began, couldn't speak but just shuffled past Scott to Khadi, who was waiting for him. Khadi wrapped her arms around him and held him until Scott tapped him on the shoulder and twirled his finger to show that they were heading out.

Riley and Khadi sat down and strapped in. Scott and Skeeter sat opposite. The rest of the guys stood by the open door, solemnly watching as the devastation passed by below.

"Was it bad?" Khadi asked after adjusting a pair of headphones to fit her.

"It's bad," Riley replied. "And probably much worse outside. I mean, honestly, inside the stadium is so much better than what I'm sure is going on out in the city. But no matter how much I tried to explain things, those people have no idea what they should be expecting. I think we're all so used to the government watching over us and providing for us that the whole idea of the authorities being impotent and unable to help just doesn't compute."

Silence filled the helicopter as Riley built up the courage to voice the question that he was dying to ask but dreading hearing the answer to. Finally, taking a deep breath, he said, "So how bad is it?"

Scott nodded as if he had been expecting the question, but he still paused for a moment before answering. "Sort of a best of times, worst of times. You know—it could have been so much worse, but it's still unimaginably bad."

"What's the geographic extent?"

"Mr. Ross," the pilot's voice interrupted, "I have the president on the line."

"Thanks; patch him through." A click sounded; then Scott said, "Sir, I'm here with Riley Covington and Skeeter Dawkins, along with my recovery team, Khadi Faroughi, Kim Li, Gilly Posada, and Carlos Guitiérrez."

"Good morning to you all," came President Lloyd's voice through the headphones. "Riley, I'm glad we were able to get you and Mr. Dawkins out."

"Thank you, sir," Riley replied, trying to keep his voice calm and businesslike. He looked at Khadi with his eyebrows raised. She gave him an encouraging nod, so he said, "It's good to be out, but it was hard to leave. There are a lot of really good people down there who are in for a rough go."

The president's voice sounded quite different from the last time Riley had talked to him—more somber, more weary. "I know it. We're doing everything we can to help them out. What can you tell me about being on the ground?"

Deciding not to pull any punches, Riley said, "It's bad, sir. We had sixty-seven dead in the stadium alone, and I lost count of the injured hours ago. People are scared and confused. But as bad as it was in the stadium, from what I could see, it looked a whole lot worse in the city. Fires are shredding whole city blocks. And I would guess all but a small handful have absolutely no clue what's going on."

"I understand. With information, people can have hope. No information, no hope. We're working on that already—trying to get the facts out."

"That's good to know, sir," Riley said.

"So here's how it's going to go," the president went on. "You and Agent Ross and the rest of your team have full access to whatever information you want and whatever resources you need. Even though there are thousands of others pursuing this, your little band there seems to have a way of always showing up where the bullets are flying. Also, I have given Agent Ross my private line. You and he have 24-7 access to me.

"You and Ross were right, Riley. I won't forget that. Now good luck to you, and Godspeed."

"Thank you, sir," Riley said, not knowing if the president was still on the line to hear him. He sat there for a moment looking at the floor. Finally he lifted his head and coughed. Now that he was out of the stadium, the smell of smoke on his clothes was so strong it was starting to constrict his throat. Scott handed him a water bottle, which he drank in one pass.

"Thanks," he said, wiping his mouth with the back of his hand. "Now, you were about to tell me how big the affected area is."

"There was just the one detonation over NYC. Remember we were wondering about the DPRK having the technology for a non-nuclear EMP? Well, now you have your answer. That is the one piece of good news in this whole thing—it was a lower-altitude blast from a lower-yield bomb. The affected zone is approximately seventy miles from Manhattan in all directions. Southern New York, most of Long Island, half of New Jersey and Connecticut, and eastern Pennsylvania up to the suburbs of Philadelphia."

"All the way to Philly? So you're talking, what, 15, 20 million affected?"

Scott shook his head. "Try 25 million. It's an absolute nightmare. If you figure on the fires from the air crashes, plus the medical issues—which are only going to get worse as time progresses—plus the impending disease from unhealthy food, tainted water, and exposure to dead bodies, plus crime . . . let's say conservatively there's just a one percent casualty rate. Well, even with that lowball figure, you're still talking about 250,000 dead."

Riley couldn't speak for a time. He looked out the window. The landscape below was so dark, he had to remind himself that they weren't flying over water. *How can a quarter million dead be a conservative number? How could this have happened?*

"What's President Lloyd doing about it?"

Khadi jumped in to answer this question. "He immediately grounded all air traffic. As far as addressing the disaster, he's had FEMA activate the National Incident Management System, so you've got both public and private groups involved. Unfortunately, quite a few of the major law enforcement agencies are being distracted by the other incidents."

"Other incidents?"

"Oh—sorry, I forgot; you don't know about them," Khadi said, turning more fully toward Riley. "In the past few hours, thirteen major cities have had suicide bombings—mostly singles, but Los Angeles, Chicago, and Philadelphia have had two each. Also, there are forty-seven state and federal prisons that are experiencing major rioting. It all seems to be a coordinated effort. Obviously, all these incidents are drawing resources that would otherwise have been allocated toward New York and Newark."

Smart; very smart, Riley thought. *We're not just dealing with some Afghani cave rat.* "What's Lloyd doing about North Korea?"

Scott took this one. "Well, until we can get positive proof that the weapons are theirs, he's doing nothing. However, he is putting out word that the United States will not tolerate nations taking advantage of the situation to pursue any long-simmering imperialistic notions."

"I.e., Russia and China."

"And India and Venezuela and any number of African nations," Khadi added.

"We are getting offers of help from around the globe, particularly Western and Central Europe," Scott said. "This is the time you really learn who your friends are."

A thought occurred to Riley. "Speaking of our friends, what's happening with Israel?"

Scott shrugged. "That's obviously a big concern right now. If we're too hurt to help them, then they're truly on their own—David against the giants. Not that it's much different from the way things have been lately anyway. Lloyd's policies have already been pulling us further and further away from Israel, so they've been preparing to go it alone for a while now."

"According to my sources," Khadi jumped in, "Israel has a three-strike plan lined up to take out Iran's nuclear capabilities. One Jericho ballistic nuke to Esfahān to take out their nuclear research center and uranium conversion facility, another to Natanz to take out their uranium enrichment facility, and the third to Arāk to destroy their heavy water reactor. Three Israeli nukes and Iran's nuclear program goes almost back to square one."

Scott waved a hand as if he didn't even want to consider that possibility at the moment. "Thankfully, right now they are only posturing. They've let it be known that if anyone, particularly Iran, tries anything, they reserve the right to bomb them to hell and back."

Riley raised his eyebrows. "Well, that must have made them even more popular among our Middle Eastern friends."

"No doubt. The Iranian president is already declaring the words to be statements of war."

Riley side-armed his fist into the helicopter's shell. "I'll give you ten to one he's got a finger in this somehow."

Khadi shook her head and said, "I don't think so. This is too . . . I don't know . . . too creative for him—too out of the box. He's such a one-track Twelver that all he can think about is getting nukes so that he can drop them on Israel and America and in the ensuing destruction usher in the Mahdi."

"Okay, so if it's not Iran, then who is it—the Saudis?"

Khadi put up her hand. "I didn't say it wasn't Iran. I just don't think it's state-sponsored Iranian. It could still be a Persian terrorist organization or a Saudi group. There's got to be some oil money involved somewhere; that's the only way they could afford to buy these weapons."

"You mean someone like bin Laden?"

"Someone like him, but not him. He doesn't have the infrastructure anymore to pull something like this off. I think we're looking at a new group that is well respected and well connected. That's why we're seeing the bombings and the Wahhabist riots—and I'll guarantee you that it is the prison Wahhabis who are behind the riots."

"What about the other EMP?" Skeeter asked.

Scott looked at the floor, frustration evident in his voice. "The president has got every intelligence agency working on this—CIA, FBI, CTD, everyone—but still we haven't been able to track down the second warhead, and we have no clue as to the location of the replacement delivery device. We haven't even figured out the planned location of detonation. So, basically, we have—"

"Squat," Riley said. "Swell."

Turning back to look out the window, Riley could see the ragged edges of the affected area down below. Relief flooded through him as the Blackhawk passed from darkness into light.

"Touchdown in twenty," Scott said. "Oh, and, Riley, I got this for you."

He tossed something to Riley. When Riley looked at it, he saw it was a new cell phone.

"Got it programmed with your number. Figured you'll probably want to make some calls to your family after we land."

"Thanks," Riley said, slipping the phone into his jeans pocket. Suddenly something sparked in his mind. He grabbed hold of Khadi's arm and said, "Have you heard anything about the Mustangs? They played earlier in the evening. I've been praying they weren't in the air yet."

Khadi placed her hand on Riley's and said, "No, I figured you'd be asking about them. I checked on it, and they hadn't arrived at the airport yet. I don't know where they are, but they weren't in the air."

"Praise the Lord for that," Riley said, taking his hand back and leaning against the Blackhawk's frame. *Being stuck in the city is bad, but at least it's better than dropping from the sky.*

Somberness spread through the helicopter, and everyone was quiet for the rest of the flight. After landing, the seven agents piled into a government Suburban. Riley slept all the way to the RoU.

CHAPTER FIFTY-FIVE

MONDAY, SEPTEMBER 14, 1:30 P.M. IRDT
TEHRAN, IRAN

The car slowed as celebrants mobbed the street. Ayatollah Beheshti heard drums and tambourines all around, and dancers surrounded the car. A woman walked past the window, and Beheshti took great pleasure in seeing the elation on her face as she clapped, chanted, and ululated.

Not far away, an effigy of American president Lloyd hung from a light pole, and as Beheshti watched, a man with a salt-and-pepper beard set fire to it, hitting it with his shoe as it began to burn. In front of the burning mannequin, the red, white, and blue of the American flag was laid on the ground, and men and women waited their turn in line to walk across it.

But as Beheshti widened his gaze, he noticed that outside of this celebration, far more people stood on the outskirts looking in. Some watched in amazement and some in amusement, pointing and laughing. Others seemed to be shaking their heads in disgust. A few were calling down curses or were being restrained by friends from attacking the celebrants below. Not surprisingly to Beheshti, most of those in the larger group were young people—students from the University of Tehran just a block to his left, up Nosrat Street.

We are starting to lose this new generation, he thought, furious at what he saw. *The recent elections proved that! They know nothing of the debauchery of the shah and the way he tried to turn us into a little America. They don't know what it means to suffer or sacrifice for Allah—to make a difference with their lives. Instead, they sit in comfort, watching their American shows on their satellite televisions. They yearn for all things Western. They don't see how they are being infiltrated—corrupted—by the very things they venerate.*

Two of the young men watching began performing a mocking impersonation of the dancers, causing those around them to laugh. Soon they tired of watching the demonstration, and wrapping their arms around each other's shoulders, they departed toward the university. *Starting tomorrow, I will redouble my efforts with my young students to ensure they don't turn out like those children of Satan.*

"Let's go," Beheshti said to Bahman Milani, who sat in front of him driving the silver Iran Khodro Sarir. Milani honked his horn and tried to weave his way through the people who had spread themselves across Kargar Avenue. But the people were too wrapped up in their celebration to take notice.

Milani turned around, frustration on his face, and said, "They won't move. They are ignoring me."

A bang on the roof startled Beheshti. A smiling man looked in the window, but his smile was quickly replaced by recognition and fear. Pressing his hands together, he bowed his apology to the religious leader. Then, elbowing his way to the front of the car, he cleared a path, pushing, kicking, punching—whatever it took to get people out of the way.

Finally the car cleared the mob. The man came around by Beheshti's window and again bowed his apology. Beheshti lowered the window halfway, placed his hand on the man's head in blessing, and then tapped the back of Milani's seat, signaling him to drive off.

At least some people are celebrating as they should, unlike those lying hypocrites I just met with.

That morning he had been summoned by the Grand Ayatollah. When he arrived at the Supreme Leader's opulent offices, he had been made to wait in the outer room for two hours before he was called in.

When he entered, he saw that Iran's president was there as well. The two leaders had just finished an elaborate lunch, and the president seemed to make a special effort to wait until Beheshti was inside before dabbing his mouth with his napkin and rising from the table. That was just the first of many disrespects shown that morning.

While the president and the Supreme Leader sat down, Beheshti was made to stand, as if he were an inferior being interrogated.

"Is this attack on America your work?" the Supreme Leader asked.

"You know it is, *sayyid*. I spoke to you of it, if you will remember."

"I remember you bringing me some ridiculous idea, and I also remember telling you not to follow through with it."

So this is the way it's going to be. "Begging *sayyid*'s pardon, but your exact words were, 'We have chosen not to sanction or participate in your plan. However, if you decide to proceed on your own, neither will we block your efforts.' I took that as an implicit go-ahead for the plan; I would just be on my own in carrying it out."

"Is that what the Grand Ayatollah said—go ahead with the plan?" the president asked, taking over the fight as if he had just been tagged. "Or did you just assume that was what he meant?"

"It seemed clear to me—"

"Is it what he said? Answer the question!" As the president said this, a projectile of spit flew out of his mouth and landed on his shirt.

Pig! "No, it is not what he said!"

Firmly established with the upper hand, the president turned up the attack. "So you took it upon yourself, a mere cleric, to launch an attack upon America, virtually destroying their most important city, then causing additional havoc with multiple incidents across the country. Do you know the danger we are in, and how much worse it will get if your part in this is ever discovered? We are not a terrorist nation!"

Beheshti had to bite his tongue at that last statement. *How much money do you funnel off to terrorism? What percentage of this country's GDP is designated to disrupt the West in any way possible?* But instead of saying what was truly on his heart, Beheshti said, "Of course not, Mr. President. If a trail ever led back this direction, I would make it very clear that I acted on my own in a rogue capacity. You could do with me what you willed."

"Do you think you would be believed? Don't you know the world would simply determine that we were setting you up as a scapegoat? And by the way, we do not need your permission to do with you what we will."

And so the conversation went for an hour. Accusation after accusation, disrespect after disrespect. Of course, they gloated over the pain caused to America. They rejoiced over the green light this gave them to launch the centrifuges in Natanz so they could begin transforming their low-enriched fuel-grade uranium to the highly enriched weapons-grade. They exulted over what they saw as the impending destruction of Israel.

But did they give me any credit for that? Never! Beheshti thought as he took hold of the grab handle above the door to steady himself as his car cleared the Kargar-Azadi roundabout. *I have brought America to her knees in a way no one else could. 9/11 was about a couple of buildings and a few planes. Now that first attack will be forgotten as a small coin is lost in a cavern of riches.*

And that, ultimately, is what that meeting was all about. It was jealousy, pure and simple.

Beheshti's cell rang. He reached into the deep pocket of his robe and pulled the phone out. "Yes?"

Nouri Saberi's voice was on the other end. "The package is in the neighborhood. It should be delivered tomorrow afternoon."

"Very good," Beheshti said, then hung up the phone.

As he held the grab handle again for the turn onto Jomhuri-Ye-Eslami, the one-way street that took him to his mosque, he couldn't help but let a smile creep onto his usually stern face.

America may think things are bad now, but they are about to get a lot worse. Praise be to Allah, the Mighty, the Powerful, for not letting one small setback destroy his divine plans.

CHAPTER FIFTY-SIX

MONDAY, SEPTEMBER 14, 6:20 A.M. EDT
NEW YORK, NEW YORK

Four years ago, Keith Simmons had been up in his cabin near Silverthorne, Colorado. For most of the night he had been awake, glued to the news, watching as a wildfire gradually made its way toward him. Out in the driveway, his Range Rover was packed and ready to roll at a moment's notice.

When dawn arrived and the morning had just started to lighten, even before the sun made its appearance through the trees, Keith had gone outside to hose down his roof one more time. He had walked out the door and then stopped. There was an eerie silence—all the animals had fled; all the birds were gone. As he closed his eyes and focused his hearing, he faintly picked up the snapping and popping of the oncoming flames.

When he breathed in deeply, he experienced the deep, tangy smell of the smoke—wonderfully rich yet utterly unnerving. Then, in the brief window between the time he opened his eyes again and when they started to burn and water, he saw the most beautiful, frightening colors out to the east. The low blackness faded to pale brown, which gave birth to a burnt orange, which yielded itself to a dirty yellow, which finally lost itself in a rich, dark blue that spread seemingly forever above his head. That blue was what gave him hope that day—the promise of something bigger and better waiting for him if he could just survive.

This morning, in the heart of the city, as he followed the colors up the identical palette, he locked on to the patches of blue that managed to peek through the smoke. *Gotta try to remember that God is in His place. He's still on His throne and He hasn't forgotten about us. His mercies are new every single morning!*

Yet even with that assurance, Keith found himself on edge. He was distracted, unable to focus or to concentrate on his prayer. The reason for that struggle was obvious to him.

The noise—complete, unceasing. Unlike back at his cabin when the eerie silence had lent the sunrise peace and focus, the din arising from the streets below made Keith dread the sun's appearance. He did not want clarity as to what was happening below.

Keith had grown up in the city, so noise was his default mode. Even after he had signed with the Mustangs and moved out to the suburbs, he always had to have a television or a radio going—something to satisfy his deep-rooted need for ambient noise.

But this noise was different. There was the low mumble of thousands of voices mixed with the screams of the injured and dying. Every now and again, a loud rumble would roll through the streets below and up to the freeway as another explosion rocked a neighborhood or another building collapsed in flames started by a downed aircraft. Together all these horrific musicians blended into a soul-draining symphony of hopelessness and despair.

In the first light, from his vantage on the elevated thoroughfare, he surveyed the damage to the city. The fire nearest them must have burned itself out sometime in the early morning hours because now it just smoked as the structures smoldered. But the same wasn't true other places. He could see fires everywhere through the towering high-rises around him.

The most disconcerting thing about the fires was that no one was doing anything about them. Here, in New York City, fires burned as if they were out in the most remote, inaccessible reaches of the Rocky Mountains. As far as his eye could see, smoke poured into the sky, eventually merging with the gray cloud that hovered over the city.

On the streets below, there was a mass of movement. It looked like many residents were already beginning their migration out of town. Many were loaded with backpacks; some pushed pilfered shopping carts. Others just milled about, unsure where to go or what to do. Many more seemed to still be sleeping, stretched out on the sidewalks, apparently afraid to remain in the dark confinement of their buildings.

Interspersed with these groups were bands of people carrying boxes and bags of items they had looted. Keith couldn't help but smile as he saw two teens struggling to carry an enormous plasma television box. *Serves the idiots right to be wasting all that energy on something that is already internally fried!*

A shoe scuffing the pavement caught Keith's ear, and turning, he saw Coach Burton walking toward him. Without saying anything, the coach came and stood next to Keith, arms crossed, looking out over the city.

After what seemed like a long time, Coach said, "Thanks for last night."

Keith assumed he meant for bringing him the information and helping to keep the team under control. "No problem."

Again, silence.

"Sounds like we've got protein bars to last us the day and drinks if we really ration, *and* if we turn down all the people sleeping in the cars around us—something I'm not sure I can do. But either way, if we're still here tomorrow, we're going to have to go out looking for supplies like you suggested. I think you're the one who should coordinate that effort. Think you can do that?"

"Sure, Coach," Keith said, feeling anything but sure.

"Good. Get together a team—make sure it's got both coaches and players—then figure out a plan so that you're ready to hit the ground running at first light tomorrow."

"Got it."

They stood there silent again. Gunfire rang out from somewhere down below them. As Keith watched, a young man ran out from an alley. People parted around him like the Red Sea, letting him pass through. He stopped in the middle of the street and looked around him. He waved the gun at a nearby couple, and a huge smile spread on his face as the woman screamed and the man cowered. Keith then saw the man taking the full backpack off of his shoulder and handing it to the gunman. The youth fanned his gun at the onlookers, causing them all to shrink back, and then he tucked the gun into the front of his pants and strutted away.

"Be careful down there," Coach said.

"Will do."

After another minute of silence, Coach Burton walked back to the first bus.

"What did Coach want?"

Keith turned to see Afshin walking up to him. He stopped next to Keith, put his hands into the small of his back, then leaned way over backward, sending audible pops rifling through his spine.

Considering how stiff he felt from sleeping on the bus, Keith felt a momentary twinge of spinal envy. "Wants me to prepare some foraging teams for tomorrow."

"Tomorrow?" Afshin said with his eyebrows raised. "Don't you think that everything will be cleaned out by then? I think we need to go today to get what we can while it's still there."

After what he had just seen on the street below, Keith wasn't so hot on going today *or* tomorrow. But he had to agree with Afshin's logic. "I'll go talk with Coach in a little bit. Then we've got to think about pairing guys up, Assistant Head Forager-Guy."

"A title I aspired to my whole childhood. Now that I've achieved it at such a young age, what's left to strive for?"

Keith smiled. "Yeah, you truly are a shooting star, my friend."

As the sun continued to rise, Keith was able to see the crowds below in more detail. From his vantage point, he could see people crying and holding on to each other. Others, surveying in the morning light the damage done to their neighborhood, began calling out curses—one man in particular was shaking his fist at the heavens, then at anyone who walked near him.

There were still bodies in the street, and people gave them a wide berth—obviously expecting the city or the department of sanitation to eventually come along and clean them up.

One thing that surprised Keith was the number of businesspeople who came out carrying their briefcases or their satchels, intent on a day down at the office. Whether it was denial or just the desperate need for normalcy, he couldn't tell. Either way, eventually they would have to face the reality that business and commerce were not important anymore. Survival was the one and only priority.

Keith could hear movement in the bus behind him and knew that soon it would empty out—the guys inside wanting food, drink, and a bathroom, not necessarily in that order.

Next to him, Afshin shook his head at what he saw. "I don't know, man. This is just insanity. What are we doing here? How did we get in this situation?"

When he saw that Keith wasn't responding to him, Afshin asked, "Dude, what's going through that brain of yours?"

Keith was silent a moment longer as he breathed deep the smoky morning air. "I hate road trips."

CHAPTER FIFTY-SEVEN

MONDAY, SEPTEMBER 14, 10:45 A.M. EDT
WASHINGTON, D.C.

Tara passed out Starbucks cups to everyone around the table, ignoring the inevitable questions.

"Is mine skinny?"

"Do I have soy milk?"

"Did you remember the four extra shots?"

"Wasn't mine supposed to be a venti?"

"Come on, gang," Scott said, coming to her rescue. "You guys are like a bunch of baby birds complaining that mama didn't regurgitate the right kind of worm."

"Thanks for the visual," Khadi said, checking her drink and then replacing the plastic cap on her cup with a disappointed look on her face.

"Don't mention it. Now, say thank you to Tara, everyone."

"Thank you, Tara," everyone around the table said together.

"You're welcome," Tara answered with as much meaning as they had put into their thanks.

"But, seriously, did you remember my extra shots?" Joey Williamson asked, setting off a whole new round of questions.

"Knock it off, or I'm going to make you pass the drinks again!" Scott said, trying to get control.

"Oh, man, and I had to sit next to Evie today! I hate soy," Virgil Hernandez said.

A week ago, the complaining about the drinks had gotten so bad that Scott had made them all pass their drinks to the person on their right. They were all so thrown off-kilter by not having their "usual," the whining had stopped for several days. *Not that I can blame them for whining. How can someone as bright as Tara find a way to mess up the order every single stinkin' day of the week?* Scott thought, taking a sip of his and cringing at the latte's flavorless nonfat milk.

"Please don't make us pass our drinks again. We'll promise to be good, Scottybear," Evie Cline said.

"I asked you not to call me that anymore. It's beyond creepy."

Evie pretended to pout. "I can't help it. You're just so big and cute and cuddly. Don't you think so, Tara?"

Scott's face flushed, just as he saw Tara's do the same. "What I think is that we should get down to business," Tara said, looking down and shuffling some papers.

Evie winked at Scott.

Okay, I've got to put an end to this whole Tara thing once and for all . . . although her face did flush too. I wonder what that means. Maybe I should let it ride out a little longer.

"Scott. Oh, Scott," Khadi was saying. "We're in a meeting. Do you think it might be a good idea if we actually meet?"

"What? Oh yeah. Right. Let's get going. Khadi, can you give us an update on what's happening in New York beyond what the talking heads are saying on the screen?"

Pushing her untouched drink to the side, she began, "Not too much yet. Uncle Sam's still getting organized. They've begun a leaflet campaign, letting people know what's happened and assuring them that the government is still standing. Apparently, they're also asking people to stay put until someone comes to evacuate them. That way they can keep the roads clear for the buses."

"We'll see how long that lasts," Hernandez said. "Once food and water start getting low, everyone's going to be hightailing it out of there."

Crumpling the top paper of her stack and throwing it over her shoulder, Khadi said, "Yeah, I kind of shook my head at that one too. Just another example of the boneheads at FEMA not thinking things all the way through.

"One thing they do seem to be getting right, though, is the start-up of the evacuations. They're beginning on the fringes and working their way in. They've got refugee camps already set up around Wilmington, Delaware; Middlesex County in Connecticut; and Lancaster County in Pennsylvania."

"Lancaster?" Williamson said. "Isn't that where the Amish are?"

"It is. And most of them are opening up their homes and their barns, even allowing tents out in their fields."

"You know, when you think about it, they could have been hit by an EMP and not even known it," Williamson said.

"Exactly," Hernandez said. "Some family'd hitch up the horse and buggy one day and ride into town. And when they saw all the cars abandoned and all the lights out, the dad'd be like, '*Ach*, Rebecca, finally the English are catching on!'"

"Guys, seriously, may I finish?" Khadi asked.

"Sure; sorry," Hernandez said.

"Beyond that, they're starting food and water drops. By the way, Scott, I did put a call in to that girlfriend of mine who's involved in the supply distribution. She's going to make sure that Liberty Stadium is well taken care of."

"Thanks, Khadi. Anything else?"

Khadi leveled her papers on the table, then laid them flat.

"I'll take that as a no. So let's get down to finding that second EMP. What's the latest?"

Here Tara stepped in. "We're absolutely clueless when it comes to the warhead. As for the delivery system, we know it's a rush job, so we don't expect it to be going by sea. That means air. Our friends at NORAD gave us the rundown of every flight that came out of North Korea into the Western Hemisphere over the last six days. Evie, you have the list?"

"Right here," she answered, quickly shuffling through her papers and pulling one out. Scott had no doubt that she had everything on that paper memorized, but she was always very cautious against mistakes. "Because of flight restrictions, the number is very low.

Pretty much anything of size that goes in and out is Air Koryo, the national airline of the DPRK. Used to be they had routes going as far west as Budapest and Prague, but those have all been terminated. They don't have anything regularly scheduled that goes outside of Asia-Pacific anymore. However, they do run charters. And in the last six days, there have been exactly three charters to the West—one to Caracas, one to Havana, and one to Mexico City.

"The one to Caracas was interesting because we all know how Chávez feels about America. But as soon as that plane landed, it spewed out enough people that there'd be no room left for a delivery system of any sort.

"The one to Mexico City seemed more unlikely because we still have a decent relationship with them. However, it suspiciously taxied directly into a hangar and hasn't been seen since. NORAD's keeping a bird above it, just to see what comes out.

"The last one was Havana. It came yesterday. The weird thing about this plane is that it was a big ol' Ilyushin Il-62. It can seat like 170 people. So it lands, and the next day on the front page of *Granma Internacional* is a picture of this little North Korean delegation deplaning and being met by some Cuban government reps."

"So maybe they wanted some elbow room," Scott said.

"You're jumping the gun. The point is that the event in the newspaper never happened. The picture's a fake—at least according to our aerospace defense friends. When they run the tape, they see the plane landing and pulling into a hangar just like the Mexico one."

"And NORAD's sure about this?"

A mischievous grin spread across Evie's face. "Well, to make sure, we did a little experimenting ourselves. Gooey?"

Standing up and looking very professorial, Gooey said, "Let me put it this way; there ain't no Gooba down in Cooba."

Gooey had a way about him that, no matter how much Scott told himself he wouldn't encourage him, he still ended up laughing. "Actually, Gooba, why don't you put it another way, because I have no idea what you just said."

"Scotty, Scotty, Scotty, where's the poetry in your life?" Gooey said as he fanned copies of a photograph across the middle of the table.

Scott picked one up. In it were the same Cuban government reps. But this time the delegation they were meeting was made up of John F. Kennedy and J. Edgar Hoover, arm-in-arm.

Scott stared at the picture, amazed. It was better than the work Gooey had done on Operation Keep the Lie Alive. And it was a far sight better than what the Cuban newspaper had done. When he compared that farce with Gooey's pic, the blurred edges and incorrect depth lines were obvious.

"Nice touch on Hoover's wedding gown," Scott said appreciatively.

"Yeah, I figured he'd go simple yet elegant. Nothing ostentatious," Gooey said proudly.

"Excellent work, gang. So did something come to pick the Cuban cargo up?" Scott asked, getting a little excited.

"That's where the problem comes in, boss," Evie answered. "There was a three-hour window when we didn't have a bird keeping an eye out. It had to have been unloaded at that time, because two hours ago, the plane took off back to Kim-land."

Frustrated, Scott slammed his fist down onto the table, bouncing the coffee cups and causing Tara and Khadi to reach for theirs to keep them from tipping. *So close and still nothing!*

"Sorry, guys," Scott said, looking around at the wide eyes. "Wee bit stressed here and needing something other than Diet Code Red and lattes to keep me going. Let's talk about potential targets for both the Havana and Mexico City possibilities. Havana, you've got Miami and Orlando."

"Not Miami," Khadi said. "Not enough impact. Maybe Orlando—could be a big women and children toll. What about Atlanta?"

"Still probably not enough impact," Tara answered. "I think East Coast, you've got to go all the way up to Washington, D.C. Or maybe they're going to truck it over to Chicago."

Scott closed his eyes and tilted his head back. "Chicago. I hadn't even thought of that."

"I think we need to keep the Mexico City option open—there was an hour-long blind window there, too," Hernandez said. "Besides, the Cubans are doing freaky stuff all the time, so the faked picture isn't that big of a deal. But imagine what an EMP would do to Southern California. You've got almost 25 million people down there—the same as you had with this first hit. Add to that the fact that it's a whole lot harder to get aid to. I really think we should keep an eye on the West Coast."

"Okay," Scott said. "Let's divide our efforts. Virgil, Evie, and Joey, you focus on the West Coast. Tara, you and Gooey take the East Coast. And let's all just pray that it's not Atlanta. The last thing Riley needs is to get hit with one of these a second time."

CHAPTER

EIGHT

MONDAY, SEPTEMBER 14, 3:15 P.M. EDT
STONE MOUNTAIN, GEORGIA

Muhammed Zerin Khan walked to the edge of the observation deck and looked out over the city. *Just gotta make a short run, clear a couple fences, and over I'd go. It would be so easy—so quick.*

He hadn't come up onto Stone Mountain since before he had gone away to college, and the view he saw now took him back to his childhood. Some people said that if you looked close, you could see all the way to Tennessee from up here, but he could never tell. When he was a kid, he would try to spot the state line, thinking it had to be out there somewhere like it was on the maps. When he got older, he forgot about things like that and just focused on the city—his city.

Out to the west, he could see the apartment block he grew up in—shabby-looking even from this great a distance. A fourteen-minute run from there (thirteen minutes twelve seconds, on his best day) was his alma mater, Crim High School, where he had managed to find himself on the good side of the 32 percent graduation rate—the side that didn't involve prison or a bullet. It was at Crim that his life could have gone either way. But with the encouragement of his football coach and the tough love of his mother, he had made the right choices.

And now I've thrown it all away! How did I let Dad talk me into this? How was I so stupid?

When his father had called him last Thursday and told him it was time, Zerin had agonized over the decision. He knew what he could be giving up if he went. But his dad was so insistent, so earnest, so determined that Zerin not go on the road trip to New York.

Way off to the west he spotted the Georgia Dome, a giant white blob in a field of gray. When he had come up here as a teenager, his eyes had always settled on the Dome. He had dreamed of pulling up to the players' lot and parking right next to the stadium. He'd envisioned getting his bag from the back of his Escalade and walking past the security and into the locker room, then, with his uniform on, jogging out onto the field to the sound of tens of thousands of fans chanting his name.

That—that is what I've lost. My dad said, "Jump," and I immediately asked, "How high?" And I ended up jumping clear out of my career—out of my dream.

Still, I guess I should thank him. Without his summons, I'd be trapped in New York instead of here, on my mountaintop. I also wouldn't know who I really am deep inside—what my character really is, for better or worse.

Zerin hiked around to the southeast side of the mountain. Far out beyond his sight line was the Georgia State Prison. He had no idea whether his dad was okay or not, and he wasn't sure how much he really cared. The stories of the rioting there and at other penitentiaries around the country had been hard to find amid the near-constant coverage of New York City. And when the media weren't talking about New York, they focused on the suicide bombings in all those cities. The plight of a bunch of rowdy convicts was a distant third on the news viewers' list of things they cared about.

The snippets he did hear, though, were bad. Scores of guards had been killed along with hundreds of prisoners. It was an all-out revenge fest with everyone finally acting on their long-held grudges. Over thirty prisons were in flames; one in Colorado and one in Texas had burned to the ground, each condemning over a hundred prisoners to a fiery death sentence.

There was no doubt that America was under attack. He continued to be amazed that *his* father was actually a part of it.

His plane had landed Friday evening, and early the next morning he had made the four-hour drive to Reidsville, arriving just after the weekend visiting hours had begun.

Hamza Yusuf Khan had looked nervous but relieved when he saw his son on the other side of the glass. Dispensing with the usual niceties and small talk, Hamza had gotten straight to the point. In the most cryptic terms possible, he had warned Zerin that the thing he had been talking about was coming the next day. He told his son that they might never see each other again, but if something did happen to him, he had no doubt that he would go straight into the presence of Allah.

Zerin tried to pull details out of his father, but that day, rather than pushing the limits of what he could divulge, Hamza seemed to want to say as little as possible.

That is, until it was mini-sermon time. Hamza recounted to his son his conversion to Islam, and then his disillusionment and fall. He spoke of how one day, a fellow inmate had shown him what true Islam was—an Islam of commitment and strength, honor and vengeance.

"That is what beats in my heart and runs through my veins," Hamza had said. "It is my life's blood—the essence of my being and the very purpose of my life. And because you are my son, it runs in your blood too. I wish I had more time to talk to you about this, but my time is short. So you must accept what I say to be true. You must step off the fence of half belief and come fully into Allah's service. And you must do what I ask of you—for the love of Allah and for the memory of your father, not the failure that I once was but the warrior I have become."

At that point they had pressed each other's palms through the glass.

"What do you want me to do?" Zerin had asked, ready to follow his father into the depths of hell if need be.

But when his father told him, Zerin was stunned. He quickly pulled his hand away and stood up.

"Is that . . . is that what this has all been about?" he had asked.

His father convinced him to sit back down. Then he spent the next ten minutes trying to convince Zerin to obey him. He yelled;

he apologized; he pleaded; he promised spiritual rewards. As Zerin sat listening to him, he was torn between guilt and disgust, loyalty and contempt.

Finally, without committing one way or another—without even saying good-bye—he got up and left the room. Now, two days later, he still didn't know what he was going to do. No matter what he chose, there would be betrayal—whether against his father or against his own character or against his very life.

He looked at his watch and saw that he had only fifteen minutes until his scheduled meeting time.

When he had first tried Riley's number on Sunday afternoon, his call had gone to voice mail. *You lucky little idiot,* he had thought, *he's in New York! I guess that takes care of that!*

Zerin had gone ahead and left an urgent message, figuring that had fulfilled his obligation. *I tried, but I just couldn't reach him! Allah is not unreasonable; he will understand.*

But early this morning, when his phone rang and he saw Riley's number on the caller ID, he felt like the main character in a story he had read as a teen about a woman getting a phone call from her husband who had died in car crash earlier that evening. Zerin's heart started racing, and he felt nauseous. Unsuccessfully trying to steady his shaking hand, he picked up the phone and pressed Talk.

Riley seemed to sense immediately that something was wrong. He initially balked at Zerin's request for him to fly down to Atlanta to meet with him, even after Zerin had convinced him that he had very important information about a possible second attack. Riley pleaded with him to tell him what he knew over the phone, but Zerin held his ground. It was in person or not at all—you never know who's listening. He had even convinced Riley to leave his giant bodyguard behind, threatening to clam up if he saw any sign of him.

But can I do it? Can I really go through with it?

As he walked back toward the gondola that would take him to the bottom of Stone Mountain, the Colt Defender .45 ACP that he usually kept hidden away in his mom's apartment rubbed gently against the small of his back.

By the time the cable car had cleared the road and cut through the trees, Zerin had steeled himself for what he knew he had to do.

CHAPTER

FIFTY-NINE

MONDAY, SEPTEMBER 14, 3:50 P.M. EDT
STONE MOUNTAIN, GEORGIA

"I don't want to hear you crashing through the brush or see you popping up behind some bush," Riley said to Skeeter as he put the Lincoln Navigator in park.

"This is stupid," Skeeter said.

"You know what? I'm not even going to argue with you. You're right! This is stupid! But what other choice do I have?"

"I told you! You go out on the path; I circle through the woods. At least you're covered."

"Come on, man, you know that's too big a risk," Riley said, pulling low the 94th Airlift Wing cap that he had borrowed from one of the guys at Dobbins Reserve Air Base. He hoped that the hat and the dark glasses would be enough of a disguise so that his presence wouldn't cause a stir. *Guess it better be; it's all you've got!*

Riley continued. "First, you don't know these woods well enough to 'circle through' them. And second, look at you—you're built for 'Scare the Bejabbers Out of Them,' not for 'How Not to Be Seen.'"

"I still say it's stupid!"

"We covered that already," Riley said, exasperated and way past done with the conversation. "Listen, Skeet, I appreciate you more than you'll ever know. But this one I've got to do on my own. Sometimes I gotta trust God, too, not just you."

Riley opened his door to get out, and Skeeter opened his, too.

"Skeet!"

"I know! I'm just gonna be sitting right here on the hood of the truck. But if I hear anything—*anything*—I'm out there whether you want me there or not."

Riley smiled. "Thanks, buddy."

Skeeter didn't say anything. He just slid himself up on the Navigator's hood, causing the metal to buckle loudly.

Great! Guess I'll just tell the folks at Dobbins that a rock fell on the truck, Riley thought as he jogged off. *A very large, very smooth, non-paint-chipping rock that . . . On the other hand, what do I care what they think?*

He looked at his watch and saw that he had seven minutes to get to the rendezvous. Zerin's instructions were to follow the Cherokee Trail under the three Confederate figures carved into the face of the mountain. Then, as soon as he passed the Studdard Picnic Area, he was to turn left toward Stone Mountain Lake. Zerin would be looking for him there.

This B movie, cloak-and-dagger stuff is so incredibly frustrating. What could have taken five minutes by phone is instead costing me nearly a full day. This is stupid! This is stupid! This is stupid! This is stupid, he repeated in his mind, keeping time to his steps.

It was hard for Riley to believe that just over twelve hours ago, he was trapped in the aftermath of an EMP attack. *No wonder I'm so tired,* he thought, feeling the ache in his legs and up his back. Following his promise to himself to pray for the people in the stadium every time he thought about New York, he again entrusted them to God's loving care.

Riley and Skeeter's homecoming to the RoU had been a special moment. As soon as they walked through the door, the team mobbed them. There were claps on the back from the guys and hugs from the girls. It was the first time that Riley had really felt like one of the team—a member of the family.

Not until everyone had gone back to their workstations had Riley remembered the phone in his pocket. He turned it on and—not to his surprise—found thirty-seven text messages and nineteen voice mails waiting.

Knowing that one would be from his mom and one from Grandpa Covington, he went out into the still-dark courtyard and made a call home. Grandpa was staying with Mom, so they both got on the phone. She had cried through the whole conversation, and both Grandpa and Riley had struggled to keep their emotions in check and stay strong; neither had met with much success.

After hanging up, Riley sat on a picnic table with his feet on the bench and began listening to his messages. Zerin's was number seven or eight. *You're the last thing I need right now,* he had thought. But as he listened, he was drawn in. There was something about the man's voice—fear, desperation—that forced Riley to dial his former adversary's number.

It wasn't long before Riley was glad he did. At first he had serious doubts about the genuineness of Zerin's claim of special information, but then he told Riley about his father's incarceration and how he knew that it was his dad's Wahhabi brethren that were behind the riots—a fact that had not yet been told to the press.

So here he was, a day later, jogging past the sparse crowd, heading for the unknown. As Riley passed under the enormous depictions of Stonewall Jackson, Robert E. Lee, and Jefferson Davis that were carved into the mountain's face, he hoped that the ultimate outcome of his mission would be more favorable than theirs.

Twenty feet after he rounded the picnic area, he heard his name. "Riley!"

Riley turned to see Zerin tucked back in the woods. He jogged over to him and stuck out his hand. "Hey, Zerin, good to see you."

Zerin ignored the hand and said, "Follow me." He didn't move right away but looked over Riley's shoulder for half a minute.

Please don't be there, Skeet!

Abruptly, Zerin turned and trudged off. Riley followed.

After about three minutes of winding through trees and fording two streams, Zerin stopped. Without saying anything, he reached behind his back and pulled a white envelope out of his pocket.

"What's this?" Riley asked.

"Read it after you leave."

"Sure," Riley said, more than a little curious. Tucking the packet into his own rear pocket, he asked, "So can you tell me what this is about?"

Zerin took a deep breath. Riley could see that he was pale and perspiring. There were tears in his eyes as he began speaking.

"First off, you need to know how hard this is for me."

Riley put on his compassionate look—the one he reserved for women who broke their nails and men who four-putted. "I understand. I—"

Suddenly Zerin's hand drove hard into Riley's chest, pushing him back a step.

Take it; don't strike back; let him vent.

"No, you don't! You don't understand, Riley! My whole life I've been taught to respect my father. 'Yes, Son, your father is a low-life drug dealer, but still you have to respect him!' 'Yes, Son, your father traded your childhood for an addiction to rock, but still you have to respect him!'

"So I did all I could to keep my true feelings for him stuffed down. I drew him cards when I was a little kid. I tried to sound happy to hear his voice when we got the monthly calls. But all the while I secretly hated him; I was ashamed of him."

Zerin leaned back against a tree, propping a foot against the trunk and letting his left hand pick at the bark. "But then, all of a sudden, things started changing with him. He got religion. He was a Muslim again. I saw him cleaning up his act. I saw him making a difference in prison. It's like one day he's this low-life drug pusher and the next he's an imam.

"That respect for him that had eluded me for so long started creeping up on me. I heard him talking about Islam, and it made a lot of sense to me. Before I knew it, I became a believer in Allah *and* in my father."

Riley tried not to let his impatience surface, but if Zerin had any important information, then this little autobiography was just delaying its getting to the right people. "Listen, Zerin, I don't mean to—"

"Shut up," Zerin yelled, standing straight up again. "Just hear me out . . . please. A number of months back, he starts talking about this big thing that's going to happen—something that will teach America—the Great Satan, he calls it—a lesson. At first I think, 'Wait, aren't you an American too?' But then I realize he's not. He's not an American; he's a Muslim—first and foremost. He's found a higher calling—something that transcends nationalities and borders. And suddenly I discover I want that too. I want that same kind of passion—that same kind of purpose! I tell him so, and he smiles and tells me to be ready to be used by Allah.

"Then, about six weeks ago, he tells me to be prepared to come down to him at the drop of a hat. I tell him I will, not truly expecting that he'd call. But last Thursday, he did.

"So I dropped everything and came down. I didn't even tell Coach that I wasn't going to make the road trip. Dad said come, so I came. You see, I knew he had something big for me to do—some major part for me to play in this big plan.

"Well, when I visit him on Saturday, he tells me what he wants from me. You want to know what it is? Money! That's the glorious imam's marvelous plan—his great vision for his son! That's how he says Allah is going to use me! I'm a PFL player; I must be loaded. Who am I to hold those resources back from the ones who are doing God's work?"

"I'm sorry, man." Riley had been on the receiving side of enough insincere, manipulative requests from people he'd least expected them from to know how much they could hurt.

"Stop it! Don't patronize me! You patronize me, and I swear I'll walk, and you'll never hear from me again! Do you understand?"

Riley nodded. Zerin seemed to be getting more frenzied—more out of control—as the conversation continued. Riley decided to just ride it out and say as little as possible.

"I stormed out of that visiting room with him calling out behind me—yelling so loud I could hear it through the glass. 'It's time to be a man, Son!' 'Don't disappoint me, Son!' 'Don't disappoint God, Son!'

"Well, you want to know who's disappointed? Me! I thought my dad had changed, but he hasn't. He's still just out for the coin."

Zerin paused. Riley could see the emotion on his face and knew that whatever he had to say next would not be easy.

"And then comes Sunday, and I see what his big plans were, and I spend the whole day crying and throwing up! How could . . . Does he really think that's what God wants? Because I don't think so! That's not the Allah that I've read about! I think that whoever planned this whole thing is just using Allah and the Koran to get power or to—I don't know—to indulge in some twisted bloodlust."

Zerin started laughing—dry, bitter laughter. "You want to know something? I think that's why my dad's doing it. I think the old man just wants an excuse to put a shank in some guards before he gets too old to give any payback.

"So here I am. I called you because I know that you know people. If I went to the cops myself, they'd hold me—they'd pry; they'd ask questions I don't want to answer. That ain't for me. I've got what I want to say, and I don't want to say any more than that. I've got other plans past this, and interrogations and protective custody don't fit into them.

"So that's why I called you—Superhero Riley Covington. Captain America, right? Isn't that what they call you? I had to call someone, and I figured you . . . you would be able to get the information to the right authorities without asking too many questions. Maybe by talking to you I could even save a few lives. That's a good thing, right? Everyone knows saving lives is a good thing!"

Zerin walked up to Riley and whispered to him, "But you want to know just how screwed up I am? I actually feel guilty about not doing what my dad asks, and I'm afraid that if I tell you what he told me, I'll feel even worse. If I betray him that way, I honestly don't know if I can live with myself. The loss of honor will be too much."

Riley put his hand on Zerin's shoulder and was surprised when he didn't pull away. "Listen, I'm not patronizing you when I tell you that I feel for you. That's not patronizing; that's just plain old compassion. You are in an unbelievably tough place. But you have to know that if what you've got to say saves lives, that's not betrayal; that's doing the right thing—that's doing the honorable thing!"

Tears welled up in Zerin's eyes. Then, suddenly, he backed away. He steadied his voice and said, "I don't know. . . . Whatever, it doesn't matter. I've made up my mind, and I'm going to deal with the consequences.

"On Saturday, my father, using the coded language he always uses to talk about this stuff, tells me that things are going to be tough for him at home because the Wahhabis are going to stand up. So I figure that this whole big thing that he's been hyping for the past months is a riot. No big deal. But then he goes on to say that their business is just one play in a bigger game. The biggest plays are going to take place up north. I ask him what he means, and he says that the lady's going to lose her wallet and she's going to lose her head.

"I'm still not getting it, so he repeats it. Only this time when he says *wallet*, he traces the letters *NYC* on the glass partition. And when he says *head*, he traces *DC*. The next day, New York City goes off-line. I don't know why Washington hasn't taken a hit yet, but I have no doubt it's coming."

Riley's heart pounded. *It makes so much sense! Take out the financial systems of America while at the same time collapsing the governmental structures! Talk about chaos! How long would it take America to dig out of that hole, especially with summer recess ending and all of the decision-makers just getting back into town for today's reconvening? How many congressmen and senators would be in planes that would drop from the skies in Washington?*

"Did he say anything else, Zerin? anything at all about the timing of the Washington attack?"

"Like I said, I think his belief was that everything was going to happen yesterday," Zerin said, now sounding utterly exhausted. "Sorry, that's all I have."

"No, there's no sorry. What you've given me is huge. Zerin, you have to know that you're a hero. A true, honorable hero. You may have saved tens of thousands of lives by what you did today."

Zerin chuckled bitterly. "Funny, I don't feel like a hero." He leaned against the tree again, and his hand recommenced picking the bark. "I've said all I'm going to say, Riley. Leave me alone now, okay?"

Riley was anxious enough to get this information to the RoU gang that he didn't need to be asked twice. Still, he asked as he backed away, "You sure you're okay? You want to come with me?"

"No, just go."

Riley nodded and turned to go.

"Riley! Don't forget about that envelope!"

Riley gave a wave over his shoulder as he began sprinting through the woods. While he ran, he called Scott Ross. "Scott, it's D.C.! The second target is D.C.!"

"You sure?" Scott asked, excitement in his voice.

"That's what he said. And it makes perfect sense. First you hit the wallet, and then you hit the—"

A loud *CRACK!* sounded through the woods, bouncing off the granite mountain and echoing back. Riley stopped in his tracks. *Oh no! Zerin!*

He reached into his back pocket and snatched out the envelope. Tearing it open, he pulled out the tri-folded piece of paper. At the top was the word *Mom*. That was all Riley needed to see. He folded it back up without reading any more.

Riley started running again, still heading toward the parking lot.

"Scott, call the Stone Mountain police or security or whatever they have around here. Tell them they have a 10-56 in the woods between the Studdard Picnic Area and the lake."

"Oh, Pach, man! You mean Zerin just . . . Oh, man! I'm sorry, dude!"

"Just make the call, but do it after you get the team going on D.C. I'll call you back from the truck!"

"Got it!"

As Riley hung up, Skeeter came bursting through the trees next to him. His gun was in his hand.

"I heard a shot," he said, stepping into Riley's path so that Riley had to quickly brake to keep from plowing into him.

"I'm fine. It was Zerin. He shot himself."

That was one piece of information that Skeeter was obviously not expecting. He paused for a moment, then said, "I'm going to go make sure."

"No, Skeet, we need to leave right away, and the last thing I need is for us to get stuck down here in a police investigation! I'll fill you in on what Zerin said on the way back to Dobbins. Come on!"

Riley's head swam with questions, prayers, and emotions as he ran, but in the midst of it all, one thought loomed above the others.

If the EMP is going to hit, please, please, please don't let it blow until our wheels have touched the tarmac!

CHAPTER SIXTY

MONDAY, SEPTEMBER 14, 4:00 P.M. EDT
NEW YORK, NEW YORK

"Do we just go?" Afshin Ziafat asked Keith Simmons while mopping his face with a T-shirt.

Keith, sitting on the freeway with his back against the bus, stewing both from the afternoon heat and from his anger at Coach Roy Burton, said, "Let's give it another half hour. If he doesn't give in by then, we'll go anyway."

Complaints were running rampant through the Mustangs. And with each passing hour, their volume increased. While there were still a few protein bars left, no one could bring themselves to eat them—all warm and chewy and nasty.

What they really wanted—really needed—was liquid. The bottled water had run out early this humid, end-of-summer day. There had been a couple of cases of Gatorade, but they were in the little bottles that might as well have been shot glass samples to these big men. Someone desperately needed to go out and find some supplies.

But despite the complaints, Burton kept holding out. It almost seemed like it was turning into a power play. Keith could understand Coach's desire to keep discipline. And there was the very real worry that players would wander off and disappear. However, things were going to get ugly soon. Even the quietest, most acquiescent rookies were grumbling. Pretty soon there would be a disorganized revolt. Keith's hope was that if it came to that, he could somehow morph the anarchist rebellion into a well-planned mutiny.

Keith had warned Burton that the players were getting restless, but Coach had dismissed him roughly—although Keith could see an uncharacteristic uncertainty in his eyes that belied his words. Coach was holding out hope that the information in the leaflets that had been dropped a few hours ago was correct, that relief efforts would come soon in the form of air-dropped supplies.

He just doesn't understand the size of the problem. Even if they do come, the chances of them coming here are slim. We might as well be out buying New York lottery tickets.

Keith shifted on his cushion and tried to keep his legs from falling asleep. The cushions were far from ideal, but they sure beat the asphalt they had been sitting on. Everyone had endured the unforgiving surface throughout the morning until Donovan Williams had stood up, walked onto the bus, and come walking out again a few seconds later with a seat bottom. Keith and the other players from bus three watched as he dropped it to the ground, planted his oversize backside firmly on the middle of it, and let out a huge sigh.

Like a gunshot, all the rest of the guys were pushing their way onto the bus to rip up more seats. Soon it spread to the other buses, and before long Keith had even seen some people in the surrounding cars removing backseats and stretching out on them.

The posterior adjustment didn't quite do it for Keith, so he stood up and stretched, sucking in a deep breath as he did so. Immediately he started coughing. The smell of smoke was still heavy in the air, and other smells were beginning to mingle in.

One smell was obvious. About ten car lengths down, some Good Samaritans with a camper on the back of their truck had pulled out some of their supplies and rigged up a privacy shield around a drain port in the side of the freeway wall. Right now there was a line of at least twenty people waiting to use the makeshift latrine. Keith, however, like many of the other men, had just thrown dignity to the wind, standing up against the low wall, looking over the city's dark skyline, and hoping no one was walking directly below.

The other smell was less defined, but Keith was afraid that in this heat it would soon become more and more pungent. It was an odor that Keith remembered from his cabin. He had gone up one weekend only to find a horrific stench. Searching out its source, he had tracked it to a hole under his porch, where he eventually dug out a family of dead raccoons.

Keith nodded to two men who came walking past, then settled himself back down on his cushion. He had recognized them from the Q&A last night. They were from two different families but had apparently decided to team up for a venture into the city.

He watched as the men carefully stepped their way through the mass of human bulk spread out in the bus's shade. Each was carrying bags filled with food, milk, and water.

"Yo, dude, do me a favor and give me a bottle of your water," Keith heard Gorkowski say.

"I'm sorry, really, but we've both got kids back at our cars. We've got to get this to them," one of the men said apologetically.

Gorkowski stood up and stepped into the men's path. "Come on, just one bottle," he said a little more firmly.

The men looked at each other, and the first man said again, "Really, I'd love to help, but we've got to get this to our kids."

"I said, give me a bottle of your water," Gorkowski said menacingly, stepping toward the two men.

Billy Gaines, another offensive lineman, stood up next to Gorkowski. "Make that two," he said.

"Listen, we don't want any trouble," the second man said, reaching into his bag. He pulled out a couple of bottles and was preparing to pass them over when Keith leaped to his feet.

In four steps he was between the players and the men, nose to nose with Gorkowski.

"Sit down, Snap," Keith said.

"Back off, man," Gorkowski growled. "This ain't your deal."

"Really, it's okay," the second man said.

"Put your water away and walk back to your car," Keith said, never taking his eyes off of Gorkowski.

"You're making a big mistake, Simms," Gorkowski threatened.

"I am? Really? I'm the one making the mistake?" Out of his peripheral vision, Keith saw the two men scurry around the confrontation. When they were clear, Keith suddenly drove his hands into Gorkowski's chest, pushing him back hard enough so that he tripped over Donovan Williams, landing flat on his back.

"What are you? A thug? You out street-hustling here, Snap?" Then, turning to Gaines, he said, "You better sit down right now, son, or I swear I will slap you into next week!"

"Whatever. Ain't nothing off me," Gaines said, retreating.

Gorkowski was just getting to his feet. His face was dark red from rage and embarrassment.

"You gonna come at me, Chris?" Keith said. "Come on, do it! Take me down for keeping you from thieving some poor kids of their water! That's what you wanna do, right? So come on!"

Gorkowski stared at Keith, the anger making beads of sweat drip down his face. But he didn't move.

Keith turned to the rest of the players around. "Anyone else? Anybody else want to steal food from babies? How about we all band together and start raiding the cars around us? Bet we could come away with a good haul! How's that for an idea?"

He scanned the faces, letting his anger slowly cool down. "Let it be known here and now that if I hear of anyone stealing anything from anybody, I personally will throw you off the side of this freeway."

Keith settled his stare on Gorkowski and held his gaze. Eventually the center dropped his eyes and sat down.

Keith turned and almost bumped into Afshin, who was standing right behind him.

"Whoa, didn't know you were there."

"Of course I'm here. I told you I'd always have your back, my friend. Besides, do you think Snap would have backed down if he hadn't been so intimidated by my rippling pythons?" Afshin said, lifting his arms and kissing his biceps.

Keith was too steamed to laugh, but he did say, "Yeah, I'm sure that was it. Anyway, thanks. It's good to know you're there."

"No, thank you for doing what the rest of us should have done."

"Look!" someone yelled.

Unsure who had spoken or where he was supposed to look, Keith glanced around. Afshin spotted it before Keith and pointed it out to him, although by that time, Keith, along with everyone else, had begun to hear what was coming.

Off to the south, the sky was filled with helicopters—mostly twin-rotor CH-47 Chinooks, but a variety of other military choppers were mixed in as well. A low rumble filled the city, and the sound grew until everything around the players was vibrating. There were too many for Keith to count, but he guessed that there had to be more than a hundred.

People started jumping up and cheering, and Keith couldn't help but join in. Everyone screamed and waved and danced around. Then, at a little distance from the heart of the city, the helicopters began fanning out, and everyone quickly became quiet again. The fear that they would be passed over was strong in the hearts of those on the freeway.

But after a time, they could see that one was coming their way. Elation filled the crowd again, and the cheers began even louder than before. Soon, the huge Chinook was passing slowly over them. Keith was waving along with everyone else. As it glided over their heads, a mass of people suddenly came pouring into their little bus camp.

What the—? Who are all these people? Keith thought as the helicopter cruised past. Then he joined the crowd trying to keep up with the helicopter.

People everywhere desperately yelled, "Stop! Wait!"

Keith could see the edges of a large wooden pallet hanging over the side of the cargo bay. *Why don't they . . . ?* Before he finished his thought, he knew the answer to his own question. There was no place to put the pallet down. It was too crowded on the freeway—too many cars and taxis and buses filling every inch of the road.

As Keith wove his way through the cars, the helicopter pulled farther and farther away. Still he kept pushing, but the tight crowd of people and the litter of cars kept him from gaining any speed.

Finally, when the helicopter had drifted about a half mile ahead, Keith saw the pallet slide out and begin its descent.

"No! Wait," he yelled with hundreds of others. Hopelessly, he watched as the supplies slowly drifted to the ground. *Lord, please help me get there! Please let me get something for the guys!*

Before he even arrived at the site, though, he knew his efforts were futile. People were already turned around, walking dejectedly back to their cars—some angry, some in tears. But Keith didn't stop. He had to see it for himself.

When he finally arrived at the pallet, he understood the reason for its location. It had been dropped in the gap where an on-ramp merged onto the freeway. All around, people were cheering and dancing as they drank bottles of water and tore open military MREs. Others were milling about, begging for something from some of the lucky ones. Keith could see two fights taking place, apparently started over dual claims on some provisions.

A majority of people still there, however, were simply looking to the skies in hopes of another drop.

Keith knew that wouldn't happen. *This city's too big. One hundred helicopters—even a thousand helicopters—are just a drop in the bucket. We were lucky to have gotten one this close.*

As he turned and began the long walk back to the buses, his will strengthened and eventually steeled. He knew what had to be done. He knew they couldn't depend on anyone else for their survival. He knew it was time to go into the city.

When he arrived back at the bus camp, he immediately started searching for Coach Burton. He didn't have to look long because Burton was looking for him.

"Coach, we have—"

"Go," Burton said. "Now!"

Then he turned and walked away.

Well, that was easy, Keith thought as he went to gather his teams together.

CHAPTER SIXTY-ONE

MONDAY, SEPTEMBER 14, 4:45 P.M. EDT
WASHINGTON, D.C.

"So do you guys want a little added incentive to get your work done fast?" Scott Ross asked the members of the RoU team who had gathered around the conference table. Gooey continued at his workstation.

The gang nodded their impatient affirmation. Scott could tell by the way they kept glancing back toward their computer monitors that this impromptu meeting was nothing but a distraction. *Oh, well; you gotta do what you gotta do.*

"Actually, first, can you guys bust down the net? It's a little in the way," Scott asked.

"Aw, come on, Scott. We finally got it just right," Joey Williamson complained.

Recently the team had attached an improvised net to the conference table, creating a long, narrow Ping-Pong table. During their infrequent breaks, they had used the game to stretch their cramped muscles and get some activity in. While Hernandez and Williamson were strong with their fast game, nobody knew what to do with Evie's spinning serves, and she reigned as the RoU Ping-Pong queen. Gooey was banned from playing due to his tendency to sweat quickly, profusely, and pungently.

"Okay, whatever," Scott said, deciding that this certainly wasn't a battle that needed to be fought right then. "They say there's no incentive like self-preservation. I just—"

"Who?" Evie interrupted.

"Who what?" Scott said impatiently.

"Who says that?"

"Who says what?"

"'There's no incentive like self-preservation.' You said 'they' say it. I was just wondering who 'they' is."

Looking around the table, Scott saw that all eyes were on him. "I don't know who 'they' is . . . I mean, are. What does it matter?"

Taking a scolding tone to her voice, Evie said, "Do you really think you should be quoting someone you don't even know?"

"Samuel Butler said, 'Self-preservation is the first law of nature,'" Gooey called out from his work area.

"Shut up and get off Google," Scott called back. "Evie, do you mind if I move on?"

"As long as you promise not to—"

"I promise! Now, what was I saying?"

As Scott tried to regain his train of thought, he saw Williamson slip something across the table to Evie.

"Wait! Lift that up!" he said, pointing to Evie's hand. Evie hesitated, then revealed a folded five-dollar bill.

Scott sighed. "Let's hear it."

Williamson spoke with a barely suppressed grin. "Evie bet me she could totally derail you within thirty seconds. And I'm a man who always pays my debts."

"Sorry, Scottybear," Evie said, giving Scott a coquettish bat of her eyelashes.

Scott shook his head and tried not to smile. He had given Jim Hicks the same sort of hard time, and Stanley Porter before him. *I've created these miscreants in my own image, and whatever I get probably serves me right.* "Back to what I was saying. I heard from Riley after his meeting with Muhammed Zerin Khan. Washington, D.C., is the second target."

"I knew it," Tara exulted, her hand coming down hard on the table.

"Yes, you did," Scott agreed. "That was an excellent call, Tara."

The young analysts snickered at Scott's unnecessarily strong affirmation.

"Keep it together, kids," Khadi said, unsuccessfully suppressing her own smile. "Did Riley get anything else from him? Is he bringing him back?"

"Unfortunately, no. Khan is dead."

"What about Riley?" Khadi quickly asked. Then, almost as an afterthought, she added, "And Skeeter?"

"They seem fine. Riley said to report to the authorities that Khan had killed himself. That's all I know."

Khadi leaned back in her chair and ran her fingers through her hair. "I tell you, the guy's going to drive me insane."

"You should have been with him in Afghanistan," Scott said. "It was like this every day. Dude's got an angel on his shoulder, no doubt about that."

"Where are Riley and Skeeter now?" Tara asked.

"They're on their way back here. ETA is a couple of hours. By the time they arrive, I want to have something to tell them. So let's talk this through."

Khadi shook herself from her Riley Covington worries and jumped back into the conversation. "Before we do that, what's Stanley Porter telling you about the world situation?"

Scott shook his head. "Apparently we had our ears in a quickly convened meeting between some of the major Middle Eastern and Central Asian countries, along with Russia, China, North Korea, and Venezuela. Let's just say that things are not good. A weak America means international anarchy, and everyone is clamoring to get their piece of a newly available pie. China's got their eyes on Taiwan and Southeast Asia. Russia's looking at the Baltics and at Israel."

"Israel? What does Russia want with Israel?" Evie asked.

"Resources. An absolutely enormous natural gas reserve has been found off the coast of Haifa, and Israel's hush-hush discovery of oil around the Dead Sea is turning into the worst-kept secret since . . . well, since worst-kept secrets were kept track of."

"Good one, Scott," Williamson said.

"Sorry I'm not living up to your standards, Joey. I'm a little tired."

"And cranky," Evie offered.

"And cranky," Scott confirmed. "Anyway, all the bad guys of the world are waiting for our eventual demise. Already Iran is massing troops on its western border. Egypt, Syria, and Lebanon are moving military equipment to their respective borders with Israel. If we don't stop this next weapon, I think Iran, with Russia's help, is going to plow right through Iraq and Jordan, and Israel will finally get pushed into the sea."

"I wouldn't count on it," Khadi said. "Not with their record. At least not before nuking every Middle Eastern capital as a parting gift."

"Which means that Russia will probably nuke Israel in retaliation," Tara continued.

"Which means that we'll probably nuke Russia, who will have saved plenty of warheads for us," Scott agreed. "The scenario keeps getting rosier and rosier."

"Well, it just means that instead of only getting to save America, we get to save all of mankind," Evie said with a smile.

"No pressure," Williamson said.

Scott's insides twisted, and he bit his tongue. No matter what he had told Secretary Moss about using humor to deal with the pressure, sometimes the jokes just didn't set well with him. *But the kids need it. Just try to keep yourself under control and get the job done!* "So what are we doing yakking about this! Let's get back to business!"

"My thinking is—," Hernandez began.

Scott put up his hand. "Hold on, Hernandez. Khadi, while we're talking, can you message the 'D.C. is the target' tidbit up the chain? Just tell them you'll give them all the details later."

"On it," Khadi said, picking up her smartphone.

"Sorry, Virge. You were saying . . ."

"Okay, my thinking is that we need to focus almost exclusively on water transport again. With all air traffic grounded, they aren't going to fly it in. I also don't see it coming in by truck because there are too many weigh stations along the route up."

"Good call," Scott agreed. "This is too big and too heavy to hide behind a false wall of Little Debbie cakes."

"Exactly," Hernandez continued. "That means we look for water traffic—fishing-boat size and up—that's making the trip from Cuba up to the waters outside of D.C."

"Which is a wide range," Williamson jumped in. "The Chesapeake Bay and the Potomac River are closest, but the device could conceivably be launched from all the way on the other side of Delaware, out in the Atlantic."

"I don't think so," Tara said. "Remember, they tracked the New York City launch to a boat just off of Sandy Hook. That's less than twenty miles from the heart of the city. I think they're keeping the launches close because they don't necessarily trust the North Korean Scuds. Or maybe because it's better to be close to land for the uniting of the missile and the warhead."

"Would have been nice to have talked to those dudes on the New York City boat before they blew themselves to kibbles and bits," Scott said.

Khadi agreed. "From what I hear, President Lloyd isn't too happy about how Secretary Moss handled that one. I have a feeling we'll be called in next time before Moss has the chance to choke another op."

Scott snapped his fingers. "That's one other thing. Text them again and remind them to keep Lloyd off of Air Force One and Marine One—no tours of the affected areas or anything."

Khadi started working her smartphone again.

"Back to what Tara was saying," Scott said. "While we need to be looking all around the Maryland and Delaware coasts, we really want to focus on the Chesapeake and the Potomac. What we're looking for is a midsize boat that's come up from Cuba."

"Got it!" Gooey yelled from his work area.

Instantly, Scott was out of his chair, sprinting to Gooey's computer, which, given the small size of the room, was a very short run. He arrived just in time to see Gooey closing a window on his computer.

"Seriously? You got it?" Scott asked excitedly.

"Got what?" Gooey asked.

"The boat."

"What boat?"

By now everyone had surrounded Gooey. "I was describing the boat we're looking for, and you called out, 'Got it!'"

"Oh, *that* boat. No, I don't got it."

Scott glared at Gooey, then said, "If that wasn't it, can you please tell me what you did 'got'?"

"It was nothing," Gooey said, seeming to shrink in his chair.

"Gooey . . ."

"Okay, I got a Death Knight."

Evie, Williamson, and Hernandez all made noises of disgust and walked away.

"What's a Death Knight?" Scott asked.

"It's the first hero class in *World of Warcraft*. This one had been lurking around for a while and really bugging me. I finally found a way to take him out. You should have seen it. I . . ." Gooey stopped when he saw the look on Scott's face.

"Tell you what, Gooey. How about we make a deal? You save our world first; then I'll give you a whole week of paid office time to go saving other worlds."

Gooey's face lit up. "Seriously? A whole week? Consider the boat as good as got!"

Gooey swiveled back to his computer.

The guy's too good to get rid of. You just got to know the right incentive to make him work. Scott watched as Gooey pounded away on his keyboard. *Nice work, Ross; you might just make a good suit after all—well, minus the tie . . . and the jacket . . . and the dress pants, nice shirt, and fancy shoes.*

Turning to get back to the meeting, Scott saw that everyone was already working. "Uh, meeting adjourned," he said weakly.

Tara walked up to him. "Khadi's in her office giving details to the higher-ups. I've got Virgil and Joey scanning satellite images, trying to track a boat up the coast. Evie is continuing to try to find the container with the warhead."

"Wow—you're good," Scott said admiringly.

Tara held Scott's arm, flashed a smile that he felt down to his knees, and said, "Well, thank you. You're not so bad yourself."

As she walked back to her desk, Scott thought, *Was that a moment? Did we just have a moment? Yeah, I think that was a moment!*

Whistling, he went back to his office to devise a new plan for saving Western civilization.

CHAPTER SIXTY-TWO

MONDAY, SEPTEMBER 14, 5:30 P.M. EDT
NEW YORK, NEW YORK

"Everyone back here by 7:30. And don't forget to wind your watches!" They had found enough mechanical watches among the players and trainers for each of the five pairs to carry one.

"Got it, Keith," they said.

"And remember, don't talk to anyone if you can help it. Your goal is to be as invisible as possible. Oh, and never, ever let anyone see what's in your envelopes!"

Keith's biggest concern was that someone would see the loot that each of the pairs was carrying and try to forcibly take it. With the amount they all had, combined with the lawlessness that seemed to be taking place down below, that wasn't far from the realm of possibility.

Earlier, Keith and Afshin had circuited through the team and asked for all the cash the guys had. The first time they tried it was early in the morning. During that initial pass, they found the players reluctant to give up their hard-earned money. Later in the day, however, as the sun rose and the water depleted, the wallets began to open.

Getting the cash had been the easy part. But then Keith had started thinking that cash was probably becoming less and less valuable, so he had gone back through one more time, asking for jewelry that he could use to barter with. The guys had been even more hesitant to honor this request until they noticed the two trademark two-karat diamond stud earrings gone from Keith's ears. Soon the clink of gold chains and the plink of rings and earrings sounded in the various bus groups.

Each team now carried a minimum of three thousand dollars in cash and about five thousand worth of jewelry—enough to buy whatever supplies they wanted, but also enough to tempt even the smallest of criminals to go up against these big men.

One last safety preparation Keith had made was to carefully plot the path that each pair would take, using a borrowed map from a nearby car with Missouri license plates.

Scanning each pair one last time and saying a quick prayer for their safety, he said, "You guys know your routes. Don't deviate! We want to be able to find you if for some reason you don't come back on time. Buy as much as you can carry, but remember you have a long walk back here. Now gather in."

As they huddled around him, Keith said, "Remember, we're not in a life-and-death situation yet, so there's no reason to put yourselves at risk. Get out there, get stuff, and get back. Got it? Now, 'scavenger rats' on three. One, two, three!"

"Scavenger rats!" they yelled in unison, smiles on their faces.

As they walked past bus three, Gorkowski flashed an obscene gesture at Keith. Keith had removed the center from a pair with Travis Marshall and put Donovan Williams in his place.

Keith didn't even bother acknowledging Gorkowski. *You make your bed . . .*

It took about eight minutes to weave their way to the off-ramp. A strange feeling slightly disoriented Keith as the ten men walked down to the city below. It felt like they had been up on that freeway for days. It was hard for him to believe that it was less than twenty-four hours since they were all on top of the world, having won their season opener on the road.

What a difference a day makes, twenty-four little hours, he sang to himself with a wry smile.

At the bottom of the off-ramp, they split up. Two teams went left to fan out over the next blocks. Two other teams went right. Keith and Afshin went straight ahead.

The first thing Keith noticed as they walked was that the air was denser down here. They were at a lower elevation than the freeway, and there was less of a breeze to keep the air moving. So the smoke hung thick and gritty. All around them things had a grayish tint from the ash that continuously floated to the ground.

Because the sidewalks were filled with people, Keith and Afshin kept to the street, winding through the yellow cabs and beater cars. This was definitely not a limousine section of town.

One thing that surprised Keith down here was the amount of debris along the blocks of shops. Mailboxes had been toppled, benches had been broken, cars had been overturned and burned. So many windows had been broken out onto the sidewalk that there was a bizarre tinkling, crunching sound that blended in with the din of the city as they walked.

Another thing that Keith noticed was a tension among the people. There was nothing outwardly visible, necessarily. But there was a palpable feeling in the air—an electricity almost, although Keith thought that comparison was an odd choice given the circumstances. It was as if, with a word or a sound or the pull of a trigger, everyone would riot.

"Can you feel that, Afshin?"

"What? That we're on the brink of violent anarchy? that we better do what we came to do and get ourselves out of here before we end up like him?" Afshin answered, nodding toward a guy curled under a bus stop, either sleeping or dead. "No, I don't feel a thing."

"Well, let's get a hustle on. Here, let's try this one," Keith said pointing to a corner market that still had most of its windows intact.

But even as they approached, it was clear they were too late. Stepping in, Keith was appalled by what he saw. The store had been stripped bare. Most of the display racks had been toppled, and the glass cooler doors had been shattered.

"Keith, look," Afshin said, pointing toward the register.

Next to it lay a man, his open, sightless eyes still registering shock and pain. His fingers clutched a crowbar, and a stream of blood wound its way from the back of his head to a small pool that had formed under the ice freezer.

Taking a deep breath, Keith walked over and took hold of the end of the iron bar. After a couple of tugs, he pulled it free from the dead man's grip.

As he walked back toward the front door, he saw Afshin's look of shock.

"Close your mouth, Rook. We might need this," Keith said, fighting to ignore his own revulsion at what he'd just done.

The next two stores they checked were similar to the first. Thoroughly cleaned out, though thankfully no sign of the owners. Just when they were about to lose hope, they saw a store with all of its windows in one piece. The sign above the doors identified it as Grissom's Market—Your Friendly Neighborhood Store.

As they approached, a man at the door leveled a shotgun at them.

"What do you want?" he asked.

"We're just looking for some food and some water or Gatorade or something like that," Keith answered.

"Let me see your money," the man demanded.

Afshin started to reach into his pocket, but Keith stopped him. "My name's Keith Simmons, and this is my friend. We're both with the Colorado Mustangs. Believe me, we've got money."

The man lowered his gun a touch. "Yeah, I thought I recognized you. What's your friend's name? He looks kinda familiar, too."

"Don't you worry about him. You just need to know who I am. So are we coming in or not?"

The man motioned with his gun and said, "Yeah, you can come in. But leave the bar with me."

"You got it," Keith said as he leaned the crowbar against the doorframe and walked in with Afshin in tow.

The doorman called into the store after them, "Keith Simmons from the Colorado Mustangs and some mystery date. They're cool."

A man came from the back room and held out his hand. "Keith Simmons! How're you doing? Sorry about the precautions. I'm sure you can understand."

"No problem. It's a nightmare out there."

"It's been a nightmare in here, too. Last night was insane, and I'm expecting tonight to be worse. By the way, my name's John Grissom. I own the place. Everyone knows you, Keith, but who's your friend, if you don't mind me asking."

"His name's Matt," Keith said before Afshin had a chance to speak. "He's one of our trainers. I told him to let me do the talking." Then, turning to Afshin, he said, "It's okay, Matt. You can say hi to the man."

"Hey," Afshin said, shaking hands with Grissom.

"Good to meet you, Matt. So what does a trainer do? You like a coach or something?"

After a quick glance at Keith, Afshin answered, "No, I mostly work on guys like Keith—rubbing them down and taping them up. That kind of stuff."

"Huh," Grissom said, giving Afshin a strange look. "Well, to each his own."

"Listen, John, we gotta get going as quick as we can. We have a whole team up on the freeway waiting for us," Keith said.

"No time for chitchat right now, huh? Hey, I understand. No problemo. As you can see, we don't have a whole lot left. I'm afraid we're totally out of bottled water."

Keith scanned the store's meager stock. "Do you have any Gatorade or Powerade or anything like that?"

"Not out here, but I do have some in the storeroom that I've been holding back. How much you want?" Grissom asked as he walked toward the cooler door.

"Just bring what you've got," Keith called out, making his way to where a couple boxes of PowerBars were.

"What's with the 'Matt' thing?" Afshin whispered to him.

"Think about it. How popular do you think the names *Afshin* or *Ziafat* are right now? Don't mean to offend, bro, but the more white American you can be, the better."

"Suppose you're right," Afshin said as he started pulling some small cans of food off the shelves. "But couldn't you have given me a better name, like Rock or Thor or something? Hey, maybe that could be my last name. Matt Thor . . . Rock . . . son."

"Okay, Mr. Thorrockson. Check it out, unless you see a can opener or those things are pull-top, don't bother with them. Snag any nuts you can find and some Snickers. . . . Oh, and see if there's any beef jerky left."

Grissom came out carrying two cases of Gatorade. "Hang on; I've got two more."

While Keith looked to see if there was anything behind the counter they might need, Afshin came up with an armload of nuts, Snickers, and PayDay bars.

"They were out of jerky."

"Yeah, I had a feeling they might be. Nice haul, though."

Grissom came back out with the other two cases. "Wow, you guys really loaded up."

"Got a lot of big, hungry mouths to feed. Now, how much do we owe you?"

A sly smile spread across Grissom's face. "How much you got?"

Oh no! Here it comes. Greedy little gouger. "No way. You give me a price, and I'll tell you if I have enough."

"Tsk, tsk, tsk," Grissom said, shaking his head. "That's not the way things are working these days, Keith. I'm almost out of stock, and who knows when the next shipments are going to reach the city. I'm afraid that's caused a bit of inflation."

A scuff behind him caused Keith to turn around. Shotgun guy was now standing just inside the door. Angrily, Keith reached into his pocket and threw his cash on the counter. "There's more than two thousand dollars there. That should be more than enough for this, even with 'inflation.'"

"And how much might you be carrying, Matt?"

Afshin threw the other half of their money on the counter.

"That enough for you?" Keith asked.

"Almost. It's just that cash ain't buying what it used to. I noticed you've got those two empty holes in your ears. You wouldn't happen to have on your person what used to be sticking through them, do you?" Grissom asked.

"You're serious?"

"As a heart attack."

Disgusted, Keith reached into his shirt pocket and tossed the diamonds onto the counter. They bounced on the hard surface, and Grissom stopped them with his hand.

"Looks like we have ourselves a deal," the storeowner said with a big grin. "Do you want paper or plastic with that?"

Moments later, each man threaded three bags on each arm, then lifted two cases of the Gatorade.

On the way out, the guy with the shotgun asked, "Hey, where do you want me to put your crowbar?"

"You really want me to answer that?" Keith said as he slammed out the door.

They both stormed down the street, but after they had gotten half a block, Keith began laughing.

"What's so funny? We just got shafted back there!"

By now, Keith was laughing so hard that he had to put down his boxes. "So what? Look at the haul we've got! Besides, I just keep picturing his face when he tries to trade those studs to someone who really knows jewelry."

Now Afshin started laughing. "You mean they're fake?"

"The best $200 can buy. I never take the real ones on road trips," Keith said as he picked up his load. "Come on, Mr. Thorrockson, let's get our tails back home. I don't want to still be down here after dark."

CHAPTER SIXTY-THREE

MONDAY, SEPTEMBER 14, 6:45 P.M. EDT
NEW YORK, NEW YORK

"So how do you think all this is going to end?" Afshin asked Keith as they walked down the street.

"Beats me. My guess is that we're all going to have to hike on out of here eventually. Otherwise you're talking like half a million bus trips to evacuate everyone—more if they're using helicopters," Keith said, huffing a bit. They were about halfway back to the off-ramp, and Keith was starting to envy Afshin's stamina and younger legs.

"Yeah, but look around," Afshin said. "How would they even get any buses in here? No, I'm with you; we'll be doing some walking."

"Excuse me, sir, but could you spare any food?" said a female voice next to Keith.

"Sorry," he mumbled without looking down. "Got a bunch of hungry mouths to feed back home." He picked up his pace, hoping to escape his guilt a little faster.

Even before leaving the buses, he had covered this eventuality with his teams. "People are going to be trying to get your food from you—asking, begging, demanding—but you can't give in. If you give in to one person, you'll be swamped. Just say sorry, make yourself look as big as you can, and keep walking."

Fine words those were, he thought now. *Easy to say; a lot harder to do. It kills me to walk past those in need, but I have to take care of my team! There are guys counting on me! So toughen up and keep walking!*

Sweat poured down his face, and Keith longed to crack open one of the Gatorades he was carrying. In order to distract himself, he asked, "How you holding up, Z?"

Afshin puffed a little laugh. "Doing better than you, old man!"

"No doubt about that. These knees have seen a few more games than yours. But I mean, how are you feeling—like how're your spirits and stuff?"

"You know, I'm doing okay. Really. Story time?"

"Sure," Keith said. Why Afshin always felt the need to ask permission before talking about himself, he'd never know.

"I remember my dad telling me about when he fled Iran. He waited a little too long, so when the time came, it was cut and run. He and my mom left with basically nothing, and when they arrived in America, they had to start all over again. But in all that time, never did he get angry or discouraged. He told me he just kept thinking that nothing had really changed for him and my mom. Sure, they had less money, and their immediate future was less certain. However, they knew that God still loved them. They knew that Jesus Christ was still on His throne. With that knowledge, they felt they could handle anything."

A little ways up, two guys moved into Keith's path. Keith stared them down with his "I'm taking the quarterback's head off this play" look and never quit moving forward. Eventually the would-be banditos slipped away in search of easier prey.

"I remember Riley saying something like that," Keith said to Afshin. "It was a couple of weeks after his dad's funeral. I asked him how he was surviving, and he said, 'As long as I know that God loves me and that I'm doing what He wants, nothing's really changed.' Then he talked about how if life is falling apart around you, it didn't really matter—not in the grand scheme of things. This life is just a blip on the radar screen of our eternity.

"I don't know. I mean, of the two of us, you're the theologian.

But I'm just thinking that God's got us in this mess for a purpose. And as long as we're doing what He wants, then we're good. Right? There are a lot more comfortable places we could be. But whether we're here or there is no biggie. The biggie is that in either place we're doing what He wants us to do. What do you think?"

"I think you're more of a theologian than you think you are. What you're talking about is called contentment. The apostle Paul put it this way: 'I know what it is to be in need, and I know what it is to have plenty. I have learned the secret of being content in any and every situation, whether well fed or hungry, whether living in plenty or in want. I can do everything through him who gives me strength.' Memorized that one for a camp scholarship," Afshin said proudly.

"Nice. I like Paul. He wasn't no weak-kneed girlie-skirter."

"'Paul wasn't no weak-kneed girlie-skirter.' I actually think that was one of John Calvin's original ten points before he pared them down to five."

"Bummer. Didn't make the short list, huh?"

"Nope. Must be tough getting cut."

"I wouldn't know," Keith said with a grin.

As they walked, dusk began to descend. A rainless cloud-cover had begun to blanket the city but was barely visible through the thick haze of smoke. Four blocks up, Keith could see the freeway. Walking up the off-ramp, recognizable mainly because of their size, were Donovan Williams and Travis Marshall. Both seemed to be carrying boxes.

"Dude, you see—"

"What do we have here?" a voice interrupted Keith from behind.

Keith just kept walking.

"Hey, you two deaf or something?" the same voice asked. Something big and round pushed hard into Keith's back, causing one of the boxes of Gatorade to slip off.

Keith whirled around and saw eight young thugs standing behind them. Each held an aluminum baseball bat. As soon as Keith and Afshin stopped, the group fanned out into a circle, surrounding them. Carefully, Keith put his bags and the other box on the ground. Afshin followed suit.

"You don't look like you belong in my neighborhood, Mr. Fancy Shirt," the leader of the pack said, using his bat to flip the collar up against Keith's chin. "What you doing around here?"

Keith's heart was racing. This situation was bad. *Just get out of this. It doesn't matter what it costs you; just get yourselves out of this.* "Listen, we're not looking for trouble. We were just up on the freeway when whatever happened happened. We just came down to do some shopping."

"Oh, how nice. Did you hear that, D. B.? They just came down for a lovely afternoon of shopping." D. B. and the rest of the guys started laughing. "You sure seemed to shop a lot for just two dudes."

Suddenly D. B. burst out, "Hey, I knew I recognized him! This joe's Keith Simmons—you know, from the Colorado Mustangs!"

The first pulled his bat back and began laughing. "Seriously? You really Keith Simmons?"

"Yeah, that's me," Keith said, relief starting to flood his body.

"Well, why didn't you say so? I'm Dizzy, and these are my boys. Imagine that—Keith Simmons walking through my hood. Tell you what, you leave one of those cases of Gatorade here, you can grab the rest of your stuff and go."

Keith put on his best smile and said, "Thanks, Dizzy. That's a solid thing to do."

The leader laughed again. "Check out Keith Simmons—getting all old-school on me. That was a 'solid' thing to do."

The rest of the group started laughing. Keith's hands shook slightly as he and Afshin began to pick up their bags. Then Dizzy put his bat under Afshin's chin and lifted his head up.

"Hold on a second, my man. I said Mr. Keith Simmons could go. I didn't say anything about your ragheaded self."

Keith's heart sank. He dropped the bags. *This is really, really bad!* He could see the fear in Afshin's eyes.

Keith stood back up and forced a chuckle. "Ragheaded? Matt? Come on, Dizzy, he's just one of the team's trainers. I brought him along to help carry stuff. Seriously, does Thorrockson sound like an Arab dude?"

Dizzy laughed harder. "Thorrockson? Did you guys make that up yourselves? Thorrockson?" Suddenly Dizzy turned serious. "You disappoint me, Mr. Keith Simmons. Why'd you go lying to the D-man? You see, I know who this is," he said, pushing his bat hard into Afshin's chest. "This is that first-rounder camel jockey, Zifanat or Zinafat or whatever his funky, suicide-bombing name is. Look around! Don't you know that his buddies are the ones who did all this to us? And you go lying for him?"

Keith looked for help from the crowd that had gathered around the confrontation. Many of the people seemed troubled, some even on the verge of tears. But others, at the revelation of who Afshin was, had something else in their eyes—hatred and revenge.

"Come on, Dizzy. Listen, I'm sorry I lied. Afshin has nothing to do with this. You know that. He's caught in it just like the rest of us. Just let us on our way. You can keep all—"

Keith's words were stopped by a blow from Dizzy's bat to his midsection. Keith doubled over, gasping for breath.

"Leave him alone," he could hear Afshin saying from above him. "It's me you want. Let him—"

Afshin's words were cut off by a metallic ping, and suddenly Afshin dropped flat next to Keith. Blood ran from a gash in his cheek. His eyes were glazed, but they managed to look in Keith's direction.

"Run," he mouthed, before another blow landed on his shoulder with an audible crack.

A cry rose up from the depths of Keith's soul and burst forth as he lunged at Dizzy.

"AUUGGHH!" He caught Dizzy under the chin with his head. The group's leader was out cold even before his skull cracked the pavement. Keith spun around to find his next victim, but something slammed into the back of his head. He pitched forward, then took another hit on the side of his leg. He dropped to his knees. One more hit to his right temple sprawled him out on the pavement.

Although his vision was clouding over, he could still make out Afshin. Four guys had surrounded him and were gleefully raining blows down with their bats. In his mind, Keith pictured himself jumping to his feet and rescuing his friend; he could see himself snatching a bat out of one of their hands and whaling blows on them until their bones broke and their heads split open. He so desperately wanted to do something—anything—but his body wouldn't cooperate.

After what seemed like an eternity, the men tired of Afshin. Keith looked at his friend's face. Half of it wasn't recognizable anymore—torn, swollen, bloodied. But it was the other side—the side with the hazel eye that was still open, staring, empty, and lifeless—that broke Keith's heart.

"Dirty raghead," one of the attackers said, giving Afshin's head one last whack, blessedly turning that eye away.

The group walked back over to Keith, and one of them prodded his cheek with a bat. Then, wheeling back, he brought the toe of his shoe directly into the center of Keith's face.

CHAPTER SIXTY-FOUR

MONDAY, SEPTEMBER 14, 8:15 P.M. EDT
WASHINGTON, D.C.

Riley leaned back in his chair and looked at the ceiling of the open room. Kim Li and Ted Hummel were laughing about some story Li had been telling. But other than that, the room was silent. The air-conditioning was set high, and Riley felt a chill after having been out in the evening humidity.

When Riley and Skeeter had first arrived back from Georgia, they had stopped by the Room of Understanding. There had been a very quick greeting from the analysts, who all had then gone immediately back to their work. Even Scott and Khadi had simply given them a fast "Good to have you back" before they left them standing alone in the middle of the room.

Reading the invisible Do Not Disturb sign, the two went three doors down the hall, just past the men's and women's restrooms, to the area that contained the ops side of the special operations group. Kim Li, Ted Hummel, Gilly Posada, Matt Logan, Carlos Guitiérrez, and Steve Kasay were all in the brightly lit room—geared up and ready to bolt at a moment's notice.

After exchanging greetings, Riley and Skeeter had changed into the all-black uniform that the SOG team favored. Then Riley gave a brief rundown of the events at Stone Mountain.

"As soon as we get a location on that boat, we're out the door. After the way Secretary Moss's people botched the New York City operation, Stanley Porter's got us first in line. But let's not forget what happened to those other guys. We lost four of our brothers when that boat blew. There's no reason to think that couldn't happen to us, too. So we go in fast, quiet, and hard. If you even think there might be trouble, pull the trigger and let God sort them out."

That had been an hour ago. Everyone had checked and rechecked their gear and their weapons. Now it was just the nerves, the anticipation, and the waiting.

Riley looked for patterns in the acoustic ceiling tiles in a vain attempt not to think about what was floating out on the water somewhere east of the city. The very real possibility of another EMP launch twisted his stomach.

However, if he were being honest—totally, deep-down, bottom-of-the-heart truthful—he wasn't really thinking about all the people who would be affected, the tens or even hundreds of thousands of possible casualties. Sure, they were there somewhere bouncing around his cluttered mind. But standing out in the forefront of his thoughts was none other than himself.

I do not want to go through that again! Especially this time without an escape hatch—no Scott to come rescue me. Yet here I am again, smack-dab in the middle of the possible ground zero.

The fact that it could happen anytime kept every muscle tense. He was just waiting for the lights to go out—to be again caught up in that impossible nightmare. *But if it is going to happen, it's better for it to happen now than when we're in the middle of the city—or worse, when we're in a chopper.* That thought gave his insides another twist.

Why am I here, Lord? Why can't I just be having a normal life with a normal career living in Normalsville, U.S.A.? I hate where you've got me! And it's not like this is the first time you've put me in a situation like this, where not only is my life in danger but I also have the lives of thousands of others on my shoulders.

Honestly, I'm tired of it! I'm tired of the responsibility! I'm tired of the danger! Despite what everyone says, I'm not Captain America. I'm still just the little kid who was scared of the ghosty tree that swayed on breezy nights outside my window.

He looked at Skeeter, who was calmly loading another polymag for his Magpul Masada. *He's gotta be feeling it too. How can he not? But look at him—all cool, calm, and collected—and here I am sweating bullets! The guy's amazing!*

Seeming to sense he was being watched, Skeeter looked up and saw Riley looking at him. With the faintest hint of a smile, Skeeter brushed his hand across his forehead like he was wiping away his sweat. Riley smiled back and nodded.

Maybe he's human after all, Riley thought as he watched Skeeter insert another round. Tilting back up toward the ceiling, Riley prayed, *Lord, I know You understand my lack of faith and my fears. Please give me the strength to fulfill the mission You've placed before me. Like You prayed in the garden, 'Not my will but Yours be done.' Whatever You want from me I'll do.*

Li had finished his story, and the room was silent again—every man lost in his own history, his own family, his own role on the team.

Suddenly Scott's voice cut through the silence. "Mount up! We've found the boat," he said over the intercom.

Instantly the room was a flurry of activity—each man grabbing his equipment and running for the back door that led to the helipad. Riley picked up his gear and Khadi's as well. He had insisted on being the one to check her pack and her weapon while she continued her work in the RoU. Skeeter had done the same for Scott.

As they exited the room and ran across the lawn, Riley could see the two jet-black, MH-6J Little Birds bringing their rotors up to speed. These helicopters, which had been brilliantly modified for special-ops infiltrations and exfiltrations, could carry up to six troops on a bench-looking external personnel system that hung on the chopper's sides. Because of their shape and their deadliness, the MH-6J had also been given the nickname "Killer Egg."

Running to his designated position, Riley seated himself, then held on tightly as the Little Bird lifted off the ground. Next to Riley was Skeeter; Scott and Khadi were on the opposite side of the aircraft. Looking below, Riley saw the second Bird beginning its ascent.

Once they leveled off, Riley reached behind himself and found his headphones. He slipped them on and shouted, "You on, Scott?"

"Been waiting on you," Scott responded.

"We're heading north," Riley said, more as a question than a statement.

"Yeah, the National Reconnaissance Office was able to track a midsize fishing trawler up from Cuba to where it's sitting now in the Chesapeake Bay right at the mouth of the Patapsco River."

"Baltimore?"

"Baltimore," Scott confirmed. "Its present location is less than forty miles outside of downtown D.C. Well within range to make a serious mess."

The chopper was reaching its cruising speed of 135 mph, causing Riley to hold tightly to the bench and lean back into the helicopter. "So the NRO found it, huh? Didn't that tweak the kids?"

"They were mostly all right," Khadi answered. "They were just happy it was found. Well, all except for Gooey, who was vowing revenge on the NRO folks using something called Avool's Sword of Jin."

"I've really got to get him away from *World of Warcraft*. He's getting a little bit addicted to that thing," Scott said.

"Gee, you think?" Khadi responded.

As they sped through the sky, Riley tried to think of something to say to the team to pump them up for the task ahead. The only problem was, the image in his mind of the chopper losing power and plummeting to the ground made it a little hard to focus.

Finally he said, "Well, this is it, guys. We take care of this thing, and it'll be time to start figuring out who caused all this mess. But if we blow this, it probably won't matter too much to us one way or the other. So let's get out there and get the job done!"

The tepid response to Riley's little speech let him know he had probably said exactly the wrong thing to get the guys psyched up. His suspicion was confirmed when Scott said, "Wow, Pach, for a second there I was picturing General Patton in front of that huge flag giving the speech to the Third Army. Very inspiring!"

That was followed by an "Ow!" as Khadi most likely gave Scott the elbow to the ribs that he deserved.

Well, good speech or bad speech, these guys know what to do. Lord, please, just let them all come back alive, Riley prayed as he watched the city lights pass by under his boots.

CHAPTER SIXTY-FIVE

MONDAY, SEPTEMBER 14, 8:20 P.M. EDT
NEW YORK, NEW YORK

Keith came awake with a gasp. His nasal passages burned, and the sensation traveled back down his throat. He flailed about and tried to get to his feet.

"Keith, stay down," a voice said.

He tried to open his eyes and found that he could only get any movement in one. As his vision began to clear, he saw Ted Bonham leaning over him. He had an ammonia strip in his hand.

"You need another hit?" Bonham asked.

Keith tried to say no but only managed a grunt. He pushed Bonham's hand away. Looking around in the flickering light, he saw Chris Gorkowski and Donovan Williams standing over him. Turning his head farther, he saw Travis Marshall and Danie Colson. They were kneeling next to . . .

Afshin's body was alongside a Dumpster, and suddenly Keith realized why he was so disoriented. He had been moved into what seemed to be an alley. It was hard to tell with the only light coming from a fire that someone had lit in that same Dumpster. He tried to drag himself over to Afshin, but Bonham kept him still.

Rage filled him, and he pushed Bonham,

sending him flying onto his back. Gorkowski and Williams attempted to hold him down, but he was twisting back and forth so hard, trying to pull himself up, that they called for Marshall.

Marshall scooted over and placed his hands on Keith's shoulders. Keith connected a hard right hand to the lineman's head, but his friend didn't let up.

"Stop, Keith! Come on, stop! He's gone! There's nothing you can do about it! He's gone!"

Keith finally looked Marshall in the face and saw tears in his eyes. He stopped fighting, closed his one good eye, and dropped his head back to the ground. Marshall's words echoed in his mind. *He's gone! He's gone!*

Pushing his friend's hands off his shoulders, Keith laid his arm across his eyes. The pain of touching his face was excruciating, but he figured it was the least he deserved. *I let them kill him! He always told me that he had my back, and the one time he needed me, I let him down.*

A sob escaped his lips and convulsed his body, but that was all he would allow himself. After using his arm to wipe his tears, he looked over at Bonham, who was just getting himself back up.

"Sorry," he said, his slowly recovering voice sounding distant and slurred.

"Forget it," Bonham said, pulling a bottle out of his pocket. "Let me give you something for the pain. Then we'll get you out of here."

"Wait," Keith replied, holding up a finger.

He nodded to Gorkowski and Williams, and they took their hands off of him. As he sat up, the alley spun around him. He put his head between his knees and took a couple of deep breaths. When he felt a little more stable, he started to stand. Marshall quickly took him under the arm and helped him up, steadying him on his feet.

With a jerk of his head, he indicated that he wanted to go see Afshin. Danie Colson still squatted next to the body. He was naked from the waist up. The shirt he had been wearing was now draped across Afshin's head.

Keith knelt down—Marshall never taking his arm off of him—and lifted the shirt. What he saw caused the anger to swell again. But it was just as quickly overtaken by a profound sorrow.

What a waste. At a time when all of America should be coming together, a handful of ignorant bigots tear a life apart.

If only they knew . . . If only they knew how much good you did for people. If only they saw your love for the hurting—the hours you put in at the children's hospital, the anonymous cash you'd drop off in the mailboxes of financially strapped people from your church. Remember that time on our way back from practice? You were dropping off an envelope and saw the door opening. You panicked so bad that you came diving through the passenger window as I burned rubber down the block! Oh, man, that was crazy. What a memory. What a guy. . . .

Keith gently put the shirt back. *You were always trying to beat me at everything—more tackles, more sacks, more QB pressures. Well, now you did beat me at something. You finally won! You're the first one to see our Savior's face. You're the first one to experience heaven, while I'm still stuck down here in this hell. It just ain't fair, Rook,* Keith thought with a sad smile, placing his hand on Afshin's cold arm. *It just ain't fair.*

"We need to get moving," Marshall said sympathetically. "It's dark and we've drawn a crowd. It's not safe here anymore."

Like it was safe before, Keith thought bitterly as he rose to his feet. The pain made him want to cry out, but he wouldn't let himself—wouldn't give the onlookers the satisfaction. *Stinking cowards. Just stand there and watch someone get beaten to death.*

"Cowards!" he shouted. He doubled over from the strain his outburst caused on what felt like multiple broken ribs. "Stinking cowards," he mumbled.

Bonham stepped next to him and slipped a few Percocets into his hand. Keith pushed them past his swollen lips and swallowed them down.

Williams walked toward Afshin, but Gorkowski stopped him.

"Kid's mine," he said quietly. Bending down, he slipped his hands under Afshin's body and cradled him in his arms. Walking up alongside Keith, he said, "Let's go."

Keith gave him a nod of thanks and began walking, Marshall still helping support him.

"How'd you find us?" Keith asked Marshall after they had cut through the crowd.

"When you didn't show up on time, we decided to give it another half hour in case you had just gotten caught up. By the time that passed, Gorkowski was going crazy, saying we needed to go right away. When we agreed, Snap practically ran all the way down here. We missed you at first because we just followed the route you had marked out on the map. After we had gone a ways, we doubled back and started asking people on the street if they'd seen you. That was when a guy told us about the beating and about you two being in the alley.

"He also told us about you not leaving Afshin when you had the chance. You were free to escape, and no one would have ever known. Instead, you stood by Afshin's side. In my eyes, that makes you a hero," Marshall said, looking at Keith.

Tears stung Keith's eyes, and he didn't return Marshall's look. "Hero? I don't think so. Look at Afshin," Keith said, tilting his head toward where Gorkowski carried him. "A real hero would have stopped that."

Marshall was shaking his head. "You tried. 'Greater love has no one than this, that he lay down his life for his friends.' You were willing to do that. That's a hero in my book."

Keith didn't respond—partly because he was uncomfortable with the whole conversation and partly because the Percocet was kicking in.

Later, when he finally lay down on a makeshift bed inside the bus, he had a hard time remembering how he had gotten there. He knew there had been a long walk, and it seemed to him that nobody had really talked most of the way. Beyond that, the details were murky.

He closed his eyes and tried to picture in his mind the things that Afshin was experiencing. *Has he left Christ's side? If so, whom has he met? What does it look like? Is it a giant throne room floating on the clouds with angels fluttering all about? Or is it like here, with grass and mountains and cool, flowing rivers? And speaking of cool, what's the weather like in heaven? Is it one perfect temperature for everybody, or can you set your own thermostat, like having dual temperature controls in a car?*

Whatever it's like, the rook is one lucky dog, Keith thought as his brain finally started to shut down and he drifted into a long, deep sleep.

CHAPTER

SIXTY-SIX

MONDAY, SEPTEMBER 14, 8:48 P.M. EDT
BALTIMORE, MARYLAND

The fifteen-minute flight was almost at its end, and Riley was chilled to the bone. He took turns flexing one hand while the other held its grip. Up ahead he could see Chesapeake Bay fast approaching.

"Going dark," said Noah Jefferson, the pilot, and the cabin instantly went black. Riley's heart gave a quick start, but unlike in his visions, this time when the lights went out, the helicopter stayed in the air. He looked behind and could just make out the silhouette of the second Little Bird against the almost completely dark sky.

Riley pounded his fist into Skeeter's thigh. "You ready?"

"Let's end this thing," Skeeter said in a voice that made Riley glad he was on the good side of the man's gun.

"One o'clock," came Jefferson's voice again. Riley looked around Skeeter and saw the lights of the trawler coming up. The chopper, which had already been flying low, dropped to just above the water as soon as they hit the shoreline. Riley always found it amazing how these pilots handled their machines. He felt like he could almost reach his foot down and dip his boot in the helicopter's moonlight reflection in the water.

Slipping off his headphones, Riley readied himself. The second Bird was going to hover just above the rear of the boat, where the guys could jump off onto the deck. Riley's wouldn't be able to get low enough, though, and this chopper was not equipped with winches, so they'd have to go down drop ropes. The whole goal of the operation was to get control of the boat as quickly as possible in order to prevent some idiot bad guy from pressing a red button and turning them all into human jigsaw puzzles.

Riley barely had time to take two deep breaths before they were there. The Little Bird made a quick lift, sending Riley's stomach up into his throat. Skeeter dropped the rope, and Riley grabbed hold of it, swinging out and clamping his feet to steady himself. Then he let himself slide, quickly descending the twenty feet to the roof of the bridge. Scott landed a second after him.

Quickly, each man jumped down on opposite sides of the cabin. As soon as Riley hit the metal walkway, an AK-47 shot out the window. Riley flattened himself on the ground.

"On three, Scott," he said into his comm. "One, two, three!"

Riley stood and fired into the cabin, making sure to avoid Scott's position as Scott did the same from his side. Three men inside quickly went down, victims of the deadly cross fire. Skeeter dropped beside Riley and on Riley's signal kicked in the door. Scott mirrored the action from the other side.

Each person took a different corner of the room.

"Clear," Riley called.

"Clear."

"Clear."

"Clear."

More gunfire erupted from the deck below.

"Scott, Khadi, stay here and see what you can find. Skeet and I'll go check out the delivery system."

Skeeter and Riley ran out the door. Riley could see Kasay and Guitiérrez on the foredeck. The rest were below.

"Gilly, give me a status," he called to the leader of the second team. For this operation, Riley had decided to do away with the enigmatic call signs. His mind was already cluttered enough.

"Four down and two in custody. We've found the missile. It's a Scud."

"It's a North Korean Hwasong-6," added Matt Logan, the team's munitions expert. "Thing has a range of at least a thousand kilometers; plenty for what they intended. It's loaded with . . . oh no! It's missing the warhead! They haven't got the warhead yet!"

Riley's heart sank as he ran belowdecks. When he reached the bottom of the steps, he almost stumbled over a crumpled body, leaping over it at the last second.

The missile was huge. Fifty feet long, it took up almost all of the specially modified cargo area. Riley wondered how the boat could survive the launch, but as he ran along the side of it, he saw an elevator system designed to raise the missile and probably place it over the water. *It's a little scary that Cuba's got these boats sitting around waiting to be used!*

But the *hows* of the delivery system were not as important to Riley at the moment as the *what nows*. He reached the front of the Scud and saw that indeed the nose was flat—just waiting for something to be attached to it.

"Where are they?" he asked Posada.

"Starboard," Posada replied, nodding to the other side of the missile.

Riley rounded the front of the Scud and found Li and Hummel with their weapons pointed at the heads of two very frightened men. Next to them was one of their dead comrades.

Hummel said, "I tried to talk to them, but I think they were speaking Arabic."

"Where's the warhead?" Riley said to the nearer of the two men, avoiding the puddle of blood that was spreading across the floor.

"Motavajjeh nemisham," he responded in a shaking voice.

"That's not Arabic; that's Farsi. Khadi, get down here quick," Riley called into his mic. Then to Li, he said, "Get that one around to the other side of the missile."

Moments later, Khadi arrived.

"We've got two, both Iranian," Riley explained. "Ask this one where the warhead is."

Khadi did. "Loosely translated, he says to go have relations with your mother," she reported.

Riley slapped the man hard across the face, drawing blood from the corner of his mouth. "Tell him to watch his language in front of a lady."

Khadi looked at Riley.

"Tell him," he insisted.

Khadi did. The man stared at Riley with hatred in his eyes.

"Now ask him again."

Khadi reported back another unsatisfactory answer.

This time, rather than hitting the man, Riley stood, whispered something in Skeeter's ear, and then fired his weapon.

When Riley rounded the front of the Scud, mopping at the blood on his face, he saw the other man. He was shaking and his eyes were wide. Li's eyes were just as wide.

Riley placed the barrel of his Magpul against the man's forehead. The man whimpered at the touch of the hot barrel against his skin.

"Where's the warhead?"

"We don't have it," the man said through Khadi.

Riley pushed the barrel harder. "I know that! So, since we've established that it's not here, tell me where it is!"

"In a warehouse in the city! I don't know where!"

"That's not good enough, cowboy. Tell me!"

Riley felt a hand on his shoulder. Angrily, Riley turned around to see Matt Logan. "What?"

Logan cupped his hand to Riley's ear and said something to him. Riley nodded, turned back to their captive, and decided to take another tack.

"What can you tell me about the warhead?"

"I don't know," the man replied.

"Is it nuclear?"

"No."

"Is it EMP?"

"Yes."

"Do you know the size of it?"

"No. I'm sorry."

"When were you supposed to receive it?"

"Tonight."

"How were you going to receive it?"

"A boat was to bring it, and we were to rendezvous."

"And how would you know where to meet up?"

"They were going to call, and—"

The man stopped suddenly, as if he knew he had said too much. When Khadi finished her stunted translation, Riley said, "Bingo! Where's the phone?"

The man clammed up.

"Tell him that if he does not answer me, I'm going to shoot him in the knee," Riley said as he pressed and rubbed the Magpul painfully against the man's joint.

Still the man said nothing.

"Have it your way," Riley said, standing and pointing the weapon at the man's knee.

"Nakheyr! Nakheyr!" the man pleaded, waving his hands.

Riley lowered his weapon.

The man began speaking rapidly.

"He says the phone is in the cabin," Khadi said.

"Scott, there should be a phone up there somewhere," Riley said into his mic.

"Yeah, I've got it. I was just checking through the calls sent and received."

"Bring it down here ASAP! Gilly, go relieve Scott on the bridge. Kasay, contact Porter's office and catch them up. Carlos, you do the same with Tara Walsh."

As they waited for Scott to arrive, Riley remembered what Matt Logan had whispered to him and said to Khadi, "Ask him whether or not the warhead can be converted to be detonated without the missile. And tell him that if he lies to me, I'll shoot both his knees."

Khadi did. "He says that it can be, but he doesn't know anything about how. He thought he heard the captain saying something about the conversion taking fifteen or twenty minutes, but he doesn't know for sure."

"Great," Riley grumbled. The good news was they had taken care of a serious threat. The bad news? There was still an NNEMP hiding somewhere in a metropolis of 2.5 million people. So little was still known about these new North Korean weapons, no one had a clue as to what kind of havoc a ground-level detonation could create. Placed in the right location, it was possible that the blast alone could kill several hundred people, to say nothing of what the EMP effects would do to the city.

Riley was anxious to get out of the hold. The air was stale with the scent of metal, gunpowder, sewage, and blood. Finally Scott arrived with the phone. Riley filled him in on the new information and told him to have the team disseminate it to all who needed to know.

"Does Gooey have the number of the phone?"

"Yeah, I have him checking it out through all of his databases."

"Tell him that we're about to make a call. I want him to give me a location on the receiver."

To Khadi, he said, "Let the guy know that I want him to place a call to whoever has the warhead. He should tell them that the boat is having engine problems, and that they'll need to bring it all the way out. Tell him that if he gives them any sort of warning, I'll shoot him in the gut, then throw him overboard for the sharks."

"Sharks?" Khadi asked doubtfully.

"He doesn't know. Just tell him."

She did, and the man quickly nodded his agreement. Riley handed him the phone and watched as he dialed. Khadi gave a running translation.

The man started out speaking rapidly, but Riley signaled him to slow down. "Who is this? . . . This is Kazem Vaziri. I am a friend of your friend. I . . . Father is indisposed trying to repair our transportation. He asked me to call you to tell you that you will have to come all the way to us. . . . I know, but we cannot come."

It seemed to Riley that as Vaziri spoke, the man got more and more nervous. Sweat was pouring down his face, and he couldn't keep still.

"I will tell Father. He'll . . . he'll . . ."

Vaziri locked eyes with Riley.

Oh no! Riley thought just before Vaziri started frantically yelling. Khadi quickly swatted at the phone, sending it skittering across the floor.

"What'd he say?" Riley asked, trying to resist the urge to drive his gun butt into Vaziri's temple.

"The words won't translate precisely," Khadi said between angry breaths, "but let's just say it's the equivalent of 'Plan B! Plan B!'"

Riley snatched Scott's phone out of his hand. "Gooey, I know it wasn't two minutes, but were you able to triangulate the signal to a location?"

On the other end of the call, Gooey laughed. "Quit acting so *24*, Jack. The Gooman don't need no two minutes."

"Seriously? You can do that?" Riley wanted to reach through the phone and give the man a hug. But then, after picturing Gooey, he figured he'd settle for a fist tap. "Where is it?"

"Patience . . . patience . . . paaaaa-tiennnnnce. Got it! Looks like 39 degrees, 16 minutes, 18.6 seconds north, 76 degrees, 38 minutes, 17.55 seconds west, which puts . . . us . . . at . . . 1600 S. Monroe St. in the beautiful metropolis of Baltimore, M-D."

"Gooey, you're a rock star! Tell Tara to notify the Baltimore police, but have her tell them not to do anything until we get there. Let them know we're ten minutes out. And how difficult would it be for you to get a real-time satellite image in case they bolt?"

"For me? Half the time of anyone else. I'm working on it as we speak."

"Thanks, Goo," Riley said, handing the phone back to Scott.

"Great work, Gooey. Next bag of pork rinds are on me," Scott said before hanging up.

"Okay, let's get topside," Riley said, moving toward the stairs. "Li, Hummel, I want you to stay with these guys until someone comes along to claim them."

"You mean this guy," Li said. "Didn't you . . ." He stopped when he saw Hummel lift the other terrorist to his feet. There was blood running down his forehead, and his eyes were only half-open.

As Riley walked away, he could hear Hummel laugh over the comm system. "Nah, Riley fired through the side of the boat, which is why our friend here is a little moist. Then Skeet clocked the dude, and Riley borrowed a little blood from their less fortunate brother whose vital signs you deemed fit to end and flicked some on his face like a splashback."

"Sweet," Li said. "Who's better than Pach?"

But Riley didn't answer. He was too focused on the next steps.

They reached topside just as the Little Birds were making their approach. The first one hovered a foot above the aft deck, and Riley, Skeeter, Scott, and Khadi slipped onto its benches. As the chopper lifted off, Riley prayed they'd be in time.

CHAPTER SIXTY-SEVEN

MONDAY, SEPTEMBER 14, 9:02 P.M. EDT
BALTIMORE, MARYLAND

"Come on, Gooey, what are you doing?" Riley yelled into his mic.

"I said hang on," Gooey's frustrated voice answered in his headphones.

"Don't give me 'hang on'! You know, you're quickly losing your rock-star status! Get a satellite on that building or pass it off to someone who can!" Riley knew he wasn't being fair with the quirky analyst, but it seemed like appealing to Gooey's pride was the one thing that really lit a fire under him.

"If I can't do it . . . ," Gooey grumbled.

The dark water passed rapidly below as they flew up the Patapsco River. To Riley's left and right were the lights of Baltimore's suburbs. Suddenly the Little Bird dipped down. Riley looked up to see a boat's-eye view of the Francis Scott Key Bridge flash overhead.

"I got it," Gooey cried out. "Wait, looks like there's a truck that's just accelerating northwest on Monroe!"

"Did it come from the building?" Riley asked.

"I . . . I . . ."

"Answer him, Goo," Scott ordered.

"I'm not sure," Gooey cried out. Riley could hear the exasperation in his voice. "There's a Penske truck rental right across the street. It could have been from there."

"'Could have' is not good enough," Riley yelled. *Great! Do we hit the building, or do we follow what might be a wild-goose chase? Come on, no time to think; just make the decision!*

"Gilly!"

"Yeah, Pach!"

"I want your chopper to go to the building on Monroe! When you get there, storm it as quickly as you can. Don't take any chances; we don't need prisoners. Just make sure that if the warhead is in there, there's no one left who can set it off!"

"Roger!"

"Goo, where's the truck?"

"It just turned northeast on Washington," Gooey said, the resentment he felt toward Riley showing in his voice.

"Come on, Gooey, I don't know the streets. Just point us in the right direction!"

Finally Gooey blew. "Listen, if you've got a—wait a second! I've got an idea! Let me patch myself in to the chopper's GPS."

"You can do that?" Riley asked, impressed.

"Puh-lease," Gooey gloated, all the frustration out the window with this new challenge. "Evie, follow this truck while I work a little Goo-gic."

"Goo-gic? Ewww," Evie said from just beyond Gooey's mic. "Should I be wearing protective clothing?"

"Okay, guys, how do we do this?" Riley asked the other three who were with him.

"We dropped our ropes after the rappel onto the boat, we don't have winches, and dropping onto the roofs of trucks only works in the movies," Scott said.

"Thanks, buddy. That answers 'How don't we do this?' Now, if we can get back to my original question . . ."

"Northwest on Carey," Evie said. Riley felt the chopper veer to the right. Back behind, the second chopper remained on its course.

"We're going to have to set down somewhere," Khadi said.

"But where?" Riley answered. "If we choose the wrong place, we're toast. Even if we have a vehicle meet us, we're playing catch-up!"

"Can we get the cops to pull it over? No, that might lead to a high-speed chase that could turn out really bad," Scott said answering his own question.

"Exactly," Riley said. "And speaking of the cops, we need them to hold back. Our best advantage right now is the bad guys thinking that we don't know where they are."

"Evie, have Tara tell the police to follow at a distance. We don't want to spook the target," Khadi said.

Evie did, then said, "He just turned east on Baltimore. He's definitely heading downtown and at a fairly decent rate of speed."

While that news wasn't necessarily a surprise, it still sent a chill down Riley's spine. *They always have to go for the maximum damage—always have to see just how many innocent civilians they can kill.*

Below him, land suddenly appeared. First a freeway, then a rail yard sped by just a hundred feet below.

"You're only two miles out," Evie said.

"Jefferson, go dark," Riley commanded the pilot, and the lights on the Bird went out again. "Okay, guys, I think our official plan is, wing it. Let's trust our training and let instinct kick in."

Riley hated going in without a set strategy, but he also knew that three out of the four of them were former members of the Air Force Special Operations Command. To get to that elite level, you had to train and train and train. And when you were done with all that training . . . you trained some more. It was all about making the unnatural natural—reprogramming instinct. Riley just had to believe that when the time came, they'd know what to do.

Coming into view to the west was M & T Bank Stadium, home of the Baltimore Predators and site of one of Riley's better games during his rookie year. Looking around Skeeter, he spotted Camden Yards on the other side of the freeway. They were both dark, as Riley knew they would be. All sporting events had been canceled indefinitely following last night's New York City attack.

"North on Eutaw," Evie reported.

Jefferson said, "We're only a half mile back, sir."

"Cut your speed and drop to rooftop level. Let's see if we can sneak up on him."

The pilot made two quick turns, then throttled back and actually dropped lower than rooftop, following the street just twenty feet up.

"There it is," Jefferson said. "Twelve o'clock."

Riley again looked around Skeeter and saw the moving truck. It was a sixteen-foot, bright yellow Penske. *Hmm, maybe I* could *drop onto the back of that. . . .*

But the closer they got, the more foolhardy that idea seemed.

They were just four car lengths back when a man leaned out of the window of the truck and started firing an automatic weapon at them.

Oh, come on! Who am I—007? This is something right out of a Bond movie!

The helicopter quickly pulled up, causing all four of the team members to almost tumble to the pavement below.

"Jefferson, you two okay up there?" Riley asked.

"Yes, sir."

"Good! Now keep it together! You almost sent us swan diving!"

"Yes, sir!"

As the chopper began to descend again, Riley could see the truck speeding up. Ahead he could see a bunch of people milling around a courtyard in front of what looked like a giant, enclosed farmer's market. *Just what we need, the truck plowing into a crowd of bystanders!*

Think! What now? You're in a helicopter, some maniac is firing at you, and there are people all around. What would Bond do?

"Jefferson, after the truck clears all those people, I want you to drop down in front of it and face it."

"Yes, sir," Jefferson said calmly.

"Skeet, you hang on to me. Scott, you do the same to Khadi. When the chopper levels, Khadi, you take out the driver, and I'll take care of the guy with the gun."

"Shouldn't I be taking the shot?" Scott asked, appealing to his greater training—and probably his masculine pride.

"You're too big for her to hang on to. Besides, she's a better shot."

Jefferson had taken them up over the truck, and Riley could see the passenger following them with the gun. Suddenly the truck began swerving back and forth in a desperate attempt to make itself a difficult target.

In a movie, this would be when the tunnel magically appears and the helicopter slams into it while you make your escape! Looking at the open streets ahead, Riley thought, *Sorry, boys, wrong movie!*

At the next intersection, the chopper spun 180 degrees and dropped to fifteen feet above the ground.

Instantly, Riley planted his feet on the skids and let his body lean out into open air. As soon as Skeeter's grip on his vest halted his movement, he opened fire with his Magpul. The passenger was firing wildly, and out of the corner of his eye, Riley saw bits of glass poofing up from the Little Bird's front bubble.

Khadi scored a hit on the driver, and the truck pulled wildly to the right. Riley, finally, found his mark, sending the gunman flying from his perch on the doorframe, but not before he heard Scott cry out. Riley looked back through the open chopper and saw that both Scott and Khadi were gone.

As the truck careened into a Food 7 Mart in a hail of brick and dust, Riley called out, "Skeet, pull me in!"

Skeeter did, and Riley scrambled through to the other side of the chopper. Looking down, he saw Scott sprawled out on the asphalt below. Khadi, however, was hanging upside down on the skid by her knees. Taking hold of the side of the chopper, Riley reached down, grasping for her hand. All those years of childhood gymnastics finally paid off for Khadi as she rocked herself back and forth, then swung up and caught Riley's arm. He pulled her back in.

"Get us down!" Riley commanded. "But watch out; Scott's down there!"

Khadi held tightly to Riley as the chopper slid back and dropped. She was shaking and breathing heavily. As much as Riley wanted to comfort her, he instead grabbed her face and said, "Stay in the game, girl! We're not done yet! Check Scott! Skeet and I need to open the back of that truck!"

Khadi nodded an acknowledgment of her assignment.

As soon as the chopper settled, Riley was out, following right behind Skeeter. While Skeeter went to the truck's mangled cab, Riley ran to the back.

"Clear!" he heard Skeeter yell.

As soon as Riley's hand touched the handle for the rear door, bullets started flying out. Pain stabbed the side of his head as he dropped to the ground. Skeeter slid down next to him.

"Do you know whether a bullet can damage this warhead or not?"

"Don't know, sir," Skeeter said, looking at the blood on Riley's head.

"I'm fine—just grazed my ear," Riley said, heading off the question before it was asked. "We can't take any chances. Door goes up, you take left, I'll take right; pick our shots, double tap. You ready?"

"Yes, sir," Skeeter said as he took hold of the handle.

Riley counted down with his fingers . . . *3 . . . 2 . . . 1!*

The door flew up. Bullets whizzed past them, and Riley heard a scream from the crowd that was diving for cover on the opposite side of the street.

Okay, ready . . . okay, ready . . . now! Riley jumped up from his crouch and centered his red dot. With two quick pulls of the trigger, he placed a round in the man's chest and in his head.

Riley and Skeeter jumped into the truck. The bomb was built into a metal frame that was welded onto the truck's floor. Electrical tools were scattered, and Riley spotted a metal plate that looked like it belonged on the device.

"Over here," Skeeter called out.

Riley swung around to the other side of the warhead and saw an open section. There were wires hanging out. He would have loved to see some digital countdown clock to know whether it was definitely armed or not. But the fact that there were loose wires in the open was enough to strongly suggest that they had made it in time.

Scott! Riley ran to the back of the truck and jumped out, the night air cooling the blood that had trickled from his ear and soaked into his shirt. Up ahead Khadi was kneeling on the ground with her back to him. She was hunched over, and it looked like she was slowly stroking Scott's close-cut head.

Oh no! Not Scott, too.

As he ran, he could see the crowds filling the intersection. One person called out, "Hey, that's Riley Covington!" Immediately, shouts of "Get 'em, Covington!" and "Go, Riley!" filled the street.

Scott was flat on his back, and his right leg was twisted at an unnatural angle. Riley dropped down next to Khadi and grabbed his best friend's arm, checking for a pulse.

Scott's eyes popped open, and a tight grin appeared on his face. "Your adoring public. . . . So no big boom means you got it, right?"

Riley could see that Khadi was smiling widely too, the relief very apparent on her face. "Yeah, we got it."

Then Khadi twisted Riley's head. "What happened? Are you okay?"

Remembering his bloody ear, Riley chuckled and said in a bad British accent, "I'm all right. It's just a flesh wound."

Scott replied with an even worse accent, "I've had worse!"

"Listen," Khadi said, "if you guys are going to start quoting Monty Python, then you can comfort your own selves."

"Speaking of comfort, what's all the head stroking about?" Riley asked, not quite as casually as he had hoped.

Sucking in his breath through gritted teeth, Scott answered through the pain. "Back off, Jealous Boy. Khadi just feels sorry for me, and I told her that it feels nice." Looking up at Khadi, he said, "Mix it up a bit so you can comfort my whole head. There's a good girl."

Khadi reached down and gave Scott's goatee a solid tug, then went back to what she had been doing.

"Ow! Tough girl, Riley. Someday you'll realize she's a keeper."

The intersection was alive with activity, and the sound of screams, chants, and sirens filled the air. Baltimore cops began flooding the street.

In the midst of the chaos, Riley looked up at Khadi, and their eyes met for a moment before she looked back down.

Yeah, someday I'll realize she's a keeper. Someday.

CHAPTER SIXTY-EIGHT

WEDNESDAY, SEPTEMBER 30, 11:45 A.M. IRST
TEHRAN, IRAN

Cower before the world! That's the way to usher in the Mahdi! Hide behind the skirts of your mothers; the West is coming! Throw them a scapegoat! Bow before America and kiss the Zionists' feet! Cowards! The Supreme Leader, the president—all cowards.

Ayatollah Allameh Beheshti closed his eyes as he slowly walked, knowing that the men who walked alongside him would make sure he continued in the right direction. In the darkness of his mind, he could see the Grand Ayatollah and the president as they sat watching the last day of his trial. They had come to witness the verdict and the sentencing, another weak attempt on their part to show the world their commitment to justice.

Justice! Making me pay for having the courage to follow through what was in your very own hearts? That may be man's corrupt version of justice, but it is not Allah's!

He smiled with satisfaction, however, when he visualized the faces of those two hypocrites. The lines on their faces had become deep crevasses. They looked tired, worn, worried. Beheshti had also noticed the way the Supreme Leader had kept his right hand on his left wrist—a sure sign that the shaking that plagued him under times of pressure was attacking him full force.

You deserve to shake! You deserve to tremble! Live your life in fear, for your days may not be long.

The Sleeping Giant had been awakened. America had been temporarily stayed with the trial and convictions of Beheshti, Bahman Milani, Nouri Saberi, and the rest of Beheshti's team. But that would not last long. There was blood in the water, and the shark was circling.

A week ago, an American air strike on the North Korean presidential palace had killed Kim Jong Il. The next day, they had taken out Kim's youngest son and successor, Kim Jong Un. That second strike had immediately triggered a revolution in the country. Government leaders were dragged into the streets and beaten to death, and military and police commanders were assassinated by those under their command. A de facto government free of Chinese influence was established until elections could be held, and the border with South Korea had been opened. Already cries for reunification echoed through the streets of the North and the South.

Now many American government leaders were hoping for the same thing to happen in Iran. And the calls for revolution were not just coming from the West. Hundreds of thousands of adults and students carrying signs with slogans like "Death to the Dictator!" and "This Is for the World to See!" marched in the streets each day, dwarfing the size of the recent election protests.

As he opened his eyes, Beheshti thought, *Yes, you have every reason to be trembling, O Supreme Leader. Your time in this life will not be long, and then you will be forced to answer to Allah for your weakness and hypocrisy.*

There was one area in which Iran's leaders and the protesters found agreement, however—the attacks on America must be paid for. *That's okay; I can accept the hatred of the world, as long as I have Allah's favor. Let all the people of this earth direct their derision toward me; I have done God's will. He will vindicate me for all eternity.*

At this moment, it wasn't hard to believe that all the world hated him. The thousands of angry screams surrounding him were representative of tens of millions of others watching on a live Al Jazeera broadcast.

Beheshti lifted the hem of his robe as he ascended the steps. He had worn his best *qabaa* for the event and didn't want to soil it on his way up to the platform. When he reached the top, the jeers and calls exploded.

Let them see that you are at peace. Show them your confidence in the vindication of Allah. Standing straight, with his head up, he slowly scanned the crowd that had gathered in the stadium. As his eyes passed each section, the screams wilted under his hard stare until only a low murmur was left.

Then one voice called out, "Death to the traitor!" and the entire stadium erupted again.

So be it, he thought as he knelt on the rough wood and leaned forward. *I am not afraid.* As the sound of the rapidly descending sword cut through the din, he said, "Into your hands, Allah, I—"

[illegible] lifted the front of his [illegible]

[illegible] up to the platform. [illegible]

[illegible] exploded.

[illegible]

[illegible] without [illegible] again.

[illegible]

CHAPTER

SIXTY-NINE

WEDNESDAY, SEPTEMBER 30, 4:30 P.M. EDT
NEW YORK, NEW YORK

The first time Keith had seen a C-5 flying overhead, he had cheered along with everyone else. It happened the fourth day after the attack, and his stomach had been growling nonstop for the previous twenty-four hours. The helicopter supply drops had continued to bring water and MREs, but with the massive number of people in need, there was not enough of either to satisfy. Seeing an enormous plane like the C-5 meant that the airport runways had been cleared, and clear runways meant supplies coming in and refugees flying out.

Forty-eight hours later, passenger jets began to be interspersed with the cargo planes. Soon it was evident that a regular schedule had been established, and Keith began to expect a plane overhead every ten minutes like clockwork.

That same day, a massive wave of people began pouring through their makeshift bus camp and onto the Triborough Bridge. All were making the hike to LaGuardia, a five-mile trek along the Bruckner Expressway and the Grand Central Parkway.

After a while, Keith decided to walk alongside

one middle-aged couple, each loaded with a backpack and a rolling suitcase. They were suspicious of him at first and didn't want to talk, especially with the sorry state of Keith's battered face. But once they connected his name with his profession, they opened up.

Tom and Laura Webb had lived in a very high-end apartment at 96th and 5th, overlooking Central Park. They had been home watching the football game when the lights went out.

At first there was nothing to indicate that it was anything other than an ordinary blackout. Then the first plane had dropped. The explosion shook the whole building. They ran to the window, where they could see the fireball rising from the other side of the reservoir. Then, as they watched in horror, another fireball rose no more than a hundred yards from the first. Then another and then another. Soon the whole park was aflame.

Laura had tried to call their daughter, Maddie, who was at an evening biology lab at NYU south of their apartment. That was when they discovered that the phones weren't working. Telling Laura to stay put until he got back, Tom had left to find Maddie. At first he planned to catch a cab, but when he ran out the door, he saw 5th Avenue packed with dead cars. So he began running.

The streets had filled with people. Panic was everywhere—people afraid to stay in their buildings, but terrified to be in the street. Twice Tom had to go around the wreckage of fallen planes. Bodies and pieces of bodies littered the blocks surrounding the crash sites. But Tom didn't have time to be horrified; he just wanted to find his daughter.

It took him three hours to run the four and a half miles to the university. When he was still five blocks away, he saw smoke billowing into the air above the buildings ahead. Dread filled his heart. He prayed the smoke wasn't from the university.

When he finally came around the last corner, his legs gave out and he dropped to his knees. Flaming wreckage filled Washington Square Park, and the university buildings surrounding it were burning uncontrollably.

Tom pushed through the crowds of people, calling out Maddie's name, constantly passing other parents and spouses and boyfriends and girlfriends who were doing the same. Tom stayed there searching until noon of the next day. When he had started his long, lonely walk back to Laura, he hoped beyond hope that he had somehow missed his daughter and that she was now back safe with her mother.

But when he finally arrived home, Laura was still alone, anxiously waiting for him. She burst into tears when she saw that Maddie wasn't with him. Tom told Laura that witnesses had reported to him that students had flooded out of the buildings when the crash first happened. Maybe she was with them, hiding in a girlfriend's apartment. For five days Tom and Laura had waited, hoping and praying that their daughter would come walking through the door. She never did.

After 9/11, Tom and Laura had had a long conversation with their only child. They all agreed that staying in New York City was like living under a giant bull's-eye. So they had decided together that if another terrorist attack should ever happen and they had to evacuate the city, they would find a way to get to Laura's sister's place in Charleston, South Carolina. And if, for some reason, they got separated, that would be their rendezvous.

Now they were heading to LaGuardia to try to get on a plane so they could eventually find their way down to Charleston, where hopefully Maddie waited for them. But even as Tom said the words, Keith could see despair in the other man's eyes. He knew the words were most likely only for Laura's sake. Tom had been there. He had seen the devastation. He knew the truth.

Keith had gone back and reported what he'd learned to Coach Burton. The next day, the whole Colorado Mustangs organization had joined the flood of refugees—all except for him. After talking with Tom and Laura, he had spent a long night wrestling with what he had heard. When the morning came, he realized that he couldn't leave. There was too much to be done here. There were too many hurting and needy people.

He couldn't blame the others for leaving. If he had a wife or kids, he would have fought to get the earliest flight available. But as things stood, it was just him. His epiphany had come when he recalled that for nearly a year now he had been praying for a purpose, a way to leave a lasting legacy. Now he had the chance to make a difference.

Keith had heard from passersby that a large refugee camp had been established near Penn Station. The Army Corps of Engineers had cleared the tracks of the Northeast Corridor and had replaced the electrical engines with diesel locomotives. Now they were running trains every half hour north to Boston and south to Philadelphia. As word got out, tens of thousands of people flooded the area. Soon a large tent city had been established. Food and water were provided by volunteers, and security by the National Guard. That was exactly the kind of opportunity Keith was looking for. So after letting a surprisingly understanding Coach Burton know what he had planned, he said his good-byes to his teammates and set off on the five-mile hike.

As he walked through the devastated city, he felt himself passing from celebrity to obscurity, from selfishness to selflessness. He was amazed that in the midst of the horror he saw all around him, he was finally discovering peace.

The past ten days in the refugee camp had been the most difficult of his life. However, he wouldn't have traded them for anything. One of the blessings of working so hard was that now when he closed his eyes at night, he was too tired to dwell on the vision of Afshin's lifeless stare or the horrible morning when he had led a solemn procession of his teammates to deliver his dear friend's body to the gruesome bonfire that had been created to protect the city against disease.

Keith walked toward the tracks and waited for the approaching train to pull into the station. *If Riley could see me now, he would absolutely crack up! I'd probably never hear the end of it.*

He wore a black-and-white checkered vest and a big straw hat that was adorned with a checkered band. His first reaction at seeing the getup was to absolutely refuse to wear anything so ridiculous. But after taking some time to think about it, he swallowed his pride and put on the giant chessboard. Because of the job he had been given, people needed to be able to spot him.

When he wasn't serving meals, he was charged with welcoming the volunteers who arrived with every new train. While still on the train, new arrivals were told to look for the greeters in the checkerboard vests. They were there to answer questions and direct them to the processing tent, where everyone would be given their assignments. Regardless, it still didn't make him look any less like a buffoon.

The long train slowed next to him. Usually they kept the volunteers in the first car or two, so he made his way in that direction. As he walked, he thought about Riley, as he often did. He picked up a lot of news from the people coming off the trains, and anytime anyone had information about his friend, he stopped them for a longer conversation.

It was through the new volunteers that he had heard about Riley's part in stopping the attack on Washington, D.C. It was also through them that he found out about Scott's injury.

When satellite communications were first set up in the camp, Keith had sent off an e-mail to Riley to congratulate him and to see how he was doing. Since that time, though, the lines at the computers had been ridiculously long. *Besides, those people need it more than I do. They're trying to set up the next steps for their lives.*

I, on the other hand, don't have any next steps. Which, when you think about it, is actually not that bad of a place to be. That pleasant thought put him in just the frame of mind that he needed as he walked toward the opening doors and the shell-shocked volunteers who were in the middle of dealing with their first glimpses of just how bad New York City really was.

EPILOGUE

Riley's stomach fluttered with excitement. It always seemed that the last leg of any journey took the longest. Now, as he looked out the window at the familiar sights, it seemed as if he would never arrive.

Khadi had not been happy about his leaving. In fact, no one had, except for Skeeter, who was as ready to get out of Washington as Riley. But Washington wasn't his home—would never be his home. His time in that city was a result of duty, not desire. And once his duty was done, he couldn't wait to put the place behind him. His departure disappointed a lot of people, but he was only doing what he felt had to be done.

Scott was the first one Riley had seriously disappointed. He had tried to convince him to stay, claiming that he needed his best friend around to cheer him up while in traction at Georgetown University Hospital. But spending the next however many weeks hanging out and playing cards in a sterile white room sounded like pure torture. Besides, Scott was getting daily visits from Tara, so Riley figured he would be well taken care of.

Leaving Khadi was much more difficult. Her

sadness affected him most of all, but it was something Riley knew he had to do. The two of them had been getting closer and closer, and it was obvious to him that if he stuck around much longer, commitments would be made that would take the relationship to a level he could no longer justify with their differing beliefs. Khadi didn't see it that way—or, as Riley suspected, she did see it that way but just didn't want to admit it.

So, obviously, part of what I'm doing is running away, which typically isn't a good reason to do anything. Sometimes, though, it's necessary. And I know myself too well to think that I could keep the status quo with her indefinitely.

His hand reached to his chest, where, through his shirt, he could feel the ring Khadi had given to him before he left. It hung on a leather thong and was inscribed with the Farsi words for *truth, integrity,* and *honor.*

"These are the words that fill my mind when I think of you," she had said as she closed his hand over the ring. "The only other man I knew who held these qualities as strongly as you was this ring's previous owner—my grandfather. He would be proud to know that now you will keep it for him."

Riley had struggled to say something, anything. His hand reached to her cheek—her beauty, her strength, her character all overwhelmed him.

"I . . . I . . ."

Khadi smiled—a smile full, deep, and rich enough to sear itself forever into his memory.

"I know," she said as she took his hand from her face with her two hands. "I do, too."

She tilted her head and kissed Riley's hand gently on the knuckle. Then, after one last long look with tear-filled eyes, she put his hand down, got up, and walked out the door of the coffee shop.

Oh, God, please let her see Your truth. Bring her into Your Kingdom—first for her sake, but selfishly, for mine, too. I truly believe she's the woman You have chosen for me, but honestly, I'm getting tired of hearing "not yet."

The final person he had disappointed was President Donald Lloyd. Five days after recovering the second warhead, Riley, Khadi,

Skeeter, the ops team, and the twentysomethings from the RoU had all been invited to the White House. As they entered the Oval Office, they were greeted by the president, his cabinet, and the majority and minority leaders of the House and Senate. The president expressed his appreciation on behalf of the whole nation and personally shook everyone's hand.

"Good to see they took you shopping," he said to Riley.

The occasion almost passed without incident. However, when Lloyd was shaking Gooey's hand, the analyst pointed to the only cabinet member with a scowl on his face and asked, "So what's with Grumpy Gus?"

The president turned, then started chuckling. "Secretary Moss does seem a bit ill-tempered today, does he not?"

Gooey's voice dropped to a stage whisper. "Honestly? Dude's always like that. Personally, I just think he's in want of a mother's love. Either that, or he's just naturally a . . ."

Riley couldn't hear Gooey's final word, but evidently President Lloyd could because he burst out laughing. After he stopped, he leaned forward and whispered something in Gooey's ear.

"Right on, Lloydster," Gooey said when the president finished. "But like I said, this is just between you and me."

Gooey gave the president a conspiratorial wink.

For the next two days, the RoU gang had tried to get Gooey to give up what the president had told him, but he remained tight-lipped. Finally the secret was revealed when late the second day it was announced that Secretary Moss had been fired and Stanley Porter put in his place.

Everyone in the office had started cheering, but Gooey just tilted way back in his desk chair, laced his fingers behind his head, and said, "Yeah, ol' Donny let me know it was coming down the pike."

The day after their White House meeting, Riley had been called back into the Oval Office. There, President Lloyd had offered him a position as special adviser to the president on the global terrorist threat.

Riley was blown away. He thought he was just going there to fill the president in on the details of the operations. It was a very tempting offer.

The world was a very different place now than it had been just a few weeks ago. Russia, Iran, and all the Arab countries had tipped their hands with their military buildups. It had taken some serious American and United Nations threats to get the various sides to stand down.

Riley's mind went back to the telecast of the Iranian president standing in front of the United Nations. All his usual arrogance and bluster were gone. His hands visibly trembled as he spoke:

"The Supreme Leader of Iran, the leaders, the people, and I myself deeply regret that one of our own people was involved in the horrific and detestable attack upon the nation of America. It was cowardly and against all our nation's principles. Rest assured, the ones responsible have received the just rewards for their criminal acts.

"As a nation of peace, we look forward to putting this incident behind us and demonstrating to the world our true desires to be friends and allies to all. As such, we pledge our financial assistance to the people of America, and we put our vast resources at your disposal."

At the time, Riley had wondered if the man truly believed the words he was saying, because no one else in the world did. General opinion was that he was forced to speak by the ayatollah, who in turn had been forced by international pressure to ensure that some kind of mea culpa statement was made.

Ultimately, putting "our vast resources at your disposal" meant a four-dollar discount per barrel of oil. President Lloyd rejected out of hand the discount, as well as any other "assistance" Iran had to offer.

Word was that the protesters who were filling the streets of Tehran and Esfahān and Tabriz were not going away this time without a sacrifice, and when the president returned to Iran, the Grand Ayatollah would be all too happy to give them their disgraced political leader.

Riley sighed and shook his head. *This was the closest I've heard of the world coming to a nuclear holocaust. But I'm sure it won't be the last.* He knew all it would take was another hard hit on America, and the sworn enemies would be back at each other's throats. And he knew that if he knew it, the terrorists knew it too.

There's clearly a need and a job to fill. The question is, am I really the guy to fill it?

After taking a little time to collect his thoughts, he told the president, "Sir, it would be quite an honor to serve you and my country in this way, but I am finished with this world of special ops and terrorism. I'm very sorry, but I'm afraid I'm going to have to decline your generous offer."

The president had raised his eyebrows and nodded. "I understand. You have been through one nightmare after another this past year. But would you do me a favor and promise me one thing?"

"Of course, sir."

"Don't say no yet. Take some time. Get away from all this," Lloyd said, circling his hand in a way that seemed to include his office, Washington, New York, and terrorism as a whole. "Then, in a few months, we'll talk again. Is that a deal?"

Riley reached over and shook the president's hand. "That's a deal. Now, if I could be so presumptuous as to ask a favor from you."

"Anything."

When Riley told him what he wanted, President Lloyd started laughing. "Believe it or not, I've already got that in the works."

Later that afternoon, Riley got a call from Scott.

"Dude, I'll give you three guesses who was just here!"

"Frank Sinatra."

"Too dead."

"Jerry Lewis."

"Too French."

"Cap'n Crunch."

"Too animated. But that does remind me that my supply is getting low."

"Gotcha covered."

"Cool. Anyway, the president of these here United States, Donald Lloyd, was just here . . . in my room . . . to visit me, little Scotty Ross, only son of crackhead Martin Ross and meth tweaker Julia Ross. He only stayed for like ten minutes, but, I mean, dude, it was so unbelievably awesome!"

When Riley hung up the phone, he had immediately called the president's office and left a message with his secretary thanking him.

All that, however, was days and miles behind him. As he gathered his bag and prepared to exit, he knew someday he would have to face the president's offer and his feelings for Khadi. But not today. Today he had other business to attend to.

As Riley stepped to the ground, he looked around. Skeeter elbowed him and nodded to his right. Even with his back to them, there was no doubting who it was. Greeting people as they stepped out the other door of the train was Keith Simmons in the most ridiculous-looking outfit Riley had ever seen.

Slowly, Riley crept up on him. When he was right behind Keith, he said, "Excuse me, but would you mind lying down? My friend and I have got a real hankering for a game of checkers."

Keith spun around. "No way," he yelled as he picked Riley up in a bear hug. Next he managed to get Skeeter off the ground too, albeit with a lot more effort.

"What are you guys doing here?" Keith said when he caught his breath.

"What do you mean what are we doing here? When I got your e-mail, I e-mailed you back and told you we were coming."

"Well, no wonder I was clueless. It seems a couple weeks ago my BlackBerry suddenly went on the fritz," Keith laughed. "But my question still stands. What are you doing *here*?"

Suddenly Riley turned serious. "Honestly, Keith, I don't know. It's just . . . after all that's happened, after what I've seen, I can't just go back home and pretend it didn't happen. You know what I mean?"

Keith smiled sadly. "I know exactly what you mean."

"Besides, Skeeter here lost my keys when I left Alaska, so I wouldn't be able to get into my house anyway."

The three men laughed; then Keith said, "Tell you what, let me show you around. Then we'll get you two on the work roster."

They walked off the train platform together. Riley knew each of them had a lot more to say to the others, but as if by silent agreement, they all decided that the talk of bombs, planes, beatings, and dead friends could wait for another day.

ABOUT THE AUTHORS

JASON ELAM is a seventeen-year NFL veteran placekicker for the Atlanta Falcons.

He was born in Fort Walton Beach, Florida, and grew up in Atlanta, Georgia. In 1988, Jason received a full football scholarship to the University of Hawaii, where he played for four years, earning academic All-America and Kodak All-America honors. He graduated in 1992 with a bachelor's degree in communications and was drafted in the third round of the 1993 NFL draft by the Denver Broncos, where he played for 15 years.

In 1997 and 1998, Jason won back-to-back world championships with the Broncos and was selected to the Pro Bowl in 1995, 1998, and 2001. He is currently working on a master's degree in global apologetics at Liberty Theological Seminary and has an abiding interest in Middle East affairs, the study of Scripture, and defending the Christian faith. Jason is a licensed commercial airplane pilot, and he and his wife, Tamy, have four children.

STEVE YOHN grew up as a pastor's kid in Fresno, California, and both of those facts contributed significantly to his slightly warped perspective on life. Steve graduated from Multnomah Bible College with a bachelor's degree in biblical studies and barely survived a stint as a youth pastor.

While studying at Denver Seminary, Steve worked as a videographer for Youth for Christ International, traveling throughout the world to capture the ministry's global impact. With more than two decades of ministry experience, both inside and outside the church, Steve has discovered his greatest satisfactions lie in writing, speaking, and one-on-one mentoring.

Surprisingly, although his hobbies are reading classic literature, translating the New Testament from the Greek, and maintaining a list of political leaders of every country of the world over the last twenty-five years, he still occasionally gets invited to parties and has a few friends. His wife, Nancy, and their daughter are the joys of his life.

TURN THE PAGE

FOR AN EXCERPT FROM THE PREVIOUS

RILEY COVINGTON THRILLER

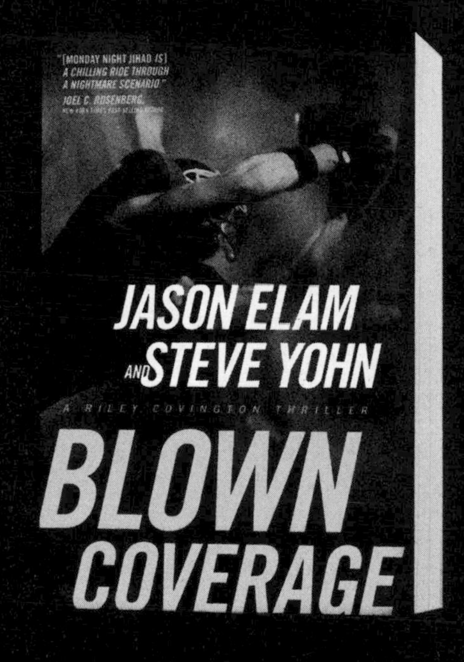

AVAILABLE NOW IN

BOOKSTORES AND ONLINE. VISIT

WWW.RILEYCOVINGTON.COM

FOR MORE INFORMATION.

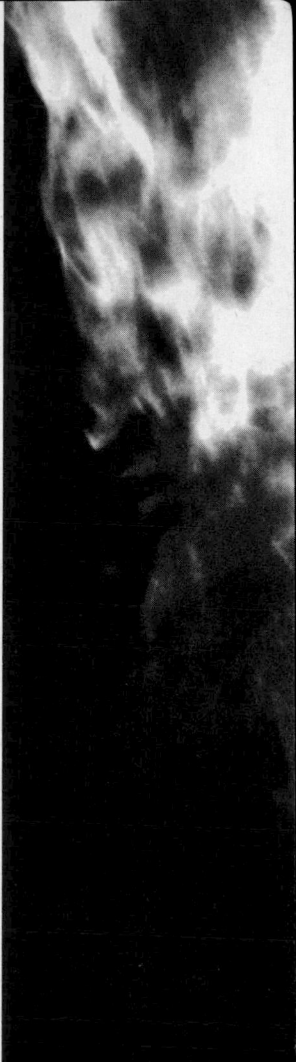

FRIDAY, APRIL 24, 11:45 A.M. CRST
SAN JOSÉ, COSTA RICA

There was not much that could give Riley Covington the heebie-jeebies—moldy sour cream, chewing on tinfoil, the music of Barry Manilow—but looking at what was in the tall fountain glass that had just been placed in front of Scott Ross was seriously making his skin crawl and his stomach dance the mambo.

"You try it," Scott said as he slid the glass across the table with his fingertips.

"You ordered it; you drink it," Riley countered, sliding the sweating glass back across the polished wood. The two friends were sitting at an outdoor table at Las Fresas restaurant in San José, Costa Rica. Skeeter Dawkins and Khadijah Faroughi rounded out the foursome.

"When I ordered guanabana juice, I thought I was going to get some sort of guava and banana mixture. This looks like they took curdled skim milk, added water, and then took the glass to the back so that the cooks could each hawk a big, honkin'—" Scott stopped when he noticed Khadi looking at him.

Riley grinned. He knew Scott had been trying

really hard to use his verbal filter on this trip, albeit with limited success.

"Let's just say that it looks like the guanabana had a bad head cold just prior to being juiced."

"Thank you, Scott. Although I'm not sure that was much of an improvement over what you were going to say," Khadi laughed. "Just try it. You might be surprised."

"My lips and this twisted tribute to postnasal drip will never meet this side of—"

Scott's pledge was interrupted by a large hand grabbing the glass from in front of him. Bringing the glass to his lips, Skeeter downed the juice in one continuous motion. Riley's huge self-appointed bodyguard slammed the glass onto the table, wiped his mouth with Scott's napkin, then without a word turned back to the spot he had been watching down the street.

"Dude, that was my juice you just drank," Scott whined. "What's up with that?"

Riley took a sip of his fresh pineapple juice as he laughed. At the next table over, a little *tico* girl with enormous brown eyes and her hair in ponytails shyly turned for the fourth time to watch this big, happy American man. She jumped as Riley caught her eyes, then quickly spun back around when Riley shot her a quick wink. The girl's mom gave Riley a smile and a nod in appreciation of his acknowledging her daughter's attention.

These last two weeks in Costa Rica had been exactly what each of the four had needed to physically and emotionally recover from the events of the beginning of the year. This group had experienced a lot of pain and had shed—and spilled—a lot of blood in the search for Hakeem Qasim. Only now was Riley finally feeling ready to go back to Denver to face life again.

Riley Covington knew he faced a decision when he got home. Three months ago, he was an all-pro linebacker for the Colorado Mustangs. Then, suddenly, his old life had literally blown up in his face when a terrorist group bombed Platte River Stadium in Denver during a Monday night game. Nearly two thousand people were killed in that suicide attack.

Because of his post-Academy years in Afghanistan as part of the

Air Force Special Operations Command, Riley had been pulled back into the Special Forces life of guns and death. *Can I really go back to the Professional Football League as if nothing ever happened? I've been franchised by the team, so it's obvious they still want me. But do I have the passion anymore?*

"Riley . . . earth to Riley," Khadi's voice drew him back from his thoughts. She motioned to the waitress who was trying to put his food down.

"Oh, sorry," he said to the woman as he dropped his elbows off the table. His jaw immediately followed his elbows when he saw the plate that was put in front of him.

"Holy Mother Russia, what is that monstrosity?" Scott asked before realizing that two more were being delivered to him and Khadi.

"Pastor Jimenez told me, 'Order the *Ensalada de Fruta con Helado*,'" Riley said. "He told me it's just a simple fruit salad with ice cream." But Riley had never seen so much fruit. His plate was overflowing with strawberries and huge chunks of pineapple, watermelon, and mango. And if that wasn't enough, three enormous scoops of ice cream topped off the tropical explosion.

"I'll never be able to finish this myself," Khadi complained. "In fact, I would never forgive myself if I did."

"Don't look at me. He never told me to get just one for all of us. I just assumed."

"Yeah, well we all know where that gets us, Pach," Scott said. *Pach* was Riley's nickname back from his Air Force football days, when his speed and hitting power drew comparisons to the AH-64 Apache attack helicopter. "If I try to eat all this, it could make for a long, painful flight home. This stuff will shoot through me like . . . like . . . like refuse through a Canadian waterfowl," Scott finished lamely. "Khadi, this whole verbal filter thing is really a pain."

Khadi reached over and patted Scott's arm. "I know it is, and I appreciate it."

Scott called the manager of the restaurant over and had him take a picture of the three of them with their fruit salads and Skeeter with his Cuban sandwich.

"Nice smile, Skeet," Scott said as he checked out the picture in the digital viewer of his camera. "You look like someone just stole your brass knuckles."

"Mmm," replied Skeeter, who turned his attention back up the street.

"It's always great having you part of the conversation, my friend."

Riley, Khadi, and Scott attacked their fruit salads, effectively halting conversation other than the occasional "Oh yeah" and "That's good."

A passing box truck spewed black diesel exhaust into the sidewalk café, causing Riley to cough and look up for the first time in five minutes. As he waved his hand in an attempt to clear the air in front of his face, his eyes were drawn to Skeeter, who was so intent on something up the street that he had completely ignored his plate. "Hey, Skeet, you okay? What's up?"

Skeeter turned around and noticed his sandwich but didn't take a bite. "I don't know, Pach. There's a couple of guys halfway down the block. Caught them looking this way a few times."

"Where're they at?"

"Your eleven."

Riley casually looked around Skeeter's big frame and saw the two men. One was sitting on a car, and the other was leaning against a building. Their close-cropped black hair and full beards seemed out of place on a Costa Rican street. Both men were smoking. As Riley watched, a third man walked out of a *farmacia* and joined them. "Don't look now, but your two have turned into three."

"Will you two relax?" Scott said as he turned around to look at the men. "You guys have been seeing bogeymen behind . . . Whoa, hold on. They do look a little more *hajji* than *tico*."

Khadi spotted the men also. "They sure do. And I've asked you to please quit using that term."

"What? *Hajji*? That's just what we called all the Middle East folk when we were out on patrol in the 'Stans."

"First of all, this isn't the 'Stans. And second, if that's true, then I'm a *hajji*, too." Khadi was from a Persian family who had fled Iran just prior to the fall of the shah.

"Come on, Khadi, that's ridiculous. *Hajji*s are guys. You'd be like a *hajjette* or something."

"Thanks, Scott. That's far less demeaning."

"They're moving," Skeeter broke in. As the four watched from the table, the three men walked to the far end of the block and turned out of sight.

"There! Did you see that last guy take a quick glance back before he rounded the corner?" Riley asked.

"I'm kind of getting a bad feeling about this," Khadi said. "We need to think about making ourselves scarce."

"Good call." Riley caught the waitress's attention and made a scribbling motion on his hand indicating he was ready for the check. "Skeeter, what are you packing?" As Riley's official bodyguard, Skeeter was the only one allowed by Costa Rican immigration to bring in firearms.

"Got my HK45 and a Mark 23."

"Good. Pass your Mark to Scott under the table. Now, there's no way anyone could know we're here, so this is probably total paranoia. But still, it's not worth taking chances. Scott and Khadi, as soon as I settle up, I want you two to walk to the corner and hang a left. Skeeter and I will cross and head up the next street to the right. We'll meet back at the hotel as soon as we can get there."

Khadi laid her hand on Riley's wrist. "I don't feel good about us all splitting up."

Riley knew that by "us all," Khadi meant the two of them. The feelings between Riley and Khadi had continued to grow over the months since they had met in the aftermath of the Platte River Stadium attack. The only thing separating them now was the only issue big enough to keep them apart—their religious beliefs. Both Khadi's Koran and Riley's Bible prohibited cross-faith unions. But, while both could control their actions, it was much harder to control their emotions.

"I understand, Khadi. But if these really are *haj*—bad guys, I don't want you or Scott anywhere around me. Skeeter can take care—"

A screech of tires made Riley jump.

"Don't matter now! Here they come," Skeeter yelled as he pushed Riley to the ground. Scott and Khadi dove for cover.

"Get inside," Riley yelled to the next table. The mother grabbed her daughter and ran through the front door.

A rusting red sedan tore around the corner where the three men had disappeared and sped up the street. One masked man was leaning over the roof of the car, and a second was hanging out the rear driver's-side window. Both were armed with AK-47s.

The sound of the assault rifles combined with the shattering glass of the windows sent screams up all around the restaurant. Riley prayed that the mother had made it to the ground in time. Scott and Skeeter returned fire with their handguns. A shot from Scott put a hole in the knit mask of the man leaning over the roof. He flew off his side window perch and exploded the rear glass of a parked car.

All of Skeeter's shots were directed at the driver, with one finally hitting its mark. The car swerved, caught a tire, and began to roll. On the third spin, Riley could see the other gunman ejected from his window. The last Riley saw of him was when the car landed on top of him, then skidded up against a delivery truck.

Riley quickly turned toward Khadi. Blood streamed down her cheek from a shard of glass. "You all right?"

"I'm fine. How'd they know we were here?"

"I have no clue. Scott, Skeet, you guys okay?" Before they could answer, all four heard the familiar *whoosh* of an RPG launch. "Incoming!" Riley yelled.

They dove to the ground just as the rocket plowed into the restaurant, showering them with pieces of the building. The explosive wave slammed hard into Riley's body and drove the air out of his lungs. Plaster dust hung like a fog, burning his eyes. He lay there gasping for breath, trying to clear his brain. People screamed around him, but they sounded like they were down a long tunnel.

He didn't know how long he remained in that state before the sound of automatic weapons fire snapped him back to full consciousness. He looked to his left and saw Khadi moving slowly. Beyond her, Scott knelt behind two large fern planters, returning fire. Next to him, Skeeter was stretched out. There was blood on his forehead, and he wasn't moving.

"Scott, sit rep," Riley called out, looking for a situation report.

"Minimum three bogies with AKs hoofing it down the opposite direction from our first batch. Skeet's out but breathing. I've got two more clips for his Mark, and three for his .45."

"Got it! Slide me the .45 and the clips!"

Scott complied.

Riley picked up the weapon and lost his fingers in the thick grooves of Skeeter's custom-made grip. However, Skeeter's gun was not unfamiliar to Riley, and he made a quick adjustment to his hold. Turning to Khadi, he said, "Scott and I are going to press these guys back. Soon as we're forward, I want you to check on Skeet."

Khadi tried to respond but started coughing instead. Tears from her grit-filled eyes were making streaks down her dusty face. She put a thumb up instead.

Turning back around, Riley said, "Okay, Scott. Just like back in Afghanistan, except this time we're outnumbered, outgunned, and surrounded by innocent civilians."

Scott grinned, "Look out, *hajji*, here we come!"

"On *go*, you cross the street and split the fire! Three—two—one—GO!" Riley began firing up the street as Scott bolted across. His peripheral vision caught Scott suddenly veering course. He turned in time to see Scott grab the first casualty's rifle off the pavement and dive behind a car. *The guy's good,* Riley thought.

He signaled Scott, who began to lay down cover fire. Running past the corner restaurant and across the intersection, Riley could hear the whiz of bullets all around him. The discordant scents of fresh baked bread and gunpowder hung in the air as he flattened himself against the side of a *panadería*. Chunks of pulverized brick showered his face from the corner of the building.

Riley looked back to see Scott ejecting the magazines that had been taped together and shoving the fresh box into his AK-47. *That'll give him thirty more rounds,* Riley thought as he slid a new clip into his handgun. *Not much, but it'll have to do.*

Suddenly, he saw Scott's eyes get big. Scott quickly signaled to him that there was another RPG ready to fire but that he wasn't in position to get a shot at it.

Riley leaned out just a touch and used the glass of the buildings up the street to give him a picture of where the gunmen were. His eye caught a dark shape with a long cylinder stepping out into the street.

Riley signaled Scott to lay fire and then spun around the corner. His first two shots were wild as he tried to get his bearings, but the next three hit their mark. As the man fell back, his RPG fired wildly into the sky. *Lord, don't let that land in a schoolyard,* Riley prayed as he quickly advanced. Running ahead, he saw another bogey lose half his face courtesy of Scott.

Where's the third one? Riley thought as he ran. *Scott said there were three. There!* At the next corner, a man was pulling off a mask as he rounded a corner at top speed. Riley signaled to Scott, who was now across the street and trying his best to match the linebacker stride for stride. Scott nodded, and they both went toward the corner.

Just before they reached it, the sound of a motorcycle engine kicking to life echoed down the narrow side street. Scott and Riley made a wide turn around the corner just in time to see the third gunman speeding away.

The sounds of sirens began to fill the air. The two men slumped against the building and tried to catch their breath.

"How'd they know, Scott?" Riley panted. "How could they possibly have known I was down here?"

"I don't know, man. But, believe me, I'm going to find out."